HOT
PROPERTIES

Other books by Rafael Yglesias

HIDE FOX, AND ALL AFTER

THE WORK IS INNOCENT

THE GAME PLAYER

RAFAEL YGLESIAS

HOT PROPERTIES

E.P. DUTTON
NEW YORK

Copyright © 1986 by Rafael Yglesias

All rights reserved. Printed in the U.S.A.

Published in the United States by E. P. Dutton,
a division of New American Library, 2 Park Avenue,
New York, New York 10016

Library of Congress Cataloging-in-Publication Data

Yglesias, Rafael, 1954-
    Hot properties.

    I. Title.
PS3575.G53H6   1986   813'.54   85-29368
ISBN 0-525-24421-2

Published simultaneously in Canada by
Fitzhenry & Whiteside Limited, Toronto

COBE

Designed by Julian Hamer

10 9 8 7 6 5 4 3 2 1

First Edition

For Margaret

PART ONE

CHAPTER 1

Fred Tatter's dinner party was about to begin. Invitations had been mailed three weeks ahead of time, making it—apart from his bar mitzvah and his wedding—the most formally schemed event of Fred's life. Indeed, because of the guest list, Fred considered this gathering symbolic of the impending culmination of his life's ambition. Four years ago he had been a dumpy Jewish guy (his own description) who knew a lot about sports. Now he was a New York Writer, all set to entertain an important agent, an editor, and several promising colleagues. He had shucked the dusty green shell of his Long Island background, and gleamed anew in fresh rows of friends and occupation. Armed with his coffee-table spread of cheeses and fish eggs, he felt his incarnation as Novelist was imminent.

Ironically, an afterthought on the guest list—Patty Lane—was the first to arrive. Patty used to work with Marion, Fred's wife, at Goodson Books. They were assistant editors until a few months ago, when Patty was fired in a general cutback. Knowing this blow had come on top of Patty's breaking up with her boyfriend, Marion felt sorry for Patty, and invited her without consulting Fred. Patty's presence might have irritated Fred, especially in her current condition of unemployment (Fred wanted this evening to gleam with success; any tarnish on his guests might dull the general glow), if it were not for her considerable charms.

Marion was busy in the kitchen while Fred brought Patty a drink. She had come a half-hour early—in her state of mind, she tended to mishear things—and so Fred was alone with her, nervously sipping wine while he watched Patty hungrily eat cheese and crackers from the tray of hors d'oeuvres. Fred began to lean forward for the food as well when he discovered an incentive to do so.

He leaned forward in time with Patty: this choreography allowed him a clear view down the front of her pink cotton top. She wore no bra; thus Fred could conduct a detailed inspection of her white slopes. That is, until his vision reached her nipples. There the soft cloth resumed its task of mild disguise. Only when Patty had taken her piece of bread from the coffee table and relaxed back onto the couch did the two hard points her nipples made in the material become the focus of his attention. For Fred, hors d'oeuvres had suddenly become exhausting.

"Are you looking for a job?" he asked, forcing his eyes *up:* to look at her eyes. That wasn't unpleasant. Patty's eyes were enormous, their color green, their setting moist; she had the bewildered and astonished appearance of an innocent shocked by a corrupt world.

"Oh," Patty sighed. Her eyes strayed to the window. She gazed at the view of the East River. Then she suddenly seemed inspired. "Are there any?"

"Jobs?" Fred said, laughing. "Of course there are jobs. What do you mean?"

"No." She laughed at herself. "I mean, are there any openings? Why don't they fire somebody besides me?"

Fred laughed, delighted by her dizzy and courageous good cheer. Patty leaned forward (reaching for the cheese board) and the forms of her breasts again appeared against the material of her top as she began the movement, gradually billowing out at the neck, until, as her knife sank into the cheese, Fred's clear view of mammary mountainside made him catch his breath. Patty cut a slice and paused, looking up at Fred.

"Fred? Any for you?"

He was speechless.

"No, no," he said abruptly, forcing his eyes away from the scenic route back onto the duller highway of cheese board, coffee table, large standing fern, and dark brown couch. "No one's been fired."

"Fred!" Marion yelled from the kitchen.

"Yes," Fred said instantly. He got to his feet. Patty's eyes widened with surprise at his prompt attention.

"Whoa!" she commented.

"My wife calls," Fred said, and left the room.

She sure has you trained, Patty thought, munching her Brie and cracker. She was famished from her long day's journey, all done on a ration of coffee, cigarettes, and one pastry, the last eaten more than six hours before. But once finished with the cracker, Patty reflected on Marion's married life. Do I envy her? she asked herself. Should I like to work all week and then spend all day Sunday slaving in the kitchen to entertain my husband's friends?

Fred appeared again, looking sheepish, with his arms burdened by a large bag of garbage. Patty laughed but repressed herself when she saw that Fred looked embarrassed and angry. He let the heavy metal door slam shut behind him as he carried out the load.

Men and women aren't meant to be together, Patty decided, and sliced herself a huge piece of cheese. "Jeez," she commented out loud. "I've got to have bigger breakfasts."

"What?" Marion called from the kitchen. And then appeared at the doorway, dressed as if she were going to the office instead of giving a party: gray woolen skirt, a light pink ruffled blouse, a plain gold chain around her neck—a junior executive in drag. However, Marion wore an apron over her business outfit and this contrast made her seem more domestic: a modern Doris Day.

Patty believed Doris Day presented a comical and demeaning image for women; nevertheless, Doris' movies were her favorites as a girl. She wanted to disdain Marion's life, but she felt envy and admiration instead. "I'm eating all your cheese."

"Good," Marion said with Doris Day's cheerfulness. "Do you have enough crackers?"

Fred opened the front door. "Yeech," he said, holding his arms out and away from his body while he studied his pants.

"Did it leak?" Marion asked.

"Ow!" Patty said sympathetically.

"I've got to change," Fred said, and disappeared down the hallway leading to the bedrooms.

"I'm sorry," Marion called after him with a worried look. "I didn't see it was torn."

"Those plastic bags are treacherous," Patty said with exaggerated solemnity. "They come apart all over me. My neighbors are used to seeing me outside my apartment covered with garbage."

Patty's gift for making the simplest statement funny through the contrast of her melodramatic language with a deadpan tone was enjoyed without remark by her friends. Marion resented this talent. Patty wasn't wittier, Marion thought, she simply made a clown of herself. Marion was rarely able to make others laugh and yet Patty could keep a room of people amused for hours, effortlessly, merely by discussing the most ordinary and routine events of the day. And, indeed, Marion herself laughed now from the vivid image she got of Patty smeared with trash.

The doorbell cut her short. Marion went to answer it. Patty got up, heading toward the hallway.

"Hi," said the fellow at the front door.

"Hello, Tony," Marion said.

Tony looked cheerfully and expectantly at Patty as he stepped in.

He had an air of accomplished sociability: he neatly removed his coat in the same movement with which he entered and kissed Marion on the cheek. Yet there was enthusiasm in the routine—as if to say that although he had stepped into a million living rooms, he could still greet this one brightly.

"Excuse me, Tony," Patty said. "I have to use the john immediately or I'll ruin the rug." Patty turned away and walked down the narrow hallway, past a recessed bookcase (filled, for the most part, with books that Marion had edited, which meant there was a surfeit of exercise and cookbooks), and on past the master bedroom into a small bathroom. There she closed and locked the door. She felt breathless and sat down on the closed toilet seat. She had lied about the condition of her bladder. Patty had felt panic out there in the living room. Presented with Marion, with her plumage of domesticity, proudly showing off her bright-colored apron and dutiful husband (gallant carrier of garbage), Patty felt inadequate. Marion's calm, settled tone, so different from Patty's harassed, eager-to-please party voice, intimidated her. Watching Marion was like getting a phone call from Mother: silent rebuke and disapproving pity for Patty and her screwed-up life were behind the kindly tone and tentative questions.

I have no money, no prospects, no boyfriends, and I hate all the men I meet. Patty recited these facts—she was *not* discovering them, this had become a daily litany—to herself. Oddly, listing her problems calmed her. They sounded foolish, unworthy of the panic they inspired. Her heartbeat slowed to a regular pace and she could take a deep breath of air that was enjoyable, even though it smelled of ammonia. Across from the toilet was a photograph of Marion's parents. Patty studied it with a detached air. What an odd spot for an icon to parenthood, she thought, and suddenly felt both loathing and contempt for Marion's and Fred's lives. She didn't want to return to the evening outside the bathroom door: a roomful of people sure of what they wanted and in the midst of getting it. Such people, no matter how kind, made Patty feel her life was undisciplined, and she an eccentric and silly person.

Fred had noticed, while he stepped into a clean pair of pants, that Patty had gone to the bathroom. He rubbed his penis self-consciously when he tucked in his shirt and remembered the vista over hors d'oeuvres. He wanted Patty. His teeth ached from the wine he had drunk, but Fred mistook the burgundy's richness for uncontrollable lust. Fred felt the seven years of sexual fidelity to his wife—they had married immediately after college—had become an unbearable burden, as well as an embarrassment. He lied to his male friends on that score. His lies were never direct or detailed, merely a series of unfinished sentences, winks, sheepish grins, and lustful laughs. Fred wrote regularly for *American Sport* magazine, which meant there were regular trips with basketball and baseball teams. The widespread belief that athletes screw around on the road helped Fred's deceptions.

Even Marion had come to the conclusion that Fred must have participated in at least one "orgy with the boys." Marion lectured herself sternly: men are faithless; a mature married woman (who expects to remain married) accepts these flirtations without comment. In fact, the thought rankled and throbbed with the pain of an untended wound, but Marion rebuked herself for such a provincial feeling. For Marion, feminism's lesson was that men were unredeemable scoundrels. Of course Fred had screwed around on the road.

But he hadn't. The athletes drank with him while they picked up girls, and sometimes a woman would flirt and put her arm in his, even grant him a wet alcoholic kiss. But, in the end, he was passed over in favor of the trainer, the assistant coach, anyone, anyone at all, who was nearby. Fred's chubby face and bulbous nose, his loud laugh and stumpy body, made Fred at times adorable, but never a Casanova. He was faithful to Marion, but, as he told himself, it was the loyalty of a coward and a failure.

Fred stepped out into the hallway and overheard Tony explain to Marion why Tony's wife, Betty, couldn't come.

"You know, Betty's father recently died . . . from cancer. Awful. Well, we've neglected her mother terribly since the funeral and she desperately wanted a night out with her only child."

Bullshit, Fred thought, she doesn't like us. On the two occasions Betty had favored Fred and Marion with her presence, she hardly spoke and looked miserable, developing headache and fatigue by eleven in the evening. She's stuck-up, Marion concluded. Marion might have made that judgment out of envy, because Betty's position in publishing was superior to hers. Betty had the title associate editor and got to work on the manuscripts her boss acquired (novels and major works of nonfiction) instead of the cookbooks that were Marion's lot. Fred, regretfully, had to agree with his wife's opinion. He wanted not to: he wanted Betty to like them, because Tony was by far the most successful, glamorous, richest, and influential of the writers Fred knew.

Tony's allure began with his family history, which Fred knew in detail, though Fred had not been told by Tony—it was gleaned from mutual friends. (The few times Fred had tried to provoke Tony into telling the story himself, Tony had answered curtly and then diverted conversation elsewhere.) Tony Winters was the son of Maureen Winters, the celebrated Group Theater actress who had been ruined by the anti-communist blacklist of the 1950's. Unable to work during her prime years, she had had a nervous breakdown (or so everyone said), but returned to acting gradually in the mid-1960's, becoming nationally famous as Aunt Hattie in a series of detergent commercials, and finally, in the mid-1970's, starring in the number-one-rated situation comedy on television. Tony had been raised by her, except (everyone said) for the year his mother was institutionalized. Tony lived with his father that year.

Tony's father only added, in Fred's eyes, to his allure. Richard Winters was the president of CBS's Business Affairs Division, but discussion about him was also barred. "We're not close," was all that Tony would comment.

Tony's reticence added to the general strain on Fred's nerves when in his company. Fred felt they were merely acquaintances, and he wanted to be close friends—he would have called it "best buddies" in high school. Tony, on top of the fame and success of his parents, had the added attraction of having had three critically praised plays produced off-Broadway by the age of thirty-two. He was generally thought of as a most promising young playwright, somebody for whom great success was a matter of time, not luck or greater effort. So Fred worked hard on his potential friendship with Tony. He boned up on what plays were grossing well, what Mike Nichols was directing in the fall, all the things that were for Tony the gossip of daily life. For a moment Fred stood in the hall and tried to swallow the resentment Betty's absence made him feel. I have to be charming, he told himself, and walked toward the living room.

En route, the bathroom door opened.

Patty came out and stood in the hall. She looked tentatively toward the living room. She hadn't noticed Fred. Her large green eyes made her look as vulnerable as a confused child. Fred moved toward her.

"Ow," she said, startled by his presence. Her small lips made a circle. They were moist. Fred's vision was in tow to them, will-less and enslaved. The small round mouth was like a flower half-open; its dishabille tempted Fred to explore the partly hidden interior. He put his arms around Patty (she was only an inch shorter than he, so a kiss was now merely an inch away) and awkwardly pressed his mouth against her fluted, blooming lips. They widened as he made contact: instantly he was swimming in them. Her mouth had swallowed his: cavernous and hungry, it became huge; her teeth gnawed at his lips; and she pulled and sucked on his tongue so hard he felt as if it would be pulled out by the roots. Unpleasant though this might sound, he was hard. Instantly! A response from the shameful and sensitive days of adolescence. Violently hard. Erect. Extended. A shaft of weight and power. He was stunned by both events —her elastic, starving mouth, and his astounding physical excitement.

What am I doing? Patty asked herself. I'm not attracted to Fred, she added, squeezing his buttocks in her small hands. Fred's cheeks felt fat and formless. I'd like to get my hands on something decent, she thought, and then wanted to laugh at this peculiarly macho reaction.

"Fred!" Marion shouted.

The kiss ended. Fred thrust Patty against the wall, banging her head.

"Whoa," Patty exclaimed.

"Are you okay?" Fred whispered.

Patty nodded.

"Fred!" Marion called again.

"Wait a couple seconds before you come out," Fred said to Patty as he started to go. "I'm coming!" he shouted back to the kitchen. "That was beautiful," he said in a throaty, desperate voice to Patty and then quickly kissed her on the lips. His eyes were shining. "Thank you," he said fervently (to her astonishment), and then walked briskly toward the living room.

"Tony!" Fred said as he entered. His voice was full of enthusiasm, an unconscious parody of Tony's somewhat affected and theatrical speech.

"Hi, Fred!" Tony boomed back at him, his teeth showing, a cigarette waving in the air, with his wrist cocked backward. "It's good to see you. I was just explaining to Marion that Betty couldn't make it."

Fred pouted. He meant his exaggerated facial response to show genuine disappointment and sympathy. "Yeah, I heard. Her mom's not feeling good, huh?"

Tony shook his head. "Betty's mother is young to be widowed. What am I saying? I'm thirty-two, it's time I considered a woman of fifty young for anything, not merely widowhood."

"Yeah, it's rough," Fred said, and continued, his compassion depleted: "Do you want something to drink?"

"Love it. What's available?"

"We have everything." Fred had spent a hundred and twenty dollars that morning to make sure of his boast.

"What are you going to have? I'll go along with you."

"I was going to have red wine. Okay?"

"Terrific."

Fred made his way into the kitchen. His heart raced, he was sweaty, and his stomach felt both light and cramped. His whole system seemed to be under attack by a virus, except for his groin, which was warm and stimulated. He couldn't look Marion in the eyes. This is terrible, he lectured himself. I love my wife. Marion stood at the counter, her hair up (the way he liked it), dressed just like the wife he always wanted: sensible, potentially maternal, and profoundly middle-class. Fred's mother was a hysterical immigrant. Marion never shrieked or wailed or turned beet-red, as did his mother with tedious regularity. Marion, when faced with defeat or despair, simply crawled into bed and slept, as if frustration and depression were a flu that merely required rest and plenty of fluids. However, sex with Marion was boring. And Fred was bored with her body, despite Marion's newly trim figure. Her lovemaking was too passive. She never touched him with any enthusiasm and certainly never serviced his body with anything like the diligence and seriousness with which Fred treated her physical needs.

Those were Fred's polite words for his love life: passive, needs, servicing. They were new. Actually, his old vocabulary was more honest, though crude, when he thought privately: she doesn't give good blow-jobs.

Lately he had tried to censure even his private feelings about Marion in bed. He now thought to himself in the jargon of popular psychology: servicing, needs, caring, experimentation, spontaneity. The last, spontaneity, was Fred's new favorite for lunches with male friends. Marion and I aren't spontaneous in bed anymore, he'd say, hoping, while honestly confessing how bad it was now, to give the impression that he and Marion used to screw in various rooms, in tortured positions, using exotic objects, playing roles. Thus Fred aggrandized his past sexual history while telling the truth about the present. He was glad to have so clever and handy a line available and there wasn't a friend invited to tonight's dinner who hadn't heard him say, "We aren't spontaneous in bed anymore."

The line occurred to him now as he pulled the cork out of a new bottle of wine. "I didn't mean to yell," Marion said in a whisper. "I just don't like Tony sitting alone in our living room. I can imagine him making up witticisms about our furniture."

Tony called out to them while Marion was whispering to Fred. "Who's coming tonight?"

"David Bergman, my buddy from college who's a big shot at *Newstime*, Karl Stein, the novelist, and my new agent, Bart Cullen." Fred said this as he began to exit from the kitchen. He whispered to Marion as he passed her: "It's okay. I understand."

Tony took the glass of wine. "Do they have dates?"

Patty entered. "Mmmm, wine," she said.

"Hello again," Tony said to Patty with such vehement cheerfulness that one might imagine he knew Patty well. In fact, they had met only a few times, through her friendship with his wife, Betty.

"Hi, Tony," Patty said. "I was in a state when you arrived!"

Fred poured wine into a glass for her, ashamed to look her in the eyes.

"Really? Why?" Tony's questions were disarming, his voice almost squeaked with curiosity and good will.

He's handsome, Patty thought. "Oh! I'm so miserable. I've bored Fred—"

At the mention of his name, Fred lost track of the rim of the glass and pointed the nozzle past it, spilling wine on the table. He caught it quickly. Tony's light blue eyes took in Fred's embarrassed movements while he mopped up the wine and then handed Patty her glass. Tony's eyes, while observing Fred, were cold and intelligent. Patty paid no attention to Fred's actions, but she did observe the sudden transformation in Tony's look, from empty-headed attention and charm to the clinical, almost heartless stare with which he evaluated Fred's state of mind. "I have no job, I'm broke, I don't know any good men," she was saying.

Shut up, Fred thought, and nervously watched Marion enter with another plate of cold vegetables and dip.

"You don't?" Tony said. "How shocking!"

"All the *decent* men," Patty said—her small pouting lips attacked the word—"are married."

"Or gay," Marion said.

"That's right!" Patty said. "Tony! Why are all the men"—she lowered her voice and even managed to peek about as if the walls were bugged—"*fags?* Why don't you do something about it, Tony!"

Tony and Fred roared, or so it seemed to Marion, at this speech of Patty's. Marion was irritated by their amusement. After all, she had said the witty thing first.

"Well," Tony answered, "the Moral Majority has already done something for you."

"They have?" Patty said in a tone so awed that Tony had to laugh at it.

"Yes! They invented AIDS."

"Don't joke about AIDS," Marion said, almost wincing. "Someone I know has it."

"You're right. I shouldn't joke," Tony said, transforming his face into a solemn mask, like a chastened schoolboy. "I also know two people who've got it. You know"—and he couldn't help but start to laugh—"in the theater world it really could be like the Black Death. It's possible it could finish theater."

Fred, who had been embarrassed by Marion's correction of Tony (her attitude might seem unsophisticated to Tony), laughed hard at this, hoping to defuse the bomb of seriousness she had dropped.

"Is everybody in the theater gay, Tony?" Patty asked, again with an innocent awe that provoked laughter.

"No, no," Tony said with great conviction. "Only half. The problem is, that half are all the males. Only the women are heterosexual and naturally after a few years in the theater, they become intensely frustrated and start screwing movie executives or owners of baseball teams."

Patty and Fred laughed, but Marion frowned, leaned toward Tony, and said in a scolding tone, "I really don't think it's funny. This twenty-three-old editorial assistant has it. He was told to take a permanent sick leave—they're paying him so they won't get sued. His lover, his family, no one will see him. And the people who worked with him are busy making jokes about replacing all the coffee cups in the office. Jokes that aren't so funny, and maybe aren't even jokes, because somebody did buy new coffee cups and even a new coffeepot."

Tony leaned forward eagerly, smiling. "You're kidding! Who?"

Fred had felt his stomach tighten while Marion reproved Tony—he wished briefly she was dead and he had Patty hosting the party—but Tony's response, completely ignoring the criticism and enjoying the facts, calmed him. Not only calmed him, but impressed Fred once again with Tony's social skills. Tony deflected his wife's crabby middle-class criticism into an anecdote in which other people were the villains and Tony became a partner in her disapproval.

"We don't know who," Marion answered. "Yesterday we came in and somebody had thrown out all the old stuff and bought new things."

"Incredible," Tony agreed, shaking his head. "It's incredible how primitive people's reactions are. An actor I went to Yale with got it and I visited him in the hospital last week . . ."

Fred met Marion's eyes, his look telling her what a fool she'd made of herself. Marion returned the glance defiantly and looked back to Tony.

". . . and even though I argued with close friends of his who refused to visit, I must admit it, when I walked in I was scared to even sit down, much less shake his hand."

"You didn't shake his hand!" Patty said.

"Patty!" Marion warned.

"Well, we don't know. They don't know how people get it."

"Oh, for God's sake—" Marion started.

But Tony cut her off. "Patty," he said gently, "if AIDS could be communicated by a handshake, millions of people would have it. And not only that, there would be no way to protect against getting it. The world would have to sit back, let those who die, die, and like the Black Plague, only those with natural resistance would survive." Tony leaned close to Patty. "Nevertheless, I didn't shake his hand."

At this Fred and Patty laughed hard. Marion leaned back with a disgusted look, as if giving up on all of them.

The intercom buzzed. Marion got up and answered it. They all heard the amplified voice of the doorman. "Bart Cullen to see you."

"I didn't know you had a new agent," Tony said to Fred.

"Yeah, Bart Cullen. He handles Fredericka Young."

Patty whistled.

"Who's Fredericka Young?" Tony asked.

"You don't know?" Fred said, amazed. "I guess she doesn't go to Elaine's."

"Maybe she does," Tony said dryly. Fred, envious of Tony's ability to be seated at Elaine's (the renowned show-business, literary, and amorphous-celebrity restaurant), often teased Tony about his regular attendance there. The kidding irritated Tony because he knew Fred's real complaint was that Tony didn't invite him along. "Doesn't mean I know her. Who is she?"

"She wrote *All My Sins*."

Marion, at the door, called into the hallway, "This way, Bart."

Tony, recognizing the title as the number-one bestseller of last year, said in a whisper, "My God, and he got ten percent?"

Fred nodded solemnly.

"Fred!" Patty said with excitement. "He'll make you rich."

Fred guffawed nervously, getting up to greet Bart, who at that moment appeared at the front door. "That's the idea," he said to Patty and Tony.

They turned to look at Fred's hope for success. Bart was the opposite of the caricature of the agent: he was tall, thin, with a full head of red hair. His long nose, pale blue eyes, and thin unsmiling mouth made him look like a Flemish painting: a mournful, industrious, and religious man. But his companion fit the image of a wheeling-and-dealing agent: she was a tall blond model with the perfect features of modern surgery and the brilliant white teeth of industrial enamel.

While Fred introduced them (the model's name was Brett, which Tony thought was probably acquired at the same time as her teeth), the intercom buzzed again and soon they were joined by Karl Stein. Karl was also represented by Bart—indeed, Karl had provided the introduction that led to Fred becoming a client. Karl was a short, sad man with black and gray hair that hung from the center of his head like draperies. His thick black beard gave the impression of religious commitment: a martyr.

In a sense he *was* a monk of the Order of Novelists. After college, Karl had begun his first book, finished it within a year, and sent it to publishers. He got fifteen rejections. Meanwhile, he began work on another novel. Over the next ten years he wrote six manuscripts, none of them finding a publisher. A friend persuaded him to meet someone he knew at *Penthouse* magazine and Karl wrote a piece for them on a sex club in New York that led to the first check he received as a writer. After a few more pieces for *Penthouse*, other assignments followed—from *Playboy*, then *Esquire*, and so on. A piece for *Playboy* on stewardesses attracted Bart's attention. Bart called Karl, suggested he fire his current agent, hirt Bart, and write an outline based on the notion of tracing three generations of a family of stewardesses, from the prop age to the Concorde. Karl's ten-page proposal on this idea won for him the book contract that his six devotions did not. He had finished *Stewardess* by the time he walked into Fred's dinner party and had only five months to wait for his first novel to appear.

The last guest to arrive was David Bergman, someone Fred knew slightly in college and had cultivated after he spotted David's name listed on the masthead at *Newstime* as a senior writer. Marion had invited Patty partly because of David. He was single and a good catch. To be a senior writer at his age was a remarkable achievement, and besides, Marion liked David. He looked responsible and decent. In his double-breasted pin-striped suit, white shirt, and red tie, he didn't look at all like a writer, she thought, without any irony or self-consciousness that she, the wife of a writer, was so impressed by that.

Other than David, who asked for bourbon, the new arrivals asked for white wine. Fred couldn't resist a gibe. "Well, I'm glad I read the Living Section of the *Times* this month."

Blank looks.

"Everybody's drinking wine!" Fred said with the tone of Sherlock Holmes naming the murderer.

"I'm not," David said mildly.

The rest looked puzzled and there was an awkward silence. Tony broke the tableau: "Fred, this is a most provocative remark. But we don't understand it."

Patty laughed violently, mostly at Tony's tone of utter contempt and the embarrassed look on Fred's face. She started to cough and choke, trying to stop herself, knowing her laughter was insulting—indeed, Fred's face turned red.

"I didn't mean it as a put-down," Fred stammered. "Don't you remember the piece a couple of weeks ago saying that hard liquor before dinner was passé?" Fred said this, appealed it really, to Karl, who (generally worried by any gathering larger than three) peered about in a bewildered and suspicious manner. He looked startled by Fred's question. In fact, he was made nervous by Fred including him in something that seemed to be an embarrassing mistake.

"No—I didn't hear what you said," Karl answered in so guilty and halting a manner that when Tony leaned forward and patted Karl on the knee, saying, "Don't worry, Karl, we'll give you a makeup test later," everybody laughed. They laughed nervously, because they were acquaintances burdened with the need to pretend intimacy and friendliness, and the strain needed relief.

Fred, knowing he had somehow made a fool of himself, desperately grabbed at a new subject. "Say, we got to get Patty a job." Fred's foot jiggled anxiously. "Come on, this room is full of people with connections. Patty's terrific. She's smart, she's cute, she knows editing."

Patty wished she was back in the bathroom again—this time to slit her wrists.

Karl frowned at her, increasing her discomfort. "You're sure you want to go back into publishing?"

"Of course!" Fred answered for her. "We have to make sure all our friends become important editors so they'll publish our books!" Fred guffawed, scanning the room with glistening eyes for others who would enjoy his open statement of opportunism. Fred suffered from the delusion that to confess to calculation was disarming and sophisticated. He believed it simultaneously revealed himself as aware of such conniving, disapproving of it, and yet showed he was prepared to take advantage of it himself—a combination of attitudes that Fred thought was self-aware and humorous (like a Woody Allen hero, Fred would have said) rather than the tail of the comet of self-doubt that raged constantly throughout the galaxy of his insecurities.

"I guess you're right, Fred," Tony Winters said to cover the embarrassed silence that threatened the room. "That's probably the only way we'll get any of our stuff published."

"No!" Patty instantly protested.

"I don't think you should go back into publishing," Karl said in a grave and considered tone.

"Hear, hear," Marion said.

Tony smiled at her. She returned his glance demurely.

"See," Tony said to Patty. "And Marion's an editor. Ask her how lucky you are to be out of it."

"You know the problem with being an editor?" Marion said, leaning forward eagerly.

Fred broke in, flashing a look at his new agent, Bart. "Just don't say it's agents who ruin the business." Again he guffawed.

"Well, they're not a big help, Fred," Marion said.

Tony smiled at Marion admiringly.

"Business," Karl mumbled into his drink, unheard by the others.

"But they're not the big problem," Marion continued, looking into Tony's handsome eyes. She felt encouraged by them: this kind of declamation was difficult for Marion. "It's the mixed messages. Nothing is straightforward. They hire you and say, 'Oh, we want you to aggressively acquire books, discover young writers, and demand big printings.' Then they reject every unknown writer you bring in, while agents only give the track-record authors to the big boys—"

"Well, I don't know if I can agree with that," Bart said quietly. His still manner made the words impressive: Marion shut up and the room gave its attention to Bart. "Bob Holder at Garlands & Company is only twenty-eight. I give him a crack at all my six-figure authors."

"Gosh, doesn't that sound nice," Tony Winters interrupted with a show of greed. Patty, Marion, and David Bergman all laughed instantly. Karl also laughed, but so violently that it seemed more like anger. The others looked puzzled, except for Fred, who was torn between appreciating Tony and not offending Bart. "It's like a chest measurement for women," Tony went on. "What's sexier? A high six figures or a low seven?"

Patty's lips made a small circle. "Oh, a low seven, for sure."

"I bet you say that to all the boys," Tony said. "That should be a hint to the National Book Awards, or TABA, or whatever the hell it is now."

"TABA," Karl said into his drink.

"TABA." Tony nodded. "Well, anyway, they should have a swimsuit competition in the future. Can't you see Bill Styron in a bikini?"

"How about Mailer?" David Bergman offered.

"No, no. Mailer stays in shape," Tony argued. "You want the real slobs, the people who have gone to seed."

"Mailer!" David Bergman called out again, laughing. "His writing fits."

"That's not true," Karl said, so exercised that he raised his head and spoke clearly.

"Despite your joking, that is the idea," Bart said to Tony. His serious tone again caused everyone to focus on him. Once they had, he continued. "TABA is an attempt to create superstar writers and superstar book events, like the Academy Awards. I think it's a good thing."

"Yeah, yeah," Fred said. His leg bounced up and down nervously. "I don't understand why you guys at the Authors Guild and PEN voted against it," Fred said to Tony and Karl.

"I'm not a member of the Authors Guild or PEN," Tony protested.

Karl wasn't either, but he didn't like to admit it.

Fred stayed on Tony. "Yeah, but you know the presidents of both of them."

"You make me sound like Secretary of State," Tony answered, smiling. He stubbornly resisted Fred's attempt to link him with a literary establishment, not out of modesty, but fear that if he admitted to Fred he had access to such people, within twenty-four hours he would get a call from Fred requesting introductions.

"It seems to me," Marion said, "writers objecting to TABA is typical of how hypocritical writers can be. Authors want to be celebrities, they want their books advertised, and all the rest, but God forbid they should participate in the selling, or admit that it's a business. Only writers can decide who are good writers, is what they're saying. It's bullshit."

Karl coughed. "Excuse me." He cleared his throat. "But that's silly. Writers have always decided who are good writers. What do you think literary critics are? Painters? They're writers." He laughed and looked around for support, but the vehemence of his tone caused only worried looks.

"Karl." Bart said the word like a parent: a warning against throwing a tantrum. "With your first novel coming out, you can't have that attitude."

David Bergman, unaware that Bart was Karl's agent, and irritated by his arrogant manner, got up from his chair and walked around the couch to face Bart, saying, "Why the hell shouldn't he? Seems to me with his first novel coming out, it's the best possible attitude. Artists can't take the judgments of businessmen to heart—not if they hope to continue to be artists."

"Editors aren't businessmen," Marion said.

"Of course they are!" Karl sputtered. His drink spilled as he put it down on the coffee table. "That's why—"

Bart's commanding voice interrupted: "So are writers."

Karl shut up and looked at his agent with the wide-eyed, trusting, and slightly frightened expression of a dutiful student.

"Never forget it," Bart said in the sonorous tone of a newscaster signing on: "A writer is a businessman first. And then, if you're lucky, you can be an artist too."

David Bergman looked at the other writers. Tony, though he wore a slight smile to indicate distance from Bart's judgment, looked at the floor. Fred, his leg bouncing up and down nervously, nodded his enthusiastic agreement. Karl simply closed his mouth, clamping down on his unfinished objection. And Patty, for the first time, looked at David with wide-eyed interest.

"Look," David said. "I know I'm a hack journalist. One of the advantages I have over other writers at *Newstime* is I admit it to myself. But I'm not a businessman. And these fellows, they're not hacks. They can't be businessmen. It would kill them to even try."

Bart looked up at David slowly. "To get what they want—they'd better be."

There was a silence, a few seconds of embarrassed uneasiness at Bart's dramatic tone.

Brett, Bart's date, stood up, her long blond hair swinging like a slow-motion shot for a commercial. David stepped back, startled.

"Excuse me," she said. "Where's the little girls' room?"

No one answered at first. Then David put his arm out—a gentlemanly escort. "I'll take you there."

Brett was astonished. "You're going with me?"

"Yes. I have to throw up now," David answered with a charming smile. The room broke up—except for Patty, who continued to stare at David with intense interest. As far as anyone could remember, that was the party's last interesting moment.

CHAPTER 2

Everyone left Fred's party only a half-hour after coffee had been served. Tony started the exit, announcing he had an early appointment. Having been shown the way out, they all developed early appointments and left within a few minutes of each other.

David Bergman was pleasantly surprised to find that Patty lived near him in SoHo, and offered to split a cab with her.

"How long have you lived in SoHo?" David asked after giving their addresses to the cabdriver.

"Two years, but I lost my lease."

"Oh. You found another apartment?"

"No, I'm apartment sitting for two weeks. I lost my lease because of a lunatic."

David smiled at her deadpan delivery.

"No one believes me. My friends think I must have done something horrible. But I'm innocent, I swear!" She clutched David's arm and begged: "Do you believe me?"

David laughed at her desperate gesture and language, because while she pleaded, her eyes twinkled mischievously, hinting, like starlight, at tomorrow's unseen and powerful sun.

He was drunk. The party had made him uncomfortable. Tasting the bourbon over and over helped, and by the time Marion's heavy meal of crab croquettes and lasagna arrived, his stomach felt full and he only wanted more cool liquid. But the booze didn't soothe his uneasy memory of his behavior. He had heard himself arguing with every opinion the guests pronounced. It had begun with Bart about writers and businessmen, but he even found himself telling Fred the Yankees couldn't win this year, quoting half-remembered opinions of Harold Yeller, *Newstime*'s sports columnist, as if he had thought them himself, or even understood them. David hadn't watched a ballgame in years. Yes, the general feel of the evening had disgusted him. There was something pathetic about Fred's formal arrangements: forcing them into some sort of community. Worst of all was the pretense that they were important, when, in fact, other than Bart (who, after all, was merely an agent), they were mediocrities. All of them standing in line at the New York cafeteria of young professionals: stuffed with opinions before the meal of life had even begun.

Patty had noticed David's succession of bourbons. No one else was drinking hard stuff, for one thing, and David also seemed to cling to his glass in a somewhat tragic and desperate manner. She liked him for it. She felt he would understand her own desperation. Besides, Patty was raised in a Philadelphia suburb, and David's drinking summoned a more manly image than seeing a shrink or complaining endlessly, as it seemed to her most New York men did when they were unhappy.

Their cab took Second Avenue down from Fred's and Marion's apartment on Sixty-seventh Street. They were passing the gaily colored Roosevelt tram, parked in its cocoon like a children's toy of a giant race. They were through the midtown traffic and would be at David's stop on West Broadway in ten minutes. She wanted him to ask her up, or at least suggest they go for a drink at the Spring Street Bar. It would be hours before Patty could sleep.

"What time is it?" she asked dishonestly, having seen eleven o'clock flash when they passed the Daily News Building.

"I don't know. It feels like four in the morning, doesn't it?"

"Oh, no. I'm speeding. I feel like I just got up."

"I didn't mean I was tired," David said.

"Good. I want you to buy me a drink."

David turned to her and showed surprise. Patty held her breath. She hadn't planned to make the invitation. Everything, these days, seemed to fly out of her: not merely indelicate invitations to men, but also intimacies, anxieties, confessions of guilt, of meanness, details of her bowel movements, all sorts of high-security information that was normally guarded closely by censors.

"Okay." David didn't mean to sound perfunctory. He had been so caught up by the image of himself sniping and nattering at the party that seduction hadn't occurred to him. But the surprise was pleasant. Patty's blond hair, wanton mouth, and big eyes were excellent lures.

"If you're tired, don't—" she began.

"Don't be silly," David said, turning his attention to the possibilities. His voice deepened; he shifted toward her and smiled agreeably. "But let's not go to a bar."

Patty pursed her lips. "Your apartment?" she suggested, batting her eyes.

Tony expected his wife to be in bed reading. She was.

"Dollface," he announced at the bedroom door.

"Hi!" Betty said, her high thin voice making this word gay and ringing. She spoke in flat tones usually, but greetings were her strong suit. She lay in the bed wearing a long pin-striped nightshirt. Ensconced in the big pillows, her short curly red hair framed by the bright colors of the linens, she looked young—a dutiful daughter waiting for Daddy's good-night kiss. Tony always felt slightly startled by his wife's girlish face. Her short nose and pale blue eyes were eager, almost naive, whereas he knew her interior to be different: cynical, cautious, and mature. It was the latter, internal picture of her that he carried out with him to the world and subconsciously expected to find on his return.

"You're awake," Tony said, pleased. He took off his jacket and opened the closet door.

"Let me see you," Betty said.

Tony turned around. "What?"

"Put your jacket on. I want to see how you look."

He obeyed with boyish sheepishness: showing himself to Mom for inspection.

"You're putting on weight," she said.

Tony sagged. "Great. For this I put my jacket back on?"

"Aw," she laughed. "Don't disappear," she called after him as he went into the closet.

"How was your mother?" Tony asked, reappearing, with only his Jockey shorts on.

"Your greenies!" Betty said, delighted. She referred to the color of his underpants.

"I wore your favorites," Tony said in a lofty tone.

"My mother! What about my mother!"

"Aha! I knew you'd forget. Tomorrow, when Fred calls to say he was sorry you couldn't come, he'll ask how your night out with Mom was."

"Oh, that's right. I'm sorry. I'll remember."

Tony closed the closet door and hurried under the covers, his hands immediately playing, ticklishly, up and down his wife's body. She squirmed and giggled like a girl.

"Oh—oh—don't! You're waking me up!"

"God!" Tony shouted in his deepest and most dramatic of voices.

Despite its masculine low register, whenever he used that tone, Betty heard Tony's mother talking—Maureen Winters, a drink in her hand, standing atop the stairs, her hair prettily disheveled, calling out in a throaty voice: "God help me!"

Tony had abruptly rolled away and over onto his back. He stared at the ceiling. "We're so damned domestic."

Betty rearranged herself, retrieving her book. "Tell me about the party."

Tony groaned. He rolled over again to his side, facing Betty. "Nothing happened. Boring." His hand sneaked under the cover, heading for Betty's thighs.

"Was Fred's new agent there?"

Tony nodded. "Bart What's-his-name." His hand touched her thin, smooth, and elegant leg.

"Bart Cullen." Betty pursed her thin lips with disapproval—a snobbish mannerism Tony disliked. "He's a bizarre person."

"He's psychotic. I think he believes he gets ninety percent of his clients, not ten," Tony said in a seductive whisper. He ran the flat of his hand up her hip to the side of her belly.

"Who else was there?"

"Your good friend Patty."

"Oh! I have to call her!"

Tony moved closer. His hand moved over Betty's stomach and up to her breast. Despite the frown she put on, her body undulated with pleasure. He gently followed the slight rise of her collarbone to her neck. There was a faint trace of a line just above her Adam's apple and he touched it lightly. She shivered. "Fred and his wife, Bart and his girlfriend. A writer named Karl Stein—"

"Karl Stein? That sounds familiar."

"He's under contract to your colleague Bob Holder. Bart is his agent."

"Right! Yeah, Bart only deals with Bob. Supposed to be a terrific novel."

Tony dropped his hand to her hips and pulled her toward him, speaking softly as he warmed himself against her body. "Can't be. He's a frightened rabbit. He listens to Bart like he's God."

Betty closed her eyes and ran her hands down Tony's back. "I don't have any books."

"You still get only two for the fall list?" He kissed the faint line and then moved up to her small, delicate ear

"You're terrible," she said flatly.

"Hmmm."

"You say Fred and his wife. Bart and his girlfriend. That's terrible. Probably they talk about me that way."

His penis stretched against the elastic band of his greenies. His immediate desire for her surprised him. When would he tire of her? He felt like a teenager on a date: barely one kiss and he was ready to climax.

Marion had cooked, so the cleaning-up was Fred's job. This chore suited him. He suffered from insomnia, and mechanical activity helped stop him from percolating his anxious thoughts. Marion, exhausted and tense, had drawn herself a hot bath and was now happily soaking. Fred made good progress, revved up by the five cups of coffee he had nervously drunk after dinner. Half an hour after his guests departed, Fred had meticulously cleaned everything, even drying to a sparkle the stainless-steel sink.

He knocked on the bathroom door tentatively, worried that Marion wouldn't allow him in. He liked to watch her in the bath, lying naked in the soapy water, but Marion was shy of exhibition. Fred argued that her reluctance made no sense: they had been married for seven years, surely he knew what her body looked like. "It's my right to be private and have a bath alone," she would answer, striking a note of finality that implied she would resort to hysteria if he pressed his point.

"Hi," Fred said in a meek voice. "Can I come in?"

He heard her move in the water, a soft languid splash. "Sure," she said. I should get my cigarettes, Fred thought as he entered, but he was too eager to see his favorite nude pose. There she lay, fitting neatly into the tub, her head resting against its sloping lip, in water made faintly blue by bath oils. "Wow. Hot enough?" Fred said. The steamy room seemed to be weeping. The wall of mirrors over the sink was fogged and dripping moisture.

"Mmmm," Marion said, closing her eyes, relaxing into the soothing bath.

"So. What do you think?" Fred asked, staring at the spooky and sexy levitation of her pubic hairs to the water's surface.

"What do you mean?"

"The party. How'd it go?"

Marion laughed. Her nipples punctured the water, floating like pink buoys. "It was okay."

He reached forward. His hand penetrated the liquid and touched her stomach. She accepted this without movement or comment. "You think everyone had a good time?"

"I think so. Don't you?"

Her skin, or the water, or both, felt oily. His hand skimmed over her belly and up to her breasts like a sleigh skimming on ice, gliding on her hilly countryside. "I don't know. Everybody seemed stiff. Didn't they?"

Marion ignored his massage and answered in a polite tone. "Well, nobody knew anybody very well. Patty was crazy, throwing herself at every man." Fred's hand covered her groin, gathering her floating wisps of hair, and he pressed, one finger splitting her lips and entering briefly.

She winced.

Fred removed his intruding finger and stroked her thigh. "She's lonely."

"She acts horny, not lonely," Marion said, frowning. She reached down and lifted Fred's hand off her. "I'm trying to relax," she said, placing his hand on the cool rim of the bathtub.

David Bergman's loft was impressive. He knew that. The twenty-five hundred square feet he rented had had its beautiful oak floor sanded and sealed to a glistening shine with polyurethane. The meticulous tape job done on the plasterboard ceiling made the seams invisible. His cast-iron columns, standing in a dramatic row down the center of the space, were painted white, highlighting their fine details against the planks of glistening oak. His kitchen was a self-contained unit of handleless black Formica cabinets above a shimmering row of stainless-steel appliances. His large bathroom was outfitted with an elaborate marble sink, its faucet handles saying HOT and COLD in delicate blue letters. His bathtub could fit two and he had the luxury of a separate shower stall. Otherwise, the space was open. Wide open: eyes could look upward, past the gay yellow sprinkler pipes to a fourteen-foot ceiling; and then scan, when standing at one end, across the twenty-five hundred square feet to a set of windows at the other end. Even his furniture (though there wasn't nearly enough to fill the place) was fine. Two large Oriental rugs floated on the floor like exquisite lily pads; two huge couches made an angle bordering one of the rugs; there was a long French country table near the kitchen exit, accompanied by a set of Breuer chairs; and, at another end of the loft, a king-size bed rested against one wall. In this cavern, it looked like a big pillow.

The effect of this splendor on Patty was increased by the deceptive prelude of the building's seedy entrance. Three of the floors were still used for industrial purposes and thus the elevator was a dark, unfinished shell, roofless and spooky. It didn't even operate automatically. David started it up by manipulating two cables, and the loud whirring noise of the elevator's engine sounded labored. It lurched at the start. "Whoa," Patty said, startled, and staggered backward, balancing herself against the rear wall.

David smiled. "It's okay. Don't worry. That's the way it always sounds."

Thus she was dazzled when David swung open the tall metal doors of the dim and scary elevator (she imagined rats and spiders and all sorts of horrible things lurking about) into the sweeping, brilliant loft.

Touring it made conversation natural. David had inherited the loft from his older brother, who had been a SoHo pioneer. David called him that with a sneer. "At the time, everybody thought he was crazy. There wasn't a name for this area and this place was a filthy mess, the ceilings sagging, the oak floor a dirty, unrecognizable brown." David's brother had gotten a lot of work when SoHo conversions became fashionable. He made enough money to realize his dream: he moved to a penthouse apartment overlooking Central Park.

"Maybe one day I'll be that lucky," David said as they settled on one of the couches. He had supplied her with wine and reheated a cup of that morning's coffee in a desperate attempt to sober himself up. When Patty leaned forward to replace her glass on the coffee table after taking a sip, the pink cotton top billowed away from her breasts like a sail picking up a gentle breeze, and he saw (in astonishing detail) the firm creamy white terrain that had so discombobulated Fred. A green-blue vein ran vertically across her right breast, winding like a stream down a mountain's face, disappearing into the chasm of her cleavage. On her left breast, a startling brown beauty mark was frozen in orbit about her nipple. All this he saw in the time it took for her to reach forward. Her big eyes rolled like a doll's, down and then up, as she straightened. He saw her see that he was seeing. He felt his face flush. His pale cheeks were all that his dark glasses and brown beard exposed, but they were enough—they turned red. His blushing wasn't unusual. David liked to think of himself as a sophisticate, but nature had given him the cheeks of a bride. Years ago, he had made peace with them by training himself to talk through their flare-ups. "It's a beautiful place," he said loudly, noticing that she was smiling and staring at the display. "But I feel like I'm part of a warehouse sale. Or a parked car. It's too big." He paused, hoping she wouldn't call attention to his embarrassment.

For a moment, she was going to, but instead she let her eyes roam, looking at the clear open space surrounding her. "I love it." She squeezed her shoulders together. "I'm from the suburbs and these New York apartments make me claustrophobic."

"This isn't like a suburban home. In fact, I can't think of anything more typically New York than a converted loft. The whole city is full of ex-rag-pickers who have entered the middle class. I know it's all scrubbed but this still doesn't feel like a residence to me. Can't you see them"—he stretched out his arm and pointed to the empty space, between two of the columns, that bridged the living and eating areas—"the immigrant women in their caps, under rows of those big globe lights, sewing their garments?"

Patty liked this dramatic gesture and poetic idea. David had seemed sour at the party: a stiff, slightly obnoxious young man who believed he knew everything. That also attracted her. She liked to win the good opinion of difficult people, but this blushing and fanciful David was even better. Patty believed sensitive men were easier to go to bed with, because, though their performance was sometimes problematic, they made more lenient judgments. Patty looked at the empty space and tried to imagine David's scene. She couldn't. The dazzling floor, those delicate columns, the beautiful peacock-colored rugs, all spoke to her of money, ease, self-assurance; things that had eluded her since she came to New York. She had grown up in this kind of comfort in suburban Pennsylvania and, so far, no one she knew in New York had it. No, for Patty, this loft was not haunted by immigrant women.

She turned herself toward David, kicked off her shoes, and put both feet under her. This made her into a small package that David could easily imagine carrying to his bed. "I don't like to think of them," she said looking sad.

"My grandmother was one of them," David said quietly.

"She worked here!" Patty's eyes opened in alarm.

"No, no," David said, laughing. "She worked in a sweatshop in the city. I don't know where."

"Maybe it was here," Patty said, her eyes scanning the loft as if she might find David's grandmother in the shadows.

"No, I doubt it," David said. He thought this last remark of Patty's impossibly dumb. His penis had begun to warm and swell in his pants (he could feel the tip press outward, like mercury rising to show fever) but this one dizzy comment chilled his passion. "Do you want more wine?" he asked. She nodded. He leaned forward to get the bottle. As he did, their bodies were now touching, and Patty's hand landed on his thigh next to the thermometer of his lust. He almost tipped the bottle over, though her touch was gentle.

He steadied his grip and carefully poured her more wine. Her hand now crept onto his penis and passed down and then back up its length

once, like a blessing. He tried to think of something to say. A casual
remark. But nothing was in his mind other than the sensation of his
rapidly rising mercury. Heat, growth, his pants suddenly tight: a clatter
of feelings that pleasurably shouted down any thought.

He fought it off (he didn't want to show pleasure, he never liked to)
and managed to finish pouring and replace the bottle without letting a
moan of smoky joy emit from the furnace below. He turned his head
toward her, ready to say something noncommittal, but when his eyes
met hers, he discovered she had leaned toward him, and now his lips
were only inches from her wet and fluted mouth.

They kissed.

While they did, her hand covered his groin. She gripped him as if
his penis were a handle with which she could pick him up and carry him
anywhere. He felt intensely excited by this dominated sensation; that she
was ruthlessly feeling the merchandise, ready to squeeze for a reward or
depart as a punishment.

Now, as their mouths opened and flattened and pecked, he was
growing, growing so hard that she could bunch his wool pants around
his prick and stroke.

It's wearing a mitten, he thought, and wanted to giggle at this silly
idea. He was happy! He felt like a gurgling infant, secure in the grasp of
this small woman who seemed to see right through his dark suit, tortoise
glasses, dark beard, and formal manner. She knew how to handle him:
with the confidence of a mother soothing her baby, and a whore's precise
manipulation. He was at her mercy.

He had become so fascinated by the drama below that he lost interest in returning her kiss and became a receptacle: her tongue probing his
mouth restlessly. He closed his eyes and rested his head back on the
couch. She leaned over him, her mouth covering his, her hand rubbing
and stroking his penis. I'm being raped, he thought with a thrill of delight.

Her hand left. He felt his stiff member twitch, begging for more
contact. But it was only a pause for her to unzip him. His pants sighed
open as if exhausted by her. He felt cool air while her fingers scurried
under the elastic band of his Jockey shorts, and, awkwardly, pulled them
halfway down. She nudged his ass, again with a combination of moth-
erliness and business practicality; with another yank his underpants were
off. How completely he was in her spell: flattened against the couch, his
tail wagging in the air, waving shamelessly for love!

Her small hand took his penis by its base, and her fingers twined
around it. While she kissed, pressed, tongued, and bit his lips and mouth,

she ran her grip up and down its length. His position and her matter-of-fact manipulation struck David as comic, but nonetheless pleasurable. His penis arced in the cool air, yearning for more, and yet was soothed with each stroke. The world was obliterated but for one sensation: the planet had been reduced to an appendage.

Her mouth was gone. But he didn't care. His head was thrown back, his legs spread and turned outward . . . and then, a hot liquid touched the head of his penis. When it departed, the cool air was cooler. And then lava covered him again, became a sea, a sauna, a sucking furnace, a bath—he opened his eyes and looked down to watch her blond head move up and down, her cheeks puffed, her lips opening and closing on the tip of his aching sex.

"This is rape," Betty said. Laughing, she tried to wriggle away and, in the attempt, her short red curls tickled Tony's neck. He was on top, pressing his pelvis onto hers, groaning melodramatically.

"Love me like a rock, oh baby," Tony said, but in a basso classical actor's voice. "Let me put the pedal to the metal."

"What!" Betty laughed helplessly, her body trembling from her giggles.

"Whoa," Tony said, gripping the bed to steady himself.

"Pedal to the what!"

"It's a macho phrase, darling. Oh, that's right, you didn't come to the screening of *Smokey and the Bandit*. Pedal to the metal. It means floor it."

"Floor what?"

"The car. The accelerator. My God!"

"Oh. I'm sorry," she said, and now kissed him languishingly, her lips lingering as she ended the contact, pulling away reluctantly.

"More," Tony said.

Betty moved her head back to get a more distant view of her husband. Her pale blue eyes studied him lovingly. But there was pride and possession in the look also, as though she was contemplating a family heirloom. She brushed his hair off one ear. "You need a haircut."

Tony leaned in and kissed her again. "Oh, that's sexy."

She winked. "It's late for me, Tony. I have to be up in six hours. Your day is just starting."

"Come on, that's not true. I have a meeting at eleven-thirty."

"With whom?"

Tony groaned and rolled off his wife. And then kept on rolling, his arms and legs flailing in the air as he went off the bed. He hit the floor with a harsh thud.

"Tony!" Betty sat up, alarmed, and peered over the edge of the bed to see him.

"Yes, darling," Tony answered casually.

"You're nutty."

"Thank you, darling."

Betty relaxed. "Who is your meeting with?"

"Gloria."

"Gloria Fowler? How did that happen?"

"She called me." Tony raised his eyebrows in an attempt to look snooty. "Said she admires my plays and wondered if we might have lunch."

Betty whistled.

"You think she wants to represent me?"

"Does she do theater?"

"No, she doesn't really. But other people in the agency do. She might want me to write movies."

"Movies!" Betty reached for a pack of cigarettes on the night table beside her. "What would make her think you'd want to write movies?"

"Well." Tony stood up and walked majestically toward the window, his legs stepping high and deliberately in front of him, a soldier on the march. "Don't you think I can?"

Betty's eyes were on his greenies. "Do you want to write movies?"

"God, you say it as if I've announced I want to fuck a leper." He peered out a window at the street tragically.

"I'm sorry. I didn't mean anything. It's fine if you want to write movies."

"Thank you. Now we just have to get a studio to agree." He turned to face her, smiling pleasantly. She looked at his flat stomach and followed the line of black hair that ran from his navel to the bulge in his greenies.

"Come here," she said.

He did, approaching with a skeptical look. When he reached the side of the bed, she took his hand and pulled him down, her arms wrapping around his broad and bony back. She ran her fingers down his spine. "You have doe's skin," she said in a whisper.

"I think I should be saying that to you," he answered.

"Let's do it quickly. I don't want to be up for hours," she said with a kiss on his cheek. She moved her way up to his earlobe and nibbled on it.

"You flatter me," Tony said. "It's never taken hours."

She smiled and slipped out from under him, opening the night-table drawer to remove the blue plastic diaphragm case, and then tiptoed quickly toward the bathroom. As she modestly shut the door behind her, she winked at him, like a girl at summer camp sneaking out of her bunk to do mischief.

Fred had left the bathroom, stung by his wife's rejection. When, with an attitude of disdain, she took his hand off her body and placed it on the cold and slippery porcelain, he wanted to smash her. That deadly look of boredom and contempt—it was humiliating.

"I have to get cigarettes," he said in a clipped voice, and left the room, closing the door behind him with a bang: hard enough to register a protest, but just short of actually slamming it.

He found a pack on the coffee table. There were only two cigarettes inside and he knew he would be up for hours. "Fuck," he said, and got his coat. "I'm going down for cigarettes," he shouted at the bathroom door.

"What?" Marion asked, her voice made faint by the closed door.

Fred opened it and said, "I'm out of cigarettes. Do you want something?"

Marion, her face a mask of indifference, shook her head.

Fred suddenly couldn't maintain his anger: his look pleaded for mercy. "Are you angry at me?"

Marion's eyes widened with surprise. "No. I'm taking a bath. I don't want visitors when—"

"Okay, okay, I get it." He shut the door and left, walking angrily, his feet stamping on the gray-carpeted floors. He stood at the bank of elevators and muttered to himself, accompanied by the hollow noise of wind rushing down the shaftways. "She really doesn't want me around." An elevator door slid open as he said this and there was a couple, dressed formally, inside. Fred suspected that they had heard him and he stepped in with his head down, embarrassed. This marriage isn't going to last, he thought to himself, peering at the logo of Otis Elevator on the floor. This thought was loud and final in his skull. He knew the marriage wasn't going to end that night, but inevitably it would have to: they had no desire for each other, they squabbled constantly, the entire relationship was joyless.

Or was it? Outside, he crossed the street along with a mass of people leaving the Beekman movie theater, and remembered last Saturday when they had stayed home and read and played a few hands of gin.

That had been fun. He cheered up, entered the stationery store, and stood behind a few people lining up for tomorrow's *Times*. Next to him, hanging by large metal clips, were copies of magazines. Many were pornographic. Fred leafed through one, pausing momentarily at a picture of a young, thin, tanned blond with her legs spread, and nothing on but black stockings. My God, is that what a woman looks like! he thought. What possible kinship could that creature have with Marion? Marion: her mousy hair, her round, sad face, her small breasts already sagging, her toneless stomach, her lumpy buttocks. And the dull look: what did Marion's blank judgmental eyes have in common with the sparkling blue gems that laughed at him off the page of this seedy magazine?

His turn at the counter allowed him only a fleeting look at the page, but he carried the contrast with him back to the apartment.

Marion was in bed. Her hair had been flattened by washing. This made her face look even rounder and more expressionless.

"Hello," she said cheerfully.

"You cooked a great meal," Fred said, undressing at the closet. He tossed the clothes on its floor. Marion watched each item: she wanted them hung up or neatly folded.

"I got it from an author. *The Fat and Happy Italian Cookbook.*"

Fred laughed. This meant he was about to say something funny. He turned to Marion, his pants in his hands. "Maybe you should convince Goodson to market the book with food samples."

"I wish we could." Her eyes stayed on the pants.

Fred, rather than using a hanger, absently hooked the pants by one of their loops on a wall bracket meant for ties.

"Fred!" Marion sat up. "What are you doing! That'll ruin them."

"Huh?" He stared at her.

"Your pants. Hang them up."

Fred obeyed. He was as thoughtless and as stupid as a child, Marion thought. "I think Bart really knows what he's doing. You know? He's psyched out what's going on." Fred finished hanging up his pants and walked to the window, opening it slightly.

"No," Marion protested. "It's too cold."

"They send up heat all night, you know."

"My hair's wet. Wait until it's dry."

He shut the window, went to the bed, took off his underpants, and got under the covers.

Marion knew, because he had taken off his shorts, that he planned to make love to her. Otherwise he slept in them.

"Why don't you do something different with your hair?" Fred said.

"Maybe you should get a perm." He was proud of himself for suggesting she change her hairstyle. If he found her unattractive, wasn't the healthy reaction a frank attempt to discuss the problem?

"A perm!" She frowned.

That was her frown of intense disapproval. It infuriated him. "You don't care enough about your appearance," he said. "We both take the way we look for granted."

"Speak for yourself, buster." Marion turned on her side, pulling up the covers to her ear. "Turn out the light, okay? I'm going to sleep."

Fred felt the disappointment of this statement keenly. He had his hand on his penis—it was already swelling. He had assumed they would screw. "Honey," he said in a small voice.

Silence.

He breathed slowly, feeling the flutter of emotion as he inhaled. He knew, or part of him knew (the tiny, huddled creature inside who was frightened by people: terrified of their judgments), that to push her would mean an argument. But nevertheless, he repeated his plea. "Honey?"

"What?" This simple question was said in a tone so harsh that a man less committed to truth would have shrunk from answering.

Fred pressed on. "Are you angry at me?"

"I'm tired."

He waited for more. Then: "You know, suggesting you change your hair isn't an insult."

"Of course it is!" Marion was suddenly animate. The covers were thrown off, she sat bolt upright, and spoke loudly, addressing the room as if it were full of listening jurors. "You're always hinting that I should lose weight, change my hair, get a winter tan—what kind of idiot do you think I am? I know what—"

"Come on, come on, come on," Fred had been saying, and went on saying while she continued.

"—that means. You're ugly! You're ugly! You're ugly!"

"Oh God!" Fred covered his face. All the pain of his marriage, the simultaneous hurt of knowing her accusation was true, and that his desire for a more beautiful woman was wrong, and yet that somehow he was a good man, and that he did love her; all this, the confusing dissonant symphony of his relationship with Marion, played while she yelled at him; and yet one clear, cold voice in the auditorium whispered: I guess this means we aren't going to fuck.

Smooth and inflamed, moist and comforted, intensely sensitive and yet inhumanly independent—David's organ occupied Patty's mouth.

Her tongue, after an especially deep pass around his penis, played lightly round the ridge of his circumcision and wrenched moans from his stomach, enraging the thick vein that coursed like a swollen river from its purple base. And then she opened wide to swallow . . .

"Oh God . . ."

She had wondered what to do when this happened. She had never stayed this long for fear that the man might climax and—now it happened: her mouth filling with the stuff, the hot brew of nature's quick mix.

Disgusted, she swallowed, almost choking because it felt so thick that she imagined her throat might be stopped up forever, cemented by semen.

She removed her mouth, despite a protesting groan from David, and gulped to get it down. Her fears had been foolish, because all of it was easily ingested. She looked at David and felt delighted with her results. He lay there, his gray wool pants and jockey shorts twisted at the knees, his red penis dwindling in the open air, glistening wet. His head was thrown back as if he had been caught in that position by an audience.

But her pleasure was short-lived when she took a second look at his shriveling member. She had assaulted him because she wanted to make love, to touch and sweat and make contact, and to forget everything that had failed and was failing in her life. She was horny. She had felt in her thighs and in her dry thirsting mouth that she wanted love: she had seduced David so that he would satisfy her, but the drooping flag of manhood before her eyes wasn't encouraging.

His eyes opened. Only a little at first. They looked sleepy, drunk, and happy. Their happiness infuriated her. She had to make clear that the fun wasn't over yet. She stood up and, looking him in the eyes, she pulled her pink cotton top up and over her head, pulling her arms through quickly. Her nipples were thick and pink-red. Her white breasts were mapped by veins, and they stuck out in the air as if held by invisible strings.

"You're beautiful," he said, his voice hoarse and yet small and innocent like a child's.

She unzipped her pleated beige pants, hooked her underpants with her fingers, and pulled off both layers in one motion, steadying herself with first one hand and then the other against the couch. She looked smaller naked: sleek and white like a boy, despite her large breasts, narrow stomach, and widening hips that poured her like champagne into the graceful stem of her legs. She got on top of him and he ran his hands up and down her, happily. She was like a stone washed and polished by the sea; his fingers ran over her back, her buttocks, her legs, as though making an assessment. Beneath her, she felt his penis harden again, and that heartened her. She liked him a little more and kissed him, forcing his mouth open with her tongue and exploring inside like a probe.

He began to turn her over, gently flipping her, so that she was under him, lying lengthwise on the couch. He kissed her neck and traveled down her collar to her breasts. That was predictable and irritated her: men enjoyed her breasts far more than she enjoyed their enjoyment.

But he surprised her, kissing her nipples only once and then proceeding south, his lips touching her lightly, raising her skin so that the sense of body was widened—she could feel her legs and stomach yearn for touch. He arrived at her belly and curved his tongue around and into her navel. That made her gasp: her belly rolled in, tickled and wounded delightfully by this invasion.

His hands had gripped her thighs, she noticed, squeezing and massaging, his thumbs rubbing inside toward her vagina. Each pass opened her legs more—he seemed to be leaving the couch, or, at least, hovering over it—and his fingers began to brush her pubic hair. He would notice that she shaved and trimmed herself so that the bush made a neat V, easily accessed, to encourage just what she hoped he was about to do.

But he resumed his whispery kisses of her stomach and breasts and neck, whooshing over her body with unexpected variations so that she wriggled away at the same time that her hands pulled his head toward her. Just when she felt his teasing would make her insane, he stopped. Her body was instantly angry, sure that he meant to betray the promise of this prelude.

Her legs were pulled wide apart, confirming her fear, but then— ecstatically—she felt his teeth scrape the insides of her thighs. She closed her legs, surprised, but quickly opened them invitingly. He accepted with his tongue and mouth. His hands went under her, squeezing her buttocks and raising her hips so that she was offered to him like a feast.

His mouth kissed her there: she felt warmth rise and suffuse her belly as his tongue and lips pressed, kneaded, and tickled. Her hands clung to his hair as if steadying herself. She was in continual motion, a thoroughbred trembling at the gate.

She heard herself moan, but nothing now felt conscious or determined. She was in pieces, floating on a sea of movement and sensation, rolling with the waves as he penetrated with his tongue, making regular passes over her clitoris.

For a moment she worried that he would stop before the climax. Men had done this much and quit when she most wanted them to go on: her fingers tightened their grip on his hair and she forced a moan, pushing his head into her genitals as well, so the message would be clear. This spurred him. His hands raised her buttocks even more so that her head and neck were firmly against the couch, and her vagina open to the air and to his investigations. Now he licked and touched and mouthed all over. Her thighs, her lips, swallowing her juice and bits of her hair, eating her with devoted passion.

And now the earthquake began! She was spun off into the universe, heat searing her insides, the air thinning, and deep within, the core of desire glowed and hardened, pulsing with the need to escape the prison of her flesh.

From her came sounds of agony and joy. Her eyes opened and she saw the yellow sprinkler pipes bounce in the air as she heaved with the expulsion of passion.

"Oh! God, God, God, God, God," she said to the sprinklers as she bucked against the merciless pressure of his tongue, darting in and over and away, with an irregular but relentless pace. She was free! She was free! She was free!

"Don't get me excited," Betty whispered into his ear.

"Mmmm." Tony was swimming. He moved to a silent rhythm, taking his strokes into the hidden stream, the warm river within his wife.

"You promised," she whispered.

Tony knew she was lying; she wanted an orgasm. He made sure he angled his behind up, under, and in, so that the pelvic bone would do its job. This was a familiar and effective choreography in their marriage: like any good dance routine, technique dominated, but the magic would come at last and transform the careful movements into inspired grace.

"Uhhh," she let out, and he knew it would be soon. His hands lightly touched her sides as he ran them up, gripping her armpits with his thumbs, and squeezing as if she were a doll. This worked for him—his thrusts deepened. He was really in the ocean now, stroking mightily toward the shore of release, sweat bursting from him, his limbs stretching with every move, his back arching, his head bobbing and surfacing like a dolphin at play.

He pushed his hand down between his member and her hard knob to emphasize the point. For a moment this interrupted their dance—and then she lifted, from the hips, off the bed, and they united, sweating,

groaning, their mouths open and yearning, as they took their long
sweetly agonizing swim together, thudding on the sand as one, exhausted
by their happy exercise.

"Oh, you're crazy," Fred complained. "That's just bullshit."

Marion reached past him and pulled the clock radio toward her. The
force of the cord coming up made the night table teeter.

"Jesus!" Fred grabbed the table to steady it.

"It's two-thirty, Fred. I have to be up at seven."

"I don't know how you can sleep—"

"I never have any trouble sleeping."

"I don't mean that. I'm churning inside. You think I don't find you
attractive when all I want is to make love—"

"You don't want to make love. You want to come inside me." She
slammed the clock radio back down and stepped over him, out of bed.

Fred stared at her as if he had been slapped. "What are you saying?"

Marion left the room.

He paused a moment to consider whether it might be safer and saner
if he didn't pursue what had already become an ugly marathon of mis-
communication. But he was juggling in his mind a variety of tormenting
thoughts: did she mean he was lousy in bed? Maybe she didn't want to
have sex as often as he? Maybe she didn't love him anymore? What was
it? For Fred, this was as maddening as not being told who committed the
murder in a suspenseful thriller. He got up and followed Marion.

He found her sitting on one of the kitchen chairs placed beside a
window that caught a partial view of the East River. The musty glow of
New York's streetlamps provided a silhouette of Marion. Her face looked
tight, as if she were holding back tears. He noticed this, but it only
spurred his desire to interrogate her. For Fred, great emotion in another
person was like a bone to a trained retrieving dog; off he went, his hind
legs powering him forward through thickets of dialogue to find his mar-
row of truth.

"Honey, let's talk about it," he said. His attempt to say this calmly
made his voice whiny.

"Fred, I don't feel well. I want to be left alone. Can't you do that?"
She turned to face him and he got a look at her staring eyes, big with
welling tears.

He sighed. He told himself to turn around and go, but his feet felt
flat and glued to the floor. The oddest thing was that he still had his
erection, though it didn't feel pleasurable at the moment. "I love you,"
he said.

She snorted with disgust and helplessness.

"What's wrong with that! I can't relax if you're not happy. I have to know what's bothering you. It's eating me up inside."

"Fred, I worked all day to cook a huge meal for your friends—"

"They're your friends too—"

"If you must know, they're not friends to either of us. It was like doing business tonight. This evening wasn't any more fun than a business lunch. I get plenty of them during the week. Goddamm it, I just don't feel like making dinner to help your career and then spreading my legs to top it off."

Fred's mouth opened in the middle of Marion's speech and remained so for several seconds afterward. She had begun to cry while she spoke, and now, biting her lips to try to stop, she was sobbing. He felt as if light had illuminated the dingy room where he stored his marriage. Everything she said sounded so right: she had given a name to what had made him uneasy about the party: both his motive for having it, and everyone else's for coming, disgusted him.

"Honey," he said, deeply moved. He went to her, knelt by her chair, and put his arm around her. She's so smart about people, he thought. "You're right. But you're wrong about why I wanted to make love. It's 'cause I felt so lonely and crummy about the way things went. Everybody was ugly and trying to get at each other. I can't believe people are so competitive."

She put her head on his shoulder and wept heartily. There was no one else with whom she could be this unhappy. And Marion believed that was the best one could hope for. Unless, of course, you had a face and body and temperament like Patty's.

"I wanted to make love because what we have is so different," Fred said. "We don't need that kind of shit. I just wanted to hold onto something real." She cuddled into his arms now, beginning to slide off the chair. Her weight felt cumbersome and he pulled her up, leading her toward the bedroom. "You should go to sleep," he said so earnestly that one would imagine she had been keeping herself up.

He put her to bed tenderly, remaking the bed and tucking her in so that she was cozy. She kissed him—her wet face lubricating their lips—and urged him onto the bed. "Aren't you going to sleep?"

"No. You know me."

"Don't stay up too late." She kissed him again, gratefully, like a wife greeting a husband feared lost.

"Un-huh," he said, pulling away. He took her hand and put it on his erection. "You keep getting me excited."

"I'm sorry. I'm too tired. Tomorrow night?" She removed her hand.

"Sure. I'm sorry about tonight. I won't do this again."

"No," Marion said, hugging him. "It's not your fault. We have to do this stuff."

Fred sighed and rolled off her. "It drives me crazy. Paying dues."

Marion laughed. She nodded at his penis, arced to the heavens.

Fred smiled proudly. "You turn me on. I can't help it."

"I'm sorry," she said, her lower lip beginning to tremble.

"Hey, hey," and they hugged again. After a while, he turned out the light. From her breathing, he knew she was falling asleep. He felt good. They had really broken through tonight. She had been resenting sex with him because she felt it was part of the jobs of her life. That was fascinating, he thought. He knew there was a novel in it: that kind of misunderstanding was what kept couples apart. People were too embarrassed to admit it; that's why so few novelists wanted to take the subject on. What had happened between them was really touching, he thought. His erection had begun to shrink several times, and somewhat thoughtlessly he had stroked himself until he was flying at full mast again.

He couldn't figure out how to plot a novel so that this lesson of marriage could be illustrated, and eventually he let his mind drift to the party. Abruptly, almost as if the image and sensation came from a different brain than his own, he vividly relived his profound excursion into Patty's fluted mouth. A warm tickling in his penis, familiar and pleasant, began. He rubbed himself very quietly, thinking of how he could have reached down into her pink cotton top and picked one of those white melons, squeezing gently, lingeringly, rubbing her hard nipples . . .

He stroked without worrying . . . he took all of Patty in front of his bathroom door. Pulled her clothes off roughly, pushed his penis down her funneled mouth, drove into her pink vagina, without sentiment . . .

Marion moved!

His heart, already pounding from sexual excitement, seemed to close his throat, thumping with fear and shame.

Marion put her head on his shoulder, mumbled something, and her hand took his hard teased penis. Her cool fingers pulled gently at the head. She had known what he was doing all the time—and she approved! This was amazing, exciting in itself. She tickled him with her icy, delightful touch, and at last he splashed his belly with the warm white liquid, and felt his manhood shrivel in his wife's hand while the vivid image of Patty's body melted into sleep. Dark, cool, wet sleep.

CHAPTER

3

Gloria Fowler looks like a greyhound, Tony Winters realized with relief. He had been frustrated in his search for a description of her: he knew he would need one when telling the story of his meeting with her to his friends. Gloria was on the phone. She had swiveled to face the window on her right (its view of a squashed Sixth Avenue and an alley of glass skyscrapers was spectacular) so that Tony saw her long flared translucent nostrils in profile. The New York sun glowed a weary red behind her and lit her nose so that he could see minute veins. Her face was gaunt, each line sharply defined. Maybe she used to be a model, he thought. Her height, her thinness, and the tasteful, casual, and yet silken appearance of her long gray skirt, creamy white blouse, and knit sleeveless vest, all spoke of fashion.

"Bill, I think we can meet about it when the revisions are in—there's no hurry. Yes! That's right, enjoy the sun. Leave that to me. That's what I'm paid for. Right, you didn't know." She smiled brilliantly into the phone.

She *is* beautiful, Tony decided, as if settling a dispute, while studying her mass of red hair (dyed? he wondered) that flowed up and back, almost as if it were startled off her head by a gusting wind. She hung up and the smile dissolved into an exhausted frown. She looked at Tony with resignation. "Actors!"

"Ah!" Tony raised his hand in warning. "Remember, my mother is one of that breed."

"Oh, your mother's a genius. Not one of these"—she gestured at the phone—"alleged stars." Her smile reprised: high cheeks were raised like a curtain, revealing brilliant teeth.

"William Garth?"

"Yes, one of my clients is doing a script for him and, I'm afraid, the script isn't quite right. Bill's not getting any younger and I suppose he can't be blamed for worrying over whether this writer can revise it properly." Gloria reached for a pack of cigarettes on the table and swiveled again so that her profile was against the gray wall. "I'm blabbing this for a reason." She paused, her big brown eyes resting on him appraisingly. This meant her body was twisted away from him, her angle haughty and forbidding, rather as if she were on a throne looking over the pages for a potential knight. The cigarette—it was long, thin, and foreign—was placed in her mouth and lit in slow movements. She spoke while exhaling her first puff: "Have you done any screenwriting?"

Tony felt his buttocks tighten, his face freeze into a mask. He shook his head no, quickly realized that was an odd way to answer, and then said out loud, "No." But his voice sounded young and tense.

"Just the plays." She laughed. This made her hair seem particularly windblown. "Listen to me—'just the plays.' I mean, of course, to say, your work has been exclusively for the theater?"

"I've written some short stories, but that's all. Only my five plays."

Gloria relaxed her queenly pose to lean forward. "Only? How old are you? Thirty?"

"Thirty-two." He said this with genuine embarrassment. He felt young, too young, in her presence.

"And you've written *only* five plays?" she said, teasing.

"Well, you know, standards have been lowered. Shakespeare at thirty-two had written at least a dozen—"

"Oh, my God," Gloria said, a hand covering her breast as if she were wounded. "You don't judge yourself by that standard? Poor thing. I couldn't bear to measure myself against genius—"

He knew this game. "I didn't mean that, Gloria," he snapped, surprising himself with his irritated tone. "I simply meant to say that writing five plays *isn't* amazing, not that it isn't an accomplishment. Of course I don't compare myself to Shakespeare. Not unfavorably. Or favorably." All this came out in a commanding though peevish tone. When he looked at her to see how she had reacted to it, he saw her smiling at him with a look of triumph and pleasure. He couldn't understand why his response should delight her. He decided she must be trying to mollify him.

"Of course," she said after a moment of gazing at him. "Were all the plays produced?"

"Yes, but only two were put on in a significant way. *Youngsters* at the Quest Guild and another production in the Harold Repertory in Chicago. The other productions aren't worth talking about."

"Gosh, I've never heard anyone dismiss credits, no matter how awful."

"Well . . ." He considered explaining, but instead he summarized: "I know those credits don't mean anything in the real world."

Gloria raised her eyebrows (they were dramatic and arched even when at rest) and stared.

Tony laughed. "What?"

"Now I understand where that toughness comes from in *Youngsters.* I saw it last summer and loved it."

"Thank you."

"I felt there were problems with the production. I don't think it did you justice. That girl, uh, the one with the funny face . . ."

"Lonnie Kane? I love her work. I thought—"

"No, no. She was marvelous. We represent her. She got some of the underpinnings in your play—I could hear strength in her. That's what makes your humor so compelling. You're not doing one-liners."

"Thank you. I didn't know you represented Lonnie. What's she doing now?"

"She's been swallowed up by sitcom pilots that don't quite make it."

Tony laughed. "The *Jaws* of acting."

Gloria frowned. "Well, she'll hit with one. Tell me, why haven't you tried screenwriting?"

"I've thought about it. I guess I worry about dealing with Hollywood. Because of my mother I do have bad associations with it."

"New York's coming back, you know. More and more projects are originating and even being produced here. I'm not sure that you'd have to even visit Hollywood while doing screenwriting."

"I didn't mean that kind of bad association with Hollywood. It isn't geography—it's the profession."

Gloria again smiled that broad toothy grin—what was it? Tony wondered. Triumph? A secret knowledge? "I thought you might mean that," Gloria said. "I can imagine what those years out there with your mother must have been like."

"Yeah, it wasn't too much fun for Mom, thinking she was about to be thrown into a concentration camp."

"But you were a baby when all that was happening."

"Yes, but the effect on me was still quite lasting." Tony laughed hollowly and instantly felt stupid that he had. He sounded as if he were being coy about the McCarthy Period, as it was referred to by his mother and her friends. The McCarthy Period, with capitals to aid the sense of dread and tackiness, sort of a slapstick Hitler. But it only seemed farcical in retrospect. At the time, with people losing their jobs, committing suicide, with the Rosenbergs dying in the electric chair, there was little of the low comedy that now remains when seeing those black-and-white TV hearings; little of the idiotic spectacle of matinee idols proclaiming their devotion to America and their loathing of "communist infiltration" of show business. "It wasn't fun," he said in a low voice, thinking of all it had cost his family: the divorce, the paralysis of his mother's career, her breakdown, his father's panic and immoral behavior. Everything else in the history of his family was a flat terrain compared to the volcanic and geological monstrosities of the McCarthy Period.

In college, Tony had used this family history to bed women, wooing with sentiment, making drama and romance out of the real pain and stupidity of his parents. He had corrupted his feelings and now suspected himself of fraud whenever he called attention to them, as if he were shoplifting from the store of his past, cheating the cash register of genuine feeling, selling the coinage of his soul.

Gloria looked off sadly. "It's hard to believe it was ever like that."

"Is it?" Tony could hear his voice take on his mother's hard inconsolable anger. "I don't think so. The man who backed the Screen Actors Guild in the expulsion of so-called communist sympathizers is now President of the United States. He was a tacky opportunist, as bad as the people whom we read about in Solzhenitsyn, the kind of person who informs on neighbors to get a better apartment. Reagan's career was washed up, so he made a career of putting his rivals out of work, and thus he accidentally landed an even better job. It was ugly and petty and immoral and yet he's President of the United States." He heard his voice ring in the room.

Gloria looked apprehensive. No, he realized, she looked embarrassed, as if he had opened his fly or thrown a tantrum. And the last was true. He had thrown his mother's tantrum.

"I'm sorry," Tony immediately said. "I don't know why I went into all that."

"No, no. I understand."

"Anyway, you can see why I might not instantly wish to write screenplays. In my subconscious, that industry is scary. After all, my mother didn't work for ten years. Ten years of her prime. She became very unstable emotionally . . . well, I mean the scars are still there."

Gloria now looked quite young and girlish. She hung her head and looked up at him, batting her eyes. He could see that she was *trying* to look sympathetic; but that didn't make him feel she was being dishonest. "Now I feel quite foolish for having asked you here."

"I didn't mean that—"

"Because I must confess I hoped to convince you that you should be writing screenplays. Not only because the money is good. I think—from your brilliant play—that your ideas are sharp, new, and very funny. Very, very funny."

Tony again felt himself tense, as if this praise concealed a trap.

Gloria continued, saying the following as if she were fully aware that it would sway him, "I'm going to come clean and tell you that I want to convince you to rewrite the script I was just discussing with Bill Garth."

"Really?" This word rolled out of him, a trill of delight and amazement.

Gloria nodded solemnly. "Now. The question is: will you join me for an early lunch to talk further?"

Patty felt tiny. She was lying under a quilt in a bed floating on an island of glossy oak. The ceiling above her was like a firmament, the sprinklers a bizarre iron galaxy. The damn place was so big she felt as if she were only inches high. Also, she was exhausted. Her mouth stuck to itself from dryness, her head felt heavy. She was hung-over. Through her swollen eyes she peered at the windows—the distance was so great she felt as if she were Columbus searching for the coast of the New World—and decided from their gray light that it was early dawn.

She heard the squeal of faucets turning and then a rush of water rattling against the metal. David was taking a shower. Maybe I'm so dry because I swallowed him, she thought, disgusting herself with the notion. I could join him in there, she mused, imagining the two of them smeared with soap, screwing standing up, banging the tin of the shower stall. I gave him a good time, she told herself, and then laughed out loud. This got her to sit up. She fumbled for the pack of cigarettes on the white Formica night table and lit up after ripping it open to find the penultimate stick.

She surveyed the loft while smoking. Its magnificent space was tempting. David's a nice guy, he was great at sex (aren't they always in the beginning?), things here might become permanent. A boyfriend and a place to live.

The faucets groaned off and embarrassed her out of this calculation. I'm horrible, she decided, pressing out her cigarette and letting her legs out from under the covers, ready to head for the john.

David appeared, his hair damp, with an orange towel around his stomach. "Good morning," he said, obviously happy. "You don't have to get up."

"What time is it?"

"Nine."

"Oh. I thought it was sunrise. Can I take a shower?"

"Of course." He shook his head to indicate how foolish her question was. "*Mi casa es su casa.*"

Patty looked blank.

"Feel at home," he explained.

"How sweet," she said, but her dry throat caught on something, and the words were rasped out.

"I'll make some juice," he said, and padded on his damp feet toward the kitchen. He left tracks. Patty waited until he was behind the partition before getting out and rushing in the chill air to the bathroom. She felt she must look awful, a conclusion that the mirror confirmed while she waited for the water to get hot.

She drenched her face with the hot spray in the shower and became more and more anxious over her appearance. She hadn't seen a hair dryer in the bathroom. The lack of one would mean she'd look like a drowned cat over breakfast. Of course she had eyeliner and lipstick in her purse, but that was all the way over at the other end of this oak-and-plasterboard desert. She never liked to go to the man's place for sex because of all this: the morning was the worst possible time to be separated from one's own possessions. At her place, *he* could be worrying about getting into wrinkled and smelly clothes while she scrambled eggs with blow-dried hair and a freshly laundered outfit.

When she finally felt as if her body had absorbed some moisture, she stepped out of the stall to find a glass of orange juice balanced on the edge of the sink. "Oh," she said.

David's voice came from outside the bathroom: "I have to leave for work in ten minutes."

"Okay, I'll hurry."

"No, no. The door locks when you leave, so you can stay. Relax. Make some eggs."

"Oh, thank you."

"Do you have appointments today?"

"Appointments?" Patty said the word as if it were both exotic and unknown to her.

"Job interviews?"

"No."

"Where can I reach you?"

That question was easily answered, but it was the job query that haunted her after David left for work. She had no job. Worse, she didn't because she had been fired. That humiliation was three months old, but she still cringed from the shame of it, as if it were only hours old. Jobs. The thought of them left her standing paralyzed in front of the bathroom mirror for minutes on end: staring into her own eyes as if they were a stranger's. In fact, she was blind. Her mind played over her last few weeks at Goodson Books.

Her boss was Jerry Gelb, a big bearded man with a deep voice and little black eyes that never showed pity, love, or even an attention span. Gelb was angry all the time. Or at least in a very bad mood. But he liked Patty. He teased Patty the way she imagined an older brother would— Patty was the eldest of three; her only brother was six years her junior. Jerry called her Patsie (her nickname as a child) and would take her along on lunches with his two leading authors. They were Harold Gould (winner of two National Book Awards) and Roberta York, the formidable and ancient intellectual, who would cheer Patty up by describing her own frustrations as a secretary sixty years ago. Roberta talked about being kept late without pay, being pressured to sleep with the boss, and how she collapsed into tears when, after having rejected the boss, he would needle her mercilessly. "Things haven't changed much," Gelb would agree in a tone that implied he was innocent of such behavior. But Roberta's talk didn't stop him from screaming into Patty's intercom when she made the mistake of letting a rejected writer through her screening of telephone calls.

"You're paid twelve thousand dollars a year to remember to say, 'He's in a meeting,' and you can't even do that right! Get in here!"

Her mouth quivered as she entered, closing the door behind her so no one could hear his ranting.

"What do I have to do!" he yelled, standing up at his desk. Behind him was a view of Fifth Avenue swarming with tiny cars and insect people. "Do you know what that asshole"—he pointed with contempt at his phone—"screamed at me? I had to listen to a nut call me a liar and a thief because you don't pay attention! When I tell you not to put some-one through, listen to the name! Remember it!" he shrieked at her. Though his voice was basso, the attitude—his arms waving in the air, his eyes scanning wildly—was hysterical and shrill.

Tears spilled from her eyes. She put up no struggle against either his accusations or her shame. She thought and felt nothing but shame, appalling shame at her uselessness.

"I've warned you over and over. How often can I make the excuse to myself and to the other editors here whom you repeatedly screw up with your incompetence, how many times can I say," and now he transformed himself into a mincing pose, holding his hands up in front of him, like a puppy begging for food, " 'Oh, poor little Patsie, she's so silly and helpless, but we don't mind 'cause she can bat her eyes so pretty.' "

Later, of course, she could answer this abuse. Later, she wouldn't agree with his evaluation of her work. But while he yelled, there was no Patty inside her to step forward and argue back. She thought it the most peculiar thing about her, the sickest thing about her, the one trait she wished she could be free of forever: she accepted any role that people cast her in. The more Jerry Gelb claimed she was a ditsie blond, the more she became one. Only when alone could she be herself. But she loathed being alone.

However, these periodic fits by Gelb were always followed by weeks of pampering. He would take her out with clients, praise her to agents, buy her a trinket, behave, in a word, like a repentant lover.

Eventually the tantrums became less frequent. Gelb selected a new assistant to yell at. Patty was grateful for this neglect and thought it was a victory. At last Gelb had recognized her worth.

And then, one day, he summoned her to the office without there having been a fuck-up.

"How are you?" he asked. This time, he was the one who closed his door for privacy. It was five o'clock. The insects below were heading home.

"I don't know," she said, staring at him with a look of shock. This formal question about her health was unusual, and so she took it seriously.

"You don't?" he looked distressed by her answer. "I thought things were going well. You have a boyfriend."

"I do?"

"I thought so. The actor."

"Oh, him. I haven't seen him in months. He was never a boyfriend. I've been dating someone else."

Gelb smiled encouragingly.

"I just broke up with him," Patty added.

Gelb again looked as if this news were a great blow to him. "I'm sorry."

Patty smiled at him languidly. "It's all right," she said, and then laughed. "Sweet of you to worry."

"Are you busy tonight?"

"A friend at Rockers has tickets to a screening of *Raging Bull*."

"Oh, good." At last an answer he wanted. He smiled nervously, cleared his throat, and said, "I don't know how to tell you this, but I think a direct approach—"

Even at this moment, Patty had no suspicion that she was about to be fired. Gelb's reputation was one of ferocity. He fired people on the spot. No leisurely hand-wringing chats in the office. Besides, he never let her feel that she was vulnerable to being fired. She was the ditsie blond, not a young turk who had to either produce or die.

"—but I'm going to have to let you go. We've had a ghastly year. One of the worst in publishing history. We overprinted on *Gold Search* and underprinted on *Jumpers,* we've suffered lower sales in every department because of the recession. Everything's gone wrong that possibly could. We have to cut down on staff and you're the choice." He said all this very quietly, embarrassed. He said it all as if she knew it.

"I don't understand."

Gelb sighed and looked away. "You know that someone has to suffer when things go bad. It isn't personal. Doubleday let a third of its staff go yesterday. You aren't the only one here who will lose a job."

She went numb to sensation, as if being in his office were a dream. Colors blurred, his voice came from a distance. FAILURE—punched onto the page of her brain. The word dominated—FAILURE. She felt as if she had been sentenced to die. All her life, she had dreaded this sort of occurrence. Getting a failing grade in school, being caught with drugs, not being accepted into a good college, meeting boys you like who reject you, and getting fired from a job. At last, FAILURE had struck. She had managed to avoid all the other calamities, she had even begun to lower her defenses . . . FAILURE. Gelb considered her so pathetic that not only was he firing her, he was doing it nicely!

"Please don't do that!" Gelb stood up. "There's no reason to cry."

She hadn't realized she was weeping. She put a hand on her cheek and her fingers slid on the wet surface.

"You can stay here for a month while you look for another job. I'll give you great references. There's unemployment insurance. It's a paid vacation."

"You just said there are no jobs," she whined.

"I did?"

"If things are so bad, then no one's going to hire me."

"Oh, there'll be jobs in a little while. Besides, you're what? Twenty-five?"

"Twenty-six."

"You don't have to stay in publishing. I think you might be happier in . . . advertising. Or maybe working in publicity at a publishing house."

"You don't think I'm any good at editing." Through her tears, she had the bitter voice of a heartbroken child, a girl on Christmas morning discovering she has gotten no toys. She hated herself for this weakness. It wasn't her real self.

"Of course you are," Gelb insisted. He wrinkled his thick brows together. This made the dark circles under his eyes more pronounced. "You need a jolt. A fresh start."

She whined and complained for more than an hour. Gelb canceled a drink date and took her downstairs to an Indian restaurant where she ate so many hors d'oeuvres that she didn't need any dinner. Gelb offered to buy that for her as well.

Now, as she stared into David Bergman's mirror, what her mind retained was the shameful memory of her childish reaction to Gelb dismissing her. And her gullible acceptance of his story that firing her was part of a general cutback. Within a month after she left, the new assistant was given her old job, and last week Patty had learned from Marion that Gelb seemed to be having an affair with Patty's successor. Only then did Patty realize how completely naive she was: Gelb had often asked her out on evening dates that she casually refused. Gelb took her rejections so calmly that Patty convinced herself he didn't mind. She hadn't put out, so he fired her. This conclusion amazed her. She had grown up reading in novels and seeing in movies exactly that scene played out, but it seemed a part of the fictional world, not the life she saw and experienced. Her father never had any affairs, she believed. And Gelb merely seemed like another version of her father: a big, disgruntled man who was frightened by tears and emotion in others. To think of him as a sexual being was both impossible and slightly revolting.

I've been a fool, she told herself, bringing her relentless replay of the scenes in Gelb's office to a close. She got herself out of the bathroom and found the pot of coffee David Bergman had made for her. He's sweet, she decided. And he wants sex, she reminded herself. Like every man, young and old—he wants it.

Fred had huddled under the covers when Marion woke him for a good-bye kiss. She was off to her job, but Fred, still waiting for Bart's reaction to his book proposals, had nothing to do. He burrowed into the bed, remembered his kissing Patty and his pleasant experience before sleep, and then, his insight into Marion's feelings. There's a novel in that, he told himself in a determined tone.

He had trouble falling back to sleep. He wanted to talk. Fred glanced at the clock—9:03. Too early to phone anyone. Tony Winters never got up before eleven, David wouldn't reach his office until ten, and Karl had let it be known among his friends that he wrote all morning until one o'clock and preferred not to be disturbed. Fred would have to wait alone for Bart to call.

It would be an important conversation, Fred thought. Bart had just taken him on as a client and the five book proposals were the first test of their relationship. Each outline was roughly thirty pages in length, and they varied tremendously in subject. There was an outline for a novel about a visiting Russian hockey team (held hostage by an insane American fan), and another called *Showcase*, about the owner of a Madison Square Garden-type organization, with a plot chock-full of corrupt boxing promoters, virile athletes, and beautiful women rock stars. Fred had one scenario that turned the kidnapped-Russian-hockey-team idea into a subplot of *Showcase*. Shifting to more somber material, *Our Baby* told the story of a couple whose response to being forbidden by court order from treating their dying three-year-old child with laetrile was to kidnap their baby from the hospital and flee to Mexico, where their son eventually dies. Back in the States they face two trials, one on criminal charges and their own divorce. In the end, they were found not guilty and fall in love with new people, providing Fred with what he believed was a compulsory happy ending. Fred's next two ideas were satirical. *Nothing But the Truth* was based on the premise that if someone existed who was incapable of any kind of deception, even the most mild white lie, that this trait would cause havoc with his friends and lovers, cost him his job, and finally leave him ruined and alone. *Kickoff*, the last of Fred's proposals, was the closest to Fred's area of expertise. *Kickoff* told the story of a middle-aged national sports columnist, divorced, with three children and heavy alimony payments, the sort of man who drinks too much and dreams of writing a novel, but instead plays poker, flirts with waitresses, and gets into fights with drunks. *Kickoff* lacked the formal plotting of Fred's other proposals. Instead, it meandered about, exploring the columnist's frustrated and blocked relationships with his ex-wife and kids, with the mounting pressure from younger sportswriters angling for his job, his own bouts with alcoholism, and his need for love. Ultimately, he finds it, but in a surprising and (Fred hoped) commercial way: he gradually falls in love with the quarterback of the Super Bowl team. Fred's proposal described his hero's gradual discovery of his homosexual longings, and his agony before he declares himself to the quarterback. *Kickoff*'s happy ending occurs when the hero finally screws up his courage, announces his feelings, and it turns out that the quarterback is also gay. The book finishes with the columnist straightening out (so to speak) all his messed-up relationships and starting work on his novel.

The five ideas were merely ideas, but having worked out the proposals almost made Fred feel he had realized them, that they were books already written. In fact, if he were to get a contract, he worried whether he would feel enough enthusiasm to write them.

Fred got out of bed and, while allowing his plots to run through his mind, followed a morning routine. He showered, shaved while coffee percolated on the stove, and sipped the coffee while he dressed. The five stories had been constantly in his mind for the last four months. Thus obsessed, Fred forced anything he did to relate to the five stories. When reading novels, he noticed any similarities of theme or character development to those he planned. At movies, he checked to see what was popular, making mental notes to himself to change this twist or that turn. He churned relentlessly, worrying whether gay themes were too shocking for the general public, whether any book that has a character die of cancer could be bought for the movies, and so on, gears of anxiety meshing uneasily with creativity, both uniting to turn Fred's great engine of commercial success.

But a new gear was in place, the story he wanted to tell to illustrate his marriage lesson of last night. Even his mashing of Patty faded as a sensual memory and became a plot point. He could tell the story of all men, basically polygamous creatures struggling to restrain themselves to achieve the more honorable state of monogamy. Women don't want to fuck around, he said to himself, and men want, intellectually, to be the same, but they naturally desire more. This, Fred thought, was a great theme, a serious and provocative idea that could trigger a great novel. But did he have the clout to sell it, never having written a novel before?

Only Bart Cullen could answer that question and Fred now began to jiggle his leg, smoke cigarettes, and distractedly leaf through the *Times*, waiting for his phone to ring.

For a senior writer at *Newstime*, Monday morning was a light day. The senior editors would meet upstairs with the editor in chief, the managing editor, the executive editor, and the assistant managing editors, a group referred to by everyone as the Marx Brothers. Potential stories were discussed, and later the senior editors would come down from Animal Crackers (an umbrella term for the main conference room and the offices of the Marx Brothers) and inform the senior writers (such as David) what they probably would write about that week. It was one of the many elaborate conventions that could easily be eliminated, but it made the corporation feel it was working a full week, rather than just the mad rush from Wednesday through Saturday, when almost all the writing and artwork were done. Only the back of the book (reviews, lifestyle and the like) was prepared in advance. In the Nation section, David's department, everything depended on the latest events, and, indeed, what had catapulted David to his early grasp of a senior-writer position was his cool ability to write cover stories in a matter of hours when a major event broke late in the week.

On Monday, David would usually arrive late with a yogurt and coffee. He's read the Washington *Post*, the New York *Times*, the *Daily News*, the New York *Post*, and the current issue of *Newstime,* as well as its equally famous competitor, *Weekly.* He would take a long lunch after his boss, Senior Editor John Syms, informed him of his assignment for the week. After lunch, David would look into his office in case (by some miracle) there was something to do, and when inevitably there wasn't, he'd head home. Monday was his favorite day.

David had finished comparing the *Weekly*'s story on the Haig news conference with his own story on it (David concluded he'd done a better job) when Syms appeared at his door.

"Are you free for lunch?"

David was a bit surprised. Syms rarely wasted a lunch on a writer; he usually angled for a Marx Brother. "Sure."

"Now?"

David followed Syms outside to a deli nearby—for some reason, Syms was cheap with his expense account, much to the Nation section's aggravation—and they chatted about how badly they had beaten the *Weekly* on Haig.

"They missed the point," Syms said. "This is an unusual breaking of the ranks for Reagan, as we noted."

As *I* noted, David thought to himself. Syms, among many other irritating qualities, always referred to a writer's work as "we" and "us" when it was good, and as "you" and "yours" when it was bad.

"Reagan has so far had his people maintain a solid front," Syms went on.

"Yeah," David answered, relieved that this lunch was not going to be a session of criticism of his work. "I didn't expect the Reagan administration to have the sort of administrative flap that Carter was always having."

Syms went on in this vein until their sandwiches arrived. Then he looked gravely at the stainless-steel bowl of pickles and said, "Have you been hearing rumors about Steinberg?"

Jeff Steinberg was the editor in chief of *Newstime*. There were always rumors, but Syms obviously meant a particular and exciting one. "No," David said, and continued eating without any show of curiosity. To evidence interest would only make Syms more reluctant to part with his information: above all, he hated eagerness.

"I'm surprised. Maybe you were so busy with the cover, no one wanted to bother you with gossip." Syms hissed disapproval on the word "gossip."

David continued eating.

"Well," Syms said with a sigh. "There's talk Steinberg is in trouble."

David looked up briefly to raise his eyebrows, and returned to his plate.

Syms frowned. "Roitman" (the managing editor) "has been spreading it—of course. But there seems to be something to it. Mrs. Thorn" (the owner of *Newstime*) "has scheduled a general meeting with the senior editors tomorrow and she's in right now with Steinberg."

David knew that Mrs. Thorn only scheduled meetings with senior editors for major announcements of change. Nevertheless, he showed no alarm or fascination. "What's Roitman saying is going to happen?" he asked coolly.

"That Steinberg is going to be fired." Syms now picked up his sandwich, bit into it, and chewed angrily.

David tried to figure out what effect that might have on him, but he couldn't. So he waited and chewed.

"I'm sorry to say," Syms finally said, "I think he's right. There's been a lot of criticism of Steinberg's soft covers—Jerry Brown, disco, and so on. After all, Steinberg is abrasive. He has alienated a lot of the old guard."

Syms meant by this that Steinberg had been slowly pushing editors hired by his predecessor out of important positions by putting people over them in newly created titles. Thus *Newstime* was now chock-full of deputies, associates, and executive editors as well as an abnormally high overhead in the midst of a recession.

"I thought Mrs. Thorn was unhappy with the old guard. Isn't that why she promoted Steinberg?"

Syms looked wise and cynical. "That was a long time ago. Nearly a year. She's probably forgotten."

David nodded. He knew enough not to agree or disagree. Syms was equally changeable. If Mrs. Thorn promoted him to Marx Brother status, Syms would think better of her, and anything David said against her now might be remembered, without Syms also recalling that he began the attack.

"Steinberg promoted me," Syms went on, "and I don't think his departure would do me much good. If she does dismiss him tomorrow, Nation might be in turmoil for a while. I felt you deserved some warning."

"I appreciate it," David said, but actually he was confused. Technically, he had been promoted by Syms and Steinberg, but David's impression was that the old guard *also* liked him. In any case, although senior writers *were* affected by changes in top management, they were rarely— if ever—fired or even demoted because of them. Besides, he didn't care: he was sure his work would be approved of by any editor in chief. His covers—he had done four in the last three months—had won two awards and general approval in the company besides. David concluded that Syms was merely trying to develop an ally, and the fact that Syms would bother with a mere senior writer was a symptom of his self-doubt. "If Mrs. Thorn is upset by all the soft covers, why would there be concern about Nation? We can't be held responsible for that."

"No," Syms said, as if that were exactly his line of defense. "But when an editor in chief is fired, everything is called into question."

After that, all of Syms's remarks were general. Only when back in his office could David tap into the grapevine. David dropped in on Bill Cane, deputy senior editor of the Business section, one of the old guard, and his first boss. Cane was jubilant:

"So you've heard! Tell me exactly."

"Only that Steinberg is leaving tomorrow. Mrs. Thorn is going to announce it at the meeting."

"Who told you?"

David hesitated, but it was only a pause of nerves; he had made up his mind to give away that fact before he approached Cane. "Syms."

Cane smiled. "He's scared, isn't he?"

David smiled back. "Should he be?"

Cane frowned and swiveled in his chair. He hit his carriage return and watched it glide back before answering. "I don't think so. You see, the story is that Steinberg really blew it with Mrs. Thorn at a dinner party in Washington last week."

"What?" David laughed.

"Kissinger was there, and Steinberg, I don't know, drank too much, something. Apparently he made an ass of himself and Kissinger took him apart, mostly over the Jerry Brown cover."

David felt himself go weak. He had written the Jerry Brown cover.

Cane noticed. "Don't worry. Kissinger made fun of putting the story on the cover, not the piece itself. You're in no danger."

David smiled. "I wasn't worried," he said, but he had already begun to reconstruct his lunch with Syms. Maybe it had been a warning.

Tony was drunk. Gloria had reordered drinks for them while he went to the bathroom—more to relieve the relentless pressure of her promises than to ease his bladder. Tony continued to drink on his return, his hands restlessly grabbing anything on the table while he earnestly nodded at Gloria's comments. He emptied four glasses of water, half of his pack of cigarettes, and three Scotches and soda. Eventually he wished he could repeat his journey to the john for a practical visit, but embarrassed to do so, Tony ended up squeezing his legs together while he ate his scallops. Gloria Fowler, one of the most important packagers in the movie business, was sitting opposite, convincing him to write for the movies, and all he wanted was to pee. He began to enjoy the contrast of an infantile sensation against the adult nature of the lunch's purpose. Irony appealed to Tony: he relished having so important and wonderful a job as writing Bill Garth's next movie put before him as if he were not only competent for the job, but had to be persuaded to take it. Wasn't this an excellent revenge on his childhood?

He had lived in terror of the moguls who forced his father to talk and barred his mother from work because she did not. Tony trembled in bed at night, warm piss spreading beneath him, not for fear of a ghostly bogeyman, but of Senator McCarthy's huge face—a face Tony knew only in black and white—with his dulled, contemptuous killer eyes. McCarthy was dead, his mother's television series was in the top ten week after week, and now Gloria Fowler was offering him a script for one of America's box-office stars.

"If you're interested in proceeding," Gloria was saying while Tony squirmed, "we'll fly you out. You'll meet with Bill and Jim Foxx, and then with the studio people."

"But there's no guarantee at this point, right? I mean, if I don't wow them with my ideas—"

Gloria leaned forward, her elegant, bony hand gently touching his arm. Her eyes blinked slowly with knowledge. "They'll hire you," she said in a low voice. "They've all read your work. And, more important, they've read your reviews. Everybody knows, no matter what else is said, that good movies can only be made if the scripts are good. They've gone the hack Hollywood route. Nobody out there knows about the real world anymore, and this script needs a writer who has ideas, convictions, and cares more about the work than the money and glamour." She leaned back and smiled. "They need a human being to write this one."

Tony was thoroughly drunk when he got home. His mouth tasted of metal, his food felt undigested, and his mind went over Gloria's promises and statements slowly, like a straight line he couldn't keep his wobbly feet on. He splashed cold water on his face and stared at his bloodshot eyes. Gloria had told him she wanted to represent him. That alone would have been a break for a writer his age. Gloria said she believed she could help get his plays to Broadway if he worked in the movie business. She cited many examples of productions that were backed by movie money, and said, with a broad look, "They protect their own, you know. Write Bill Garth's script. It will get made, the studio will love you, and buy your next play, and put it on Broadway." Gloria laughed. "A year and a half from now you'll have a Tony and an Oscar. You can use them for andirons."

Tony had laughed at her. She had laughed back. They had traded looks of superiority. "You don't care about awards and money," she went on to say. "I know that. But I know you care about mounting a real production of your next play—and Tinseltown can do it for you."

The last year Tony lived in California he was five years old. He had no ambitions other than wishing he were Superman or an airplane pilot. He liked movies, but they were commonplace. Everyone he knew had a screening room in the den: they were adult work, and they caused adults to have boring conversations at dinner. But the bogeyman had been in town, his mother had had a breakdown and disappeared from his life. When she returned, the boring conversations became shrill with rage and terror. His parents would begin their rumbling after he went to bed. Their voices, dark and terrible, would wake him. He'd creep out, carefully placing his feet to avoid floorboards that might give his presence away, and eavesdrop on their fights.

"I couldn't betray people!" his mother screamed one night.

Tony heard nothing for a long time, and then his father's deep voice said, "You wouldn't have been lying. They were communists. And they still are."

His mother screamed instantly: "Then so am I."

Tony hated his mother. She was ugly like that. Why did she get so upset? He knew she was right—he felt it—but why did she have to be so loud and silly? That's what made his father angry, Tony felt, nothing else, just her ugliness.

That was his father's last night with them. A few months later, his mother took him to New York, where he had lived the rest of his life, except for summers in California, or other parts of the world, when he visited his father. By his ninth birthday, Tony didn't want to be Superman. And he hated movies. By then, he would stay up late, worrying over why his mother was out so late again, and read plays. Soon, he spoke the parts aloud, and found himself crying, or dueling, or making love. He understood nothing of the plays, and yet he understood everything. He was still a baby, but he had become as old as humanity's literature. He had never loved, or died, or ruled a kingdom: but at night, while buses belched beneath the window, he was a king, a lover, and he died a hundred terrible and wonderful deaths.

Theater grabbed his life by the elbow, slowing its hurried pace, and replayed its exquisite arguments and loves. Plays glued his shattered loyalties together, and let him weep, not only for his brilliant and brave mother but also for his scared and weak father.

Routine knowledge told him differently, but his heart couldn't dispel the lesson of his boyhood: movies destroy.

Patty noticed him, but it was too late. At the head of the BMT subway stairs, standing in a pool of his own urine, was a bum, laughing at her. His head moved jerkily from side to side as if he were dancing, only his feet were still, like a drunk jack-in-the-box.

Patty tried to hurry past him, but the steps were steep, and she half-stumbled, preventing a fall by righting herself with an outstretched hand, placed, unfortunately, at the border of the bum's piss. Horror shot through her so palpably that her nerves were stung, and she screamed.

"What the fuck?" the bum mumbled, his eyes big and wounded and wondering, like a child's.

Before she could think, Patty was off the stairs and bouncing between hustling midtowners on their lunch break. I escaped, she thought, but that did not relieve her desire to scream or cry or beg someone—anyone—on this busy corner to hug her and take her away from this mad city and her hopeless life.

She had trouble finding the restaurant. The sun glistened on the storefronts across the avenue. The lettering on the signs wavered and shimmered, as if beguiling her to misread them. She squinted while she walked, peering across the midtown traffic. She bumped into people and worried each time that her purse was gone or that a pickpocketing genius had unlatched it and removed her wallet without her knowledge. She walked past the restaurant because she was so concerned with the opposite side of the street, and ended up in a phone booth getting the address from Information. (Even that was a struggle: at first the operator claimed she wasn't supposed to give out addresses; she relented when Patty explained it was only a restaurant, not a residence.) Thus, when Patty finally appeared at Betty Winters' table, she was twenty minutes late.

"I'm sorry," Patty said breathlessly.

"I'm crocked. I've had two glasses of wine," Betty said with a tipsy smile. "What happened?"

"I can't find anything . . . I don't know where I am or who I am." Patty waved her arm distractedly. Her frizzy and wild hair flounced with the movement. The whole picture made Betty laugh. "I mean it," Patty said in the nearest she could come to an angry tone with another woman, namely petulance.

"I'm sorry. It's the wine. So—I was talking with Howard Feingold about you. He needs an associate editor. He expects you to call."

"Oh." This made Patty feel guilty at having snapped at Betty. "Where is he?"

"Fire Books. Quality paper."

"Thank you. Do I know him?"

Betty laughed again. "I don't know. Do you?" She controlled her smile to ask seriously, "Are you okay? Tony said you seemed fine at Fred's."

"Fred," Patty repeated, remembering the kiss in the hallway. Had last night really happened? Everything in her life seemed to quiver in her consciousness, as if her memory were a poor television signal.

"Tony said you went home with someone, a journalist."

"We shared a cab," Patty said. She had intended to tell Betty of her passionate night with David Bergman, but Betty's eagerness to hear gossip turned off Patty's desire to give it. "No more talk about *me*," Patty said with pert emphasis. "I'm sick of me."

"Well, I'm very boring. I have no gossip."

"How about work?"

"I don't have enough books for my list. I had something earlier in the week, but Jeffries said no."

"How does he expect you to fill your list if he doesn't let you buy books?"

"I asked him that. He said, 'Dear, your job isn't simply to buy books, but to buy good books.' Anyway, Howard Feingold is nice. You should call him."

"Okay. But do we want to work in publishing? Have these middle-aged men saying no to our books and calling us 'dear'?"

"Yeah!" Betty said, making a fist and shaking it in the air. Then she laughed. "I should tell him to stop calling me 'dear.' My God, it's been five years. You'd think he'd start treating me like one of the guys."

"Did he ever make a pass?" Patty asked with abrupt curiosity.

Betty blinked. "No. You know that."

"I did? I'm sorry." Patty did know, but from time to time she asked, hoping Betty would answer truthfully. Patty was convinced her denials were false.

"How could you forget? That's the story of my career. Everyone thought I was promoted to senior editor so fast because I had slept with Jeffries."

"Oh," Patty said, as if that were also news. Of course, it wasn't.

Betty sighed and lifted her glass. She held it wearily. "I can't win. I only get credit because of the men around me. My uncle got me the job, Jeffries' praise has made me important within the house, and my Tony, my beautiful Tony, he gives me the authors with his contacts." Betty drained the glass.

Patty leaned forward earnestly. "Your life is wonderful! You're the ideal!"

"No, no. The ideal is me with a baby."

"You want a baby?"

"I mean, according to the women's magazines. We don't want to totally repress femininity for the sake of career drives."

"I don't know." Patty stared off. "I'd like to squash my femininity right now. Squash it like a roach and flush it down."

Betty, though she smiled, blinked her eyes. She was astonished and somewhat appalled by Patty's vehemence. "I think you'd better call Howard Feingold this afternoon. You need a job."

"Am I promiscuous?" Patty said, staring earnestly into Betty's eyes.

Betty stared back for a moment, and then laughter burst from her, as if she had been shocked into it. "What? Where did that come from?"

"I HS'ed with David Bergman last night."

"HS'ed!" Betty said in a loud, irritated tone, pursing her lips. She didn't know what Patty meant, and Betty always reacted impatiently to anything she couldn't understand.

"Had Sex."

"Oh." Betty laughed again. "You did? Great! So you did like him."

"I don't know. That's why I asked if I was promiscuous."

"Because you went to bed with one man?"

"Well . . ." Patty was also thinking of Fred's kiss. She wasn't comfortable mentioning it, but she wished she could solicit Betty's opinion—she tried desperately to think of some way to explain her situation without going into details. But there was no way. "Did you sleep with Tony right away?" she asked, which, of course, gave entirely the wrong impression.

"We met while we both apprenticed in the Berkshires during the summer. We worked together and even did a scene together before we really, you know, dated. Not dated, but spent time alone. I knew him a few weeks before we slept together. But there's nothing wrong with going to bed with David Bergman the first time you meet him. God, I sound like a decadent Dear Abby."

Patty listened admiringly. "And he proposed then?"

"No!" Betty laughed. "God, no. I had a terrible time with him for more than a year. I know he was involved with at least one other woman."

"The louse."

Betty ran a hand through her red hair—the gesture seemed defensive. "No, he wasn't a louse. He didn't want to be married that young."

"How did you convince him?"

"I didn't. I had given up. Even decided that we had only a few more months to go before breaking up." Betty paused and stared off with a glazed look in her eyes.

Patty waited. She felt it was important to know why Tony married Betty: maybe the answer to what could make a relationship work was something simple and definite, something Patty could put into action and in one sweep change her life. Marry David Bergman with all that loft space, get a job from Howard Feingold, and have a mature lifelong friendship over expensive lunches with Betty. "What!" Patty finally asked with furious impatience.

"Oh!" Betty said, startled. She laughed. "I'm sorry, I was thinking of how he proposed. He showed up dressed like an English professor and sang 'I've Grown Accustomed to Your Face' and then handed me slippers."

"Oh," Patty said with noticeable disapproval.

"It was cute," Betty argued.

"Sounds degrading."

"Degrading?" Betty straightened. "He was joking. And besides, he has a beautiful voice."

"So what changed his mind?"

"I don't know."

"You never asked him!"

"Oh, I asked him. But what makes Tony so charming at a cocktail party, that is, his gift for a pleasantly clever answer, in human terms, makes him slippery and unknowable. When I'm depressed, I think to myself that someone he truly loved rejected him, and when I'm happy, I decide that he recognized my virtues."

"I'm sure it's that," Patty said, leaning so far forward that she was halfway out of her chair. "He loves you."

Betty looked at her with cool curiosity. "Thanks. I'm glad to be reassured."

Betty's tone set off an alarm. Patty scurried for an exit. "So when should I call Howard Feingold?"

"He said anytime. He'll be happy to talk to you about a job."

"Great. Now you have to get me a boyfriend."

Betty laughed. "Maybe you've got one." She laughed again, and with her laughter, relaxed. Patty did also, now that the bells had been turned off and there was no more worry that a burglar had entered Betty's fine store to steal her prize possession.

Fred's heart was pounding so hard it felt as if it were surging up through his lungs and might hop out into the air, leaving him without nerve or confidence. But he did manage to answer the secretary without spilling any blood. "Yes, I'll hold."

And there was the silence and the loneliness of being on hold, reduced to a flashing light on Bart Cullen's phone. Fred wanted a cigarette, but the pack was on the coffee table and his phone cord couldn't stretch that far. He moved the distance anyway, and tried to reach, balancing on one foot, holding the receiver with his shoulder, and pulling the cord so tight its curls disappeared. Idiot, he said to himself, if you had put the phone down right away and got them, you would have had time. But now Bart might come on any second and Fred didn't dare risk greeting him with silence.

Why are you so frightened? he asked himself. He's only your agent. Who cares what he thinks? But they've become so powerful, his pounding heart reminded him, that publishers use them as adjunct editors, weeding out the amateurs, and, through the contracts of their successful clients, establish minimums for unproven writers. If Bart backed one of his ideas, he would get a contract. Fred was sure of that.

There was still nothing on the line but the whoosh of electronic obscurity. The cigarettes lay temptingly on the table. He tried to stretch the receiver an extra few inches . . .

. . . and the phone was yanked out of his hands, snapped back to its mother by the taut cord, flying through the air, smacking into the wall, and finally clattering to the floor. The noise horrified Fred. He grabbed his pack of cigarettes and dashed to pick up the receiver, sure that Bart had been listening and deduced it all, and was laughing even now at foolish Fred.

"Hello?" he cried desperately into the phone. Nothingness answered him. So he lit his cigarette. With the first drag, he inhaled self-assurance and a dim sense of peerage with Bart.

"Hi," a voice said.

Fred almost didn't answer because the greeting was so quiet and lugubrious. "Bart?"

"Yeah. How are you?"

"Fine . . ."

"Thanks for last night."

"You're welcome."

"I've just gone through the material—"

An abrupt silence. Then Fred overheard Bart talking to someone else.

"I'll get back to him—Fred? Sorry. Uh, I, uh, looked over the proposals. They're good, but—I don't think this kind of market is looking for this sort of book. I mean, we wouldn't be attacking the point of least resistance. This is sort of paperback-original material. You can make good money in that, but I think we should be trying for more. We are a complete agency, we like to develop books that have a long life—hardcover, soft, good foreign sales, movies, television. I don't like to automatically cut off those things. Uh . . ."

Fred stared at the edge of Formica where it met the corner of his stainless-steel sink. There was a brown line of decay caused by moisture. He had never noticed it before. He saw himself standing in the living room of a forty-story building, sandwiched between row after row of hustling baby-boom middle-class thirty-year-olds, living off their salaries, subscribing to *New York Magazine*, feeling close to the rich, close to the famous, with the roar of the main pump of life's most exciting engine in their ears. Until Bart had opened his mouth to deliver that talk, Fred thought he was about to be finely polished and screwed into the glistening motor of New York, his name typeset for the appropriate columns and invitation lists. These words of Bart's were really a death sentence, a lifetime lease in this row of plasterboard mediocrity.

Bart was still talking: ". . . we need something sharper for you, with greater—"

"I have another idea," Fred blurted.

Silence. Then, "Uh-huh."

"Would you like to hear it?" Fred asked, not sure whether Bart would say yes.

"Yeah."

"I want to write a male version of *The Women's Room*. I want to show that men aren't shits. There's all this talk about monogamy and men fucking around when they hit forty. All that. The truth, and what no one is saying, is that men aren't able to be monogamous. Women can be. Men fall in love and they're horny, but those are two different things." Fred blurted this out and then suddenly had nothing to say. He waited. This was his last flare. Either Bart slowed his huge liner and rescued him from his waterlogged lifeboat, or steered past and left Fred to die of thirst in an ocean of water.

"Well," Bart said after a moment. "That could be interesting. But I need to hear a plot, something more."

"See, I want to follow two people my age from their romance in college up to now, show all the stuff, the political years, the drug years, becoming professionals, the touchy-feely psychology of the seventies. You know I want to do all the junk that is on Phil Donahue and in the Living Section of the *Times*, and then show how it's all down to this one basic difference."

"Mmmm." Bart fell silent, then spoke as if startled. "I think this has potential. Can you come up with enough of a story to write a proposal?"

"Sure!" Fred said happily.

"All right. There are several editors I can think of who are right. Bob Sand at Flanders, Carrie Winston at Ingrams. I'll light a fire under them while you get started on the proposal."

"How long should it be?"

"With this kind of story, don't get too involved with plot details. Focus on how it's a response to the feminist novel. That's the hook. I have to go . . . get this in quickly, Fred, it could be very exciting."

"Right. Thanks. Good-bye."

He was saved! Spinning out of the darkness, from the towering deck of the luxury liner, landing with a plop in the waters of obscurity, came Fred's lifesaver. He stopped only to pour a cup of coffee before he was at his typewriter. Nothing delayed or dismayed him as the pages appeared, blackened with his ideas, littering his desk while he invented effortlessly. It had never been like this before—he knew this story by heart. After all, it was the story of his marriage. And when a doubting voice wondered how Marion would feel about her life being thus exposed, Fred reminded himself that no great writer had ever hesitated to make a sacrifice of his life. At last, it had happened. Fred was in that great company of geniuses and artists. He was struggling to get over the railing, still soaked by the brackish water—but the liner had stopped and was ready for boarding.

David Bergman felt very much in demand. Writers from every section either dropped by or phoned. Two senior editors from the back of the book asked him to stop by their offices, and when he did, they too discussed the rumor. This sort of thing was general in the building that day. No one seemed to be working on the magazine.

None of the talk implied danger for David. Someone even suggested David might be promoted because of all the shifting around that would necessarily result from firing the editor in chief and replacing him from within, namely the managing editor. Someone would have to replace him, and someone the person he had replaced, and so on, in a complicated series of moves.

After a moment of anxiety over his job, David began to feel, while having all these gossipy conversations, that he wouldn't really care if he had to leave *Newstime*. He could be hired by almost anyone. The *Times*, the *Journal*, *Business Week*, they would all be willing to hire him. Syms was sure to be hired elsewhere if he were fired, and Syms would certainly hire David. To be worried was idiotic. He had over twenty thousand dollars saved up in the profit-sharing plan, there was unemployment insurance, he would be free to do nothing for more than a year before getting a job could become an urgent financial problem. How many thirty-year-olds could make that boast?

What finally did begin to stick in his mind was Patty. Her mouth gliding up and down his penis—that took over, with mixed results. He hadn't sat at a desk with an erection since junior high school, but the excitement below seemed divorced from his thoughts about Patty. She was just a blond girl. Silly and with great tits. Of course, she was accepted by everyone: the men wanted to look at her. But could he date her seriously? He imagined Patty accompanying him to a *Newstime* function. David, the classic smart Jewish boy walking in with a breast-flouncing chippie. The Marx Brothers would certainly snicker. And heart failure (at least) would strike David's parents.

But the rigidity in his pants was unimpressed. Last night was, if not the best sex of his life, certainly the most carefree and explosive. The last of the senior editors had casually wandered in to whisper in hushed tones about the rumor. David kept his own counsel and pretended no interest in any possible promotion that might come his way. While he listened to the senior editor's anxieties over his own job, he kept seeing Patty's head move up and down with relentless mastery of his organ.

David was so unresponsive that the senior editor left him after a few minutes. David kept his eye on the door—he didn't dare close it on a Monday with rumors turning sedentary writers into talky nomads; that would be suspicious—and squeezed his right hand underneath the belt of his gray pants, stretched the elastic band of his Jockey shorts, and got his cool fingertips to the head of his hard and frustrated penis. The constricted circumstances made any manipulation difficult, but he tried, his eyes watering from the effort of staring at the door and attempting to anticipate someone entering. He began to succeed in his fingering and the pleasure made his surveillance more difficult.

The phone rang.

Startled, David sat up abruptly, his swivel chair sliding toward the desk, banging his trapped wrist against the edge. He pulled his hand out of his pants and picked up the phone.

It was Chico, the managing editor. "David. I need to speak to you. Can you come up?"

"Sure."

"Come up without mentioning it. Okay?"

Dutifully David took the stairs, assuming this would make his trip to Animal Crackers less obvious. You never knew who was in the elevators. David even went so far as to peer down the hallway from the stairway entrance toward the reception area of Animal Crackers to check whether it was clear before making his appearance. Chico's secretary told him to go right in, and Chico, standing nervously at the window, told him to close the door. All this secrecy might mean nothing: Chico loved melodrama.

"You've heard, of course."

Pretending would be dumb. "Yeah." But on the other hand, maybe David hadn't heard the right rumor. "If what I've heard is what you're talking about."

"Steinberg is gone tomorrow. Syms will also be asked to leave. The last is a big secret. Everybody knows about Steinberg. With Syms out, we'll have problems in Nation. We're thin, especially in writing. And a number of our writers couldn't possibly take over as senior editors. Bill Kahn couldn't handle Nation."

David, for the first time that day, began to realize that this shift in power might be wonderful for him. What if they made him Nation senior editor? Was that possible? Nation was the most prestigious senior-editing position on the magazine, the traditional stepping-stone to Marx Brother status and presumably the ideal background for editor in chief. David had always assumed that if Syms left, Bill Kahn would succeed him. Besides, David was very young to be made a senior editor. This notion so dominated his mind that he had trouble appearing at ease, and the trouble made him more nervous, as if his being caught thinking such an ambitious thought might make Chico change his mind. What was he thinking? Such a change wouldn't be up to Chico alone; all the Brothers and Mrs. Thorn would have to agree on a promotion to senior-edit Nation.

"You agree, don't you? About Kahn?"

Now this question from Chico seemed loaded, and with deadly bullets. David tried a traditional escape maneuver: "You mean Kahn is more interested in writing?"

"No. Kahn would love to be made senior editor. I mean, he couldn't handle it. Isn't that obvious?"

Bang, it was back in David's court. Can I agree? he nervously questioned himself. I shouldn't be hesitating. Senior-editing Nation wouldn't allow hesitation. "I only know Bill as a writer. I mean, as a writer knows another writer. I read his stuff, that's all. I have no idea how he might edit or develop ideas. He doesn't seem interested in other people's work, so perhaps he wouldn't be a sympathetic editor. He would establish a tone." Was any of that true? David wondered. Probably, he decided.

"Oh, Bill's a superb writer," Chico agreed. "But I don't think he can handle people. That's at least as important as editorial skills. That was Syms's problem. He was arrogant."

Chico citing Syms for arrogance? Chico was the most arrogant man in the world. Everything that came out of his mouth was a pronouncement, an absolute judgment, calmly delivered, with the self-assurance of a monarch. Chico could be chilling. David thought all this and noticed Chico's use of the past tense when discussing Syms.

"You liked working for him, though," Chico added, and sat down, his eyes—beady little things that seemed too small for his large body—peering at David.

"Yes." David stared back. To lie about that would be thoroughly pointless. David had flourished under Syms, drawing more and more cover assignments in Nation (and away from Kahn) because of Syms's support.

"But I get the feeling you can work with anyone," Chico said.

Was that a compliment? Or was Chico accusing David of having no taste?

"That's an important quality," Chico continued. "To put out this magazine, we need as little tension and scraping of egos as possible. Good senior editors can work with anyone."

Bingo. Something David had not expected for years was about to happen: senior editorship. And of Nation at that!

"I wanted to give you Nation to senior-edit," Chico said, "but others feel you're too young to be moved immediately, as a senior editor, into the most important and pressured position. They want to ease you into senior editing. As a compromise, you'll be offered Business."

David had had only a second to relish the hope that he might senior-edit Nation, but that moment was sufficiently captivating to make getting Business instead a disappointment. He knew that was an absurd feeling —to be a senior editor at his age, no matter what the department, was extraordinary. Besides, Business was the second-most-important position in the rank of senior editor, in fact the job that five years ago, when he first came to *Newstime*, he hoped he would someday hold. Meanwhile, he had to respond to this surreptitious and unofficial job offer, if that's what it was.

"What happens to Jim?" David asked, referring to the current senior editor of Business.

"Well . . ." Chico grabbed a paper clip and began to unravel it, almost angrily. "You understand none of this is definite."

"Of course." So he couldn't celebrate—yet.

"Presumably Jim would move to Nation."

"Really?"

"Yeah, I agree. He's not right for it. I don't think he'll be there for long."

There was a loud buzz from the red intercom resting next to Chico's phone. A disembodied voice boomed from its open speaker—in *Newstime* this intercom system, which provided the Marx Brothers and all the senior editors with direct lines to each other, had been nicknamed the Power Phone—and to David's surprise, the harassed and irritable voice belonged to the owner, Mrs. Thorn. "Bill, can you come by now? I think we're ready for a decision."

"Be right there."

David got to his feet immediately, noting the tension and expectation in Chico's face. What was Chico waiting to hear? That he had been chosen to succeed Steinberg?

"I'll speak to you tomorrow," Chico said.

"Right." And David turned, leaving this exalted floor, the home of the Animal Crackers, certain, for the first time in his career that he would one day work there. He smiled to himself, once alone in the back stairway, thinking of himself in college, not quite bright enough to be at the top, not handsome enough to dominate the coeds, not angry enough to be a radical, not talented enough to be an artist. But if tomorrow's promise came true, he would be at the head of his class.

CHAPTER

4

Tony took a seven P.M. flight to Los Angeles a week after his meeting with Gloria. He had signed a twenty-page contract with her agency, Creative Artists International, and fired his sweet-tempered but lax theatrical agent, Boris. "I knew someday you'd go with the big boys," Boris said in a resigned but friendly tone. "They may make you money—but they won't love you like I have. They won't notice that your scripts don't have peanut butter on them anymore, or that your wife likes to fluff the hair around your ears."

But it was precisely because Boris saw himself as a second mother, rather than as a businessman, that Tony wanted to fire him. He was signed with Creative Artists International for only seven days and already they had him flying first class on a 747 to LA, booked into the Beverly Hills Hotel, *and* scheduled for a meeting the next morning with Bill Garth, the actor, and Jim Foxx, the producer. All this was courtesy of International Pictures to discuss a project that was certain to be made. If Garth and Foxx liked his ideas, he would be perhaps a year away from seeing his name on the big screen. Sooner or later success in LA would get him to Broadway. That was Gloria Fowler's love, and Tony preferred it.

Tony had flown first class to LA before. His father, using his CBS expense account, used to fly Tony out and back for summer vacations and alternate holidays. He had stayed with his mother at the Beverly Hills Hotel. He had met famous actors and producers before. But Tony had never been the object, the cause of spending, the focus of a Hollywood summons. While the stewardesses kept cheerfully getting him new drinks and extra dessert (only now, at thirty-two, did Tony finally treat the experience with the greedy enthusiasm of a boy), he realized: *This is fun!*

He sat in the back of his limousine during the ride from LAX to the Beverly Hills Hotel and played with the bar and the temperature-control dial—he wanted to see if he could tell the difference between sixty-eight and sixty-six degrees—and said to himself over and over, this isn't depressing, this is fun! And though the difference between his childhood visits and this trip was obvious—to see a father who has given your mother a nervous breakdown and blacklisted his friends is presumably of a different quality than being summoned by a world-famous actor and a powerful producer to "save the script"—nevertheless, the pure thrill of it, the preposterous treatment of him by the driver and hotel clerks as if he were the scion of royalty, the silly extravagance of first-class travel, all of it, was wonderful, perhaps his first real Christmas ever.

Two messages were waiting for him at the desk, from his father and mother. Of course, their names didn't mean that to the slavish clerk. She was the star of the number-one television sitcom and his father was the head of programming for a major network. As always their stature in television land amused Tony, but once upstairs, disappointed that his room was small (writers don't get suites, I guess, he thought), the two names scrawled on the message-form slips depressed him, reminded him of the other LA, blew in to the air-conditioned room a Santa Ana of greed, cowardice, and disloyalty.

He decided not to phone, his excuse being that it was late and he had an early meeting. But he couldn't sleep and after unpacking with a meticulousness totally unlike him, he wanted to talk to someone. New York was out of the question; it was already late there. He was stumped for a while, until he thought of Billy Feldman, the son of a neighbor of his father's, also a child of divorce, with whom Tony would play during his summers in Beverly Hills. Tony's father had mentioned the last time they talked that Billy was in town working in the business. Tony found him through Information, living in Hollywood.

"Hey, man! How are you? This is incredible, I was just talking about you."

"I'm in town. I can't sleep. I was hoping . . ."

"Sure—where are you?"

Fifteen minutes later Billy arrived at the hotel entrance and waved away the valet-parking attendant as Tony approached. Billy was driving a BMW sports car, wearing a pink T-shirt and white shorts and a pair of sunglasses pushed back onto the top of his head.

"What's this?" Tony asked, getting in. "The Hal Prince look?"

Billy looked puzzled.

"The glasses," Tony explained.

"Oh." Billy seemed worried suddenly, as if he had committed a gaffe. "I forget I have them on, I'm sorry."

"I was teasing," Tony said. He slapped Billy on the leg. "Thank you for rescuing me. I was so lonely in that hotel room."

"I know what you mean, man. They're the worst. What are you doing in a hotel anyway? Between your mom and dad you've got forty-five rooms to stay in."

"I've never seen Mom's place. Think it's big?"

"I know it is. I was there last week."

"You were! For what? Don't tell me she had a party."

"Script conference. Haven't you heard? You haven't!" Billy seemed slightly miffed. "I'm a writer on her series," he continued, obviously proud of this fact, and hurt that Tony wasn't aware of his accomplishment.

"You are! No kidding. That's terrific!" Tony said with conviction. Billy relaxed and told the story of how he landed his job as a "story editor" on Tony's mother's series. His account was given in a tone that implied the anecdote had the significance of legend, the way a war veteran might talk of his participation in the Normandy invasion. In telling how he got the assignment to write an episode, Billy seemed to discount that he had known Tony's mother, as well as the executive producer, since childhood.

"So they gave me a week to write the script. I didn't fucking sleep at all. By the time I handed it in, I was sure it was shit. And I just felt—I mean, I'm sure I was overdramatizing—that this was my last shot. If this script didn't go, I don't know, I would have just given up. Gone back east or something."

"So after you wrote one episode, they made you a story editor?"

Billy frowned. He seemed both confused and irritated. "Well, the script I wrote was the car-wreck episode."

Tony nodded and waited. Billy looked away from the road to glance at Tony and saw that his explanation had been insufficient.

"You know?" Billy said, now a little doubt creeping into the tone of the war veteran: perhaps his listener had never heard of World War II.

"The car-wreck episode," Tony repeated. "That was this past season?"

"Tony, your mom won an Emmy for the car-wreck episode. Don't tell me you haven't seen that show!"

"Well . . ." Tony was about to say that he vaguely remembered seeing a few minutes of an episode about a car wreck, when he realized that such a comment would be more insulting than saying he had never seen it. Obviously Billy believed the car-wreck episode, if one saw it, would haunt the memory.

"Here we are!" Billy announced, in time to prevent Tony from saying anything.

"Joe Allen's!" Tony exclaimed with genuine delight. "I forgot they have one in LA."

"I thought it might make you less homesick," Billy said.

When they walked in and Tony saw the familiar brick walls and the long old-fashioned bar at the entrance, he said, "You're right."

"Yeah, the first year I moved out here permanently, I ate here three times a week. I would've come more, except I was embarrassed. And broke."

Billy walked past the headwaiter and on into the back room, heading for a table with two young women and room for two others. Tony followed, dismayed at the prospect of having to meet people. Billy introduced the women as Helen, his roommate, and her friend, Lois.

"As in Lane," Billy added with a grin.

"And you're Billy, as in the Kid," Lois answered in a quiet drawl. The response, and the vague suggestion of hostility in her tone, interested Tony.

While they ordered drinks, and Tony, his stomach clock disordered, first decided he was hungry and ordered a hamburger, then had no desire for it on its arrival, they discussed their reasons for being in LA. All of them were New Yorkers. Billy, like Tony, was raised by his mother and had been visiting LA for years before he moved, but Helen and Lois both came to LA after college and worked as secretaries for movie studios. Helen was now a film editor (Tony eventually was able to determine without asking directly that she was still basically an assistant film editor, which could mean anything from being the real talent behind her boss to being the person who organized the loose strips at the end of the day —the lower end of the spectrum was more likely) and Lois had become a sitcom writer. Indeed, she had made it: she was the producer of his mother's series, a title which meant that she supervised the assignments, acceptance, and final polishing of all the episodes, as well as writing four or five herself.

They all knew Tony's story, to his surprise, but it turned out his mother was fond of bragging about his plays and (when he guessed this, and asked them, they cheerfully admitted it) implying that they wrote garbage for TV while her brilliant son was a "serious writer."

Tony's wringing this admission from them made them all great friends, especially when Tony laughed at his mother's description of him as a "serious writer." Tony said, "That means I don't make any money."

While Lois laughed at this remark, Tony smiled and looked into her eyes, thinking about making love to her, and it was clear to him that she would be willing. She had been expecting to loathe him; she was someone who had little free time for meeting single men; she knew mostly television types like Billy; and, of course, though Tony made fun of talk about himself as a "serious writer," he knew that in fact he *was* a serious writer, and therefore possessed a sort of impoverished nobility that still awed people who worked in Hollywood. All this added up to her being an easy target for a seduction.

Now, despite the fact that he was already flirting with her and giving every indication that he had never met a woman so beautiful and interesting before, did he actually want to sleep with her? It was hard for him to even begin to answer this question. He always wanted people to want him. Often this concern obliterated whether he wanted them.

Even now, as he noticed that her lips, thin and bloodless, did not appeal to him, that her hair was a dull brown, her breasts were small, that she had an arrogant attitude toward Billy and Helen, presumably because they were lower down on Hollywood's totem pole, and that she was obviously dying to know the details of his business in LA—all these things made her unattractive—even so, he heard and saw himself wooing her as if nothing, nothing else on earth, could be more important than winning her.

Patty's week had been difficult. She saw David Bergman only once more. He was strangely indifferent and though they went to bed, he was passionless, ignoring her desires, while his own seemed to be satisfied perfunctorily. It had been the booze, she decided, and felt profoundly insulted.

Her problems mounted each day, because every day cost money, and she had less of that commodity with each expense. Unemployment insurance didn't cover everything, despite her efforts to economize. She had trouble sleeping until after a long struggle, which meant that she would fall asleep at four or five in the morning and be unable to wake up until noon. That made her search for a job even more difficult.

Her life had no markers. Each day resembled the last. Life's ordinary routine—sleeping, eating, bathing, cleaning—rose like dark hills for her exhausted will to climb.

She got up one morning to discover she weighed under one hundred pounds, a first since childhood. In the *Times* that morning was a long article on anorexia. Patty diagnosed herself as a sufferer, and was haunted by images of bones piercing through a shrunken body. She became too upset to eat breakfast, confirming her terror, and she called Betty in a panic.

"I need a doctor," she said without even a hello.

"What's wrong!"

"I'm anorectic!"

Betty laughed. "I wish I was."

Patty began to cry. She tried to cover it by talking, but the words caved in like a rotten floor and dropped her into a basement of sobs.

Betty's tone changed sharply. "My God, Patty, are you all right? You're *not* anorectic! Where are you?"

"In the kitchen," Patty whimpered, looking at her untouched breakfast. "I can't eat."

"I want to see you. Are you dressed?"

Patty tried to say yes, but sobbed instead.

"Get in a cab and come here."

"I can't—"

"I'll pay for it."

"I can't face midtown . . ."

"Patty." Betty said this like a mother: with stern love. "The cab will take you to the entrance. You get in an elevator and walk into my office. Midtown won't touch you."

This is silly, Patty thought. I'm not having a breakdown. I don't need to run to Betty's office for her to take care of me. But while Patty told herself she was okay, she nevertheless rushed out of the apartment, caught a cab, and anxiously watched the street numbers go by, as if her eventual arrival might be in doubt, or that the closer she came to the solace of Betty's office, the more easily she could bear life.

And indeed, by the time she stepped out of the elevator onto Betty's floor, a kind of lightheartedness took over, as if Patty's presence there was part of a different life, as if she were merely visiting a peer during some free time grabbed from the hustle and bustle, meeting Betty to play squash, or for a drink, or for any of the reasons she used to visit Betty's office. One of the editors she knew passed her in the hall, and Patty easily greeted him, and gave an impression of contentment that was genuine coin, even though the purse of its origin was otherwise dark, musty, and poor.

Betty looked relieved on seeing her. She closed the door to her office. "Are you all right?"

"I'm a wreck."

"You don't look it. You look great."

"I feel like dying."

Betty said nothing. She nodded seriously and looked expectant. But Patty didn't want to elaborate. It was truer kept simple: detailing her problems made them sound small, and they didn't feel small. In the aggregate they were suffocating, and made her want to disappear and die.

"You need a job," Betty said at last, as if this were a conclusion reached through intensive tests done by a crack medical team. "Why don't you write something?"

"Are you nuts? I need money. I have three hundred bucks in the bank."

"No, no. I mean, write a romance book, or, uh, you could do some ghost writing, something. But guaranteed money, not on spec."

"Can I write?" Patty said heavenward, with a sweet pleading air, like a child querying Santa Claus on his ability to give a special present.

"Sure! Those things? I think of doing them all the time. Those romances are a formula. It's like painting by numbers."

"I can't believe it! I'll become one of those hysterical writers screaming for more ads. I can't do it. And how do we get a contract anyway? We have no experience."

Betty laughed. "So you do want to try?"

"I can't get a job again. I'm too passive. I'd never be promoted. I'd end up being the first eighty-year-old assistant editor in publishing."

Betty stood up. "Let's go."

"Where?"

"Downstairs to the Shadow Books division. We'll see Joe McGuire. He handles romances."

For a moment Patty stayed in her chair. It seemed preposterous: could it work? Had she been worrying herself to death over nothing? Could she just take an elevator down to an assignment, money, respectability, a sense of self, a return of appetite, the ability to pay for extermination of all the cockroaches in her sublet? Had this nightmare merely been an illusion of nerves?

Betty nodded at the door. "Come on. Let's do it."

Patty opened her mouth to protest: argue that failure would surely be the result.

But Betty anticipated her: "No back-talk. I'm telling you it'll work."

Patty got up. Betty made her feel competent. That this would be fun. She followed her out and smiled brilliantly at a cute male assistant who was watching her breasts bounce while she walked.

Fred Tatter was waiting again. This time in Bart's outer office. He had handed in an outline for *The Locker Room*, his novel on the incompatibility of men and women, two days after thinking of the idea. Bart had taken the weekend to read it, called to say he liked it, and made an appointment to see Fred the next morning. So Fred had spent a sleepless night trying to deduce what Bart intended from his terse comment of praise on the phone:

"It's good, Fred. Come in tomorrow at ten and we'll talk."

A cryptographer handed a top-secret code could not have found more significant hidden meaning than Fred did in those two sentences. He began euphorically; decided that Bart was going to present him with an offer from a publisher and simply wanted to do it face to face. That fell by the wayside when Fred realized it was impossible. Not enough time had passed for Bart to get the outline to an editor and have it read. By three in the morning he had become pessimistic: Bart wanted major changes in the outline and simply wished to begin by softening up Fred with praise. By five in the morning Fred decided that "It's good, Fred" was a pretty weak compliment, so halfhearted that it was no better than saying "It stinks, Fred."

I poured my heart into that outline, Fred thought. It's got my guts in it. And all he can say is, "It's good."

Fred fell asleep on the couch at six, furious and despondent, resolved to break off with Bart if he suggested any changes, and prepared to demand why he was so abrupt and high-handed on the phone.

But by the time Fred, bleary-eyed, his back aching from sleeping on the soft couch, arrived at the town house in the Village that Bart had bought—the bottom two floors for his office, the top three for living—he felt so worthless, so convinced that his only hope of success lay with the backing of a hot, powerful agent like Bart, that he was ready to throw out the outline and apologize for having handed in such a miserable piece of work.

Fred looked at the beautiful built-in maple shelves that surrounded the marble fireplace in the waiting room. A hundred years ago it had been a fancy parlor room, and Bart's architects had kept and restored that feeling, except for the Xerox machine that glistened on top of a large oak table near Bart's secretary's elegant desk. The shelves were filled with books by clients. Even if Fred had come in cocky, the sight of seven bestsellers within the last two years would have punched it out of him. In his state of mind, it almost felled him to his knees. He felt lucky that Bart's secretary smiled at him, grateful he had been offered coffee, and terrified of the closed door to Bart's office.

When it did open, Fred got up quickly, forgetting his cup of coffee was filled to the brim and would spill. It did, most of it going on his best beige pants.

Bart's secretary exclaimed.

Bart merely stared impassively.

The hot coffee burned into his thigh painfully.

The secretary rushed over with a roll of paper towels from her desk, handed Fred some, and bent down to mop up what had landed on the white rug. She looked up at Fred. "Are you okay? Is that burning you?"

"No," Fred said angrily.

"Are you sure?"

"Yeah." He had dabbed at the wet spot on his pants, but that made the burn hurt more, so he stopped and held out the paper towel to the secretary. "Sorry about the rug."

"Won't hurt it," she said. "Maybe you should put some water on the pants. It'll stain."

"Nah." Fred waved his hand as if he usually wore a pair of pants only once and then threw them out. His leg hurt. He got an image of it swelling into an enomous pus-filled blister.

Bart, still standing at the door calmly, said, "Come in, Fred."

"Sure," Fred said, now carrying the coffee in both hands.

Bart's office must have been the dining room. It had tall, elegant windows, a large fireplace, and elegant moldings in the center of the ceiling that once supported a chandelier. There were no books in this room, but there were two large leather couches—distinctly inconsistent with the dominant motif of French country antiques—a large armchair opposite Bart's desk, and an enormous globe underneath the nearest window. The world was literally at Bart's fingertips.

Fred winced as he sat in the armchair.

"Are you all right?" Bart asked in a tone suggesting surprise that he could possibly be in pain.

"Oh, yeah."

"I just got off the phone with Bob Holder at Garlands. We were discussing your outline. I'm sending it to him this afternoon. He's promised to give an answer in two days, if I give it to him exclusive."

Bart's tone was matter-of-fact, so listless that Fred didn't react. He nodded slowly.

"I think he's a good choice, don't you?"

"Uh, Bob Holder?" Fred repeated.

"Yeah, he's the hot young editor at Garlands. And they've really been the aggressive packager of fiction in the last couple years."

"It's great," Fred said in a stunned tone.

"Off an outline I don't know how big an advance I can get—"

"You think he'll buy it?"

Bart stared at him. "Why not?"

"You think the outline's really good?"

"It's fair. You're not terrific at writing outlines. But it's been my experience the best outline writers come out with lousy novels. And vice versa. I told that to Bob. He agreed. He's had the same experience."

Fred laughed nervously. Fair. He said the outline was fair. "He knows I haven't written a novel?"

"If Bob likes the idea, he'll trust my judgment that you can pull it off. We've done very well together."

Fred nodded, stupefied by this strange conjunction: Bart thought the outline was fair, but he had given it to his big-money editor at one of America's most prestigious publishers, and was confident he would make a deal. Was Bart that influential? Could this man whose rug Fred had just spilled coffee on really announce to an editor that someone was a good writer and be taken at face value? If so, rather than reassuring Fred, it made him very nervous. He tried to think how he should react: with profuse thanks? Or was that too craven, indicative of a total lack of confidence in himself? But if he took it in stride, mightn't Bart feel Fred was ungrateful, ignorant of how big a favor Bart had given away?

"This is great," Fred said, still in the slow speech of a victim of bad news.

"Of course Bob agrees with me that you should make some changes when you get to the actual writing of the novel."

"I don't understand. Has Bob read the outline?"

"No. But I told him the story line. We both think the hero shouldn't be Jewish—"

"But I'm Jewish."

Bart paused. "Tatter?" he asked.

"My great-grandfather's name was Teittlebaum. He couldn't speak English, so the official gave him the name of Tatters. 'Cause of the condition of his clothing. By the time my great-grandfather found out what 'Tatters' meant, he had grown fond of it. He dropped the S so people wouldn't make the connection."

Usually this story brought a smile to people's faces. Bart contemplated it rather as if Fred had told him an intriguing and sobering paradox. "Why does that mean your hero has to be Jewish?"

"It doesn't. Just that for my first book I thought I should . . ." Fred trailed off. He really didn't know why. "You know."

"Do you see this as an autobiographical novel?"

"I guess not."

" 'Cause if you do, maybe we could make it nonfiction. A male answer to *The Second Sex*."

"No, no. It's definitely a novel."

"All right. Bob and I think it's better if the hero is non-Jewish. There are too many complaining books about Jewish men and sex."

"You're right," Fred agreed, embarrassed. Did the proposal give away how frustrated and inadequate he felt in bed? Just another Jewish boy upset that he doesn't have a big prick?

"In fact," Bart continued, "maybe the book shouldn't take place in New York. Seems to me almost every novel I read is located in New York. You know, I was brought up in Detroit and, uh, New Yorkers think of the rest of America as provincial, but the fact is it's New York that's insulated. New York books are too self-conscious. I think readers would be more interested to find out how men feel in the rest of the country. Maybe you could set it in my hometown. Ever been to Detroit?"

"Yeah, sure. I did a couple pieces on the Tigers for *Sport*." Detroit's a shithole, Fred said to himself bitterly, mostly because he couldn't say it out loud.

"What do think about setting it there?"

Fred swallowed and looked away from Bart's cold eyes. He felt as if these weren't merely suggestions. That the timing of this conversation—immediately before submitting the outline to Bob Holder—implied a threat if Fred didn't go along. Perhaps Bart would use his influence with Holder only if Fred agreed to these plot and character changes. He hated them, though.

"You want to set the book in New York," Bart said in what seemed like an impatient and disappointed tone.

"No, no," Fred said quickly, meaning to answer Bart's impatience. He realized—with horror—that he had just accidentally agreed to setting it elsewhere.

"You're just not sure about Detroit?" Bart prompted.

Fred nodded, abashed. Why didn't he argue? Why was he letting his novel be changed without a fight?

"Detroit was just a notion. The important thing is to keep it out of New York. As long as you agree, that's fine." Bart leaned back with a satisfied expression. "This is going to be a big book, Fred. I considered making a hard-soft deal with Bob. He already brought it up—but now I don't think so. We may get seven figures for the paperback rights if you can pull it off."

Fred was electrified. Not by the talk of seven figures; that he knew was gossamer. It was Bob Holder bringing up a possible hard-soft deal. That meant he was already partly disposed toward making a deal even before seeing the outline. Jesus, why hadn't he worked on the outine harder and longer? "Holder's really excited, huh?"

"You know, it's interesting, Fred. This idea of yours—it's hot. Minute I heard it, I knew you had something. And Holder, who has, I think, the best instincts for commercial fiction in the country, was hopping. He was terrified I was going to give anyone else a shot at it."

Fred felt scared. He learned forward. "Bart. Listen. Maybe, given all these changes, I should rewrite the outline before Holder sees it."

"I've already sent it to him. Don't worry. He doesn't expect much from the outline. I told him you'd done it in a rush, that you'll be eager to sit down with him before writing and really work out a detailed plot so there'll be no surprises when you hand in the manuscript. You know, it's best to involve an editor. Get their ego into the book. Make 'em feel almost as if they wrote it. Then they fight like a motherfucker for a big printing, ad budget. I think if you work closely with Holder, he'll go to the mat and really fight for the book."

Fred left Bart's office thrilled. He hailed a cab and gave his home address. He lit a cigarette and looked out the window at New York City —perhaps too boring and provincial a location for his novel—but the crisp fall day's sun glistened against the midtown skyscrapers and danced a celebration of welcome. Fred told the driver he had changed his mind, and asked him to steer for Brooks Brothers, and soon he was there, amidst all those insulated New York men; men who ran the banks, the newsmagazines, the television networks; powerful men, who, Fred fancied, glanced at him casually, as if he belonged, despite his coffee-stained pants. Self-confidence rose from him like a mist, obscuring that he was short, Jewish, and all those other insecurities that America had been bored to tears reading of. No, there would be no shouts of intruder from the powerful men, because, Fred believed, he now belonged.

Another major story had been assigned to David Bergman the week that *Newstime* became the subject of the news rather than a purveyor. Every day in the New York *Post* on page six (a garish page of show-business and media gossip) the "scandalous" story of Steinberg's sudden firing and the confusion over who would be named Groucho—editor in chief—was given big play.

While David puzzled over the bureau reports on Haig's problems, wild accounts of Mrs. Thorn's dismissal of Steinberg appeared, were denied, and then reappeared with new embellishments. The original story was: she had walked in out of the blue and, despite Steinberg's very profitable record, had fired him impulsively when, after she complained about a recent cover story, he told her not to interfere with his running of the magazine. *Newstime* editors and writers found themselves getting calls late Monday and early Tuesday from people at the *Weekly* trying to confirm or deny this. Everybody claimed to have no idea what had happened.

David tried to concentrate on the Haig story. His dismissal had been so widely anticipated that David couldn't find a single new element to bring in now that the event had actually occurred. By Wednesday the story that Mrs. Thorn had had security guards appear to prevent Steinberg from taking any files and that she had had him led out in disgrace was causing a lot of laughter at the *Weekly* and among newsies in general.

But the attention of *Newstime* employees was on the question of who would be Steinberg's successor. David was glad that he had his cover story to write, because he could plausibly ignore the nervous speculations in the hall. He had heard nothing more from Chico about his own potential promotion; he had tried to see Patty Lane again and had been too distracted and anxiety-ridden to enjoy her; and so he told himself to focus absolutely on the cover story and let events decide things for him.

By Thursday, contempt for Mrs. Thorn was rampant in *Newstime*'s halls. The writers decided the gossip was true. She must have fired Steinberg without thinking it through because she had not yet picked a new Groucho. By now Steinberg, for whom there had been little love and certainly no passion, was being discussed wistfully, as if his tenure had been a golden era, impossible to recapture.

Everyone's mood was worsened by the emotional state of the remaining Marx Brothers, who, made restless by a vacancy above them, were suddenly trespassing on each other's territory, as if to prove that they were qualified to head the magazine. Chico, who had been put in charge for that week's issue, behaved as though the assignment was permanent. But his manner was irritable and defensive, like someone who suspects that if he should settle on his throne, he would discover that a prankster had moved it away, and he'd end up on his ass—with a roomful of spectators to laugh at him. David found his "blues," so called because the rough drafts of articles were written on blue sheets that were edited by the appropriate senior editor and Marx Brother, coming back from Chico with crabby and picky margin notes requesting changes. This was unusual and worried David. Had someone convinced Chico that

David was a poor choice to senior-edit Business and now Chico was out to cover himself by becoming David's biggest critic?

But he, unlike the rest of the magazine, forced these worries down. He told himself that pretending lofty disinterest in the magazine's power struggle would eventually redound to his credit. (He was right. Later, the nervous, gossipy behavior of some writers was remembered bitterly by the Marx Brothers.)

On Friday, everyone was taken by surprise. All the newshounds of New York had failed to pick up even a hint of what Mrs. Thorn did. She named an outsider as the new editor in chief. He was Richard Rounder, a six-foot-five blond, blue-eyed ex-Navy commander who had no background as a journalist but had been the founding editor in chief of *New South* magazine, one of the startling successes of the last decade. Everything about Rounder was unprecedented. Editors in chief of *Newstime* had always been both Northern and Eastern—Rounder was born and bred in Atlanta—and worked many years either as journalists or as editors of strictly news-gathering organs. And all but one had worked at *Newstime* for many years before being promoted to the top job. Rounder not only had never worked at *Newstime*, and had no background as a journalist, he also had no experience with weekly newsmagazines. *New South* was a slick, glossy monthly devoted mostly to lifestyle features, with an occasional exposé.

The gossips at the magazine (namely everyone), though they were taken by surprise—few had considered an outsider as a candidate, and those who *had*, picked former *Newstime* employees—adjusted instantly, as is the habit of journalists, with authoritative explanations. Rounder's success had been with a feature magazine, therefore Mrs. Thorn obviously intended to improve *Newstime*'s "soft cover stories." A remarkable number of people who only a day before had been insisting that Steinberg was fired *because* he did too many "soft covers" were now looking wise and grave as they pronounced that Rounder was hired to ensure that *Newstime* do more. Among the political writers, David's immediate colleagues, Mrs. Thorn's decision went over badly.

"Better pack up, David," said Bill Kahn, deputy senior editor of Nation, walking into David's office on Friday at dinnertime. Kahn was the fellow whose deficiencies as a potential senior editor of Nation David and Chico had discussed so confidently only four days ago.

David smiled while continuing to glance over the latest rewrite of his cover story, checking to see if he had dealt with all of Chico's irritable changes. "Yeah. I've been fired? Just in time. I've had it with this bullshit."

"No. Worse than fired. This guy Rounder, he only likes stories about cheerleaders or how to get rid of crabs without your mom finding out you had 'em."

David got serious. He put the blues down and looked at Kahn. "Is it really that bad?"

"Listen, some people think we may not cover the eighty-four election."

Kahn was smiling, but he meant it, David knew. "Have you seen Chico?"

"What's left of him. Guy's only about three feet tall now."

David laughed. Chico's size did seem to fluctuate depending on his fortunes as a Marx Brother.

"Haven't you seen him?" Kahn asked. "You're doing the cover."

"No, I'm just getting changes from Syms."

Kahn glanced toward Syms's office and lowered his voice. "Everybody says he'll be gone too. They think Rounder's gonna clean out all the senior editors and bring in happy-time news bozos from *New South*."

Kahn left after ten minutes of gallows humor, climaxing with his claim that the only reason they might cover the eighty-four election was that the incumbent was a former actor. In a low voice, glancing suspiciously toward the hall, he wrapped up his analysis: "You know why she brought in an outsider? To get rid of the deadwood. Rounder doesn't owe anybody anything, so he'll willingly play the part of hatchet man. You'll be all right. But fat old drunks like me—we're gone."

Kahn walked out and then spoke to the other cubicle offices in a stentorian voice: " 'Never send to know for whom the bell tolls; it tolls for thee.' "

That was greeted with game laughter and David knew what they all knew: threats of change always exceeded the eventual reality. Kahn saying he expected to be fired was a lie; he was upset because he knew Rounder being hired meant he would probably become irrelevant, pensioned into a job that only a few weeks before he thought was a rung on a ladder, and now had become the zenith of a rather small ascent. For David, Rounder's hiring meant something similar. Chico would *not* become a major power, and therefore David's promotion might never come.

David's cover story was closed early, by nine o'clock on Friday. But the usual excitement that accompanied finishing a cover successfully was absent. In general that week, the actual putting together of *Newstime* had been neither newsworthy nor timely.

Although Tony had flirted relentlessly during dinner, still he was surprised when Lois boldly announced outside Joe Allen's valet parking that she should take Tony to the hotel, since she lived in Benedict Canyon and it was right on the way. Billy and Helen nodded quietly. Tony knew they would be suspicious; their place was also on the way. But that didn't matter—since their suspicions would be about her, and besides, he hadn't decided to fuck her, he had merely wanted her to want him.

In her BMW he stared at the digital clock, amazed that it was only eleven-thirty. Stupidly, he had to slowly count the time difference to realize it was two-thirty in the morning for his body. Lois pulled away sharply from the curb, her bony hand arched above the shift knob, so that she gripped it with her long fingers.

"Tired?" Her voice was cool, distant.

Maybe he was wrong. This might just be taking home the boss's son, ordinary brownnosing, not the sexual kind. Anyway, that was all wrong. Lois knew, or must, that Tony wasn't close to his mother. He had shocked them over dinner with the revelation that his parents had found out about his trip from other people in the business and that Tony hadn't returned their messages when he arrived in his hotel room.

"You don't like your parents?" Billy's girlfriend, Helen, had asked.

"They're great material for my plays—but I don't want to be an actor in their drama," Tony had said, consciously pretentious about it, because somehow he knew that would impress Lois. It had. He remembered the look of wisdom and approval in her eyes, as if she were saying: "You're so right. I understand." But his line was bullshit. He meant to call his mother and father during those three days in New York after he knew his itinerary, but kept finding trivial excuses not to. He wanted to have tomorrow's meeting with Garth before speaking to them. Why? He didn't know.

Lois laughed. "You must be tired."

"What?" he said, startled. "I'm sorry. No, I'm not tired. I'm sort of —I guess this is jet lag. My legs want to sleep but my mind wants to see the city."

"But you know LA."

"Not as an adult. Not really."

"You want to get a drink somewhere?" she asked tentatively. She meant more than merely a drink. He knew it from the slight edge of scared girlishness that crept in. She felt exposed by the question.

"Does LA have a nightlife?" he stalled. Not because he hadn't decided—it was just a drink after all, no matter what she thought: he could always cool off later. He delayed because he wanted to tease her slightly. See how eager she was.

"Not really. It has comedy clubs, discos, and massage parlors."

"No Elaine's?"

"I guess there's Spago's."

"No jazz clubs? No bourgeois nightlife?"

"I don't think so," she said doubtfully. She was embarrassed by her city's failure to provide sophistication in this circumstance. Tony knew he had her on this score: she had made it in television; it bred insecurity when faced with a tired, cynical New Yorker. At least it would until she was forty, when the simple pleasure of having money usually overcomes any doubts about its environment.

"Amazing," Tony said.

She glanced at him. "No drink?"

She was eager enough. "Oh yes. Sure. But where?"

There was a pause. Then, in a cool tone: "We could go to my house."

"Okay," Tony said, like someone concluding an amiable negotiation. They were on Sunset by now, leaving Hollywood's garish billboards and bold hookers and giving way to quiet rows of tall palms. She took a right and they began their ascent onto one of Beverly's hills.

CHAPTER

5

Patty lay on her bed staring at the stuff from Shadow Books. It had been too good to be true. Sure, as Betty had predicted, they *did* pay five thousand for a romance novel, the plots and characters *were* all a matter of formula, but Patty *would* have to write something on spec in order to land an assignment. Joe McGuire, the top editor ("word processor" might be more accurate) of Shadow Books, had been sweet. He said normally they asked for an entire novel before making a commitment, but all he would ask of Patty—since Betty thought so highly of her—was a sample chapter and an outline.

So now she lay on the bed surrounded by titles like *Dark Harvest*, clutching a guide sheet from Shadow Books on what elements ought to be in a romance novel.

But it wasn't so bad. She felt excited, like the first day of school. The formula was so rigid that the task seemed easy, and a sample chapter would mean no more than twenty pages. Surely she could do that in a few days.

Her phone rang and she picked it up expecting that it would be Betty —widowed by Tony's trip to the Coast and curious about Patty's reaction to the material. It was David.

"Hi. I'm sorry."

"Hi," she said with genuine surprise and enthusiasm. "What for?"

"Tuesday night. I was a lousy date. I'm sorry. The office was in turmoil—"

"I know! Do you still have your job?" Patty asked with naive seriousness.

David laughed. "I guess so."

"Do you like this guy Rounder? Who is he?"

"You're really up on this."

"I love page six! Read it every day."

"Well, I haven't met him. I don't think anybody has. It was a real mess this week. I was writing the cover and there were all these rumors. I know I was grumpy."

"You sure were."

David laughed. "That's right. Don't spare my feelings."

They both laughed. Patty remembered David had started to talk about the changes at *Newstime* when they met for dinner Tuesday, but she had assumed it meant little to him personally and hadn't really let him talk. Maybe the stalling conversation and bad sex of the evening were due to her lack of attention. She had been very self-concerned lately.

"Let me take you out to dinner to apologize," David said.

They met at a bar between her sublet and his loft. He was fun this time. He quickly ordered and put away three drinks while explaining his week. Patty found the names and various alliances confusing, but the general impression, that David was a dynamic force in the midst of a power struggle for control of one of America's most important magazines, was exciting. She was glad she had her romance novel to discuss when he was done talking about his job. She suspected he thought she was flighty and at loose ends (I am, she thought), but having Shadow Books alleviated that worry.

Indeed, David *was* interested. He insisted on going back to her sublet—thank God I washed the dishes before leaving, she thought—to look at the guide sheet. He was charming about the whole thing, sufficiently irreverent to read the empty and gaudy prose aloud and yet not snobbish about her plan to write one. "It's great money," he said, "if you knock them out in three or four weeks."

"And if they're popular, you can be rich!" Patty said in a tone of absolute trust that life could have dramatic and happy changes of fortune.

"You mean it can be more than just a flat fee of five thousand?" David asked. They were on the bed, Patty sitting with her legs under her, David lying down, his head propped up by pillows, his legs stretched out behind her back. He seemed relaxed, friendly. There was little of the judgmental and therefore cautious atmosphere of a date. He behaved like an old friend or lover would. It seemed so long since she had felt this at ease. When she broke up with her college boyfriend five years ago, she had told him that she wanted romance and adventure: their quiet intimacy had become too fraternal. She believed, from their perfunctory and routine sex to their dull social life of seeing movies and going to dancing parties, that their life together was more teenage than adult, and their closeness more a fearful need for company than a desire to be intimate. But in the years since, the loss of that safety had become frightening. Patty often felt desired by men, but rarely loved in the way that her family of two brothers and a sister made her feel. David was prepared to share her fantasy of writing these romances and becoming rich. It was a simple exchange of trust and interest—but it had been a long time since a man had been willing to make the bargain.

"Yes!" Patty said, unafraid to expose her greedy scenario. "If the first two I write are popular, then I can negotiate for royalties. Elizabeth Reynolds makes over a million a year writing them."

David picked up *Dark Harvest*. He had read aloud from it earlier, sarcastically intoning the puffed-up prose. He opened it to the middle and silently read a paragraph.

"Foul, isn't it?" Patty said. "Can I stand doing it?"

"For a million dollars a year? You sure can." He read another paragraph with a serious and studious air. When he was finished, he put the book down and looked at Patty. His eyes had a distant, thoughtful look. Then he laughed. "It's not any different than what I do."

"This junk?"

"Yeah. It's a formula. Take the heroine to an exotic place so the frustrated housewife feels she's taking the trips that she knows her husband will never be able to afford. *Newstime* and the *Weekly* create the feeling for their readers that they're in the know. I write my stories about the President and the government in a confidential tone, like the reader is getting inside dope nobody else gets. And it's bullshit. I'm taking bureau reports from reporters who, for the most part, get handed briefings. To be sure, sometimes some of our better reporters get a real story, but always because someone inside has decided to let the cat out of the bag, and our guy just happens to be there."

Patty put her hand on his leg and stroked him soothingly. "No, David. Don't be hard on yourself. What you do is really important." She pointed to *Dark Harvest*. "This is trash."

"Don't worry. You don't have to reassure me. I'm not depressed about my work. I just meant . . ." He stared off and didn't continue.

Patty moved her hand up his leg, heading toward his groin. Her eyes were wide open and attentive, waiting for David to finish his sentence. But he said nothing. She reached his penis and rubbed.

His eyes focused on her.

"Yes?" she said with a smile, the knowing smile of a seductress.

He smiled. "You're beautiful."

She silently mouthed "thank you" and continued her massage of his erection.

"Mmmm," David said, closing his eyes. When he opened them a moment later, he looked into Patty's eyes. She watched her effect on him proudly.

"You like this?" she asked.

"Un-huh," he said, feeling helpless. Happily, warmly helpless.

"What were you going to say?"

David laughed. "I don't remember."

"Good," Patty said with a triumphant look.

"Good!" David laughed.

"That means," she said, opening her mouth wide and leaning in to kiss him, "that I'm doing a good job."

After his meeting with Bart and his purchase of several new Brooks Brothers shirts, Fred went home and called Marion at her office. He breathlessly told her the story.

She burst out laughing when he mentioned spilling the coffee.

"I've seen that white rug. Bart must have shit a brick."

"No, no. It didn't bother him. Anyway, listen! Stop laughing."

"Sorry."

"He's given the outline to Bob Holder, who he says is already interested."

"Holder's already interested?"

"Well," Fred said defensively, "Bart said that Holder thought it was a good premise. And he insisted that he get it exclusively."

"Un-huh," Marion said.

"What?" Fred said. "That's good, isn't it?"

"Oh, sure. It's just that . . ." She hesitated.

"What?" Fred demanded.

"Don't get your hopes up, okay, Freddy? Holder likes to make a fuss. He wants everything exclusive. Doesn't mean he's gonna buy it."

"I know that," he snapped. "You don't have to tell me that. I was just telling you what Bart said. Of course I know it doesn't mean anything."

"Okay. I'm sorry. Listen. I'd better get back to work."

"Sure. Look. Let's go out tonight. To a movie or something?"

"Uh, I don't know. The *nouvelle cuisine* book is due to—"

"We'll go to an early movie. Come on."

"Okay, Fred. Call me later. I got to go."

And she hung up. He looked at the receiver in his hand as if it had spat in his face. She had no faith in him, he decided. She thinks I'll never be a novelist. He thought back to her reaction when he announced that he was going to turn down *American Sport* magazine articles for a year and try to get a contract for a novel.

"Fred, you won't get a contract for a novel from outlines," she had said with a tone of absolute knowledge about publishing. "First novels, unless they're by people who are very famous for some other reason, are always written on spec."

"That's bullshit," Fred had said. "What about Karl?"

"Fred, Karl had written six books on spec!"

Fred guffawed and jiggled his food. "If his publisher had read any of those manuscripts, he wouldn't have given him lunch, much less a contract." She had no answer for that. He told her: "Bart got Karl his contract, and if he takes me on, he'll get me one." She hadn't argued, but he knew she didn't believe it, despite the evidence of Karl and his stewardess novel. Fred knew why. Marion had once said about Karl, "I don't know if Karl's a good writer, but he looks, talks, and thinks like a novelist." She didn't believe that about Fred. He was merely a nice Jewish boy to her. Maybe she doesn't want me to succeed, he said to himself. Maybe she's scared if I become a rich famous novelist, I'll leave her.

He clicked down the buttons of the phone, got a dial tone, and called Marion back.

When he got her, he burst out, "What do you mean Bob Holder always asks for an exclusive look?"

Marion laughed. "That's what you called me back about? You're gonna drive yourself crazy—"

"How do you know that? You don't know Holder."

"I've met him. I don't really know him. But Betty works at Garlands. She makes fun of Holder doing stuff like that. He thinks he's a hotshot, so—"

"He *is* a hotshot, honey."

"Okay, so he is a hotshot. And he likes to act like one."

"But Betty didn't say, specifically, that Holder always asks for an exclusive look?"

"Fred," Marion said in a gentle but thoroughly contemptuous tone, "everybody would ask for an exclusive look if they thought they could get it. What's the harm? If you don't like it, you can still say no. If you do, then you don't have the pressure of competing interest. Maybe Bart made it sound like a great thing, but an editor getting an exclusive look just gives the editor leverage. It doesn't help the writer."

Fred stared at the window at the traffic and people below. He only noticed them when he felt like a failure or a fool. They went on with their lives, ignorant of him.

"Fred?" Marion said tentatively into his silence.

She had made him see that his excitement was over nothing. His conviction that Bart could somehow manipulate an important editor into buying his outline was a fantasy; he had sat in Bart's office and listened to him pitch the elixir of success, and bought it, only to discover it was simply the plain water of uncertain promises. "Do you think Bart's a bad agent?" he asked suspiciously, as if she had been keeping a secret.

Marion grunted. It sounded like a startled laugh. "No, I didn't say that. He's flattering Holder by giving it to him exclusively. And he's letting him know that Bart *really* thinks it's a hot idea. That's great. I was just trying to get you to calm down. Not to expect too much. Holder hasn't read it. Until he has, it doesn't mean a thing."

"I don't need that, you know. I realize I may get turned down. I know I may be a failure. I don't need you to remind me."

"Fred." Said very sternly: a warning not to continue. "I don't want to talk about this. You're paranoid. I'll call you later." And she hung up.

He let the hand with the receiver drop to his side, as if the dismal emotions of the conversation had made it too heavy to hold up. He leaned his head against the wall and looked again at the people below. A delivery truck with the New York *Post* had stopped at a corner news kiosk to unload an edition. Two boys of about fifteen, coming home from school, passed the stacks of newspapers. They were short and probably Jewish. One of them was fat. His wrinkled white shirttails were hanging outside his pants. The other was skinny and wore thick black glasses. They stopped and peered at the back of the *Post*. It would be a sports story that caught their interest. Fred at their age looked like them and also would have peered at the headline with total absorption. In those days, it never occurred to him that writing served any purpose other than graduating from school or proving that Mickey Mantle was a better hitter than Willie Mays. That dumpy kid with his shirttails hanging out was innocent. He had yet to learn, as Fred had, that his appearance would cut him off from most of the fantasies that men have: he would never be thought of as glamorous, as sexy, as profound. No one would look at him and say, "There are a poet's eyes, a sculptor's hands, an actor's voice, or the tall inspiring body of a leader." That kid, gawking with happy concentration at the *Post*'s sports headline, hadn't been faced with the certain knowledge that no tall, beautiful blond would go to bed with him— unless he paid her. "Money," Fred said aloud, as if he were hurling a curse down at the boy below. "Money and fame are the only things that will help."

He turned, despairing, and returned the receiver to its cradle. It rang instantly.

"Fred?" said a deep but tentative voice. "It's Karl."

"Hi."

"How did the meeting go?"

"You knew about it?"

"Yeah, Bart told me he read an outline of yours. He said he liked it. Thought he could sell it."

The poison of Marion's pessimism left Fred's system, as if wiped out by a miracle drug. "He did?"

"Yeah," Karl said. 'Didn't he say that to you?"

"Yeah. He did. I'm crazy. You know, it happened three hours ago. I was high as a kite. But just now I was really feeling down—"

"Why? Isn't he sending it out?"

"Yeah. He's sending it to your editor."

"Oh." Karl sounded taken aback. "You mean Holder?" he asked idiotically, as if hoping against hope that Fred had made a mistake.

"Yeah. Does that bother you?"

"No, no," Karl said so quickly that it was obvious he was disturbed.

"It shouldn't," Fred said almost pleadingly. It flashed in his mind that Karl might speak to Holder during the next few days (Karl's novel was due out in five months and contact between them was probably frequent) and say something denigrating about him. Point out that Fred has never written a novel, that his experience as a writer was limited to twenty pieces on sports—and most of those were interviews, which hardly put great demands on Fred as a writer.

"No, of course not. I was thinking whether I should speak to him, tell him I know you—"

"Oh, you don't have to do that," Fred said anxiously, but as he spoke, he looked at the situation the other way. Holder obviously admired Karl; if Karl spoke well of Fred to Holder, perhaps it would add to the favorable impresssion of Bart's recommendation. "Unless—do you think it would bother Holder?"

"Bother?" Karl said in a bewildered tone.

"I think you shouldn't. He'd think I put you up to it."

"Okay. I won't say anything."

"So," Fred said, clearing his throat. He wanted to keep Karl on the line. Talking to Karl—Karl the novelist—made him feel his ambitions were real, answered the worry inside him that he was a victim of a delusion. But there was nothing in his mind other than talk of the outline, talk of the meeting with Bart, worry over what Holder would think.

"I was calling to invite you to a poker game. Do you play?" Karl asked.

Fred was delighted. He had heard Karl, on the social occasions they had spent together, refer to his weekly poker game, whose members were all established writers. Several times Fred had mentioned to Karl, rather awkwardly, how much he liked to gamble (Marion would always exclaim, "You do?" incredulously, humiliating him), hoping to provoke an invitation, but his comments were returned with blank looks from Karl, and, more ominously, after a while Karl stopped even mentioning his poker game.

"I've told you I play poker," Fred said, to let Karl know that he knew this invitation was a symbol of a change in their relationship.

"Well, you know," Karl said, "usually we're full up. We have seven regulars. But one of them's dropped out. It's tonight. Can you make it?"

"What time?"

"Seven. And you have to play until at least midnight. It's a house rule."

"Even if I'm down a hundred dollars, I gotta stay?" Fred asked, laughing, as if that was an absurd idea.

"Yes," Karl said. "Even if you're down a hundred dollars. Nobody ever limits their winnings, so we don't let people limit their losses. I don't care if you just end up anteing every hand and folding, but you gotta stay until midnight."

"Sounds pretty serious," Fred said.

"It is. It's really serious poker. No kibitzing or stuff like that. So if you don't like that, you shouldn't come."

"No, no. That's fine. Tell me, how much money should I bring?" Fred asked, hoping in this way to find out what the stakes were without implying that he was frightened of losing too much.

Karl's voice was matter-of-fact: "Biggest loser we've ever had was three hundred dollars. The average losing night is about one hundred and fifty to two hundred. And, also, you should know, we play a lot of high-low games—"

"I've never played them."

"Oh," Karl said, as if that were a big blow.

"Don't worry. I'll learn fast."

"Well . . ." Karl sighed and paused.

Schmuck, Fred said to himself, why did you say you'd never played them? You could have announced that at the game. "Don't worry," Fred said again.

"I think you'd better come at six. I'll teach you some high-low games

. . . the guys aren't real patient about explaining while the game is going."

"Great. Okay. I'll be there at six."

"All right, see you—oh, you'd better eat before you come. There are no snacks. That's another rule."

Fred rang off ecstatic and nervous. He had wanted into that game for almost a year. Tonight would be like an audition. If they liked him he would become a regular. He dialed Marion once again.

"Fred?" she said with despairing impatience when her secretary let him through.

"Listen. Karl just called and invited me to play poker tonight. So you can edit your *nouvelle cuisine* book."

"His weekly game?" she said. "But that's a very expensive game. Karl's always talking about how much money people lose—"

"Honey," he said with great confidence, "don't worry. I've played plenty of poker on the road with the ball teams. I'm sure a bunch of writers aren't that tough, okay?"

"All right. As long as you know what you're doing. So do we have to eat early?"

"I can't eat with you. I've got to go over early so Karl can teach me how to—" He caught himself. He stopped talking and closed his eyes in frustration at his slip.

"Teach you *what?* I though you knew how to play."

"No, no. You wouldn't understand. They play some silly games— kid stuff, like wild-card games—and they don't like to slow things down to explain, so Karl wanted me to come early. I don't think that's the real reason. He heard from Bart about my outline. He probably wants to chat about that."

"Why? Wouldn't he just say he wants to talk about your outline?"

"Forget it. It's not important. Go back to work."

"So you'll be gone by the time I get home?" She sounded petulant; suddenly a neglected child.

"Yeah, I have to be at Karl's by six."

"When will you be home?"

"Honey, I don't know. It's a poker game. It'll probably go on till late."

"Oh," she said. A disappointed moan.

"What? What is it?"

"I'll miss you. I wanted to see you tonight."

"What? Earlier, when I asked if you wanted to go to the movies, you acted totally uninterested."

"I did not! I said I would go."

"After I insisted."

"Okay, I'm sorry. Good-bye. I'll see you later—or I won't. Good-bye—"

"Come on!"

But she had hung up. "Jesus Christ!" he yelled at the walls. "She's gonna drive me out of my fucking mind!"

But his anger was quickly dissipated once he got down to the business of dressing for the poker game. Jeans, a black turtleneck, and sneakers were his choices: they made him look slim and tough, he thought, like a street-smart kid. And he felt like a kid, a happy kid, going over to the Upper West Side where Karl lived. Heading for a night out with the boys—the writing boys.

The Scotch tastes like metal. Cheap metal, Tony thought. He looked around the tacky dark-wood-paneled living room. Lois, judging from the decoration of her house, fancied herself a Spanish duchess. There were big ungainly chairs with elaborate carved wood designs and a big dark wood couch with thin cushions that failed to rescue its occupant from discomfort.

"Too megalomaniacal?" she asked, indicating the room with her eyes.

So she did think it was grand, he thought to himself, feeling despair. Not simply over the prospect of being alone with her, but being alone in this city, where ugly furniture could house pathetic delusions.

He smiled at her knowingly, as if to say, "I understand, I approve, but I'm too bright to take anything too seriously." He looked out the big window behind her. There was a sweeping view of Hollywood and the valley. Lights lay below like a twinkling bed, bejeweled for a princess. "How long have you lived here?" he asked.

"A year. When I was made producer on your mother's series, I started making so much money my manager told me to buy something. I couldn't believe it. Felt weird. Being single and owning a house."

"Your manager?"

"My money manager. Not a personal manager."

"Do you have a talent manager also?"

"Well, I have an agent."

"Isn't that the same thing?"

"No. They're different."

"What's the difference?"

"Your mother's got all those things. An agent, a personal manager, a money manager, a lawyer—hasn't she told you the facts of life?" Lois asked, laughing.

"Only the sexual ones. That's why I'm happy but poor."

"Yeah." She nodded and looked off as if she had taken his comment to heart.

"So why don't you tell me?" Tony said.

"Well. A manager gets you work."

"Don't agents do that?"

"Top agents have lots of clients and you have to fight for their attention. A personal manager will do it for you."

Tony thought about this and then shook his head wonderingly. "Seems like a Rube Goldberg way of going about it. You hire somebody to watch somebody you hired. It's bizarre."

"Who's your agent?"

"Gloria Fowler."

Lois looked impressed. "She's the kind of agent who's got so many name clients that somebody like you might hire a manager to call her and bug her. Saves you the embarrassment. But it's not something writers do. Actors do it. A writer only needs attention on one or two projects at most."

There was a silence. Tony realized he had wanted to be with Lois to gather this sort of information. His mother and father could have supplied him with these details of the movie business, but he didn't want to ask them, to give them the pleasure of playing at being his teachers. She had him here for sex. Or something. Maybe just company. But he wanted facts. He was scared to walk into that meeting tomorrow without knowing something, anything, about how Hollywood operated.

"Are you tired?" he asked.

"What?" she said with a smile. She looked different now. The hard angles of her high cheeks were softer here in the dim light of her Spanish living room.

"I'm not gonna be able to sleep tonight. I don't like strange hotel rooms . . ."

She smiled, her eyes opening wide. He realized she suspected he was going to proposition her. So he hurried on:

". . . and I've got this big meeting tomorrow. I don't know shit about this business. Maybe you don't either. But I'd like to tell you about the meeting and if there's any advice you could give me, I'd appreciate it."

Lois looked him in the eyes for a moment. Searched earnestly for an answer to something. "I know the feature business. I haven't worked in it, but I know a lot about it. A . . ." She hesitated. "A guy I went out with is a top executive at International Pictures. All he talked about was the infighting, the deals. I had it coming out of my ears."

"And that wasn't what you wanted to come out of your ears, right?"

She nodded wearily. "Right." She got up and stretched. Tony looked at her thin body arch: her stomach hollowed and her ribs showed; her pelvis pressed against the fitted pants; she was lean like a racing dog or a long-distance runner. "But you knew that, didn't you?" she said casually, like an interrogator playing a trump card.

"Knew what?"

"About him," Lois said.

"The guy at International?"

She nodded, closing her eyes angrily, as if she was disappointed that he pretended not to know her meaning.

"How would I know about him? I don't get it."

"From Billy."

"Oh . . ." Tony nodded. "Boy, you are paranoid. You think I came here, pretended to be interested in you, because I knew you knew somebody at International." Lois looked embarrassed but didn't deny it. "Think about it," Tony went on. "Does that make any sense? If I needed information that badly, wouldn't I get it from my parents? Is this town that crazy? You want to know what's really going on? Is my behavior confusing you?"

Lois stood still, obviously nonplussed. She thought she had him figured twice. First, he was a philandering husband; then, a scheming opportunist. Both times she was wrong. She looked as if that was rare for her. "I work in TV," she said after a moment. "We're used to very simple motivations."

Tony laughed. He liked her a lot for that: it was clever, a quality he found sexy. "Okay, but I don't know what my motivation is. I'm scared to be here. Not in your house. I mean in LA. This place brings up a lot of bad memories. I've been having a tough time with my plays. I haven't had a hit off-Broadway. Never even been close to making Broadway. Gloria Fowler told me if I could cinch this deal, get this movie made, the studio might help finance my next play. Get some heat behind my name, maybe intimidate investors into backing me. I don't know what she meant. It was vague. Maybe I'm a fool to believe her. I wouldn't know. I don't really know whether this Bill Garth project is a hot project or not. I don't want to ask my parents. They'll be too thrilled that I'm working in their business—I don't want them to be thrilled about me. I didn't know anything about you and this guy at International. I haven't spoken to Billy in years. He drove me to Joe Allen's and we talked about some episode he wrote for Mom's show. He assumed I'd seen it. I hadn't—"

Lois laughed. "What! You mean you haven't seen the Emmy-winning car-wreck episode!" She burst out laughing again. "I love it. That's great. Must have driven him crazy."

"It did. Is it terrible of me?"

"No, of course not." She moved to the uncomfortable couch and sat next to him. Not seductively. But like a close friend, unselfconsciously, leaning forward eagerly to pursue interesting gossip. "He thinks of you as a real writer. No doubt he had this fantasy when you called that it was because you knew about his success and admired him."

"Oh." Tony thought about this. "Well, I guess I'm too snobbish to ever admire somebody 'cause of TV writing. I mean, if theater didn't have the compensation of making me feel superior, how could I stand the obscurity and poverty?"

Lois smiled. "Look, obviously I don't know you very well, but I have gotten one thing straight about you. You think playwrighting is a calling, a religion. You're not a snob. You believe in it." She said this with frank admiration. Tony was pleased: he believed the compliment. "Anyway, tell me about the meeting."

"Well, I'm supposed to have breakfast tomorrow morning at the Polo Lounge—"

She smiled. "Very good so far. Polo Lounge is good."

"Is that more important than who's at the meeting?"

"Probably."

"I see. Well, it's supposed to be with Bill Garth—"

"He's actually going to be there?"

Tony hesitated. "What do you mean? Doesn't he usually show up for meetings?"

Lois leaned back and stared at the ceiling thoughtfully. "He has a reputation for committing to projects, then firing lots of writers, I don't know for sure—my friend at International hated him. Claimed that Garth screwed up project after project by never being satisfied with the script."

"But Garth makes movies—so obviously he's eventually satisfied," Tony reasoned.

"Yeah, but usually they're not scripts Garth himself has developed. I asked if he would be there because I was hoping this was a project International was developing *for* him, rather than he developing it for *them*."

Tony shook his head as if he were trying to clear it of confusion. "Jesus, I'd better get on the next plane home."

"No, no. Don't let me frighten—"

"I'm not frightened. I don't even understand what you're talking about. Whoever heard of an actor *not* wanting to get something on? It makes no sense! It's the opposite of everything I understand."

"It's 'cause Garth's on top. He's won an Academy Award. He's had hits. Every script in town is offered to him. If he decides he wants to work, he'll work. If he doesn't like the script, they'll change it. He doesn't like the director, they'll fire him. It's a position most actors never get to —so his psychology is turned upside down. Instead of the studio vacillating, he vacillates. His power, all of it, resides in making a decision to do a movie. Once he commits himself, he loses his power. The film editor and the director can cut his scenes—"

"What? He doesn't get final cut?"

Lois hesitated. "You know, you got me. I don't know. If he demanded it, especially of a studio that needed a hit, he'd probably get it. See that?" she said with a smile, turning to him and putting her hand on his arm. "You stumped the expert."

He smiled at her. Her hand felt warm and friendly. They looked into each other's eyes. Tony's contempt and distrust of her was gone. She seemed human now: the hard-angled leanness of a Hollywood bitch had softened in the dim light of her Spanish fantasy. His suspicion that she was a dull, opportunistic, and selfish woman had evaporated in the dawning of her kind interest in his worry and her desire to advise him well. There was nothing of the one-upmanship toward Billy, nothing of the cynical pose at dinner of someone who believes that Copernicus was wrong: that the earth actually revolves around money. Once he had made it clear he didn't want sex from her, she had relaxed and become ordinary. And, of course, now he had to admit it to himself: now, as their eyes searched each other's, he *did* want to make love.

David moved carefully, lifting Patty's arm off his waist. She had gone to sleep with his wet penis in her hand, her body pressed against him, their legs entwined, and her head resting in the crook of his arm. It was as if she wanted to merge with his body, melt into him; there was something forlorn about her clinging to him. She had serviced him, her mouth loving his prick until he climaxed. There had been no complaint that he brought her to orgasm lackadaisically with his hand. She had acted grateful for his presence, as if she felt lucky even to have him there.

David got her arm off him and then slowly disengaged his leg. She stirred at that and turned around, her slim silky buttocks angled into him. She has a beautiful body, he told himself wonderingly. Wonderingly, because it was the kind of body that he had lusted for in high school and college and had never succeeded in getting. Now he had it and there was no sense of triumph or delight. The fantasy was no better than the reality—Patty was fabulous in bed. Her golden-haired vagina was moist and pink, her breasts firm, her stomach flat and yet soft, her hips smooth but flowingly curved.

And she was so yielding! Her mouth was a willing slave, opening abjectly for his tongue, his penis, swallowing whatever he chose to inject. Why didn't this thrill him? Wasn't it his dream?

He couldn't claim, as he tried to convince himself after their first and second dates, that she was merely a dumb blond, a mind and soul too numb to feel deeply or understand his life. Patty was bright, maybe not intellectual, but he had never liked that in women or men. She exuded cheerfulness and wit, qualities he not only enjoyed but also considered rare. Why weren't these additions to her delicious body a cause for celebration? He ought to be madly in love, he told himself. To have this beautiful and charming woman cling to him was a great piece of good fortune. But he felt lonely in her presence. Lonely and false, as if he weren't really experiencing the sex and the conversation, as if he were in disguise, reaping rewards that justly belonged to someone else.

This thought frightened him. He felt a chill of horror, as if his soul was about to break out and spin into the black universe, divorced from human life.

David moved and hugged Patty's back, putting his arms around her waist. She moved and hugged his arms to her, saying, out of a half-sleep, "Mmmm."

He put his cheek against her smooth back and pushed out any thought, absorbing her warmth. His fingers stroked her soft belly. He brushed her pubic hair and she arched up, catching his hand in her pelvis.

He moved quickly, in the dark, down, pushing his face in her buttocks. She opened her legs and rolled on her back, moaning in a sleepy voice as he put his mouth to her vagina.

He knelt on the bed and quickly, in desperate and frightened movements, licked her. Almost immediately she was wet, with that ferocious moisture her body could summon instantly. He pushed his mouth and nose and chin up and down, from side to side, obliterating the terrible memory of that vision of spiritual death.

He had no idea how long it took. It seemed only moments before her body kicked and heaved, her mouth making sounds of release. He felt intense pleasure at her pleasure, at letting her squeeze his head between her thighs.

After her climax, she pulled him up and kissed his mouth, wet from her sex. He looked into her eyes and said with great feeling:

"I love you."

He was astonished that her reaction was to hold him close, hugging him as if he were a long-lost savior. He glanced at her face and saw there was the beginning of tears in her eyes.

Seeing her happiness, he felt the dreaded emptiness return, and regretted that he had spoken.

CHAPTER

6

Fred looked at his checkbook. In the dim fluorescent light of Karl's bathroom he saw that the balance was one hundred and twenty-four dollars and sixty-seven cents. It was eleven-thirty, a half-hour before people would be permitted to quit, and he was down, by his rough calculation, close to two hundred dollars.

He had the money. Marion and he had a ten-thousand-dollar certificate of deposit, and he had eight thousand in stocks with his broker. But when he had told Marion he was going to forgo magazine assignments for a year, they had done a strict budget so that they could live on her salary with only occasional intrusions into the eighteen thousand they had in the bank. Fred had repeatedly gone over the set limits, using up four thousand in three months. This two hundred would be seen by Marion as an idiotic extravagance, if for no other reason than that he would have to break the ten-thousand-dollar C.D.

"But I would have had to break it for the rent check anyway," Fred argued to Karl's bathroom mirror. "It's ridiculous," he answered the imagined rage of Marion. "We have fourteen thousand dollars and you're making me feel poor."

He heard his name called from the dining room, where Karl had set up the game. He stared into the mirror and said, "Wake up!" and then yanked open the bathroom door and stormed down the long narrow hallway. He saw a bubble of paint at the end of the hall. Karl lived in a pre-World War II building on West End Avenue. And though many elegant details remained—marble fireplace, elaborate moldings, sliding wood doors that separated the large dining and living rooms—the building wasn't being kept up, and Karl's place had many patches of peeling and cracked paint. Karl was the big winner that night, up over two hundred dollars, and as Fred made the turn out of the hallway, he hit his fist against the bubble of paint, shattering it into pieces that fell on the floor.

Entering the room, Fred could see a cloud of cigarette smoke that hung like an evil ghost over the table. There were several cups and plates swollen by mounds of ashes. The dead butts lay in them like drowned insects. The blue, red, and white poker chips blared their colors in this fog, either arrogantly stacked for precise counting by winners, or slumping, disheveled, in front of losers. Fred had a messy pile, a very small one, in front of his empty seat.

The other players were all writers he had met casually once or twice before at dinners with Karl or at publication parties Marion had been invited to. They were, in order of prominence, Sam Wasserman, the former investigative reporter who, with the publication of a bestselling book on the murder of a middle-class young woman, had become more than a reporter and less than a novelist, and, while writing additional factual but very melodramatic books on other fancy murders, wrote a regular column for *Town* magazine that had a broad range from political commentary to complaints about the service at Bloomingdale's; next down the ladder of success was Tom Lear, also a former reporter, who had sold a piece on a crack New York city detective to the movies, wrote the screenplay—while several carping stories appeared claiming the detective in Lear's article had taken credit for other people's achievements—and it was now being shot on location in New York; a rung farther down was Paul Goldblum, who had published two highly praised but unprofitable novels, but had received a National Endowment grant and a plum creative-writing teaching job at Columbia University; staring up at his rear end was Richard Trout, a New York *Times* Metro reporter and nothing else, but he talked ceaselessly of a book he planned to write on the recently notorious murder of a local congressman who was rumored to be gay; and, last, William Truman, a childhood friend of Karl's, who was a poet—publishing mostly in academic journals no one read—and supported himself with the aid of an enormous trust fund whose source was his grandfather's investment in real estate (Fred had been told that Grandpa Truman once owned half of Ohio).

"Bong!" Sam Wasserman said on Fred's entrance. "Final round."

"Come on!" Paul Goldblum said. "You're not quitting at midnight."

"I gotta get home and finish my column," Sam said in a grave tone, like a surgeon announcing he had a patient on the table waiting for an emergency operation.

Tom Lear, the only writer present who felt himself equal in stature to Wasserman, let out a loud Bronx cheer.

Karl smiled nervously. "It's your deal, Fred."

"Those of us who still have to write prose, instead of that stuff with skinny margins—" Sam Wasserman began to say angrily to Tom Lear, the reporter turned screenwriter.

William Truman, the poet, interjected quietly, "Don't forget, poetry has skinny—"

But Lear was already answering Sam: "I'm sorry, Sam, I forgot. You're still a serious writer. You haven't sold out like me."

"Damn right—" Sam began.

But Lear rolled on, "What's your column this month? Comparing lambskin rubbers to ribbed rubbers? Or maybe you're gonna take on somebody heavy, like another attack on Joe Garagiola?"

Fred guffawed, opening his mouth and leaning back with enjoyment. Wasserman looked at him: it was a cold and angry look. Sam's attitude toward Lear was combative but friendly. When he spoke now to Fred, it was with the contempt people reserve for irritating inferiors: "Deal the cards. Or don't you know how to do that either?"

This comment silenced everyone—it was *too* openly hostile, cruelly dismissive, exposing Fred's vulnerability. Everyone knew that an attack on Fred's playing was really a statement directed at his being a social interloper. At least Fred thought everyone believed it was.

"Okay, okay," Fred said, his face reddening.

"That's what I like about you, Sam," Tom Lear said. "You win so gracefully."

Fred shuffled and dealt in silence. Most of the game had been that way. The dialogue was limited to macho exchanges referring to the strategies or outcomes of hands. But it was the just-completed exchange, until it was suddenly directed at him, that Fred had hoped would dominate the evening. He loved being with these guys. Even Sam's contempt for him didn't lessen his desire to hang on to this group. If anything, it whetted his desire to stay.

He found himself up against Sam in the hand he dealt, as if a writer were controlling the events. As he raised and was raised back at the climax, Fred convinced himself that he would win simply because Wasserman had been unfair. But he didn't win, and Sam let him know he thought Fred entirely merited his bad luck.

"I'm showing a boat, I'm betting a boat. Haven't bluffed a hand all night. What the hell you doing staying in—and raising at that?"

Karl spoke softly. "All right, Sam. You won the hand. That's plenty. A lecture isn't necessary."

"Let him go on," Tom Lear said. "Maybe it'll be his next column."

"Don't you know," Sam said to Fred, "that you don't raise a possible lock hand? You shouldn't've been in there, but if you were in there, you shouldn't've been raising."

"Yeah," Paul Goldblum said, "you got some nerve, Fred. Making Sam's winning hand really pay off. He was actually trying to let you win."

"Look, don't listen to these assholes," Sam said. "I'm trying to help you out a little bit. It's basic poker. You don't raise a possible lock."

"Okay," Fred said earnestly. "Thanks for the advice." What he didn't say was that he didn't understand Sam's terminology, didn't know what a lock hand was, or what he was supposed to avoid in the future. But he behaved contritely, hoping to make himself so docile that Sam would feel he was too pathetic to attack. Fred knew he couldn't face him down directly, but he swore to himself that he would someday. Get a book contract, write a bestseller, a bigger bestseller than Sam's was.

The game ended at twelve-thirty. Goldblum forced Sam to agree to stay an extra half-hour and Fred went along, embarrassed to be the only one to leave at midnight. When they totaled up and Fred found himself writing two checks—one to Sam, one to Karl—for a total of three hundred and fifteen dollars, Truman asked, "That's a record loss, isn't it?" and the others smiled to themselves.

It was then that Fred swore to himself that at the very least, he would learn this stupid game and beat the shit out of Sam. Hell, out of all of them.

Patty and David spent Sunday together. She kept him busy advising her while she got started on her sample chapter for Shadow Books. She had half of it written by Monday morning when they separated for the first time in thirty-six hours.

By then they were so intimate Patty felt as if they had been a couple for a long time. David hadn't repeated his "I love you" of Saturday night, but he hadn't withdrawn either. Indeed, his desire that they be together seemed intense—he didn't want to go out for a walk, or to a movie, or even for dinner. To her delight, he went to the supermarket and cooked her a suprisingly good meal. He made her take seconds, claiming (the first time a man had ever said this to her) that she was too skinny.

He wasn't her romantic ideal. He showed signs of a middle-aged potbelly. His curly black hair was receding, and baldness by forty seemed inevitable. His skin was white and puffy, his eyes beady, his lips thick. But somehow the overall impression was better than the parts: he dressed well and carried himself with confidence. And his voice was pleasingly resonant; a calm fatherly tone came naturally to him. But most of all, what mitigated his physical ordinariness was his intelligence and his genuine interest in her. He listened to her hopes, her opinions, her reminiscences, with pleasure; taking part in her inner life as if it had become his own. He was a partner, discussing his career problems not with a mind to impressing her, but with a desire for advice and support. When she commented on the magazine, he weighed what she said carefully, never dismissing her perceptions as being ill-informed or silly.

That was not to say he didn't fuss and fondle her body like other men. Indeed, it was the combination of his sexual and intellectual interest in her that pleased: they were usually divided. Since her college romance, men had either wanted her as a lover or as a friend. It had been integrated with her college boyfriend for the first year, but slowly his sexual interest waned. Or did it? Maybe her sexual interest waned. Could that happen with David? After a while, would she notice only the stomach and the disappearing hair and not the respect for her?

This debate went on in a distant whisper in her mind while they played house together—writing her chapter, cooking, cleaning, screwing, and watching television in bed. For the first time in a long while she felt at home in New York.

She called Betty fifteen minutes after David left for work.

"You're up early," Betty said.

"I'm in love!"

"Really?" Betty lost all her usual reserve—abandoned for the thrilled joy of a teenage girl.

"I spent the weekend with David. We had a fabulous time."

"That's great!" But now Betty's reserve, her inherent skepticism of anything extreme, had crept back into her tone.

"Is it real?" Patty asked her pleadingly. "Or am I just boy crazy?"

Betty laughed. "Don't ask philosophical questions. Enjoy. You've just met him."

When Patty hung up, she felt the ease and calm in her body. Her confidence radiated steady warmth. She straightened the apartment quickly, not resenting the task, and settled at her desk to finish the sample chapter.

It flowed from her as if she had waited her whole life to write the life of a demure virgin who longed for a dark, handsome, and possibly brutal man to awaken her passions. She wrote though the morning and early afternoon and found, to her surprise, that she had finished a rough draft.

She read it over, only occasionally wincing at the florid language and cartoon characters. In fact, most of the time she was proud of her work. Just that she had written twenty pages impressed her. And that it seemed right, as professional as the books she had sampled, was thrilling.

She reread the pages, wondering at her heroine's wild shifts in mood, riding a crest of hope like a surfer, covered with the spray of vigor and romance, only to crash ominously on the shore as the chapter ended, so the reader would turn the page eagerly . . . so Shadow Books would hire her to write the rest.

Maybe it isn't such bullshit, Patty told herself, thinking of the past week. After all, she had paddled out into life's ocean, stripped naked, and trusted herself to cold waves, been slapped and rebuked by them, only to rise glorious and young at last, commanding nature to carry her safely to the sun-blessed shore of love and work and happiness.

Tony Winters returned to the Beverly Hills Hotel at five-thirty in the morning still innocent of adultery. Only their talk had progressed to intimacies: Lois told him about her one-year marriage to a TV producer who went from taking cocaine once a week to a restless snorting that left him hopping with enraged incoherence by two o'clock every afternoon.

She asked a lot of questions about his mother, and he answered them honestly, not worried that to tell Lois (the producer of his mother's series) such things might be indiscreet. Lois was too vulnerable, obviously scarred by her marriage, bluffing toughness, for Tony to believe she was capable of misusing such information.

But when he got back to the hotel, drunk with fatigue, his legs aching, his eyes watering, suffering from what felt like a broken back, his sinuses clogged and his throat sore from too much smoking, and stood himself under the shower, he abruptly lost his confidence in her. I'm a rube, he thought. She probably went out to dinner with me to get precisely that kind of gossip. He could vividly imagine her at work tomorrow telling the gang all the scandals, laughing at the pretentious, ignorant New York writer with two parents in show business who didn't know a thing about movie deals.

He ordered coffee from room service to keep himself up until the eight-o'clock breakfast with Bill Garth and . . . and whom? He sat on the bed and realized with dread he had forgotten the producer's name. One of the few powerful independent producers in the business, Lois had called him, claiming *he*, rather than Garth, would probably decide whether to hire Tony.

Room service arrived looking as sleepy as he, with the pink-and-green linen motif of the hotel, and he drank his coffee, his stomach rumbling angrily at its arrival. There was a wave of nausea moments later, so severe that Tony thought he was not only about to vomit but also that he was fatally ill. Could he cancel? he wondered, writhing on the bed while fighting off the queasiness.

But that passed.

What was that producer's name? His cheek lay on the rough bed-spread, and he felt warm about his eyes. He closed them and remembered being on the plane—the steady hum of the motor, the keen promise he had felt about the trip. It seemed like weeks ago, but it was only yesterday afternoon, a little more than . . .

There was ringing. Lots of ringing. Shut up. Shut up. I'm sleeping.

He gasped and sat up. There was bright sunlight all around him, so bright the sun seemed to be inside the room. He had overslept!

He grabbed the phone. He said something into it. It was supposed to be hello.

"Tony?" a female voice said doubtfully.

"Yes!"

"Hi, it's Lois. I just wanted to make sure you were awake. Did you fall asleep?"

"Oh, God. Thank you. Yes. What time is it?"

"Seven-forty-five. You've got fifteen minutes."

"Okay! Bye!"

"Call me," Lois said eagerly. "Let me know what happens."

"Sure." He started to hang up and then caught himself. "Where?"

"The number is—"

"I don't have a pen—"

"Call the network at Studio City. Ask for the show. Then ask for me."

He shaved as quickly as he could, given that the floor seemed, every once in a while, to buckle and wave beneath him. He wondered if it was an earthquake, but his puffy and pale face and his bloodshot eyes told him otherwise. When he bent over to rinse off, he almost pitched into the sink. He rubbed hot water into his skin and then stared into his eyes. "You're a mess," he told himself. "If you can't handle a breakfast, how the fuck are you going to write a screenplay?"

He groaned and rested for a moment, trying to settle his erratic breathing and his uncertain stomach. When he looked back in the mirror, he had an answer: " 'Cause it's the breakfast that's really tough."

He laughed at himself, as if he were in an audience, not feeling his anguish and tension, but merely observing how childishly he was over-reacting.

That's what you've got to do. Play this like it's a part. A role you've written.

Tony walked out of the room, his back straight, and ambled casually toward the stairs, his feet moving silently on the thick green-striped carpet. You're smart, modest, pleasant, and sure of yourself, he said as he appeared in the lobby and turned toward the elevator banks.

You're smart, modest, quite pleasant, and impossibly sure of yourself, he told himself as he approached the narrow arched entrance to the Polo Lounge. A woman dressed in a silk blouse and a tweed skirt came up to him.

"Reservation?" she asked languidly.

Only then did he realize she worked there. "I'm meeting Bill Garth."

"Yes," she said with anxious eagerness, "he's here."

Tony ignored the glances—evaluating ones, he was sure—as they walked toward the back, heading for a bank of booths against one wall. Garth was there along with the producer (his name! what was it?), and as Tony approached they broke off what appeared to be a serious discussion. Garth's face, that famous but relatively ordinary face, with his slightly bent nose, high forehead, and darting clever eyes, looked up at him.

You're very smart, very modest, extremely pleasant, and utterly, totally, eternally sure of yourself, Tony said to himself.

David Bergman tossed his yogurt into the black plastic wastebasket under his desk and stared at his typewriter. It was an old Royal, a rattling gray manual that writers at the magazine insisted on, believing it created more than a superficial kinship with the great journalists of the past. David had gone along with the tradition, just as he had adopted their style of dress, their drinking hours, and their political attitudes. He had become a member of the club, body and soul, but now that he was recognized as a top writer, a power hitter who could win the ballgame in the late innings, he wanted out.

For a day, he thought he had crossed the line from the playing field to the front office. The weekend with Patty had overwhelmed such thoughts. But when he entered the building that morning, walking past the huge blowup of that week's cover, the disappointment of Chico's promise falling through made him sag unhappily. He loathed the routine: carrying his paper bag with coffee and yogurt, reading the competition, admitting to himself that their story was very similar, indeed almost identical to his, and waiting for orders from above as to what his subject matter for the week would be.

He picked up his phone and dialed Chico's extension. He hadn't decided what he would say—a unique approach for him, normally he mentally rehearsed every conversation with a boss—but he felt there was nothing to lose by complaining. His job was secure and his chances for a promotion, if they had been scuttled by the hiring of Rounder, couldn't sustain any further damage.

"Hi, Linda," David said. "It's David Bergman. Is he there?"

"He's in a meeting with Syms and Rounder. He'll get back to you."

"Syms and Rounder?" David said. He had—he made a point of having—a good relationship with all of the Marx Brother secretaries. "What's going on? A triple suicide?"

Linda laughed sharply and quickly caught herself. She whispered: "I don't know. But it's something."

"Hmmm. Well, get your boss to call me back. Tell him I've taken poison and unless I get his call within a half-hour, the antidote won't have enough time to save me."

Linda laughed. "Okay, but if I were you, I'd take the antidote."

He hung up and stood, walking to his one window with its view of Madison Avenue. The city looked gray, dressed for work in a law firm, presenting an unemotional face, a face that could look upon misery and greatness as one. He knew that the meeting upstairs would have a pro-found effect on his life. If they were firing Syms, that meant Chico was influencing Rounder's decisions, and David's promotion to senior-edit Business was likely. If they weren't, then there would be no openings on the senior-editor level, and Syms, given a chance to toady to Rounder, would clog up things for a while, and probably insist on keeping David as a writer, knowing that to surrender a good writer would only weaken his section.

It was all garbage, David thought with disgust. They dangle jobs and promotions as if they were cheese for experimental mice: to convince the poor trapped writers that the maze could be escaped someday. I'm here forever, he pronounced over himself, a judge delivering the sentence.

"Good job, David," a voice called at his door.

It was Kahn. For a moment David didn't know what Kahn meant, and then remembered he had written the cover story. "Thanks. I read *Weekly*'s. Seemed no different."

Kahn raised his eyebrows. This was the sort of criticism that, if someone else made it, would be considered insulting. "You're selling yourself short. Your piece is much better."

David nodded and returned to his chair, sitting morosely.

Kahn looked at him. "Something wrong?"

David shook his head.

"I liked your tag," Kahn went on, as if David's problem was that he needed more praise. He looked at David's piece and quoted, " 'While the President lay on an operating table, Haig took the microphones at the White House to reassure the nation that "I'm in charge here." Although the assassin's bullet thankfully proved not to be fatal, Alexander Haig will not soon forget its deadly political ricochet.' "

"That was Chico's suggestion," David said coolly. He didn't believe Kahn's praise. That tag was a routine gag, nothing special.

"Oh," Kahn said, taken aback. "Well, it's good," he went on lamely.

David had never been anything but polite to Kahn, who, after all, was his elder and for many years had been the heir presumptive to Syms. But he didn't conceal his irritation now: "Give me a break. It's crap. And you know it."

Kahn's mouth opened to answer, but nothing came out.

David smiled maliciously. "Yes?" he prompted. "Going to argue about it some more? There's nothing in this magazine worth the paper it's printed on. The only thing that separates you and me from them"— he pointed outside his office, meaning to indicate the less prestigious writers of *Newstime*—"is we process the crap faster."

Again Kahn opened his mouth, but before he could say anything, behind him Chico, Syms, and a tall blond appeared.

Chico entered officiously. He introduced David and Kahn to the tall blond, who was, of course, Rounder, their new boss. David, rattled that the two most powerful Marx Brothers had entered so hard upon his critical remarks, got up awkwardly.

"Pleased to meet you," Rounder said to David. "Just finished reading your cover. Good job."

David glanced nervously at Kahn, momentarily fearing he would tell on him. But Kahn looked pale and apprehensive. David was dismayed at how little strength Kahn's age and experience gave him to resist the uncertainty of this moment: meeting a man who controlled your fortune seemed to frighten everyone regardless of age or rank. Was there no escape, David wondered despairingly, from this craven insecurity? Even Chico, grinning like a court jester and nervously pretending that being with Rounder delighted him, was obviously eager to please the new editor in chief.

David studied Rounder. He seemed alien. He was at least four or five inches taller than Chico, and Chico was over six feet. Rounder, however, had none of Chico's stockiness. He looked trim and muscled, at ease with his body, and that, combined with his blond hair and brilliant blue eyes, gave an impression of command, of absolute self-assurance, and implied that he was judgmental, perhaps harshly so. But more than that, he was physically atypical. Not dark, or short, or pudgy, like most of the ethnic types. And not florid-faced or distracted like the usual magazine WASP. Rounder was an American. The talk had made fun of his image: former Navy pilot, all-American in college. But he looked the part, and his steady eyes, his coldhearted blue eyes, convinced David that Rounder *was* the part.

"I'm making an informal tour," Rounder said. "Wanted to meet the key personnel. I know there's a great deal of worry when a new man comes in. I hope to put that fear to rest. Of course, there'll be changes. But only some shifting about at first. We do intend to make organization changes eventually, but only after I've had a chance to learn how the magazine operates. After all, *Newstime* comes out every Monday, so you all must be doing something right." Rounder smiled and they reflected the light of his bright big teeth with their own duller versions. "You're both essential to what makes this a terrific magazine," he said, looking first at David and then at Kahn. "I'm a newcomer. Never been a writer. So I need input from men like you. If you've got ideas, or maybe just good observations, about how to improve things, I'll be grateful and glad to hear 'em."

Rounder looked expectantly at them. David, still stunned by the coincidence of their entrance into the middle of his complaining, nodded stupidly. Kahn looked at him, though, as if he should talk, and David plunged in: "Well, we only know about our little corner of the universe —"

"But you know it very well. Better than anyone else can," Rounder said, his voice eager, jumping on David's words as if trying to force them open with a knife. "I don't care if it's just meaningless bitching"—he smiled brilliantly at David, his blue eyes staring into David's eyes—"I want to hear it."

"Well, to tell you the truth," David began. He saw Chico straighten. He was standing behind Rounder and he looked alert, as if he might have to wrestle David to the ground, a Secret Service agent protecting his Chief. "Just as you came in I was in the middle of meaningless bitching. But it's nothing you can do anything about. I wasn't happy with my cover story. The *Weekly*'s was almost identical, and that always bothers me."

"I liked your piece," Rounder said, as if someone had challenged him about it. "And there's not much you can do on a major national story to distinguish your stuff from the *Weekly*. What fellas like you need are more chances to do think pieces, more general stuff that'll allow you to grow and shine." Rounder smiled at him dazzlingly. "So you see, your bitching wasn't all that meaningless."

David smiled back stupidly, a dog eagerly waiting for more petting. Rounder said it was good to meet them, that he had to continue his tour, and they would talk more soon. Chico winked at David when he left behind Rounder. Syms followed them outside to the hall and said good-bye there.

David and Kahn looked at each other. The visit had the feel of a presidential tour and they both felt like naive visitors to the White House. Golly gee, their faces seemed to say, we just met the commander in chief. Steinberg had never had that effect. Rounder was radiant with energy and confidence. David felt, abruptly, that *Newstime* was going to be a very good, very exciting place to work.

The phone rang and Fred picked it up casually. He had been standing in front of the stove, pouring water into his coffee filter, thinking bitterly of Friday's poker game. Regret, resentment, and anger over his losses had snaked itself around his trepidation about Holder reading his outline. By Sunday night his obsession with his defeat at the hands of those successful writers had strangled his own career anxieties. Fred had lied to Marion about the game, telling her he had lost a little, which forced him to call Karl and ask him never to mention that he had dropped three hundred bucks.

"You shouldn't play, Fred," Karl had said, "if you can't afford—"

"Are you kidding? I got fourteen grand in the bank—"

"Really?" Karl said with a tone of surprise—annoyed surprise—that worried Fred.

"Well, yeah, I mean, it's our savings, but still . . . Look, she would bust my ass about it—"

"Don't worry. I won't tell her."

"And I want a shot at getting my money back, right?" Fred said, his irritation at losing overcoming any delicacy he might have felt about demanding another invitation.

Karl had tried to convince him he shouldn't play again. When Fred pressed him, Karl told him flat out that he was a terrible player and would consistently lose.

"Well, let's just say I like losing to famous writers, okay?" Fred said, somehow thinking this would put Karl in his place.

And so Monday morning, while pouring the boiling water into his Melitta, when the phone rang, for once Fred didn't anticipate that it was his million-dollar call, the career-transforming moment. Usually, when he was waiting for news, his heart skipped every time the phone rang, but this time the fantasies of pulling an endless succession of full houses on Sam Wasserman opiated him, and he picked up the receiver dully. "Hello?"

"Fred Tatter?" It was the neutral voice of a secretary.

"Yes?"

"Bob Holder calling. Could you please hold?"

"Sure," he said, and his soul knew despair, triumph, terror, and awe —all within the few seconds it took for Bob Holder to come on.

"Hi!" said a young aggressive voice. "Fred?"

"Hello."

"Glad I got ya. Read your outline last night. Had to talk to ya first thing. I love this concept. Think it could make a great book. What do you think?"

Fred said nothing, confused, thinking momentarily that a third person must be on the phone somewhere, and that Holder's question was directed at this stranger. But the silence told him it was meant for him. "Oh. Yeah," he said. "I think it's great."

"Well," Holder said. "I don't think it's great now. See, your outline doesn't hit it, doesn't hit it hard enough. I want to meet and talk about it. Okay?"

"Sure."

"I got some free time this morning. That's why I called first thing. Can you come up at eleven? I have a lunch at twelve-thirty. But that's all the time I'll need."

"Sure."

"Great. Know where we are?"

"Sure."

"Great. See you at eleven."

And Holder was off the phone. Fred hung up slowly. He had the feeling that the call hadn't occurred. He stood in front of the stove watching the water drip through, his mind unable to apprehend what had been said by Holder.

The phone rang. Fred picked up sluggishly, a woozy fighter dumbly wading in for the final punishing blows. "Hello?"

"Fred? It's Janice. Bart's calling."

"Okay," he said slowly, but she was already off and Bart was on:

"Fred? Did you hear from Bob?"

"Yes. He just called."

"He's really excited. I think we've got a deal."

"Really?" Fred asked in disbelief.

"Wasn't that your impression?" Bart said, his voice impatient. "What did he say?"

"Well, he said he liked the idea—actually he said 'concept'—but he didn't think the outline had—"

"Oh yeah," Bart said, bored, as if this came as no surprise. "He doesn't think the outline is right. You and I discussed that. Remember, Fred? Not making the hero Jewish. Setting it somewhere other than New York. Bob has some other ideas. He said he wanted to meet with you. Did he arrange a meeting?"

"Yes. I'm seeing him at eleven. But he didn't say why."

"Well, that's the reason. He wants to tell you some of his ideas and see if you guys are in sync. If so, then I think you've got a deal."

"Huh," Fred said. He wanted to ask if he would have to write another proposal after talking with Holder about his ideas, but he felt inhibited, as if the question was impolite, as if he were prying into affairs that weren't his business.

"Okay, Fred. I think we're rolling. Call me after the meeting."

"Sure. 'Bye. Thank you." But Fred was already talking into silence. Was everybody else speeded up, or was he moving in slow motion?

He finally poured himself a coffee—it seemed a century ago that he had decided to make himself a cup—and drank it. He stood there like the victim of an accident: in shock, unable to fully remember the details or understand the consequences of a terrifying crash. Was this good news? Or was it simply no news? If Holder wanted a brand-new outline with all the plotting changed, why did that mean he was close to a deal? If he failed to write the new outline satisfactorily, Holder would end up turning it down. Why was Bart so pleased by these events? Why was Holder behaving so eagerly and expressing so much excitement, if he didn't like the outline? There was nothing to be excited about except the outline. The situation made no sense to Fred.

And yet he wanted to believe.

He finished his coffee and realized the meeting was only an hour away.

He began to feel alive. His senses seemed to turn on all at once. His stomach growled, his heart pounded, his mind began to replay the two telephone conversations, and soon he was hurrying to shower, shave, and dress, worried he would be late, worried he wouldn't be sharp and clever at the meeting, worried that he would blow it, blow his one chance, his only hope.

By the time he hailed a cab to go to Holder's office, he was a nervous wreck. He entered the editorial reception area for Garlands and asked for Bob Holder tentatively, prepared to be told that Bob Holder had no idea who he was or why he would want to see someone named Fred Tatter.

But he was cheerfully informed that he was expected and that Bob's assistant would be right out to guide him through the tortuous dusky-glass-walled, gray-carpeted halls to Bob Holder's corner office with its canyonlike view of Sixth Avenue. And all this happened quickly, too quickly almost. Fred found himself seated across from Holder, nervously fumbling for a cigarette while telling the assistant that he wanted milk in his coffee. Holder sat at his desk, leaning forward on his elbows, looking at him with keen delight, like a kid eagerly ready to play a tough game of Monopoly.

Holder was a plump fellow in his early thirties, his curly hair cut short, so that it seemed tense, a boiling surface for a restless overheated brain. He was squeezed into a gray woolen sweater that made his biceps look powerful and outlined his well-fed belly; and the elbows were well-worn, the right one even showing a bit of his white-and-red-striped Brooks Brothers shirt. His desk was clear, but behind him on built-in shelves beneath his windows were mounds of manuscripts. A large appointment book was open beside the phone and the month was marked with meetings—a whole hour with him seemed luxurious.

"You're just as I pictured you," Holder said with a mischievous, energetic smile. Fred kept expecting to be challenged to a friendly arm-wrestling contest.

Fred nodded uncertainly.

"Tell me how you see your book," Holder went on, and leaned back, putting his arms behind his head and looking pleasantly expectant.

"Uh . . ." Fred lit his cigarette. He felt like a teenager doing it. As if he were unused to smoking. "Well, I think I say it in the outline. I want to show how all this modern stuff about women and sex is basically bullshit. You can't fight the fact that men, when they start feeling old or beat in some way, feel like screwing around. And it doesn't mean they don't love their wives or that their lives are bad."

"Are you saying—"

The assistant entered with a cup of coffee for Fred. Holder went on talking. Fred took the cup and felt embarrassed that she might have heard what he said. She was a woman. What if she told Holder it was a disgusting idea? He made a point of thanking her, remembering Marion's bitching about how casually assistants are treated. She did seem pleased, but Fred missed what Holder said.

"I'm sorry," he said. "What did you say?"

Holder frowned and let his chair tip forward so he was back to his combative attitude: arms on the desk, leaning toward Fred aggressively. "You're going to go after . . . you know, marriage counseling, therapy—be honest—all that."

Fred hesitated. Maybe Holder didn't agree with his point of view. Maybe Holder didn't like the outline because he once had an affair, now regrets it, made up with his wife—he looked and saw a wedding ring on Holder's left hand—but it was too late anyway because Fred had already nodded yes.

"Great!" Holder said, leaning back and smiling. "That's what makes this a good book. Get a lot of controversy. Get people talking. We can even get something that's always a marketing problem with novels, namely some talk-show appearances, if we present it as a kind of confessional from you about how modern young men are. You know, the women writers always get that kind of subsidiary publicity on their books, 'cause they can go on talk shows and discuss their books like their books teach you how to live. Know what I mean?"

"Like *The Women's Room?*"

"Yeah! Exactly. Though with you, we got a much better, much more salable presence. You know? You'd be great on Phil Donahue. Man, does that show sell books. I've just brought out *Greenhouse*. About the earth heating up, the ice caps melting. Well, we got the author on Donahue last week. Put the book right on the bestseller list."

"Really? His show does that?"

"His show. *Nightline, Good Morning America*. The *Today Show* used to be great—"

"But since the ratings went down, they're no good?"

"They're still good. I don't mean to say they don't sell books." Holder said this as if he were speaking in public, like a politician afraid to make clear statements. "But they're not a top priority. Anyway, your book could attract all of them. And that's great for me. I can really push within the house. I mean, it's a terrible thing to admit, but a novelist who can get on a talk show is worth the talent of seven Tolstoys."

Fred laughed appreciatively. "I gotta remember to quote you to my wife. She's an editor at Goodson—"

"What's her name?"

"Marion Tatter."

Holder squinted. "I don't know her."

"Anyway, she'll like that."

"It's true. Sad, but true. Anyway, getting back to your book. I've got a few problems with it, and I wanted to see if we put our heads together whether we could solve them. First, I don't like it being set in New York."

Fred nodded.

"I don't like the sense," Holder went on, "that it's a poor man's Philip Roth novel—you know, Jewish introverted hero who really, deep down, wants to be fucking his brains out, only he's too guilty about the Holocaust or something. That's a distraction from what we've discussed. We want this to be the male answer to *The Women's Room*—"

"We could call it *The John*," Fred said out of nervousness. He felt left out, lectured to, and he wanted to show he had some intelligence.

It must have been the right comment, because Holder banged his hand on his desk and laughed. Laughed hard, his mouth open, issuing staccato bursts of sound. "Not a bad idea," he said. "Anyway, the point is, let's stay away from any superficial resemblance to a whiny Roth book. Make the hero a WASP, set it in the Midwest or maybe California—LA might not be a bad idea, after all that's where all the fads come from. What do you think?"

"I think you're right."

"Good," Holder said, with a touch of surprise, as if he had expected a hassle. But the victory sat uneasily on his head. "You're sure you agree? That's not giving up anything important to you?"

This worried Fred. He wanted to make it clear he would do anything Holder wanted, but without seeming like a hack, a whore who would spread his legs for even a hint of payment. Instinctively Fred knew that no matter how much they junked up the plot of the book, he must convince Holder that he was a serious artist (I am, he insisted to himself), and make even the most calculated and topical novel read like literature. "Well," Fred said, and pressed out his cigarette. He wanted to say: I can do it, whatever you want, I can do it. "The minute you said to me that the outline made it sound like a Roth novel, I understood. That isn't what I'm going for. I guess I was worried people wouldn't think I could do a non-Jewish, non-New York book. Fact is, I'd rather it wasn't."

"Good," Holder said, now convinced Fred's concession was sincere. "I have another problem with the outline." He paused, as if this were a delicate moment. "I don't think it should start in the late sixties and follow the couple up until our hero's crisis. It should start with the crisis. And stay in the present, using all the current pop psychology that's around."

"You mean, start with him having an affair?"

"Or wanting to. Yeah."

This bothered Fred, but his mind was blank as to why. He had adjusted to the notion of changing the setting and the ethnic background of the hero—after all, were those really changes?—but to throw out the first ten years the book was supposed to cover . . . ?

"I'll tell you why," Holder said after Fred's silence had gone on for a while. "You want the book to be about this biological incompatibility between men and women, right? Men aren't monogamous, that's your thesis, right?"

Fred nodded uncertainly, like a witness being interrogated by a crack lawyer, afraid to admit even the most harmless and obvious fact, lest it lead to a damning conclusion.

"See," Holder said, leaning forward earnestly, pleading his point, "then doing it with our hero being young, meeting his wife, marrying her, and so on, takes you down the wrong road. You want it to be that he's happy, he's settled, all that crap. Deciding to get married, establishing a career, is behind him. His life is settled, he's okay. He's got it all. Only—" Holder held up his finger suspensefully and lowered his voice ominously. "Only he wants all those beautiful young bodies out there!"

Fred was smiling and nodding throughout all this, as if he loved it, and agreed. Agreed so heartily that he was on the edge of his chair, almost ready to leap into Holder's arms. "Un-huh," he said, not wanting to say anything, because he didn't know what he thought, he just wanted to encourage Holder's enthusiasm.

"See what I mean? Starting it in the present focuses it. Makes it an advocate for your statement. And that gets us a tight narrative and"—he winked cynically—"maybe on the Phil Donahue show."

Fred nodded solemnly and looked thoughtful. However, his only thought was: I have to rewrite the whole outline. Nothing has been accomplished.

"I know that makes the book shorter, but that's good, I think," Holder went on.

"Definitely," Fred said.

"So basically you'd start the novel about halfway through your outline."

"Okay," Fred said, bobbing his head like a doll.

"Okay. Now that's settled, I'll tell you my plan. We usually submit proposals to the ed board—which I'm on, along with five other editors and Tom Paulson. But I can go to Paulson directly if I tell him we only have your outline exclusively for twenty-four hours. That's what I'm gonna do. So you should have an answer by tomorrow morning. How's that?"

The Resurrection of Christ, Bobby Thompson's home run, the Parting of the Red Sea—no reversal of fortune in history could compare with the shock, followed by delight, in Fred's heart at this statement. He said, "Great," with his first natural smile of the meeting, and floated out back onto the street feeling as if he had never lived before, never seen the intense beauty of real life, never known true respect for himself.

Finishing the chapter excited Patty. She calculated that if she were able to type it quickly, she could deliver it before five to Joe McGuire, the editor in chief of Shadow Books. She was a fast typist, the only skill she possessed that her old boss Gelb never found fault with, and even going slowly (to be sure there was not a single typo), she had the twenty pages done in an hour. It was two-thirty.

A pause of insecurity slowed her progress to McGuire's office. After all, Betty knew what he would want, and she was on the floor above, so Patty called from the lobby extension and got Betty, asking if she could read the pages immediately.

"Sure. But what's the rush?"

"Don't we want to get it in and over with? You know how we hate suspense."

"We sure do," Betty agreed, laughing. "Okay, I've got a meeting at three. So let's do it."

Patty went upstairs and paced restlessly back and forth past Betty's window while she read. Twice Betty told her to sit down and once she burst out laughing at something in Patty's chapter. "Whoa, that's hot," Betty said toward the end of the chapter, and Patty knew she must have reached the moment where the heroine was roughly kissed by the dark, handsome, and possibly brutal love interest.

At last Betty swiveled in her chair and said, "It's great! I knew you could do it."

"Okay. But what should we change? What's wrong with it?"

"Nothing! Absolutely nothing. It's fine."

"Come on," Patty said, frowning. "I need this to come through. I can't start a relationship with a man and be broke. I don't want to depend on him for money."

"It's that serious?" Betty asked, not concealing her amazement. After all, only last week Patty hadn't even discussed David with her. To Betty no weekend, no matter how magical, could be that dramatic.

"I told you I was in love. I don't know. Am I crazy?" Patty's eyes looked big and forlorn, like those of a misbehaving dog approaching head down, asking for reassurance from its owner.

"I didn't mean that," Betty hurried to say. But she did.

"I feel like it's serious," Patty said in an unusually somber tone.

"That's terrific," Betty said, and felt moved for Patty. In all the years she had heard Patty discuss men, never before had she allowed herself to speak so simply, to make it clear that she was vulnerable. Several times Betty had concluded that Patty was incapable of real feeling, of being in love unselfconsciously, without burlesque. It had made Betty think less of her, and so this moment was impressive. "Well, I think Joe will give you a contract on this."

"Really? 'Cause if it needs work, tell me—"

"I think it's fine. You should give it to him. Does he know you're bringing it up?"

Patty blinked, confused.

"You didn't call ahead and tell him you were delivering it?"

"Oh God," Patty said, looking distraught.

Betty couldn't help smiling. "It's not a problem. Call him from here. Just give him a little warning."

McGuire took her call right away and sounded delighted that she had finished. "Jesus! You could probably write a whole book in two weeks. Bring it on down. I'll read it tonight."

His friendliness puffed her up with confidence. She breezed into his office and tossed her manila folder with the chapter inside on his desk.

"I'm telling ya. I should pay you by the hour. Save me a fortune." McGuire got up and moved around his desk, heading for her. He was short, five-six, only a few inches taller than Patty. He had a plump face, with benign red cheeks and small twinkling eyes that seemed to think everything was funny. He wore jeans and a wrinkled white dress shirt with a narrow tie that looked too small for him, as if it belonged to a prep-school boy's uniform. He had thin bloodless lips that now kissed her full on the lips, staying only a fraction of a beat longer than was polite. She smelled Scotch on his breath and backed quickly into a chair to make sure nothing more happened.

"God, you look great!" he said loudly, as if he were only a drink away from throwing all caution to the winds. He reminded Patty of her alcoholic uncle who, by the end of every evening, would tell rambling, incoherent stories with punch lines that would cause him to go into gales of laughter and leave his listener frozen with a mystified and embarrassed smile.

"Thanks. I'm in love," she said, to prevent a repetition of that slobbering kiss.

"Oh," he said with a puzzled look, as if he were smelling something bad but didn't know its origin.

She felt despair, realizing that Betty was with her when she met McGuire and that he might have decided to give her a chance with a quickie in mind, and hadn't made that clear because they weren't alone. His reaction to her announcement seemed to confirm this fear; and that meant he would turn her chapter down now. "Isn't that great, Joe?" she said, looking at him slyly. "Aren't you happy for me?"

"I don't know," Joe said, encouraged by her teasing manner. "At your age, I fell in love every afternoon. Didn't mean a thing."

Patty crossed her legs. She was wearing a light blue skirt, slit up the right side, so that her action showed her thin and graceful leg. McGuire's amused eyes went to it and focused. Patty did this without reflection, although, if she had thought about it, she wouldn't have lied to herself about what she was attempting. Sometimes, with men, it was possible to let hope spring eternal without letting them actually do any springing. She didn't reflect because she would have disapproved of herself; and her disapproval might not have been sufficient to stop her from flirting. Better to do it without allowing any self-criticism. "And now you don't fall in love every afternoon?"

"No, no," McGuire said, not bothering to conceal his stare at her bare leg.

"What a pity, Joe. How unromantic. Especially for a romance-book editor."

This reminder of his job—which Patty assumed was a bitter fact for him (Betty had said being made editor in chief of Shadow Books was considered being kicked upstairs)—seemed to kill his sexual drive. His eyes left her leg and drifted boozily up to the shelves behind her chair. "Right! I only sell the stuff. Don't buy it."

"You must buy mine. I'm desperate."

"Ah. I like desperate women."

"Oh, Joe. You're so cruel."

It went on like this for what seemed an eternity to Patty. An unpleasant, forced, and silly flirtation that made her so irritable she almost wished he would simply unzip his fly so she could hitch up her skirt and let him get it over with. At least that would be the end of it. Sitting there and having to fake interest was sickening and quite difficult. But she lived in dread of not playing the game. She had lost one job because she didn't have the brains to go along. If an hour of imbecility with Joe was going to get her a contract to write this romance novel, then why not do it?

There was one reason to prolong the foolish chatter. Ending it meant Joe had another opportunity to kiss her. So when his secretary entered with some papers, Patty got to her feet and said, "I'd better go."

But McGuire was more brazen than she thought. He said when she moved to the door, "What? No good-bye kiss?" winking at his secretary, who looked bored, as if she also knew that he was not only repulsive but also inffectual. McGuire got up, walked to Patty, and when she moved her head to give him her cheek—despite the presence of his secretary— he put his arms around her, and under the guise of giving her a big hug, put his hands on her buttocks and gave them a hard squeeze, allowing a quiet but ridiculously intimate moan to escape his lips.

Patty wriggled out of his arms, saying with lilting cheerfulness—and yes, maybe a hint of promise—"Talk to you tomorrow, Joe."

Jim Foxx, Tony said to himself with a wave of relief. His name is Jim Foxx. He had slid into the booth with Garth and Foxx after they had transformed their solemn looks into radiant smiles when he appeared, and was now accepting Foxx's offer of coffee, which he poured himself from a pot on the table. Tony judged from the empty juice glasses, half-empty coffee cups, and full bowls of fruit in front of the actor and the producer that they must have arranged to meet earlier. To discuss Tony? It didn't matter. At least he had remembered Jim Foxx's name, though what good it would do him, he couldn't say.

"How was your flight?" Garth asked. His tone was serious, compassionate almost, with the earnest tone Garth had had in his Academy Award-winning performance about the Legal Aid lawyer who successfully defended an innocent young black farmer accused of raping a white woman.

"Good." Tony gulped a sip of coffee. "But I guess I don't travel well. I had terrible insomnia. Got less than an hour's sleep."

Foxx nodded. "Happens to me too."

"You mean you never get over it? I assumed it was because I don't do much traveling."

Foxx signaled to a waitress. "First night on the road, can't sleep. I must travel"—he looked at Garth as if he had the answer—"hundred and fifty thousand miles a year. Probably more. Never get over it." The waitress reached them. "Do you know what you want, Tony? We've already ordered."

Tony asked for French toast and bacon. "Okay, honey," the waitress said, which struck Tony as being odd in an expensive restaurant. But it did make him feel more protected, in a strange way, as if she had let him know that he belonged.

"Ah, to be young," Foxx said about Tony's order.

"You don't want any juice or melon?" Garth asked. "They have great melons here."

"I've always heard that about Hollywood. Lotta great melons."

They all laughed. Foxx, especially, was taken by surprise and enjoyed the joke. He assumes I'm a pretentious playwright, Tony thought to himself.

The waitress hesitated.

"But no, I'm fine," Tony said to Garth, and she went. He felt slightly baffled but pleased that they treated him like a nephew they were taking out. There was no sense of the truth, or at least what Tony understood the situation to be, namely that this was an audition of sorts. The writer showing off his legs to the big producer and box-office actor.

Garth looked at Foxx expectantly in the pause that followed. Tony, taking the hint, was silent, and also looked to Foxx to say something.

"Did, uh . . ." Foxx spooned an enormous strawberry out of his bowl and held it near his mouth. "Did Gloria tell you much about the history of this project?" He ate the strawberry.

"No. She said she thought it would be best to leave that to you. All she mentioned was that there had been a script written which you weren't happy with."

"Five," Foxx said. "We've been through five drafts and three writers. It's tough," Foxx added, looking off philosophically.

"There's something I wondered about," Tony said. Both Garth and Foxx seemed surprised and curious that he wondered about anything. Maybe writers aren't supposed to wonder, Tony wondered, but he pressed on. "How come you didn't send me the latest script before this meeting?"

"We want to totally throw them out," Garth said in the tone of a betrayed lover speaking of the mementos of his ruined romance.

"Even if you were to come onto the project," Foxx said, "we wouldn't want you to look at the earlier drafts. We've had a lot of meetings—"

"Bullshit. All bullshit," Garth said. His thin shoulders were hunched, his head hanging low, like a fighter's. He had just taken a sip of coffee. He set his cup down on the saucer with a harsh clatter. He looked Tony in the eyes. It was transfixing to look into them: Tony felt as if he had become a character in a movie; or that he had been seated in the front row of the theater. They were dark and suspicious. "It's hard for me to accept, but you gotta leave the writer alone. Every draft, we've gone step by step. Giving notes, doing it page by page. Doesn't work. All we want is to pick a writer we like, tell him—in general—what we want, and then leave him alone. Only thing that makes sense."

Foxx nodded gravely, but Tony saw that he really wasn't paying attention to Garth, like a wife who has heard her husband tell a particular anecdote over and over. "Yeah. This is a special idea. It needs originality. And you can't get originality writing a script by committee."

"And you can't get originality from a Hollywood writer," Garth said. "They've spent their lives writing to suit other people. They have no idea how to be their own man. That's why we wanted a playwright. You know, in the theater you guys have the final say. So"—Garth smiled, and his famous boyishness abruptly took the curse off of his cranky tone—"that's what we want. Someone who'll go off, write us a great script while we lie in the sun." He banged his fist on the table. "No more script conferences until there's a script to confer about."

Tony laughed. Garth smiled mischievously. "Okay," Tony said to him. He felt completely at ease with Garth. He seemed bright, accessible, and reasonable. "So how do I convince you to hire me?" Tony said. He didn't know if it was too bold a remark. But it was what he wanted to know, and Garth's honesty made him feel that truth was the best approach.

"You don't have to," Foxx said.

"Let me tell you why you're here," Garth said. He ran a hand through his straight black hair, another gesture straight out of his roles. "I saw your play last year in New York—"

"*Youngsters?*"

Garth smirked. "Yeah. Did you have more than one play on that year?"

"Yes," Tony said quietly.

Garth looked abashed. "You did?"

"I had two one-acters on at the Quest Guild right after *Youngsters*."

"I didn't know that. I wish I'd seen them. I guess I wasn't in town—"

"You might have been. They were only on for four weeks. It was a limited run."

"Anyway, I did see *Youngsters*. You know, I've seen a lot of stuff about the sixties, the antiwar movement, the sexual revolution—nobody got it the way you did. There were no preachy monologues, you snuck in the politics painlessly, you made terrible fun of all of us, and then you turned it around beautifully. I cried at her speech . . ." He turned to Foxx. "You know, the drugy who yells at her kid sister about how it was worth it, no matter how badly they failed."

Foxx nodded throughout gravely, but again with that abstracted look of someone who has heard it too often.

"Thank you," Tony said. He was astonished that Garth had been to his play (and surprised that he hadn't known it; usually the presence of a celebrity in an off-Broadway theater doesn't go unnoticed) and intensely flattered by Garth's vivid recall and detailed praise. Why he should so value Garth's admiration—hadn't the *Times* said he was "touched with genius"?—he didn't know, but he felt himself suffused with a happy warmth.

"Anyway, I had just read the fourth, the fifth, I don't know what draft of *Concussion*—"

"Is that the title of this project?" Tony asked.

"Working title," Foxx said hastily. "We need something—"

"Less medical!" Garth said impatiently. "Anyway, I'm sitting clapping at the curtain, tears coming down my face, and I think: Why the fuck didn't we hire this kid to write *Concussion*?"

Tony smiled. "So why didn't you?"

" 'Cause the studio wants people with credits, as if that proves something. *Concussion's* a thriller, that's what's gonna sell it to the public. Like a Hitchcock movie, it'll mostly be a glamorous chase picture. But—and it's a big but—what gives it resonance, some depth, is this: we take a guy in his mid-thirties, he's in Washington, he's made it, he's a partner in a firm that does a lot of antitrust work, basically fighting the Environmental Protection Agency, you know, all the regulating bodies of the Justice Department. So, he's an establishment guy. But in the sixties, he was a radical. And a real radical. Fell in love with a beautiful, mysterious woman—"

"Meryl Streep," Foxx offered.

Tony smiled involuntarily, but then he remembered who these people were. If they wanted Meryl Streep for a part, they could get her.

"Yeah, I'd love to work with Meryl again," Garth said. "She's terrific. And she'd be perfect for this. Anyway, she's very radical, and part of the reason he went along with going underground, making bombs, was that he was in love with her."

"This is all back story," Foxx said.

Garth smirked. "He says that 'cause it scares the shit out of the studio. Like I'm gonna make a movie in which I blow up the President."

"Not a bad idea," Tony said.

"Yeah." Garth winked at him. "You get the idea. It's all back story, and he's sorry he ever had anything to do with making bombs—"

"Why did he stop?"

"Ah!" Garth leaned forward eagerly. "This is how the movie begins. It's 1968. We see a quiet town house in Greenwich Village. I'm in the basement with Meryl. Quickly establish I love her while I argue with her that we shouldn't place the bomb—which we see her making along with two other characters—in a situation where anyone could be hurt. She's very hard-line. Finally, I say we need milk, or they want sandwiches for lunch—"

"He goes out for lunch," Foxx said impatiently. "He can't go out for milk."

"Whatever," Garth said. "Doesn't matter. I go out. I'm about half-way down the block—"

"Town house blows up," Tony said for him. "You're doing the Eleventh Street incident."

"Exactly. You see?" Garth said to Foxx. "Tony knows what I'm talking about. The other writers had never heard of the Eleventh Street town house."

"That's great that you know about it," Foxx said with a big smile at Tony.

"So," Garth said, again running a hand through his hair, "the town house blows up. Cut, dissolve, fifteen years later. I'm an establishment guy in a real conservative law firm. You find out that Meryl was presumably killed in the explosion, that I've never gotten over her, that I was totally turned off politics by her death, and so on. And then, Nyack happens."

"This is great," Tony said. "It'll be like *Vertigo*, only it's the sixties coming back to haunt him."

Garth leaned back with a big smile and gestured toward him, the star asking the audience to acknowledge the presence and talent of his costars. "You've got it."

Foxx, however, was frowning. "Nyack?" he said with distaste, as if someone had asked him to move there.

"You know, the terrorist bank robbery," Garth said.

"In the script?" Foxx asked.

"Yeah," Garth said patiently. "That's based on a real incident. The Nyack thing. You didn't know that?"

"I thought that was invented. Is there going to be a legal problem?"

"No, no, no."

"Do we need it?" Foxx said. "I don't think it works. Can't Meryl's character come back as something else? I don't like her killing cops and being a bank robber."

"But she hasn't actually done the robbery!" Garth said, his tone so aggrieved that Tony knew this was a point that had been argued many times.

"That distinction is unimportant," Foxx said. "All the audience will know is that she's a terrorist. Saying she's innocent of a particular act of terrorism won't change that. She won't be sympathetic. Meryl would never play the part!" Foxx burst out with abrupt impatience.

"Why make it clear?" Tony asked.

They both stared at him. Their looks were blank, as if they had forgotten he was there. "What do you mean?" Garth snapped.

"Hitchcock wouldn't make it clear. Our hero, after the flashback, would be sitting at home watching the TV news coverage of the Nyack robbery with a look on his face that'd tell the audience it frightened him, and then there'd be a knock on the door. And Meryl, beautiful and distraught, would be there, telling a breathless and confused story of how she was being set up, of her years underground, and so on. A story whose truth we wouldn't know until the end of the picture. We'd have a hero who intellectually thinks she's guilty, but emotionally needs her to be innocent." Tony turned to Foxx. "Meryl, if the part was written properly, might want to play it because it would allow her to simultaneously play a villain and the romantic lead. The best of both roles in fact."

Foxx listened. He looked Tony in the eyes while nodding agreement; his eyes were suspicious, however, searching doubtfully for a catch, a hidden trick to Tony's explanation. At the finish they flickered, and Foxx leaned back, looking up at the ceiling.

Garth, meanwhile, reached across the table and rubbed Tony's head —an affectionate big brother. "That's brilliant," he said.

Tony knew it wasn't brilliant. But he loved Garth saying so. He flushed at having his hair tousled: he knew his ego was being seduced; but he didn't care; it felt too good to protest.

Tony looked at Foxx. He knew now that Foxx was the impediment to his being hired. He had also realized that Gloria Fowler's sudden inspiration to be his agent had come from her certain knowledge that Garth wanted to hire him. She had been dishonest, pretending that she had picked him out of the haystack of off-Broadway theater; but the credit for that belonged to Garth. I'm too naive, Tony said to himself while he waited for Foxx's eyes to come back down from the ceiling. He knew Foxx wanted the political background out of the script, and therefore he would see Tony as a step backward. Tony had made it sound like he would only use it as a Hitchcockian veil of suspense: if Foxx bought that, he'd get the job.

"Well . . .?" Garth said to Foxx. "What are you doing? Checking the sprinkler system?"

Foxx lowered his eyes. They brightened at something. A smile came over his face and he seemed to straighten in readiness. Garth followed his gaze and also smiled. Tony, still waiting for Foxx's judgment, felt hands come around his head and cover his eyes. He smelled a perfume he had known all his life.

"What's the matter? You never write. You never call," said a guttural female voice. Laughter lay only an inch below its deep surface; an amusement that had cued audiences, in the subtle way only a great comedienne can, that a joke was being played, and thereby got even bigger laughs than the lines deserved.

"Hi, Ma," Tony said, playing the comedy in the harassed voice of a teenager.

His mother released her blindfold and then he was hugged violently, pressed into her substantial breasts, suffused by her familiar odor. Out of the crush, he could see with one eye that surrounding tables were looking on with self-conscious delight.

"What have you been doing to my boy?" Maureen demanded of Garth in a melodramatic tone while still crushing Tony.

"I'm innocent," Garth said. "The producer made me do it."

"He comes to town," she said, releasing Tony and slapping him on the shoulder. "Doesn't phone, doesn't tell me where he's staying. Is this a son or a viper?"

"Neither, darling," Foxx said. "He's a screenwriter."

Maureen pushed at Tony. "Let me in, you louse." Tony slid over. Maureen got in, saying, "You making a deal with my boy, or just jerking him off?"

"Around, darling, not off," Foxx corrected, while Garth convulsed with laughter.

"I always get idioms mixed up," Maureen said, winking at Tony. Her double entendre, disguised as naiveté, was an old joke between them. "Well, which is it?"

Garth smiled. "That was the question I was going to ask Jimmy. But I was going to wait until Tony left."

"Since when are you diplomatic?" Maureen said to Garth.

Tony kept waiting for an entrance into this banter—and praying that his mother would stop just short of totally humiliating him. She usually did, but there had been miserable exceptions.

"Maureen, I'm hurt," Garth said, and looked it too.

"Of course *we* want to hire him," Foxx said. "But the studio has to approve."

Garth smiled.

Tony wondered.

Maureen said, "That's bullshit, darling. If Bill Garth and Jimmy Foxx tell a studio they want a writer, the studio hires him." She turned to Tony and kissed him full on the lips. "You've got the job. Stick it to them on the negotiation. They'll pay your price."

Garth roared, throwing his head back and slapping Foxx on the back. Even Foxx couldn't control his face, beaming at Maureen.

Tony, stunned, the exhaustion of his trip and the long night of talk returning through the anesthesia of adrenaline, looked away from the group and scanned the Polo Lounge.

Most of the tables were looking at him.

Wondering.

Who was that kid with the famous actor and actress? Who was that masked man seated with Jim Foxx? Should we know him?

Yes, Tony answered silently, while the others laughed.

GARLANDS DEAL MEMO

re: Fred Tatter novel, *The Locker Room*.
$20,000 advance. Payable: $5,000 on signing;
$5,000 on delivery of a mutually satisfactory
one hundred pages; $10,000 on delivery
of a mutually satisfactory completed
manuscript. Bart Cullen, agent. Robert Holder,
editor.

NEWSTIME INTEROFFICE MEMO

John Syms will be detached from senior-editing
Nation to Future Projects for six months. Jim

Daily will senior-edit Nation during his absence.
David Bergman will fill in to senior-edit
Business.

SHADOW BOOKS DEAL MEMO

Patty Lane, flat fee, $5,000 for untitled romance
novel.

INTERNATIONAL PICTURES
DEAL MEMO

Tony Winters hired to write first-draft
screenplay on *Concussion*. William Garth, Jim
Foxx producers. William Garth star. $50,000
draft and set against $175,000. Contracts to
follow.

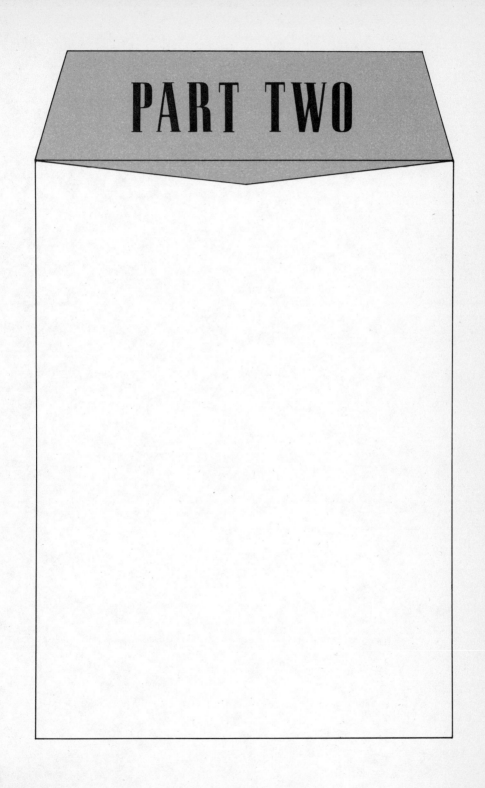

PART TWO

CHAPTER

7

For nine months Fred had lived a life once only dreamt of: he was a writer under contract for a novel. The legal agreement itself was precious. He kept the thirty-five-page document at the front of his file drawer. He saw the edge of it's nineteenth-century typeface at the start and finish of each work session, when he would remove and replace that day's writing. Sometimes, late at night, he would get out of bed and surreptitiously sneak into his study, quietly pulling open the drawer, and gaze at the contract: a teenage boy enjoying a stash of pornography.

At first the glances were passionate, their purpose to reexperience a thrill. But afer two months, bogged down in the second chapter, feeling inadequate to the task of actually producing a novel, he made the nightly excursions for reassurance. A confirmation that he, in fact, had a contract.

After nine months, Fred started to *read* the legal agreement. By then he was close to finishing the first one hundred pages of his novel. Now he worried that his prose was bad, that Bob Holder would reject the novel when he handed it in. He knew, from Marion among others, that the five-thousand-dollar portion of the twenty-thousand-dollar advance he had received on signing the contract would have to be returned only if another publisher wished to accept Fred's novel. Nevertheless, late one night he read through the document to confirm this fact.

The quest was pointless, in a way. If his novel were rejected by Holder, and then by every other publisher, not having to return the five thousand dollars would hardly compensate Fred for such a devastating failure. Better never to have gotten a deal than to have had one and blown it. He would rather have died of thirst in a desert of mediocrity than have had his lips cruelly wetted by a few drops of the rain of success.

Still, he read through the clauses, looking for the legal reassurance that, even after a hurricane of rejection, he would be left clutching his five thousand dollars. He never got there. His eye was caught by an earlier clause: "$5,000 payable on signing. $5,000 payable on delivery of a mutually satisfactory one hundred pages. $10,000 payable on delivery of a mutually satisfactory completed manuscript."

What did "mutually satisfactory" mean? For a moment he thought, illogically, it meant that Holder would have to accept his novel if he, Fred, found it satisfactory. Then he absorbed the phrase. The only protection it gave him was that if Holder liked his novel and Fred didn't, Fred could prevent Holder from publishing it. This notion delighted Fred, and not simply because of its obvious improbability: the chance that he might dislike his own work while others approved of it was fundamentally unsound. The suggestion that his opinion of his work needn't be in tow to the world's was as absurd to Fred as the possibility that he might be granted the ability to fly while the rest of humanity remained earthbound. To be a yo-yo jerked up and cast down by an unseen and whimsical giant, spinning on a string of hope, seemed an immutable natural law to him, a fate no one could escape.

He phoned Karl Stein first thing in the morning to chat about that silly clause in his contract, ignoring Karl's request, made to all his friends, that they not interrupt him before noon. Since the disappointing publication of *Stewardess*, Karl had had trouble writing his next book, and he liked to keep his mornings free of distractions. Fred had been ignoring Karl's injunction from the day he got his deal for *The Locker Room*. Fred justified his violations by telling himself that Karl wasn't serious. For although Karl would say, "Fred, I can only talk for a few minutes," at the start of the conversation, it was almost always Karl who would end up telling a story or worrying over a plot point in his new novel, thereby extending the call for an hour.

That morning Fred was startled when he had heard Karl's voice blare loudly in the phone with the telltale whoosh of a tape recorder, saying, "Hello. This is Karl Stein. I'm not in right now. But if you leave your name and number when you hear the beep, I'll get back to you as soon as I can."

"What!" Fred said, after the beep, with mock outrage. "A phone-answering machine! I can't believe it! And I certainly don't believe that you're out at nine-thirty in the morning!" Fred guffawed into the receiver. "I was just calling to tell you something I found in my book contract . . ." Fred paused and waited. He knew Karl would be monitoring the machine, listening to Fred talk. Fred thought that the suggestion he had something interesting in his book contract, keeping in mind that Karl was also being published by Bob Holder and Garlands, might provoke Karl—

There was a clattering sound. "Fred?"

"Karl? Is this you? Or a robot?"

"I was taking a shower, and I—"

"Sure, sure," Fred said. "When did you get the machine?"

"Yesterday. Now that I'm doing more magazine articles, I'll be in and out—"

Fred laughed good-naturedly. "And in case the President calls, you don't want to miss it."

"Fred," Karl said, his naturally deep voice resonating even more with suppressed anger, "I need the machine."

"Hey, I was teasing. I know. I hate the machines, that's all. I always think it's a person at first. But the worst thing is, you have to have a reason every time you call somebody. Otherwise, you're left listening to the beep and going: Duh . . . Most of the time, I call people just to chat."

"Or drive them crazy," Karl said, with enough humorous coloration to soften his voice's dark palette.

"That's right," Fred said, laughing, but he felt stung, reminded once more that he wanted Karl's frendship more than Karl wanted his. Every time Fred began to behave unselfconsciously with Karl, he was brought up short and made to feel that he had to start again, watching that his tone be deferential, careful, stepping around Karl's ego as though it were shattered glass on a clear floor: the sharp pieces might be anywhere and they could cut deep.

"So what's new?" Karl asked, friendly again, now that he had Fred bleeding.

Fred knew that Karl had heard him saying on the machine there was something interesting in his contract. He wanted to force Karl to ask what it was. "Oh, nothing. I'm stuck on the book. Is the game on this week?" There was a pause, a hesitating pause from Karl. Since Fred's three-hundred-dollar loss, Karl had been obliged to invite Fred back several times. Besides, in Fred's mind, he had a book contract now, so he belonged as much as anyone. But Fred was surprised that after three more visits, even though he had done better—not winning back what he had lost, but breaking even once, winning fifty dollars another time, losing a small amount—that Karl didn't volunteer an invitation for the next week. And when Fred asked to come, Karl stammered that an old member of the game was in town and they didn't have room for him.

Every week for a month and a half, it had been the same: Fred waiting for Karl to say something, finally asking himself, and then being given some excuse. Karl's stammer would get worse and his ability to invent was taxed into bankruptcy. By the fourth week of noninvitation,

Karl was saying that two caned chairs had been broken by a visiting overweight uncle and Karl couldn't accommodate a seventh player. Fred, of course, offered to bring his own chair. Then Karl added to his poor invention by saying that he felt tired and wanted the game to end early and so preferred holding the number of participants down. Fred, naturally, said he would leave at eleven. Karl finally had to say no without rationalizing. But Fred was not to be got rid of by even that clear an answer. He said, "Okay, but I want to come next week. I'm still not even, you know." And so Fred was back in and stayed for seven more weeks.

But then Sam Wasserman complained to Karl about Fred. Sam said that Fred was ruining the game with his cheapskate style of play. It was true that Fred, since the three-hundred-dollar loss, had become a conservative gamesman, folding nine out of ten hands on the opening cards. Karl, bullied by Sam's remarks and fearful of losing Sam, made another attempt at discouraging Fred from coming. He tried a direct lie, telling Fred that he had decided to give up playing and had canceled the game. Fred asked why. Karl said the arranging, the setting up of the table, the cleaning up afterward, all of it, was too much hassle. Fred offered to take over. Since, in fact, Karl had *not* canceled the game, he could hardly say yes and permit Fred to call the others, who were under the impression that nothing had changed. That would work only if he included the other five players in his deception. Karl was embarrassed by his own actions, humiliated both by the fact that he was telling lies *and* that he didn't have the guts to simply tell Fred he wasn't wanted. He was forced to call Fred back and say the game was on.

Karl had spent several nights unable to fall asleep, wondering why he bothered being friends with Fred. He told himself not to let Fred seduce him into long telephone calls, not to be frightened to tell Fred he was ruining the poker game, in brief, not to care about sparing Fred's feelings. But every morning, no matter how many vows he had made, Fred would call and Karl would answer, tight and tense in the early part of the conversation, until he heard himself saying something insulting or demeaning to Fred, something he would instantly regret and feel he'd have to make up for by chatting longer.

Finally he bought the phone machine to defend himself. He'd call Fred back in the afternoon, after finishing his own work, and surely then he'd be able to avoid hurting Fred and therefore . . . But then, the very first time Fred called, he had picked up anyway! Meanwhile, Sam Wasserman was bitching more and more about Fred, his hostility surfacing at the game with increasing frequency, and just three days ago Sam had phoned and said that he was feeling fluish and might not come. "But you don't need me anyway," Sam had added pointedly, "you've got fuzzy Freddy." The point was clear. After all, nobody cancels events three days off on the chance that he might be coming down with the flu. So Karl had conceived of the plan that he would buy the phone machine, call Fred and tell him an old friend who used to play in the game (this was an excuse he had used successfully in the past) was in town and he didn't have room for Fred, and then turn the machine on all the rest of the week, so as not to have to listen to Fred's plaintive questions and . . . But then he had picked up! The very first time!

And now here was the moment, here was the time to laboriously tell Fred that this old friend was coming to town, stammering throughout because he knew it sounded utterly fake, totally dishonest.

"Hello, Karl!" Fred said, laughing nervously. "Are you there?"

"Sorry. Listen, I don't think there'll—"

"What? You're not having the game?"

"No, but my old friend is—"

"Oh? Which old friend is this?" Fred said with open disbelief.

Karl opened his mouth to continue the lie, but there was no engine to power the words. They were stuck in his throat, a sailboat resting on still waters, with no wind to blow them to their destination. "Nobody," Karl said angrily.

"What?" Fred said, startled. Instantly his voice was small, scared by the possibilities of confrontation.

Karl noticed. It made him angrier. Why does Fred needle and probe and insist, if he's unwilling to hear the truth? If he's so vulnerable, Karl thought, why does he act so tough?

"The others don't like you," Karl said, wanting to wound Fred, but discovering, right in the middle of the thrust, that he didn't relish the actual moment of stabbing Fred. "They say if I keep inviting you, they won't come. I don't want to lose the whole game because of you."

There was silence from Fred. A total oblivion that almost convinced Karl Fred had been cut off and his excursion into truth had been wasted. Then he heard Fred clear his throat.

"Look. I've tried to—" Karl began to stammer, but Fred interrupted.

"I understand. No problem. I gotta go."

Fred hung up.

He stared at the phone. He had known, really, known all along. But still he had tried to tell himself it was coming from within him, his own poor sense of himself, his perpetual nervousness that he wouldn't be liked. The black receiver resting in its cradle, still and silent, possessing no identity but its own, reflected a small distorted image of his face peering anxiously into the black impenetrable world. "Let me in," it seemed to say, "or I'll die."

David Bergman's dinner party was about to begin. He had finished setting the table with his brother's hand-me-down china. It was black Wedgwood, chosen to match the black Formica kitchen, and therefore left behind, since his brother's taste had moved on, evolving backward from high-tech to Victorian wall sconces and floral patterns.

However, David had to admit that the dense-colored but delicate plates, boldly blotting the white Formica dining table, did indeed, as his brother would say, "make a statement." And David wanted to impress, to seem as adult as possible tonight. It had taken two months to find a night that Chico and Rounder (nobody called him Groucho, possibly because he was such an outsider; a restraint which ultimately added to the sense that he would forever continue to be one) were both free to come. The other guests, who had suddenly become problematic, were Tony Winters and his wife, Betty. A few days ago Betty had told Patty that Tony and she might not be able to come because Tony's father was coming in from Los Angeles on his way to London and wanted to see them for dinner. Patty had, with shameless charm, begged Betty not to cancel, complaining that she would be drowned in a flood of *Newstime* gossip. Betty called back, after checking with Tony. His father wasn't arriving until ten o'clock, and he planned to meet them at eleven, so they *could* attend, as long as it was understood they would have to leave early.

David resented this arrangement. He had met Tony and Betty on only one other occasion besides the dinner nearly a year before at Fred's —the night he had first met Patty. A few months later they had gone to a startlingly fancy brunch at Tony's and Betty's. That event, with its nakedly business-oriented guest list, the professionally tended bar, the rented coat racks, the fancy dishware, and the elaborate menu, convinced David it was appropriate for someone his age to invite his bosses to dinner. David, secretly, was irritated that Patty would never dream of entertaining on that scale (David didn't consider the possibility that Tony might have made the arrangements), thus forcing him to settle for an uncatered, relatively intimate dinner. At Tony's party he had counted at least thirty people in show business, all of whom, David assumed, were important contacts for Tony, relationships Tony needed to succeed. David wouldn't have minded having Rounder and Chico over, along with the other Marx Brothers and the important editors he knew from *Business Week*, the *Wall Street Journal*, the New York *Times*, and so on, to make the point to the Marx Brothers that David was the sort of person whom they needed to woo, if they wanted to hang on to him.

At first David had been put off by the prospect of including Tony and Betty at his dinner. Although David thought Tony was an impressive figure, he knew that Rounder and Chico were so neglectful of culture they wouldn't care about Tony until he had six Broadway hits. However, when David learned Tony would have to leave early, he worried whether it would seem like a slight to Rounder and Chico, as if David couldn't hold the attention of even minor playwrights. Who the fuck cares? David told himself as he laid down the last spoon. I hope to become Nation senior editor, not edit the culture pages.

Tony and Betty arrived first, half an hour early, bringing an expensive bottle of wine and expressing disarming apologies. "God, I'm sorry about this!" Tony exclaimed while shaking David's hand. "I know it must seem strange. But I haven't seen my father in almost two years. Last two times I was in LA, I didn't give him proper notice and ended up missing him entirely."

Betty meanwhile studied Patty. Patty had on a demure long dress, covering alluring parts of her body that were usually exposed. Her hair, which only three months ago had been permed, was now straight and gathered up in a bun, suggesting the fifties-movies cliché of a blond bombshell hiding in librarian's clothes. "You look cute," Betty said to Patty, her voice lacking conviction because her mind was absorbed by the shock that Patty had not merely unbaited her hook, but had thrown out the rod and reel as well.

Patty wheeled around, her dress billowing at the knees. "This is my taken look," she said.

Tony and Betty laughed, pleased by her admission. David looked puzzled. "What do you mean?"

"This says: I have a boyfriend."

David didn't join the others in their smiles. "You're not doing that for my benefit, are you?"

"Of course I am!" Patty said, a little sharply, as if hurt.

"You don't have to."

"Come on, David, you hated my single-girl wardrobe. Said I looked like a trollop."

David flushed, his cheeks flooding with blood. "You did," he said in a cruel tone, to cover his embarrassment at being exposed as a prude.

"Well," Tony said breezily, "that's just like Betty. After I picked her up on Forty-second Street, it took weeks to get her to throw out her hot pants."

David and Patty laughed, glad to have an exit from their tense exchange. Betty didn't. She said, "Ha, ha."

An alarm bell rang in the kitchen and Patty almost jumped. "My roast!" she said, hurrying into the kitchen.

Betty followed her, saying, "Can I help?"

"What would you like to drink?" David asked Tony.

"Nothing. I'm meeting my father later, so . . . On the other hand, he's so self-absorbed he wouldn't notice I was drunk unless I threw up on his lap."

David laughed. "Is that a yes?"

"Yeah. Give me a Scotch."

Tony followed David over to an exposed bar on a built-in shelf unit. "How's Hollywood?" David asked.

"Hot, I guess."

"I meant your script."

"Almost finished with, uh, a rough draft for Bill Garth to look at."

"And if he likes it, they make your movie?"

"Who the fuck knows?" Tony said. "I can't get a straight answer out of anybody as to how a movie gets made."

"Doesn't your mother know? Or your father?"

"Maybe I'll ask my father tonight. Mom? She's in TV land. When she worked in movies, it was the tail end of the old studio system. Everything was different then."

In the kitchen, Patty fussed over her roast, her high cheeks flushing from the oven's heat. "Where are you meeting Tony's Dad for dinner?"

"Elaine's."

"Whoa!" Patty said, standing up. A strand of hair had fallen across her face and she blew it back.

"I can't get over this picture of you," Betty said. "You look like Doris Day in *Pillow Talk*."

"Don't you love me this way?" Patty said. Her tone, slightly arch, but insistent, left Betty in doubt whether it was sarcasm or self-satisfaction.

"Are you happy?"

"Oh yeah," Patty said. "And you?"

"I'm going to be thirty-three in a month," Betty said.

Patty ignored Betty's mournful tone. She often complained about age. "You look twenty-two," she answered, glancing in her direction, noting Betty's bobbed red curls and pert (surgical, Patty assumed) nose.

"I'm talking biological clock, not vanity," Betty answered.

This got Patty's attention off the roast. "Are you trying?"

"No!"

"Why not?"

Betty looked disgusted. "What do you think? 'I'm not ready, dear.' "

"Men," Patty agreed. "For machos, they're awfully chicken."

Betty laughed. "Yeah. So, if you're happy, how come I never see you?"

"It's not my fault! You and Tony are always busy. Having dinner with Robert Redford—"

"Oh, come on—"

"It's true! You've become too fancy to see me! Look where you're going to dinner tonight—Elaine's!"

Patty's accusation was burlesqued, so Betty couldn't answer it solemnly. Betty felt the charge was unfair. Patty herself, as was typical of her behavior in the past, had withdrawn from Betty as soon as her relationship with David had become serious, and then, once Patty felt the fish was landed and her life had become dull, Betty started getting phone calls, invitations to lunch, requests for dinner. It was true, however, that a tendency of Tony's, a desire to socialize only with successful show-business people, had become more pronounced since his deal to write a movie for Bill Garth.

"And you, meanwhile," Betty said, deciding to return Patty's passing shot with a similar stroke, "entertain only editors in chief."

Tony appeared, a drink in his hand. "Break it up, girls. The big cheeses are coming."

Patty imitated a pouting child. "She started it."

"Oh, she always does," Tony said. "She's famous for brawling."

Patty laughed. Betty looked at her husband. He stepped back. Betty's pale eyes, usually placid and reserved, seemed dark with anger. "I don't think these endless jokes about my losing control are funny. If you think the idea that I could ever make a scene is so hilarious, maybe I'll start making them, and then we'll see how happy you are."

"Hello!" David called out. "Where is everybody?"

There were other, lower voices, accompanying his.

"Oh God, they're here," Patty said with open despair and nervousness.

"I'm sorry," Tony said to his wife in an abject tone. "I guess I'm on edge about seeing my father."

"Well, don't take it out on me," Betty said, and walked past him, out toward David and his guests.

At the same moment, having left his company behind in the living area, David was heading in and he and Betty collided, bumping heads. David's glasses fell off with a loud clatter.

"Oh Jesus!" Patty exclaimed.

"Careful!" David said, looking owlish, squinting pathetically at the floor. "Don't step on them!" he cried desperately to the others while his own foot moved forward and made a sickening crunching sound as it landed on his spectacles.

"Oh my God," Betty said, staring down. David removed his foot as if it had landed on a hot coal.

"You have another pair, right?" Tony asked, his tone implying that he suspected the answer was no.

David didn't speak. He knelt down, picking up the shattered lenses tenderly, his face made grief-stricken by the bewildered expression of his denuded and abandoned eyes. The others stood by motionless: sympathetic sentinels at this funeral.

"David," Patty asked gently. "Do you have another pair?"

He didn't look up. "No," he said. "These are my spares. I didn't get the others fixed." Now he peered at Patty like she was a ghostly figure. "Thought about it this week. Was going to. But I didn't."

For a moment they silently contemplated the tragic nature of this oversight. "How blind are you?" Tony said at last.

David stood. He put the glasses down on a counter. "I'll be able to find the food on my plate," he said bravely. "Come," he said, "let me introduce you." And he walked toward the living area ahead of them, his feet moving tentatively, an expert on a tightrope, his eyes desperately focused on finding each safe step, while his body pretended grace and ease.

Rounder and his wife were at the other end of the loft, standing side by side looking at the complex of elegant shelving David's brother had built around the industrial elevator shaft. Rounder's wife, Cathy, was tall, almost six feet, and blond, with the same big-boned, ruddy-cheeked heartiness as Rounder. Indeed, she was a beautiful female version of him. She had recently given birth to their second child, but she had also, making her seem even more awesome to Betty and Patty, gotten her doctorate in economics. Columbia University, as well as NYU, had offered her positions of some kind (details were unknown) when her husband was made editor in chief and they had had to move from Atlanta, forcing her to give up her teaching job. But, in a remarkably unchic gesture, she declined the offers, saying that she wanted to devote her time to her children, especially while her husband would be absorbed in getting a feel for *Newstime.*

Chico was slumped on one of David's huge couches, staring at the enormous abstract painting (it was six feet long and four feet high) of a sharply defined bright yellow semicircle. He regarded it suspiciously, as if he suspected it of picking his pocket, or, at least, of impertinence. His wife, Louise, looked half his size, though she was really only a foot smaller, with a shock of short black frizzy hair and a thin eager body, always alert, back straight, eyes forward, like a hungry little bird. She, too, had a successful career in journalism, holding the number-two features-editor job at *Town* magazine. Louise sat on the edge of the couch, also regarding the abstract painting, but with a lively look, almost as if it were talking to her wittily.

While David introduced Chico and Louise, Rounder and Cathy moved from the shelving toward the living area. The moment greetings were done with, Cathy said to David, "Your brother designed all this?"

"And built it," David said. He squinted at her briefly. "He got this place while he was trying to make it as a designer. He'd get some money together and then finish a section. Go back to work. And so on."

"It's beautiful," Cathy said. She looked at Rounder. "We should talk to him about our new place."

"If we stay," Rounder said.

This led to a tedious discussion of New York real estate. David mostly listened. He felt silenced by his blindness. A headache came on rather quickly because of the strain of squinting at each speaker. Realizing this, David stopped looking and merely absorbed the voices: Rounder, self-absorbed, wading in with attitudes toward New York neighborhoods that he obviously only dimly understood; his wife, nervously joshing about "dangerous" areas like a small-town girl; Chico, pretending he didn't care at all about the status, elegance, or comfort of his apartment (David knew that, in fact, Chico had crippled himself with a huge mortgage in order to live on Central Park West just a few years ago); Betty, dogmatically saying that only Beekman Place and Sutton Place were truly acceptable, safe, and civilized areas, an attitude that only a rich girl like Betty could afford, but which she expressed rather as if it were a matter of taste, not money; Tony, elaborately explaining to Rounder the history of various reclaimed neighborhoods, such as SoHo, Chelsea, the Upper West Side, the Village (Tony's observations were obvious, the stuff of *Town* magazine pieces and yet Tony said them as if they were brilliant, and Rounder actually listened as if he thought so too); meanwhile, Louise, the features editor of *Town*, smiled cheerfully at everyone but said nothing. And Patty? She told a horribly embarrassing story about being thrown out of her apartment because of all the crazy men she had been dating, and kidding that what made her relationship with David terribly important was that it rescued her from the New York roach-go-round of closet-size apartments at exorbitant rents.

Listening, hearing only the tones, David loathed them. Their self-satisfaction, their absorption in trivialities, disguised by an ironic self-satire which sounded hollow and insincere, was revealed by the sounds of their voices, abstracted from leavening smiles and gestures. And he loathed himself, because he knew he was so much like them. The loft, with its classy hypermodern design, had impressed Rounder and Chico, adding a layer of sophistication to their image of David. And he had said nothing to contradict their reaction, didn't admit that he would never have volunteered to live that way. That if it weren't his brother's handiwork, he would have ripped it all out.

Patty served dinner, forgiving David for the carrying to and fro, the clearing, and so on, because of his blinded state. Tony dominated the dinner conversation. They asked endless questions when he dropped the fact that his mother was Maureen Winters. The hopelessly starstruck fascination of the Marx Brothers with show business never ceased to amaze and disgust David. Here were people who had dined with presidents and kings, oohing and aahing over stories of foolishly extravagant Hollywood; listening to Tony describe meetings with Bill Garth as though he were allowing them a peek at the lighter side of God.

And then, pathetically, Rounder tried to match Tony's stories, telling of his encounters with stars. Rounder's tales were of formal dinners, charity banquets, secondhand information from stories his reporters had filed. In short, they were boring. At least Tony's stories were alive with absurd details, from the point of view of someone who knew these people when they were relaxed and off-guard.

David was sipping his coffee and squinting through his pounding headache while Rounder fumbled through a pointless anecdote about a charity banquet with Norman Lear as master of ceremonies when he put his coffee cup down and Patty did a double take and then burst out laughing.

Rounder stopped talking.

David stared at Patty, wondering if she'd lost her mind.

One by one the others looked at David. And laughed.

David quickly looked down at his shirt, expecting to find that he had spilled coffee all over it. But there was nothing there.

"Want a little sugar in your coffee, David?" Rounder said, and triggered another round of amusement.

David followed their eyes to his plate. He had shoved his chair back a foot and had to lean forward to see what they saw.

He had placed his coffee cup squarely on top of his German chocolate cake. The white china cup was sinking into the cake, a gentle coffeefall washing over the tilted rim and making his dessert into a muddy mess.

He watched them laugh while Patty explained that David had broken his glasses. She described the scene in the kitchen vividly and the sight gag of the coffee cup was a perfect illustrated page. Their laughter increased.

The whole idea of the evening was in jeopardy. David had wanted to present himself, his life, as evidence of being adult, serious, responsible. He bore the burden, as well as the glamour, of being the youngest senior editor in *Newstime*'s history. To make himself a Marx Brother, he thought, required that he seem mature. David stared at them coldly. Faced with the collapse of his plan, he felt fatalistic. He had been a fool, anyway, to arrange the evening, he thought to himself. He deserved this exhibition. To try to make it through socializing—it was disgusting and merited humiliation and failure.

"I don't know why you're all laughing," he said coolly.

They quieted, unsure of him. He wasn't certain of his own mood, either. He had, for a moment, felt hurt. But the sight of the plate was amusing.

"I think it'll make a great cover for our Health in America feature. You know—Can We Give This Up?" He pointed to the caffeine and sugar mixing: "I carefully arranged it for maximum effect, don't you think? I mean, that picture says: heart attack."

They relaxed and enjoyed his response. Chico winked at him. "You're right, David. I was against that cover, didn't think it had enough drama. But that sure persuades me."

"I told you," Rounder said to his wife, "he's our most innovative senior editor." They all smiled, but Rounder's voice had an earnest tone.

"He is," Chico said, now completely serious. "You've being doing terrific work, David. You made the *Weekly* look dull on the Conoco takeover."

"Would have been even better if," David said quickly, "you'd let me get that shot of their chief executive officer doing a pratfall into a vat of oil." David turned to Tony Winters, chic Tony with his glib talk and winning smile, and said, "I have a slapstick view of the world."

His heart began to thump again in his chest while they laughed and turned to him, warming his chilled soul back to the world and the things of it. The cold abstraction from them, the self-hatred of his own intentions and desires, melted back into the comfortable mush of life: the messy sugared world of acquisition and ambition.

Betty looked at her husband. He was a few feet away, sitting at a large round table next to the passageway that led to the bathrooms, the kitchen, and the unchic back room of Elaine's Restaurant—New York's best-known literary and show-business hangout. She had emerged from the small, cold, and rather dirty ladies' room. A fat, unshaven fellow whose bottom button on his shirt had popped off, exposing his navel, was standing in her way.

"Okay, Paulie. No problem," Tony's father, Richard Winters, was saying to the plump man.

Paulie had a small thick hand on Richard's shoulder, massaging it while he spoke in a nervous voice, its tone alternating between loud joshing and low, secretive intensity, the shifts made abruptly, and not always with apparent cause. It was now intimate, suggestive: " 'Cause, ya know, it's no fuckin' problem for me. I don't like the guy. Jesus!" he said explosively into the air. "I'm exhausted. I was up at five to see my shrink!"

"Five in the morning?" Richard said, catching Betty's eye and winking, as if apologizing for his participation in this conversation. "That's when you see your psychiatrist?"

"Six. If I didn't have him first thing in the morning," Paulie said in an intimate whisper, and then burst out: "I'd never get out of bed!"

"This is my daughter-in-law, Betty," Richard said, gently moving Paulie's body aside so she could pass. "Paul Friedman."

Paul Friedman had his hand out, ready to shake even before he knew where Betty was. As a result, he almost shook hands with the wall, since Betty went around him while Paul turned to where she had been standing.

"This way, this way," Richard Winters said, turning Paul around. The hand stayed out until it caught up to Betty.

"Who are you?" Paul said when they at last made contact.

"She's my daughter-in-law," Richard said.

"My wife!" Tony called from the other side of the table.

"My name is Betty," she said mildly, not wanting to make a feminist point, simply trying to give him a name to remember, rather than a category. Betty knew that to be identified other than as an attachment to

Tony or his father at Elaine's was hopeless, and she didn't squirm or struggle against that indignity. At her blackest, she told herself that someday she would publish a wild-eyed and brilliant young novelist, and then she'd be identified as his—or her—editor, presumably a more worthwhile secondhand fame than being a wife. It *is*, it *is*, she assured herself.

But the restaurant made her feel inconsequential. Within the ten feet surrounding her were two of the most important writers in the country. One of them was eating with the best-known woman editor; the other was pawing a model. The editor, someone Betty admired enormously, was smiling girlishly and adoringly while her author pontificated; the model was doing the same at the next table. Was there a difference? Betty wounded herself with the question. There must be, she decided.

Paul Friedman, meanwhile, had decided Betty was inconsequential. He had turned back instantly after hearing she was someone's wife—by now he couldn't have said whose—and said to Tony, "How's the script coming?"

"Fine," Tony said. He sounded self-conscious. He was. He knew he was within the hearing of world-famous writers. He felt fraudulent discussing his own work in the same room, and hoped, by his one-word answer, to discourage Paul from asking more questions.

"Who's doing it?" Friedman asked. His eyes wandered the moment the question was out, scanning the room for other people whom he needed to say hello to.

"International," Tony answered, furious that Paul wasn't paying attention, and humiliated that he couldn't think of a graceful way to deflect the questions.

Tony's father slapped Paul on the back. "Okay, Paul. Our food's getting cold. Get back to your table."

"Yeah . . ." Paul said, staring off absently. "I'm with great people," he added, his voice drained of enthusiasm. He then wandered off, stepping sluggishly, as though he were sleepwalking.

Richard Winters looked at Tony and Betty with a sarcastically raised eyebrow, and they laughed.

"What does he do?" Betty asked, having trouble believing that Paul could be competent at anything.

"PR," Tony answered quickly. He sounded impatient, as if knowing what Paul Friedman did was an obviously essential bit of information.

"He's good at it," Richard said solemnly. "Crazy job. Demands a crazy person."

"You were saying that you've heard there'll be changes at International Pictures?" Tony said intently.

"Well . . ." Richard looked down at his plate. He sighed. "You know, rumors of management changes at the studios or the networks are constant. But I have reason to believe these are true. Shouldn't concern you, Tony."

Then why did you bring it up? Betty wondered. She had gone to the bathroom when Richard did because she felt Tony tense beside her. It was unpleasant feeling his worry. When they were courting and getting married, one of the qualities she loved in Tony was his easy manner, his sense of accomplishment, so unlike other young men. True, he had a material reason for his self-satisfaction: his first play had been produced successfully, at least by critical standards. With each production failing to accomplish anything more, not winning him money or greater praise, his cheerful attitude had worn thin, and with this movie deal, desperation seemed to have crept in. She had got up from the table to avoid hearing him worry over management changes, something that in the past Tony would have joked about, sure that only his own work and worth mattered, but apparently Paul had stalled the talk until now.

"I don't care about who it is," Tony said. "As long as it doesn't fuck up International's relationship with Garth."

"If Garth wants to do your script," Richard said, "you don't have to worry who's in charge at the studio."

Tony heard the dismissive impatience in his father's tone. He dropped the subject. Richard looked young for his age; tall and elegant in his pin-striped suit, his tanned face relaxed and open. He cut an impressive figure of strength and reliability, qualities that were not reflected in the distant mirror of his past.

Producers, agents and writers began to drop by their table, greeting Richard like an old friend. They were the lesser lights of Elaine's, contacts befitting a business-side network executive. Woody Allen remained aloof at his table, the world-famous novelists flanking them didn't notice, this year's Academy Award-winning actress fluttered past, her fur coat brushing against Tony's back when she squealed and opened her arms to hug someone. Tony took a malicious delight in observing his father's second-rung status. At least in New York, TV was still TV, something you watched but didn't talk about in intelligent company.

When they left, Tony and Betty were outside alone for a moment while Richard was held up inside, collared once again by Paul Friedman. Betty looked tired.

"Are you okay?" Tony asked.

"I'm tired." She moved into his arms, burying her face in his chest.

"What's the matter? Don't you like having two dinners a night?" He felt alive, looking uptown at Second Avenue. A pack of taxis, freed by a green light, bolted, driving with menacing speed, riding the cracked, uneven road like surfers, their headlights bobbing, turn signals flickering a brief warning before they hurled in front of each other, competing for customers or the next free lane. Their machines were shameless incarnations of the city's will to win at any cost. Tony felt their delight in the loss of moral constraint, of their triumph over law and good sense: the city is ours! their rattling chassis proclaimed.

Richard swung open the door and stepped down onto the street, breathing deeply. "Ah!" he exclaimed. His overcoat blew open in the wind, exposing his pink Brooks Brothers shirt. "Remind me never to go there again," he said to Tony.

"Why does anybody go there?" Betty asked.

"To be seen," Tony snapped, as though having to give the answer was an imposition.

"Sure ain't for the food," Richard said. "Well, do I put you kids in a cab, or would you like to stop at the hotel for a drink?"

Betty felt Tony's body tense. He moved away from her to see her face. "Can you stay up, honey?" he asked with a strained note of consideration.

They had had fights over Tony's willingness to keep a social evening going beyond Betty's endurance of fatigue (and pretentiousness, she would have added). She knew he wanted to enjoy his father's room service at the Pierre, that he hoped to grill him more about the International rumors or whatever else Richard might gossip about. Normally she took the position that if she wanted to go home, Tony should go with her. Her father had taken endless business trips, leaving Betty with the romantic notion that togetherness implied happiness; in her parents' marriage, separation certainly hadn't. But she couldn't complain if Tony wanted to spend extra time with his father, especially since they rarely saw each other. What she resented, and what disappointed her, was that Tony's desire to hang on to his dad had nothing to do with filial affection. "I'll go home, sweetie," she said. "You stay with your dad."

Once alone in the cab with his father, Tony felt free, at ease for the first time that evening. He had found the preliminary round of dining at David's and Patty's wearing, and the meal with Richard irritating because of the constant interruptions. He had also felt Betty's impatience with every conversation he tried to have with his father. Why was that? She had always disapproved when Tony spoke slightingly of his father. Why was she bothered by his desire to get to know him better? Wasn't that her sentimental notion of how he should behave? Betty always seemed displeased with him since the first script conference in LA. Did she know? Was that why? Or was it coming from him: a dissatisfaction he thought he had cleverly concealed?

He looked at his father's strong jaw, flashing yellow, red, amber, in the reflected glare of New York's street and traffic lights. Richard had a distant look while he watched the streets go by. "I miss this town," he said. He looked at Tony. "I guess you always miss the setting of your youth." He looked back at the city. "I didn't have a dime when I lived in New York. I still get a big kick out of being on expense account here: doing all the things I dreamt of when I was a kid."

"You sound like a play," Tony said. From Tony, that was high praise.

Richard laughed. "More like *Playhouse Ninety*."

"Did you do any work on *Playhouse Ninety*?"

"No." Richard shook his head and frowned. Tony felt abruptly self-conscious: he had placed his father back in the shameful fifties. Their cab pulled up to the carpeted sidewalk of the Pierre and a uniformed doorman with gold-braided epaulets moved to open the door. "The Golden Age of Television," Richard said, leaning forward to give the driver money, "was mostly garbage, you know."

Tony laughed. "I know. They've been showing it on Channel Thirteen. Pretty hokey."

"It was the era of working-class drama. If it wasn't set in a kitchen, it wasn't art."

They moved through the lobby quietly. Tony felt younger with each step, more and more a child out with a parent. He kept his head down while in the wood-paneled elevator, like a shy little boy unable to meet the glances of strange adults. It all brought back vividly the discomfort he had felt when his father had had custody of him. Richard was a quiet, thoughtful, self-absorbed man whose conversational pattern with Tony was passive, waiting for Tony to begin lines of inquiry, and then supplying only the minimum amount of information necessary to satisfy. Tony had no recollection of his father ever showing any curiosity about his emotional life. There were merely the checklist questions: How's Betty? Are you writing? Do you have enough money? Have you seen your mother lately?

"What do you want to drink?" Richard asked once they were in the room.

"A Remy," Tony said, flopping onto the floral-patterned couch. He leaned forward and pushed at the low pile of magazines on the coffee table. He opened one of them to the theater guide, listing currently running plays with quotes from the major drama critics. He looked resentfully at the two comedies running on Broadway. One by a commercial slob, the other by an overrated feminist, he said to himself, and flipped the magazine closed.

Then he felt disgust at this self-revelation of his bitterly envious feelings.

Richard got off the phone with room service and slowly, thoughtfully started to take off his tie, while glancing at the square slips of phone messages he had been handed at the front desk.

"I haven't worked on a play in almost a year," Tony said. He seemed embarrassed: a sinner confessing.

Richard looked a little startled. "You've been busy on the screenplay."

"I have?" Tony laughed.

"Well, haven't you?"

"Yeah." He frowned. "Yes."

"Excuse me for a moment. I have to return a few of these calls." Richard got on the phone and placed a series of calls to California. Tony marveled at his father's manner while doing business. He sounded relaxed and confident, a pleasant man in his tone, but hard, unyielding in what he said.

"Fuck him if he wants more points," he said to some star actor's agent. "You may assume, at your peril, that we'll do anything to keep a hit series. It isn't so. If you stick to these numbers, it'll be cheaper for us to put a flop in the time slot." Richard spoke these harsh words in a slow, gentle way, looking in Tony's direction with focused, even observing eyes, as if the conversation was only marginally important. There was no tension, no fear of defeat, in his voice. Tony couldn't fit that piece of self-confidence in with the puzzle of his father's cowardly adherence to the blacklist.

"He put people out of work!" Maureen Winters had shrieked at Tony shortly after he had been returned to her upon her release from the sanitarium. He was in cotton pajamas with "New York Yankees" written across his chest, standing in a narrow hallway looking up at his distracted mother, her eyes red, her body fat and sagging. "Your father has no balls!" she shouted at her six-year-old son. "He screams at shadows!" she said moments before Maria, their housekeeper, ran out to carry Tony away. He remembered the swishing rush of Maria's slippers playing accompaniment to Maureen's strange words: "He screams at shadows!"

She was mad, Tony said to himself, watching his handsome, tanned, calm father managing millions as if they were tips. Tony always said his mother was crazy, but in a tone that implied artistic eccentricity, and that's what he had convinced himself it was, he realized now, as the weight of his judgment sank in: she was mad.

But then why did his father give him up? Why did he let a mad-woman take his son three thousand miles away?

Tony let his head fall back on the couch. He closed his eyes, because they had begun to burn with ancient grief. *He doesn't love me. That's why*, Tony said to himself, and squeezed his lids watertight.

Patty had asked aloud, shortly after Tony and Betty left, if anyone wanted to adjourn—she hesitated—to the living area. Only the women, Cathy and Louise, agreed. Rounder, Chico, and David didn't say no, but they stayed put, to continue their discussion of changes that should be made to *Newstime*, becoming so absorbed that more than an hour went by before the men spoke to the women.

Patty didn't mind the segregation, except on principle. In practice, Patty thoroughly enjoyed talking with Louise and Cathy. After she ex-plained the flat-fee payment for romance novels to them, she complained that although writing the first one had taken only a few months, her second had been coming along very slowly, and speed was what made them profitable. She quizzed Cathy in detail on the difference between having a career and staying home with the kids. They compared good shops to buy clothes, matched the assets and liabilities of male and female single friends of theirs to see if they could create a good couple, and so on, in a relaxed rambling discussion of life, love, birth, housing, and favorite TV shows.

Occasionally Patty would eavesdrop on the boys (Patty thought of men and women as boys and girls, except when she felt anger or disap-proval), and felt sorry for them that they could only discuss their jobs. She had grown used to the fact that David was obsessed with his work; she had decided that the explanation lay with his ambitious, self-critical, and demanding character. Tonight she wondered if it were a matter of gender—or at least gender training. Men are so alone, she thought to herself. To care only about one's career implied an absence of friendship to her; it meant one's companions were other people at work; bosses, rivals, or subordinates; relationships that were always fraught with ten-sion, and in danger of collapse or disintegration. She, for example, had had several close friends at Goodson Books—Marion, Fred's wife, was one—but the intimacy didn't really survive her departure. Once Patty's daily presence as a player in the office game was over, although the good fellowship of being teammates remained, the loss of common strategies, alliances, and goals made conversation either baffling or boring.

"Are you and David thinking of marriage?" Louise asked, completely within the spirit of intimacy that had evolved in their talk.

Patty stiffened. She felt invaded by the question and caught herself feeling it was rude. Her reaction was unfair, considering how she had pressed Louise and Cathy about similar decisions in their futures. Confused, Patty sat up and laughed to cover her embarrassment and irritation. "Jeez," she said, brushing a few stray hairs away from her high cheeks. "Who knows?" she added to the ceiling, as if flying off into the heavens was equally as likely or desirable.

"Do you want to?" Cathy said casually.

Patty laughed and felt herself blush. What the hell is wrong with me? she asked herself. Do I care about this? She cleared her throat, tried to look solemn, and said, "No comment." The whole effect was hilariously out of character. Louise and Cathy laughed good-naturedly.

"I'll tell my husband to issue a memo to all senior editors that Mrs. Thorn likes her senior men to be married," Cathy joked, and they all burst out laughing at this notion, this image of themselves as girls from the fifties, scheming together to bag a man.

"Hey, hey," Chico said from the table. "No fair. You're not supposed to be having more fun than us."

"Have you solved all the magazine's problems yet?" Patty asked to divert any investigation of what they had been laughing about.

"Couldn't possibly do that in a night," Rounder said, beaming like a politician at a fund-raiser. "We'd better go," he said to his wife.

Chico hurriedly seconded the notion, with a note of tension in his voice, as if staying out later than the boss was inappropriate. At the elevator door Cathy said to Patty, "Come up and have lunch with me next week. I'd like you to see the kids."

"Love to," Patty said with excessive enthusiasm.

"Don't let Cathy give her any ideas," Rounder said to David. There was polite laughter.

For an answer, Patty swung the heavy industrial doors closed on them all—David had to operate the cables—and she could hear their delighted amusement as the lights of the descending elevator cage flashed through the crack at her feet. "Doofus," she said quietly about Rounder, and reached behind her to unbutton her dress. She was tired of its heavy presence on her body. She felt hot and itchy, as physically constricted by it as she had felt constrained by the evening's formality.

She was in her bra and underpants, sprawled on the couch, when David returned. He opened his eyes at the sight, and then squinted so hard his eyes were reduced to slits. "Are you naked?" he asked, approaching.

Patty laughed. "You're so blind," she said, noting for the dozenth time how different David looked without his glasses. His eyebrows seemed thicker, his nose bigger, his eyes duller and smaller.

He sat next to her and peered at her belly. A red line circled her stomach an inch or so above her navel, created by the elastic of her stockings. He touched it gently and then bent over, saying, "What's that?"

Patty laughed uncontrollably.

"Oh," he said when his eyes were almost touching her body.

She pushed him away. "Stop studying me," she said haltingly through her laughs.

David leaned back and stared toward the dining table. He looked solemn and distracted. "God, what a mess," he said.

"What?" Patty said. "I thought it went very well."

"No," David said, and set his unfocused, squinting eyes on her. "I mean, all the cleaning that has to be done."

"Yeah, you'd better get to it."

He blinked at her. "Okay." He brought a hand up and rubbed his eyes. "Don't worry. I'll do it."

"I have to get a job," Patty said, looking thoughtfully at her slim body, wondering if it was staying slim enough. She had put back some of her weight since moving in with David, relieving her anxiety that she had become an anorexic. But now yesterday's hope had become tomorrow's worry. She patted her stomach, which was flat and firm, as though it were a beer belly. "I'm too fat and lazy," she added.

"You have a job. If you'd only finish it."

"That's not a job," she answered contemptuously.

"You wrote the first book in a few months. If you concentrated, you'd be finished with this one in a month."

"I know," she admitted. "I told you. I'm a lazy slob."

"Talking that way only stops you from working."

"I need a job. I need to have to be somewhere at nine in the morning. I can't be self-motivating."

"You were."

"But I fell apart, didn't I?"

"Stop trying to make me say what you want me to say," David snapped. " 'Cause then you turn it around and act like it came from me instead of from your cross-examination." David got up in the middle of this outburst and moved to the table, beginning to stack the dessert plates, plopping them onto each other, the clattering implying anger.

"Why are you angry at me?" Patty asked, her eyes wide with innocence as they peered over the back of the couch.

"I'm not," he snapped.

She stared at him while he carried his load of dishes into the kitchen, and continued when he reappeared to gather coffee cups. He noticed her when he turned to head again for the kitchen.

"What?" he said.

"How much money do I owe you?"

"You don't owe me anything."

"I want you to figure out how much I owe you for the rent and everything else."

"Why?" he said with a sneering smile. "Are you moving out?"

"No. I want to pay you back when I start earning money again."

"Well, you're not earning money now, so why do you have to know now?" David argued.

"I want you to keep track."

"*I* don't care about your earning money. *You* care about it."

"I know!"

David opened his mouth to say more, but her admission puzzled him. He closed it, turned to go, and then abruptly wheeled back. "Then *you* keep track of it." And walked out with a satisfied air, a lawyer closing a case.

Patty didn't believe him. She thought his attitude toward her was dominated by the fact that she wasn't earning her own keep. Within the last few months, David had left to her the doing of more and more housework. He used to make the bed in the mornings, occasionally cook dinner; often he called from the office and asked whether he should buy groceries on the way home. This party, however, had been dumped on her, like she was responsible for the domestic side of his being promoted, as if she were a suburban wife expected to focus on her husband's career, as if . . . as if she were living her mother's life.

Patty sat on the couch listening to David load the dishwasher, contempt for him filling her mind. *I* even had to supply the friends, she thought to herself, marveling at the fact that David didn't know anyone, outside of *Newstime*, who he felt was impressive enough to invite over along with his bosses.

"You know . . ." David called out in a cheerful, eager voice, startling her.

She didn't answer, unwilling to leave her abstract plane of judgments and rest on the ground with the reality of him.

"I really think Chico hates Rounder," David said, emerging from the kitchen. His pants were wet at the thighs from rinsing plates.

Patty could only look at him: she had no voice to answer him.

"I don't mean," David continued eagerly, "just that Chico envies Rounder 'cause he was passed over for being Groucho. I think Chico actually hates the man's guts." David laughed self-consciously, embarrassed by his glee at this observation.

"I don't think so," Patty said coolly. She hadn't thought about it, she merely wanted to disagree because she knew it would bother him. "It's in your head. You want them to hate each other. So you have something to gossip about."

David looked stunned. He stared stupidly at the floor for a moment. "God," he said. "Maybe you're right." He turned and went back to the kitchen.

Patty looked at the spot he had deserted as if it were a hole in the earth expanding rapidly, heading in her direction, ready to swallow her. She got up abruptly and walked to the desk near the front windows, where she wrote. She sat at the metal chair, shivering at the cold on her naked legs, but not wanting to slow down to get a pillow or clothes. She put paper in the typewriter and began to write a scene for her heroine like that night's dinner was for her: a series of small revelations about her fiancé that increased her longing for the dark, brutal stranger—a rescuer from the dull journey that life can so easily become.

CHAPTER

8

Fred made a decision. He had tried to ignore the hostility of the others at the poker game, hoping they would eventually accept him as a player and ultimately begin to socialize with him. Fred had consciously avoided making a social move first, assuming it would meet with rejection. But now, utterly rejected, he was willing to face more.

Tom Lear, the journalist turned screenwriter, had been least unfriendly to him. Possibly because of his habit of disagreeing with everything Sam Wasserman did, or said, or believed, Tom had never been discourteous to Fred. Fred looked up his name in the phone book, pleasantly surprised by the good fortune of its being listed, and dialed.

He got a phone machine.

His irritation at this left him baffled when the beep came. He hung up without speaking. Within moments he knew what his message should have been, but now he worried that if he called back immediately, Tom would know Fred had been the hang-up. He let two hours go by, assuming that the intervening messages after his hang-up would obscure any connection.

"Hello, Tom. This is Fred Tatter. I have two courtside tickets to the Knicks-Celtics playoff game tomorrow night. My fellow Knick fan can't make it. I thought I remembered your saying you love basketball. I need to know by tonight—I don't want the ticket to go to waste. Could you call me?" He rattled off his number casually, in a tone that implied Tom already had it but was being saved the trouble of looking it up. Fred laughed to himself afterward, thinking of the dilemma he had placed Tom in. Lear had gone on and on recently about how much he had loved the glory days of the Knicks and how he looked forward to their being in the playoffs this year. The game Fred had invited him to was scheduled for the night of the poker game.

Fred had done many pieces on the Knick management during their losing seasons, when they were widely criticized in the New York press.

Fred's interviews were soft, easy, and made them look good. He had earned the right to request good seats for any game. It pleased him that he had acquired this weapon in his battle to be liked by the writing boys through his own writing. He phoned the Knick office after calling Tom and arranged for the tickets, and then sat back at his typewriter, resuming work on his novel with renewed vigor, producing effortlessly for the first time in months.

He finished a chapter at five-thirty. Marion would be home soon. Tom Lear, if he had been out to lunch, would have come home by now and gotten his message. He read over the chapter, his mind distracted by waiting for a bell to ring. He thought about having sex with Marion. He'd have to ask, of course. He might get her to agree if he offered to give her a back rub. He tried to remember when he had last gone down on her and brought her to orgasm orally. Well, he told himself defensively, when was the last time she gave me a blow-job? The prospect of negotiating through all these preliminaries drained the desire for the ultimate goal. What he really wanted was for her to arrive, magically strip off her clothes, open her legs, and let him take her on the parquet foyer floor, pulling him to her with enthusiasm, moaning with joy. Fast, fast, fast, without all the garbage, the tentative shy touching. Why couldn't she come home one night and say, "Fuck me," and like it? Why couldn't she slip under him and let his penis invade her throat? Why wouldn't she get on her haunches, without being asked, without being seduced, and beg for it up the ass?

Because she doesn't enjoy sex, he told himself with anger, a saddened, dissipating fury. She doesn't really enjoy anything. Not work, or sex, or me.

Marion arrived shortly after this judgment. She rang the bell and Fred found her slumped against the hallway wall, her leather bag drooping at the end of a hand. She opened her fingers and let it drop. He said, "Hello!" valiantly, trying to discourage her performance of fatigue.

Marion closed her eyes and let her head rest against the wall.

"Come on!" Fred said, irritation erupting through his brief attempt at good cheer. "Wake up."

She opened her eyes and walked into his arms, burying her head in his shoulder and sighing. He was home to her: a safe port whose criticisms and praise were equally familiar, and becalmed of harm or excitement.

This physical request, that he be her protector, secure and comforting, made him feel hopeless. *He* needed help: rescue from the battering storms of his constructions into the dangerous world; not a plea for shelter, a plea he was both unwilling and unable to answer.

She put her arms around him and squeezed, saying, "Mmmm." But it was a sound of childish coziness, not a passionate preliminary. He eased her away, pulling her arms off. She kept her face on him, leaning forward, threatening to topple if he moved away.

"Come on," he said, trying to keep irritated emphasis out of his tone.

Marion abruptly breathed in deeply and straightened, her face impassive, and returned to the doorway to get her bag.

"Rough day?" Fred asked.

"The worst." She walked past him, taking off her trench coat and hanging it up. "Did you buy anything for dinner?"

"No," Fred said. He rapidly calculated that if he hoped to get lucky with her, he'd better compensate for his oversight. "I thought we'd order Chinese," he said casually, pretending to a carefully thought-out plan.

"Not again," she moaned. "Why didn't you buy some steaks? You never think of buying anything. What would you do if I weren't living here?"

Fred guffawed. "Order Chinese," he said, delighted by this witticism.

Marion, to his surprise, smiled. "You'd turn into a humongous dumpling," she said, patting his flabby belly. "I can't eat Chinese again."

Fred beamed. "How about pizza?" And then guffawed at himself.

"What a diet," Marion said, and walked into the kitchen, opening the freezer, only to frown at its contents. "You want hot dogs?" she asked doubtfully.

"Oh yeah. That's much healthier than pizza."

Marion laughed and looked at him affectionately. He walked over, putting his arms around her and kissing her, like he did when they dated in college, his tongue out, pushing into her mouth rudely, anxiously selling his desire to penetrate her. Marion welcomed this embrace without enthusiasm, but with a gentle touch on the back of his neck. He broke off at this response and looked in her eyes. "I love you," he said almost in a tone of apology.

She smiled sweetly.

The phone rang. Marion sagged. "You get it," she said, her eyes looking pained at the sound of the second ring.

"Hello," Fred said cheerfully into the kitchen wall phone.

"Hello, Fred? It's Tom Lear."

"Oh." A jolt went through him; a shock of transition. "Hello."

"I got your message. Listen, thanks for thinking of me. I really appreciate it."

He's going to say no, Fred thought, and he felt the dark troubles of the world stir, a monster growling in the slime.

"It should be a great game," Fred said, hoping to appease the beast, remind it of its self-interest. Could Tom be so disdainful that even to sit next to Fred would spoil a superb basketball game?

"Great? It's the game of the year! Game of the century! At least— it's the best game this week."

Fred laughed, but feebly. Suddenly he was uncertain of defeat. Tom sounded natural, at ease. Maybe he *was* going to accept.

"Anyway," Tom went on, "I do want to go to the game . . ."

Here it comes, Fred thought.

". . . and I would have loved going with you, because you're a real Knick fan, but I already accepted an invite from Sam Billings, the producer of my movie. He's invited me into the studio's box. I could beg off to do something else, but I think he'd be insulted if he spotted me there with you."

"The tickets I have are courtside," Fred pleaded. "Do you know where the private boxes are? They're way up top. In fact, they're built above the cheap seats."

"Oh, I've been in the box before. You're right, they're terrible seats. Only good thing about it is the private bar. Most people end up watching the game on the TV in the box. Most ridiculous thing in the world. Go to Madison Square Garden to watch the Knicks on television."

"I don't think your producer would spot us."

"Oh, if your tickets are courtside, the way I jump up and down, they're sure to notice." Tom laughed at himself. Fred did not. Tom cut himself off at the lack of response. "No, I'm kidding. I know he probably wouldn't. But if, by some chance, he did, it would be very embarrassing. Anyway, I was going to suggest that you come up to the box at halftime and have a drink. Meet whoever's there. Maybe a starlet or two." Tom laughed. "I assume you won't bring the wife."

Who *am* I going to bring? Fred wondered. Especially if he planned on visiting the box. He could hardly invite his old childhood friend Pete. Pete still used words like "farout" and "heavy." "Um, I don't think she wants to," he said, not loudly. Marion was standing nearby, laying out hot dogs on a frying pan. Marion might want to go but Fred wasn't sure he wanted her to come along. Not because he had any illusions about picking up starlets; he had an uneasy sense he didn't want her on his arm in a private box at Madison Square Garden. It was a peculiar feeling. Marion, after all, was bright and well-spoken.

"Well, whomever you bring, come up at halftime. It's Box Nine. All right? I have to rush out to meet someone for a drink. Thanks again for the offer. I'll be courtside in spirit."

"You're welcome."

"See you at the game." He rang off.

Fred hung up slowly. Marion opened a can of baked beans, pulling back the metal lid with a scraping noise. "Who was that?"

"Tom Lear."

"About the poker game?"

"No. He was inviting me to join him at one of the private boxes at the Garden."

"Really?" Marion looked surprised. And pleased.

"Yeah. What's so amazing about that?"

"I didn't know you were friends."

"Oh. Well, I guess I'm the only person at the game who's a basketball fan."

"So what did you say? Are we going to go?"

Fred stared at her. "Uh . . ."

Marion's eyes narrowed. "You didn't ask if I could come," she said, making an accusation, not asking.

"No, it isn't that." Fred felt stupid. He had let her think Tom had instigated this, and judging from her reaction, he would be teased if she found out the reverse was true. Now he had a particular reason for not wanting her to come. If she stayed home, he could keep her false impression intact.

"Oh, there isn't room!" Marion said, pleased, a student guessing right on a difficult quiz. "He's taking you."

"Right," Fred said. "Do you mind? I can call him back and cancel."

"No, of course not. You always get to go to the good things. I'll just stay home alone. Again." This sort of teasing was unlike Marion. Her mood had unaccountably changed since her outburst over his lack of attention to domestic details.

"Since when do you want to go to a basketball game? I can always get us tickets, you know."

"I'm kidding. I wanted to see what one of those boxes is like. And I'd like to meet Tom Lear."

"You would?" This, too, surprised Fred. Marion made fun of other people for wanting to meet the well-known. She called Tony Winter a "star-fucker" with the contemptuousness of someone who wouldn't look up from the newspaper to glance at Greta Garbo dancing with Howard Hughes.

"He's a good writer. I loved his book."

Fred fell silent at this. He watched her heat the beans and turn the franks, thinking that he should say something, lest she decide he was made jealous by her praise of another writer. He wasn't. He also admired Tom Lear. His quiet came from feeling how distant he was from being spoken of that way. He thought of his half-finished manuscript, of his uncertainty whether it had any merit, or how he had not only been made to feel unwelcome at the poker game, but had actually been barred. Tom Lear was about his age, didn't seem to know more, or to speak better—there seemed so little difference between them. And yet Fred felt that if Tom had been born a king in the eighteenth century and he a peasant, there couldn't have been a greater gulf between them.

After dinner, Marion said she had some editing to do, and he returned to his study to write more. He was still at his desk when she took a bath. He was rewriting the opening paragraph for the twentieth time when she came in her nightgown to kiss him good night.

He rubbed her belly through the soft material and felt hard immediately. He kissed her, his tongue pushing in and out anxiously, while he roughly sneaked a hand inside her neckline and reached for a breast. She pulled away, giggling at the feel of his cold fingers. "I have to go to sleep," she said, smiling to soften the rejection.

"Okay," he said, and his eyes went to the pages in front of him.

"Don't go to bed too late," she said.

"Okay," he answered, already hypnotized by his words, prepared to sit up through the lonely hours of the night, until, exhausted by the fever of his ambition, he could slide beside his wife and listen enviously to the tranquil breathing of her sleep.

David noticed an ambition had been realized without a clear moment for its recognition. He was a senior editor. Syms had moved along with his old boss to another magazine, and four weeks ago David's temporary position senior-editing Business had been made permanent. His dinner was conceived as a kind of celebration, a social confirmation of his elevated work status, but it had felt to him more like the opening gong of a new fight. Somehow, because of his eyeglasses breaking, an illusion of danger had been created in his mind. Until his joke broke the sense that he was an object of analysis by the others, a figure of affectionate amusement, like a three-year-old running in the buff through a group of loving but condescending relatives, David had the feeling that he had won nothing through his promotion.

Indeed, was he any less a prisoner of the magazine as a senior editor than he had been as a writer? The Marx Brothers now directly vetoed his story ideas instead of doing so through a proxy. True, he could now argue his own case rather than rely on the persuasiveness of someone else, but the dull logic of national newsmagazine writing always triumphed. If interest rates fell below ten percent, could he choose to ignore it in favor of a possibly more significant but less visible phenomenon such as the world-debt crisis? No, he would have to wait until Argentina or Mexico actually defaulted before ordering a piece on its significance. He could, and had, succeeded in getting a sidebar (a two-column box in a different color and bordered by a black rule) explaining that the Federal Reserve might have loosened because of the debt fears, leading to lower rates—flatly contradicting the cover story, which gave credit for the lower rates to the economic recovery. But his predecessor would have fought and gotten just such a story. Such frustrations were constant. He knew, for example, that a shakeout in the computer industry was coming—all business insiders knew it—and he wanted to do the story *now*, not in three months when the *Weekly*, *Business Week*, and everybody else would be doing it because the rash of bankruptcies had begun.

But isn't my complaint foolish? he asked himself. Here I am, a journalist, bitching that I'm a prisoner of events. The illusion of being an essayist, created by the circumstance of working at a weekly news organization whose appeal had to be one of summarizing, analyzing, and predicting the effect of events, since it couldn't compete with the immediacy of newspapers, much less television's blood-spattering "live" coverage, was just that—an illusion which made the editors of *Newstime* delusional; persuaded them that not only should they reach for a deeper understanding of American life than the rest of journalism, but that they actually possessed profound insights. Indeed, David himself could make the argument that his desire to jump the event of the computer shakeout was nothing more than publishing an insider consensus, which could, like so many others, turn out to be wrong: "experts" predicting the obvious because of its safe logic, making error easy to defend.

But is there any genius in editing by noticing what was on the front pages of every newspaper, and the lead item on the network news, and then ordering a story on the same subject? Was this a talent to be eulogized at the end of a long life? At three o'clock in the morning, staring sleepless into the impenetrable mist of eternity, could this role in life sustain him?

Patty, looking frail and cold, hunched over her typewriter, doesn't ask herself such questions, David told himself. Why do I? I make sixty thousand dollars a year, can hire and fire men almost twice my age, and, if things go well, can look forward to promotions that will lead to the top of my profession. Would he trade places with her, writing a trivial and silly entertainment for frustrated housewives? Did he want Tony Winters' life, writing a tap dance for pretty Midwesterners who had caught the public's fancy with their epoxy teeth and surgically perfect breasts? All work is contemptible if judged by my standards, David decided.

Patty's legs are short, he noticed. Thin and smooth now, but her thighs had potential for stockiness, he thought. With age, motherhood, the inevitable gaining of weight, youth sagging under the burden of time passing, they might someday be thick: the hearty legs of a Waspy, leather-skinned worshiper of a good time. Wasn't that her real nature? he challenged himself.

She liked to play tennis, lie on the beach, chat with girlfriends over lunch—what separated her from a woman of her mother's generation and class was a taste for modern clothes, dance, and sexual openness. And the willingness to marry a Jew. *Perhaps*, he cautioned himself. How did he know she'd marry him? He assumed it, of course, but was that based on anything besides egotism and a sexist assumption that all women want the legal commitment? He believed her crankiness about money was a passive request for a proposal. If they were married, his supporting her wouldn't make her uncomfortable, he reasoned. She wouldn't feel she owed him anything then, especially if she were the mother of his children.

Three months ago he would have married her gladly. She had brightened his gloomy, windowless existence, taking down the dusty curtains and opening the shutters, ventilating the smoky air of his recirculated ambitions and lighting the small lonely darkness of his obsession with *Newstime*. He felt free during the early months of their relationship. The nervous energy of sex had been drained and left him cheerful, his mind relaxed, taking all things, from washing dishes to reading and re-reading the blues, as though they were equal pleasures. Instead of worrying whether his senior editorship would become permanent, he worked at his new duties with interest and full concentration, too content with life to fuss over whether it was secure or sufficient. He handled the writers who were now under him, men who used to be his peers, many of them older (who no doubt believed they should be in his spot), effort-lessly, sure of his command. He wielded the sword of power so gracefully and gently that no one heard it cut the air or noticed its blade. He found himself complimenting and encouraging the writers, flattering them into making changes eagerly, not because he had figured this as a strategy, but because he felt generous. To them, to himself, to the city, to life— he wished everything well, wanting nothing to dispel the beautiful sur-face of his contented life. Patty, with her big eyes always there to listen as if he were a magic bird carrying jewels in his beak instead of tired office politics; with her full lips, always slightly apart, wet, as though he were a delicious candy she wanted to have melting inside her; Patty lying beside him every night with her slight slim body outfitted with the big warm breasts of a voluptuous seductress. Had he been threatened for an instant with losing her, he would have torn his clothes like a grieving peasant and raved at God for his injustice.

But now he was a stranger to that love, so far from those feelings that he would have denied he had ever had them. Patty's attentiveness began to cloy. He began to suspect her of not paying attention to what he said, despite her glistening awed eyes. He noticed she asked the same questions about his colleagues no matter how many times he had already given a definitive answer. Once he caught himself in the middle of telling her a long story about Chico that he distinctly remembered having al-ready reported. But she had leaned forward eagerly throughout, exclaim-ing at the appropriate moments, as though it were all new. He stopped himself and accused her. She flatly denied having heard the anecdote before, but from her flustered manner he knew she was lying. When he insisted, she revealed what he now believed was her real feeling about him: "All your *Newstime* stories sound the same. You can't blame me for not knowing the difference." Of course that was said in anger. She apologized later and took it back. "I love your office politics," she said in bed, opening her warm mouth and taking his mouth hungrily, as though to suck his soul out. He let her and fucked her with his usual passion, but lying awake later while she curled her legs around him and fell asleep, he decided the apology was the lie. And though the taste of her was still on his tongue, and his penis lay wet with her moisture, she had become a stranger.

The unity dissolved. He carried loneliness to work again, the job no longer a matter of killing time until he could be with Patty, but a chance to relax: not to have to watch everything he said, and judge her reaction, waiting for more hints of secretly held contempt.

Within a few weeks, every speech, every response, had become suspect. He believed her adulterous—not with another man, but with a low opinion of him. That was the lover he tried to catch red-handed, seducing her. He had had many successes at this morbid detective work. Tonight had been notable. From her joking that she had agreed to live with David because of the terrible apartment shortage in New York to her thrilled laughter at his myopic placement of the coffee cup into the cake.

Everyone had laughed when she claimed she had moved in with him because finding an apartment at a reasonable rent was impossible, as though to admit behavior so crudely opportunistic proved it was untrue. But was it? David believed Patty was unconscious of her base motives, unable to see herself clearly, but the truth slipped out past the sentries of self-esteem and tact, under the disguise of her humor. The reason she could make life sound so amusing was this half-aware truth-telling: a cheerful cynic, absolving sins even as she confessed them. If he walked over now and accused her of getting involved with him so quickly because it was convenient, she would have been stunned, outraged he could think so little of her. If he cited her own comments, she would have contemptuously told him she had been kidding. Her humorous confessions made the blade of truth retractable. She came wielding a knife, but it landed softly, a stage prop providing only a split second of real fright, releasing its audience from terror at its penetration, to childlike joy at the wonder of inventive fakery. Look at that, she left everyone saying, he isn't dead, he isn't even wounded.

David squinted contemptuously in her direction. Her spine rippled as she hunched over the typewriter. Her long hair curved away from her neck, disappearing to fall on the other side of her shoulder. He could imagine it covering her thick nipple and warm breast. He knew, though he couldn't see in his blinded state, there were very blond, almost invisible hairs at the base of her long neck right above the first rung of her vertebrae. He had often fallen asleep with his lips almost caressing them, his exhausted penis nestled in the firm silk of her ass. . . . Yes, she *is* a killer—but the gun is loaded with blanks.

David stood up, his headache pounding with the movement, and walked toward her. She typed without pause, more like a secretary copying an already written document than a novelist struggling to create. He fought off his surprise at the ease with which she invented by reminding himself it was only a stupid romance book. When he was within a few feet she stopped and looked at him. She had a blank look on her face, as though they were strangers in a public place: David someone she had noticed on the subway while she glanced up to see if this were her stop.

He put his hand on the back of her head, his fingers gripping her hair possessively. He turned her away from the typewriter toward him and pulled her up slightly to meet his lips. She was pliant, willing to be uncomfortably posed, partially off the chair, her neck back, her head paralyzed in his grasp, while his mouth and tongue fired away at her stationary full lips. She left her lips slightly open and only reacted when his tongue invaded, her teeth closing against the departure as he pulled away. David stopped to look at her, a puppet held aloft by his hand, her eyes closed, her mouth open, a fish mouthing at the water for food. She held her balance with the balls of her feet, so her belly was arched, her tight stomach flexed, her hip bones jutting out enough to open a view down her panties, her breasts thrust forward, her nipples making hard points in the soft translucent material of her bra.

With his free hand he reached inside her bra and found one erect nipple and squeezed. She moaned slightly and her hips moved from side to side as though she were a lonely dancer pretending she had a partner. He let go and roughly pulled his hand out, the bra pulling off crookedly so it covered only the top of her breast. He ran the flat of his palm over her rippling stomach down to her bony pelvis and grabbed her cunt hard. His finger penetrated like a swimmer diving; there was no resistance to his invasion, only watery absorption.

She swiveled on his hand, her body twisting and rocking, her head cradled in his hand. She was like an obscene doll designed for decadent children. She's a whore, he thought with a dark, harsh inner voice whose tone was alien. And she was so wet, so totally enthralled by sexual feeling: her eyes closed, her lips sighing to be kissed, her body bucking with desire. He could feel nothing but contempt for this abandon, it made her worse somehow that she could enjoy sex with him if she didn't love him. And he knew she didn't love him. The jokes were the truth, the protests of love were the jokes.

He pulled his hand out. She quivered sadly at its departure and her behind rested once again on the chair. There was a moment in which he stood there, over her, doing nothing. Her head was down, looking like a penitent awaiting a blessing. Slowly—he thought reluctantly—she reached up to his groin and rubbed his erection through the material. He didn't move or look down: he stared off impassively, waiting to see if she would do his bidding without even a hint. There was a moment of uncertainty, when she shifted on the chair, drawing one of her legs up under her. But then her small hands came up to his belt and began to strip him.

Silently, motionless, he stood there while she exposed his penis and took it in her mouth, her head rocking steadily below him, the warm funnel sliding with dull regularity, as though she were a sleepy farmgirl milking a cow. He could almost see her dull sense of duty as she serviced him. Flashing into his brain while he put his hands on her head and urged her to take more and more of him each time; answering his question while he felt himself emptied into her mouth: She can enjoy it when I make love to her because she pretends it's someone else. When she makes love to me, it's her job, her rent check.

She kept his shrinking penis inside and sucked and licked slowly, a pro finishing with meticulous care. He patted her on the head and walked away. Silent. Ignoring the obvious civility of doing something for her. He waited for a protest, for a demand that would disprove his theory. He sat on the couch and picked up that week's *Newstime*. After a few long moments of quiet anticipation, while he stared at the magazine typeface, the black letters dissolving into meaningless zigzags, he heard her typewriter begin again. You really earned it tonight, Patty, he said to himself, and tried to laugh bitterly. Wisely.

Instead, he felt tired. And the dull throb of his headache returned.

Tony Winters stood at the bathroom mirror studying his just-shaved face. It had the puffed whitish look of a baby's. His hair was lustrous from the shampoo. He looked good: young, open, his eyes shining with optimism. He felt almost as if he were seeing a photograph of himself as a college freshman; smooth-faced, eager, beaming cheerfully at the hostile world, confident it would welcome and praise him.

He walked out, the heels of his new shoes sounding a dramatic approach, into the kitchen. Betty was there, dressed for work, reading the *Times*. He noticed a headline slug at the top of Section C: "BUNTING, NEW PLAY AT CIRCLE REP OPENS," and decided he wasn't up to reading either a rave (depressing—it could have been me) or a pan (infuriating —why are they putting that on instead of reviving my plays?). Betty was reading the *Hers* column. He laughed at that. She glanced up casually and then steadied her gaze. "You look so handsome," she said.

"Thank you, darling," he said casually, but he was pleased she had confirmed his bout of self-admiration at the mirror.

"Why are you so dressed up?"

Tony walked to the stove so he wouldn't be looking at her when he answered. "Got a lunch date with Bill Hadley."

"Who's Bill Hadley?"

"My roommate freshman year." He poured himself coffee. "I feel like I'm in college today."

"You *do*," she said, smiling delightedly. "Your short haircut makes you look like a boy." She put out her hand as he neared the table, and her arm went around his waist. He bent over and met her lips. When he pulled away after a quick peck, she insisted, and brought him back for a longer kiss.

I should have stayed in bed until she left, he thought, waiting for her to release him.

When she did, he took Section A from her and looked at the stories, reading paragraphs senselessly, waiting, waiting, waiting . . .

"Don't you have to be at work?" he asked, unable to restrain himself.

Betty glanced at their designer wall clock with its minimalist lines instead of numbers. "Oh my God," she said. "I'm late."

She hurried out of the apartment. Tony listened for the sound of the elevator doors opening to swallow her and to remove any chance she might overhear. When he had, he picked up the phone and dialed:

"Sherry Netherland. Good morning."

"Lois Picker, please."

"Thank you."

He had been up most of the night, sleeping lightly, waiting to make this contact, but now, hearing the phone wire click as he was switched from electronic point to electronic point en route to Lois' room, he felt dread.

"Hello." Her voice was alert. She had flown in last night, arriving at ten or so. She should have had trouble falling asleep. He had pictured her still in bed, the heavy curtains drawn. Instead, he thought, she must be fully dressed, a breakfast finished on a nearby table, a flat folded newspaper now crumpled and disassembled.

"Hi."

"Hi," she said, the hard businesslike tone softening.

"Should I come up?"

"Sure."

"Okay. I'll get a cab." He hung up, his stomach rumbling. Suddenly he was falling apart—no longer eager, thrilled to have a clandestine life, his body keenly anticipating passionate lovemaking. His legs felt weak, disconnected from his torso, out of step with each other. There was tremulouness in his belly. In the taxi, when it jolted over potholes, he felt as if his intestines were a badly sewn pocket, its seams crumbling.

He got out on Madison, hoping that the one-block walk to Fifth would settle his nerves. Spring must have arrived, Tony decided, because of Central Park. Its pretense of natural beauty in the heart of New York seemed a perfect companion to his own hypocrisy. The trees were like large decorator plants rising out of an enormous stone pot set in the city's waiting room, a false gesture made by nature to prettify an arrogant manmade world. His adultery seemed just as self-conscious and showy. Betty had done nothing to deserve this: it was an act of narcissism, not desperate love. He could easily live without Lois' admiration. He would still be a self-sufficient city if he avoided elaborately landscaping his emotional life with a pastoral scene of romance.

The nervous guilt wore off while he walked aimlessly looking at the park, replaced by a petulant anger, an aggrieved feeling that he was oppressed by antique notions. To be faithful, to be honest, to sustain intimacy with only one person; they are dull bourgeois values, he lectured himself. The image of himself as a virtuous married man, living out a lifespan of sexual monogamy, was appalling, as though he were being forced to decorate his apartment with flocked velvet wallpaper and kelly-green shag rugs. He caught a glimpse of himself wearing a light-weight Burberry raincoat—tall, slim, a pleasant, wise smile—and asked the world: Would anyone really believe I could be faithful? Even if I maintained my vows, the world would think otherwise.

When he finally strode into the Sherry Netherland, it was with the self-righteous air of an injured party collecting his court-awarded compensation. Goddamm it, his bearing seemed to say, I deserve this!

In the lobby, when the deskman told him to ring up Lois' room, it occurred to him that someone who knew him might walk by and stop to ask whom he was seeing in a hotel at ten-fifteen in the morning. After all, this wasn't some out-of-the way motel. Show-biz meetings were held here, in the rooms of visiting producers, studio executives, and the like.

"Hi, it's me. What's your room?" he blurted at the sound of Lois' voice.

"Twenty-one forty-two," she answered in a startled tone.

He dashed across the narrow lobby to the elevator banks and told the uniformed boy the floor number, praying the doors would close quickly before anyone else had a chance to enter. Even in the relative security of the twenty-first floor's hallway, Tony moved quickly, glancing at the brass-plated oval room numbers in search of Lois. He found her waiting, the door open, at the end of the hall. He trotted to her, sweeping her in his arms and kicking the door closed behind him, his fearful actions making a good imitation of passionate desperation.

She hugged him hard, as if to say, "I'm here, darling, you have me," to his wild run of longing. His misunderstood performance now began to work its magic on him. He buried his head in her shoulder and nuzzled like a devoted pet greeting a long-lost master. Clasped in her thin, muscled arms, pressed against her tense bony body, he felt welcomed. At home. Celebrated. Cheered. She loves me, he thought, swelling with pride, and loving her back not out of mere politeness but out of gratitude.

There was desperation in their lovemaking. Impatient, they didn't even strip before coupling. Both her jeans and his pants were around their ankles, her blouse was unbuttoned and open but still on her arms, and though her breasts were exposed, the empty bra was on her, lewdly covering ribs and stomach.

He entered her with almost no preliminaries. She urged him to, unzipping his pants and pulling desperately at them in an awkward attempt to lower them. When he did, she took hold of his penis and guided it into an already warm welcome and then put her long fingers on each buttock and pulled him toward her, her back arching, her eyes closing, with a quiet moan of relief and satisfaction.

Tony withdrew a little and then pushed hard, not stopping when he was fully inside and felt her hard pelvic bone press on his, but shoving angrily against the impasse. Lois opened her eyes, like someone coming blissfully to consciousness in heaven, free at last from the world's cares and evils, to look in his eyes. "I missed you," she said. It was the first words they exchanged.

A part of his mind, yearning to answer her truthfully, searched for a summary to the complicated feelings he had about coming here to this physical consummation of the emotional adultery begun in LA ten months before. He had fantasized this illicit sex so vividly for so long that to leave it unfulfilled at the altar of his dreams, unwed to reality, had seemed cowardly and stingy. In LA she had seemed fascinated by him; he wanted more of her intense interest. He wanted that distillation of what an audience provides en masse: uncritical silence and admiration for the playwright's soul, ideas, and feelings. He had become fond, through months of phone calls and letters, of her outer hardness, so different from Betty's genteel manners; and Lois' inner yielding to him was just as different from Betty's secret aloofness. Lois transformed him into a new person, less cocky and sure of himself about the world, but utterly in command of the emotional war. She had broken her sword and surrendered to him in a way Betty never would or could.

Betty would die fighting to maintain her dignity, a pretense of negotiated equality: Do you love me? Then I love you. Will you help me? Then I will help you. And so on, in the dull negotiations respectable people conduct, believing that emotions can run on schedules, picking up anger here and depositing understanding there, arriving at a terminus of happy unity. For Tony, the train never seemed to go anywhere. Instead, with Betty he often felt alone, a lawyer seated across an oak table from another skilled logician, nitpicking over contractual details. I want to have a baby. I'm not ready. Let's not go to their party. I want to. They don't like me. Yes, they do—you don't like them. That's right, I don't like them and neither do you. I can't think of an idea for a new play. You will, sweetie. How do you know? You always do—I need a book for the spring list. Why don't you publish my collected plays? Ha, ha.

"I missed you," Tony answered Lois in a whisper and resumed his movements in and out, avoiding her eyes, because they looked at him with sad longing, as though their image of eventual separation loomed behind his loving body, so that each movement seemed to contain both comfort and sorrow. She pushed him in harder and harder each time, impressing him on her, as though she could stamp herself with his devotion permanently. Soon she sighed and groaned with satisfaction, her chest heaving, her feet trying to untangle themselves from her pants so she could wrap her legs around him for the final moments of orgasm.

He was amazed at her easy climax. With it, he felt abstracted. His penis felt at home, comfortable with its occupation of her. This was unusual. Normally he felt the pleasures of the vagina too awesome to control; a little boy, he lost control and peed his passion away too soon. He would repeat the act a little while after ejaculation, less out of desire to prove virility (he told himself) than a wish to screw calmly. But seconds always felt like second best. There was a loss of intensity. Now, with Lois satisfied and concentrating on him, her hands playing up and down his backside, her hips working, even the walls of her cunt contracting and loosening, her mouth teasing his neck, his mouth, soothing his eyes, there was both: the miraculous joy of surrounding warmth, an unbearable overload of pleasure, but also the calm sense of ease, unhurried passion, controlled, building, pulling him out, out of himself, widening from his groin, vibrating through his legs, washing up his belly, breaking down his observing mind, blinding his sight . . .

He slept. For an instant the narrator was silenced and he floated unconscious in her. Someone sang. No! Moaned. It's me! It's me! Oh God! I love, I love, I . . .

He absolutely lost control: he bucked against her like a wild stallion, making sounds of joy and triumph to the hotel walls, an animal seeding its mate with blind, agonized joy.

When he fell against her again, utterly drained, and noticed the sweat, the color of the carpet, he felt himself again. He understood he was in the Sherry Netherland, lying on the floor of a room with his pants cuffing his ankles. He could picture what the sight would look like to an audience: an automatic laugh, the sight gag to be revealed to a cuckolded husband or a shrewish wife; or the automatic reveal in a drama, the scales falling from the eyes of betrayed husband, or the ultimate humiliation of a neglected wife. He felt stupid. Small. An easily dismissed category of human. The arrogant, self-serving bourgeois artist, without scruples or shame. He felt shame at his lack of it; he felt belittled by his own condescension to himself. Appalled that he felt appalled. Guilty that he was guilty. And, finally, remembering how completely he had lost himself, howling like an animal while his prick jerked its liquid into her, as though she were merely a vessel, he felt embarrassed.

He glanced at her shyly. Lois was smirking proudly. There was love in her eyes, but there was also pride, the look of someone who had secret knowledge. The confident look of a person in power.

Tony laughed. "I guess I enjoyed that."

"It was great," she said, her proud smile widening even more.

He realized she thought of it as her achievement, a tribute he had paid to her. He had been shamed by the revelation that he loved sex so much, that it could so overpower him. He didn't think of it as having much to do with Lois.

"Do you always come so loudly?" she asked playfully.

Tony wondered at this strange moment. There was almost nothing in his memory (at least at that moment) of life with Betty that could compare to the nakedness of this. Lois was asking if she possessed him, owned a greater percentage than his wife's holdings. He had spent only a few days with Lois, and this was his first sexual experience with her, and yet she could ask him that. And he felt perfectly at ease answering: "No."

The seriousness of tone wiped Lois' smile away, replaced with a look of openness and interest.

"You don't come like that with Betty?"

"No," he said again in a sonorous tone, like a Shakespearean ghost.

"Ever?" she asked.

"No," he said.

Lois hugged him and whispered in his ear with undisguised greed: "Good!"

Suddenly Tony felt lost. He had come to the hotel thinking he understood everything about the action. That he could foresee every possible result, understood the boundaries. But now he was lost. Surprised at the outset, and baffled by the future.

Patty cupped his balls in her hand when he pushed her head to take more of him. David was big, far too long for her to comfortably attempt total consumption. She had often goaded herself to try, especially after reading something—was it *How to Please a Man*, or Helen Gurley Brown's book, or a Dear Abby column?—that claimed the gag reflex was responsible for making women think they couldn't do a large one. Patty responded to such challenges. She studied the suggestions for overcoming the gag reflex (gradually taking more and more, relaxing through the initial urges to choke, reminding herself that no harm could result, that ejaculation involved a small amount of liquid, and so on, in a comforting pseudoscientific rosary to buck her up against the dread of being killed by a monstrously huge penis) and had patiently practiced on David, achieving terrific results in terms of pleasing him, but not even coming close to the olympic glory of her lips reaching the base of his organ. Indeed, such a stretch seemed utterly beyond hope—judging from his length, surely it would pop out through the back of her head! So when he pushed at her, as if he too had read those damn books and had decided it was time for her to go for it, she took his balls, fighting against his hand, and lightly tickled the smooth skin behind them, knowing from experience that that often triggered David into climaxing.

And, of course, to her relief, he came instantly; like pressing a water fountain's button, the mechanism worked predictably. How dismaying the human body is, she thought. There was a definite spot (she had pressed David's finger there one night when she became impatient to come) which if rubbed lightly crosswise, alternating with irregular, harder pressure, resulted in an orgasm for her in minutes. That the dark mystery of passion had so dull a solution seemed to impoverish life. Despite her loathing for romance novels, Patty had to admit the impulse that attracted their fans, the desire for seduction and satisfaction to become oblique, shadowy, vaguely frightening, and finally benign, was something she too longed for. Bring back the priests of darkness, shatter the mirrors that teach us what our vaginas look like, let us think that the rare man who accidentally moves so the clitoris is stimulated is special, not someone blessed with dumb luck. She forced herself to drink his puddle of sex and let him shrink in her, licking the drops that were left, because those ridiculous books said these touches were important, making oral sex tender . . . or something. It's true, she had lost her horror of semen. But it hadn't become her favorite malted milk either. She had learned dutifully, and of course the actions had become duties as a result.

Before she had resorted to technique—when David had first silently approached and roughly kissed her, his hand rushing up and down her belly, her breasts, his lips touching hers lightly, then angrily—she had become excited. She sensed he was playing at something, angry at her, or himself, or just frustrated at life. There was so much passion in him, though, while he felt her possessively. His hands played on her like a baker kneading dough, treating her body like a senseless thing whose malleable qualities were merely a means to an end. He didn't even demand surrender; there was no acknowledgment that she had a say in his actions. He touched her as if she were a sexual Ouija board designed to summon ungodly things from another world. It was so appropriate to her writing. She closed her eyes and could see him in riding boots, his cheeks flushed, grabbing her by the waist in a Victorian drawing room and kissing her furiously, his crop pressed against her back, preventing an escape.

The more she stretched against the world, the harder Patty fought for a sense of herself apart from men, the richer her fantasies of being sieged and controlled became. While his index finger rubbed her clitoris —so well! he had learned so precisely how she liked to be touched—she moaned and swiveled to encourage more. He used to kneel at this point and take her panties off (furiously, as though they were made of iron and demanded extreme force to remove), mouthing at her vagina devouringly. In the early months of their relationship, he liked her to come to orgasm with abject totality, as she had that first night, but she had been unable to repeat its intensity. To be sure, the climax would happen, but a part of her stayed back to report the joy, note its individual changes, observe David's technique, and measure the force of the final quake.

She blamed the diminished involvement on him. She tried to pinpoint what he had altered from that first coupling. She decided at last that it was the fact that he had come first. That night, when he turned his attention to her, he had already been serviced. His penis sighed like a weary flag in the wind. She knew that everything he then did was for her. His enthusiasm for her body, knowing he had been drained of the natural excitement for lovemaking which always exists, that he wasn't merely trying to sell her on making love to him, relaxed her utterly: secure in the seduction, trusting his flattering tongue and worshipful lips. She had surrendered that evening to sensation, not to him; given herself up to the power of her body's lust to enjoy itself.

So when David broke off his rough handling and stood there, his erection showing in his pants, she decided to repeat the actions of that first night and satisfy him first, with the hope that his later servicing of her could flatter her subconscious into another glorious orgasm.

And though, when she unzipped him and slowly introduced his penis into her mouth, wetting more and more of him, so she could begin to slide up and down, her tongue flicking teasingly at the head during the brief separations, she had assumed that her action implied a deal (I do this, then you go down on me), still Patty felt no surprise at David simply pulling up his pants and walking off.

She felt irritated, the way one might at a broken promise, at a friend who had agreed to accompany you to a boring event in exchange for your presence elsewhere, and stiffing you when it was his turn. But there was no moral outrage. Possibly because she had chickened out once again at trying to get all of him in her throat; because she had tickled him just under the testicles to provoke a fast ejaculation; because she had done her loving perfunctorily, simply wanting to get to the good part. Whatever the reason, a sense of injustice didn't well up in her. She sat, physically on edge but still numb and weary from the effort of fighting off her slight revulsion at blowing him, and thought: You bastard. You're gonna leave me like this. But there was no passion in it. There was no exclamation point of outrage, or even a question mark of betrayed shock. They were simply words, a knowledge that she had gotten a bad deal, without a sense that she truly deserved better.

A few moments passed, she lost her sense of time and place exploring her hollow anger, and then she found herself reading the last few lines she had written. Her heroine was discovering her fiancé to be dull and yet was repelled by the dark Brian's (the potentially brutal but handsome mystery man) arrogant action of simply kissing her roughly on the veranda when she turned him down for a dance, despite her desire to accept, simply because his tone implied that he took a yes for granted. They're both David, Patty said to herself. They are both sides of him. They're the two sides of every male. Either they bore you to tears or they drive you to tears. That's funny. She wrote the sentence down. It made no sense where it was. Her heroine had just slapped Brian. I can make it what she thinks about hitting him, she decided, and did so. She rolled the typewriter up a little and read over the paragraph. The new line sounded flip after the solemn prose above it. She almost X'ed it out, but when she read it over again, her last line was the only line she liked.

Patty pulled the page out, put in a new sheet, and typed "Men either bore you to tears or they drive you to tears" as a sentence to begin something. A short story? A novel? A serious novel? Alone on the page, separated from her silly heroine with her silly feelings and her even sillier

situation—who goes to formal balls and walks out on verandas anymore?
—the sentence read grumpy; a nasty, unclever bit of whining disguised
as feminism. An image of David kneeling at her feet, his tongue straining
to lick her cunt, flashed into her self-disgust and excited her. She reached
down and pressed her hand against her crotch. She was wet. Still wet
from earlier? Or had that single image turned her on?

I should masturbate right here, she thought, and pleased herself
with the devilish notion. She vividly pictured the scene: David sitting on
the couch, glancing up in her direction, and seeing her, legs spread,
rubbing herself to climax. What would he say? What if her silly heroine
did that on the veranda after rejecting the dark Brian? This demure
creature abruptly exposing herself and fingering away madly while the
formal ball continued.

Damn this book, she said to herself, feeling imprisoned by it. A wave
of loathing for it, for the rules of its genre, for the embarrassment of
doing it, for the betrayal it represented of her sex, shuddered her resolve
to write more. Patty didn't care to identify herself as a feminist, or to get
points from women for saying and believing the obvious, but still, these
romance books really are beneath contempt, she decided. Writing one,
forced to sit with its logic inside her head day and night, staring ahead,
stony-eyed, at the narrow emotional highway her heroine was permitted,
made Patty realize how much a part of the whole scene the stupid book
was. She sits there and *reacts* to these bozos, Patty thought, enjoying her
disgust. The contempt she felt was invigorating. Her brain had left a
stuffy room; she could breathe the clean air of truth. It was almost as if
having to think like that foolish bitch had stuck to her own brain, like
cellophane to a shoe, and for months Patty had been standing idiotically
on a street corner, comically shaking herself to be rid of it, until tonight,
when she thought of the incredibly simple and effective idea that she
could pull the stuff off with her hand.

I'm not gonna write this damn book, she decided.

She forced the dozens of questions that decision provoked out of
her mind and leaned forward (I should put on some clothes, I'm freezing)
and continued typing. She added to her lone sentence, writing away,
without considering what her story was, concentrating instead on the
scene she had imagined, namely an infuriated woman answering her
mate's insensitivity by brazenly masturbating. She was enjoying it, enjoying it the way she would have if she had had the nerve to do it herself.
But as the description played itself out, she approached a fork in the
road. Either her new heroine (reborn out of the ashes of sexist caricature) was fantasizing this behavior or actually doing it. Patty knew the

choice would either infect or nourish the remainder of the work. Making it a fantasy would straighten and smooth the roadway, its destination sure, but perhaps the scenery would become dull and predictable. If her heroine, previously a sensible, reasonable, modestly behaved woman, was *actually*, worn out by years of selfishness by her mate, doing it, taunting him with her own superior ability to satisfy herself . . . But was that true? Patty wasn't most satisfied by bringing herself to climax. A man devoting himself to her body was her real thrill. What she had done for David was what she wanted for herself. That was the truth.

Could she write it?

Wasn't it . . . in bad taste? No, she wasn't worried about that, she was fearful of being hated for it. Men don't want to know those things. And women, the truth is, don't like to face them. Anyway, she reasoned, am I doing it? I have at least as much justification. Did I love myself in front of him? He's still sitting there, stupidly reading *Newstime*, no doubt in an attempt to narrow his horizons even more.

I couldn't do it. Even if I began to, I'd be too embarrassed to enjoy it. Climaxing in front of David—something she had presumably done dozens of times—seemed utterly vulgar if done by herself, especially without . . . without what? Without permission?

Do I need his permission to touch myself?

Jeez, I'm starting to sound like a dyke with hairy armpits. No, that's wrong. It's worse. That sounds like an academic who still does shave.

Sure, I need his permission to touch myself in front of him. How would I like it if he, over breakfast let's say, opened his fly and jerked off into a napkin? Or worse, onto the tablecloth?

She burst out laughing.

"Watch it," David said without looking up. "I don't think those books are supposed to be funny."

His casual, contemptuous reference to the romance genre froze her laugh. For a moment she wondered if she despised the form simply because his attitude had insinuated itself into her. No, no, I knew this was crap, she argued. David was infuriating. I should do it. Right now. Pull my panties down, and, staring into his whitish squinting face, masturbate. Who needs you, Mr. *Newstime*?

David tossed the magazine onto the coffee table. He stretched and then got up, avoiding her glare, and announced quietly to the floor, "I'm going to bed."

Patty didn't answer. She stared ahead, feeling rage, confusion about her work, a vague horniness that wandered through the other feelings like a lonely shopper browsing for the perfect purchase.

She reread her new pages. She loved them. The frank, unstylized prose, its easy access to the heroine's emotions and imagination, the clear simple lines of character. It was real. So beautifully true. No fake adjectives about scenery she had never seen, peopled only by ordinary humans with incomes under six figures, and with a heroine who had been laid and was at least the equal of the men around her. The new words seemed like a friend, an intimate with whom anything could be said, any secret entrusted, someone to stay up all night with.

But what could she do with it? She had no story. She hadn't even decided whether the opening scene was real or imagined. Certainly she couldn't continue it as a portrait of her relationship with David. There was no story in that, and definitely not an interesting one. In fact, was her new character interesting to anyone but her? Who was she?

Maybe she's Rounder's wife? an impish voice asked. Rounder had the virtue of being at the top of *Newstime*, so his obsession with the job would be more reasonable and sympathetic than David's. And Cathy Rounder was a Ph.D. and the mother of two, a much more stunning person than Patty herself. Imagine Cathy rubbing her clitoris in front of the six-foot-five blue-eyed Rounder! Send in the Marines, Cathy could say, and Patty roared at herself, followed by embarrassment at the viciousness and vulgarity of her imagination.

How could she write about a woman with two children? She knew nothing about it. I could have lunch with her, and play with the kids later, observe her daily routine. David wouldn't mind. They might even socialize regularly. It would further his career and provide her with material for the book.

She moved her chair forward, read over her opening, made it a fantasy (the mirror within a mirror of this pleased her: Cathy masturbating to a fantasy of her masturbating), and then set up the character's situation. The exposition seemed awkward, an anticlimax after Cathy's climax, and also halfhearted. The arbitrary choice of Cathy and Rounder —real people—had stunted her ability to make up anything about them, as though she were suddenly writing a nonfiction piece about them for *New York Magazine*.

What if she were?

What if the opening fantasy was a fantasy of a magazine writier while writing a portrait of these prominent New Yorkers? That character could be me, a free-lance journalist, searching for the ideal couple ostensibly through my work, but really to reassure myself that it exists, she said to herself, so tired now that after thinking the thought, Patty was unsure if it even made logical sense, much less worked aesthetically. She decided to stop and read what she had tomorrow.

Patty got up, hiding the pages under the manuscript of the romance novel. The thought of David discovering her experimental story filled her with dread. She looked at him, huddled under the blankets like a frightened animal, and resented his presence.

She was careful not to disturb the blankets while getting in the bed. After a few minutes of lying silently, listening to his breathing to make sure he was asleep, Patty touched herself furtively, secretely, loving herself to a choked and cowardly orgasm, and then bunched a pillow in her arms to fall asleep in its soft embrace. . . .

CHAPTER
9

"Fred!" Tom Lear called. He got up from a swivel chair placed in front of a television that was embedded in the paneling of a private box in Madison Square Garden. "Why doesn't Hubie play Marvin and Cartwright together against Parish and McHale?" This was asked in place of a greeting.

Fred had just been let into the box by a tall handsome man in his sixties, who, instead of challenging Fred's right to enter, asked, "Can you rebound?"

Fred had worried while on his way up that maybe Tom Lear would have forgotten his invitation and decided to wander off during halftime, or that Tom, given that the Knicks had lost the two games prior to this one, might not have come. He was startled by the distinguished man's question and then enormously relieved at seeing Tom. "He can't," Fred answered Tom.

"Why not?" asked the door-opener, not aggressively, but with a quiet undertone of authority that implied he was used to being answered.

"Because," Fred said with the nervous pride of a star pupil, "he has no backup if they get into foul trouble, and Webster can't keep up with McHale on the fast break."

"So?" Tom said, obviously enjoying this esoteric conversation, which now had the attention of everyone in the box. When Fred entered he got an impression of many people broken up into groups of twos and threes: a few on the couch at the rear; a pair by the bar; one lone person still looking out the balcony down to the court below; and others gathered around the television, studying the halftime statistics. "They won't get any fast breaks with those two in," Tom continued, "because McHale will have to keep 'em off the offensive boards."

"Nah," Fred said, shaking his head like a wise old man. "Webster isn't a good offensive rebounder. He's pretty good on the defensive boards, and he's a great shot-blocker, but he won't give 'em fits on the offensive boards. They're too slow to play together for long, and besides, it leaves you thin for the second team."

"Okay," Tom said, sighing.

"Thank God!" someone at the bar said to the room. Then to Fred, "You have no idea how he's been torturing us about this garbage. But nobody here knows enough about basketball to keep him quiet." They all laughed and Tom hung his head, but the group's attitude was friendly, indulgent, and warm toward Tom, like a family toward the favorite baby, pretending they were capable of criticizing him when, in fact, anything he might do delighted their hearts. Fred envied this with the keenness of a starving man watching another eat a feast.

"Who is this savior?" a woman by the television asked about Fred.

Fred noticed, as everybody's eyes moved to study him, that the lone figure at the balcony was Tony Winters. Tony looked at him blankly, as though he didn't know him.

"Fred Tatter," Tom Lear said to the group, and then rattled off their names. It turned out that the distinguished man who had opened the door was Richard Winters, Tony's father. Fred recognized one of the other names, Sam Billings, whom he knew to be the producer of Tom's movie, but the rest were obscure. That made Fred anxious, since he couldn't know who was important and who was not, a circumstance rather like walking through a mine field, in which any innocent twig might have the capacity to blow his career to kingdom come.

"Was Ray Williams really close to his sister or is that just bullshit?" the thin leather-skinned woman who was introduced as Melinda Billings asked. She had the emaciated body and cynical eyes of a woman who spent her life attempting to retain the allure of her youth, knowing all the while it was both hopeless and required. She referred to the Knick guard who had been playing poorly (and therefore earned the active abuse of fans) until that night. Williams had missed the previous playoff game when it was announced he had to attend the funeral of his sister, a forty-year-old victim of cancer. Tonight he returned and had played a brilliant and uncharacteristically mature half. The same fans who had vilified Ray now felt piously supportive and, presented with a good performance, were rapidly alibiing for Ray's earlier play (he had been distracted by the wait for his sister's death), and spinning out a fantasy in which the tragedy would spark a fundamental change in Ray, and he would now forever burn with the intensity of a superstar.

Fred, although he knew as a sportswriter it was an appealing angle, was also convinced that Ray was a hopelessly stupid and undisciplined

basketball player who, in time, would return to his selfish and disorga-
nized play. People don't change, most of all athletes, Fred knew. The
yearning of the Knick fans to believe in a mystical transformation
through personal tragedy was precisely the reason Fred wanted to escape
from sportswriting. Covering the Knicks, Fred would be obliged to go
along with the pretense; fans didn't want the truth, namely that whatever
makes a player weak transcends whether his wife loves him or his father
dies on the night of the big game, or all the other movie clichés. The
young power hitter who can't hit a change-up won't do so simply because
he's fallen in love, the brilliantly talented quarterback who chokes under
pressure and throws fourth-quarter interceptions will go on throwing
them even if his two-year-old son recovers from leukemia, and Ray Williams would continue to turn the ball over, despite his sister's tragic
death, because he was too dumb to keep his concentration up. But all
that has to be concealed from the sports fans. They don't want the
illusion destroyed that the games they watch possess a significant soap-
opera subplot. Why couldn't they appreciate the games as games? Fred
wondered. Why isn't the simple majesty of men able to follow a ninety-
mile-an-hour ball and hit it with a stick of wood enough to astonish and
delight? Even inconsistent Ray, twisting his muscled arms in midair and
lightly flipping a basketball through windmills of flailing arms up against
the backboard and into the basket, was a miracle of nature, an awesome
proof of humanity's ingenuity, a modern preservation of our savage past,
the physical equivalent of our evolution from painting on cave walls to
splashing paint on a canvas. Now we celebrate the warriors who toss
pigskin spears. Who cares if their wives love them, if they need cocaine
to face the modern equivalent of death (failure), or if Ray Williams needs
a sister to die in order to know he shouldn't take jump shots from the top
of the key when Bill Cartwright is loose under the basket? Watch him do
it! Whatever the reason!

"Yeah," Fred answered. "I guess he's dedicating the game to her."

There was a murmur from them at this.

"I think she kind of raised him," Fred said, making it up, but already
busy convincing himself it must be true. "His bad play this year dates
almost exactly from when she was diagnosed." That bit of sentiment
originated with the Knick publicist whom Fred had called to get his
ticket. The Garden organization was taking a truly clever tack: immediately after saying that, the publicist went on, "But Ray doesn't want that
known. He doesn't want people to think he's using his sister's corpse as
an excuse." Who knows, Fred said to himself while the others in the box

gave him their full attention, eyes wide open with the wonderment of children, maybe it's true, maybe her being sick really did bother him. But then what was bugging Ray for the previous six years?

"How come nobody said anything about it while he was fucking up?" Tom asked peevishly.

"Ray kept it from everyone but Hubie and asked him to keep it a secret. He didn't want to use her death as an alibi." Boy, is this bullshit, Fred thought, amazed that he was holding their attention so easily. I'll bet Tom isn't sorry he invited me, he thought proudly. "They're a very close family. You know," he said to the leather-skinned woman, Melinda, wife of the powerful producer, "Ray's brother, Gus, plays for the SuperSonics. They grew up guarding each other. It's great when they play in an NBA game opposite each other. Suddenly you can picture them playing as little kids on a dirty playground on a summer day in New York."

"Yeah, it's fantastic," Tom Lear said. "Straight out of a movie."

"Does sound like a movie," Sam Billings said, and for a moment the room seemed to hold its breath. By Fred's count there were certainly three writers in the room and he suspected one of the men at the bar was also. Fred almost blurted out, "I'll write it."

"Yeah," Tony Winters said. "Think of the dream casting. Richard Pryor and Eddie Murphy."

Someone murmured appreciatively. Fred cursed himself for not having thought of it.

Tony, meanwhile, frowning with concentration, went on: "Richard Pryor and Robert Redford. Eddie Murphy and Clint Eastwood—"

People began to laugh as they understood he was fooling.

"As brothers?" Tom Lear said, spelling out the joke.

"Yeah," Tony went on. "You do a movie in which Redford and Pryor are two poor brothers who grew up in the slums and who end up facing each other in the championship game. Call it *De Naturals*. Don't bother to explain how they're brothers. Just assert it." Tony looked thoughtful while people, with slight embarrassment, laughed sporadically. "Meryl Streep could play their mother. I think it would be a good stretch for her. She could play a Polish mother—"

Now the room was laughing shamelessly, except for Fred, who stared sullenly at Tony. That's disgusting, he said to himself with rage. Making fun of talent that way—it's a cheap shot.

"—she could do a Polish black accent," Tony elaborated. "Now *that* would be interesting!"

Fred wanted to say something cutting, shut off Tony from the group's admiration as thoroughly as he had been. Tony would deserve it —his smug attitude of equality with the people he made fun of infuriated Fred. Tony had no right to such a pose. What play of his had run on Broadway? Everything was so easy for men like Tony. He took his presence in the private box for granted. Probably his father had been bringing him to elite seats his whole life. Someone like Tony Winters had never sat in the mezzanine of anything. And Fred, poor Fred, he had been stuck way up in the back, in life's cheap seats, scraping ancient gum off his shoes and straining for a view of the action.

"Are you a sportswriter?" Richard Winters asked Fred in his low, calm tone while the others were elaborating on Tony's joke.

"Uh, used to be. I'm writing a novel now."

Richard nodded wisely, as though he had expected that answer. "Did you cover basketball?"

Tony called across the room, answering for him: "You probably have read Fred's stuff, Dad. He did a lot of writing for *American Sport* magazine. The interviews?"

Fred was bothered by Tony having overheard (why is he on my case?) and made nervous by his tone. He had called it "Fred's stuff," not even giving it the dignity of an "article."

But Richard Winters snapped his fingers and looked delighted at Fred. "Of course! You did that great interview with Billy Martin. First time I understood both why he was a great manager and also why he's crazy. Everything else I read about him would do one or the other, never both."

"You two know each other?" Tom Lear asked Fred, meaning him and Tony. There was ill-concealed surprise in the question.

"Oh, sure," Tony said. "We're old friends."

Fred now relaxed, decided he had been paranoid. Obviously Tony was trying to be helpful and friendly. He did not notice, nor did the others, that Tony smiled to himself after his assertion of amity with Fred, like a man contemplating an irony.

Below, the buzzer sounded to signal an end to the halftime warm-ups and the teams went to their benches for final instructions before the start of the second half. Fred moved toward the door. "I'd better get back —"

"No, stay!" Tom said, and a few others did also.

"We have plenty of room," Richard Winters added with a note of warmth sufficient to imbue his words with urgency, but not intense enough to suggest even a hint of desire.

The Knicks, although they gave their fans a good scare near the end, won the game, Ray Williams perfectly playing his role of the athlete redeeming personal tragedy through triumphant performance. He won the game with his controlled, determined leadership and showed no vulgar pleasure in his achievement or the fans' delight. He left the court with his head bowed, accepting the congratulating embraces of his team-mates with an unprecedented modesty.

For Fred, also, the evening was a triumph. While they shuffled into the elevator to take them out, Tom turned to him suddenly. "Where's your friend?"

"My friend?"

"Who did you bring to the game?"

Despite the fact that Fred had had hours to prepare a response, he still fumbled over his response: "I gave it away to one of the teenagers outside."

"You didn't sell it?" Tony Winters asked, and again Fred thought that perhaps in his tone there was an insult, a suggestion that Fred was incapable of any act that might be considered generous or good.

Before the game, when Fred arrived in a taxi outside Madison Square Garden, there was a collection of kids desperately asking, "Selling any? Anybody selling?" as there usually is preceding a hot game. Normally there are plenty of ticket scalpers available, but their goods must have gone quickly, because by the time Fred arrived—only five minutes before game time—with his spare ticket, having thought of no one he wanted to accompany him to the box at halftime, the forlorn cries, "Ticket? Anybody got a ticket?" had not been comforted. He spotted a pair of black teenagers and walked up to them, whispering, "I've got one. I can give you one."

"How much, man?" asked one.

"Where is it?" the other said before Fred could answer.

"Courtside," Fred said.

They looked startled. And then wary. "How much you want for it?"

"Nothing. Cost me nothing." He held the ticket out, leaving to them how to resolve which one would get it. One of them grabbed it, saying, "It's my turn. You said it was my turn."

"Fuck," was all the other one could say, listlessly, suggesting that his whole life had been dominated by ill fortune.

During the first half, the kid had sat next to him, in a state of ecstasy, totally into the game, shouting himself hoarse, arguing with the refs, advising the players, cursing extravagantly at the opposition. All around them, people smiled at his intensity and laughed at his expressions of agony.

Fred had felt stupid, stuck with the extra ticket, embarrassed by his deception of Marion and his inability to think of someone to invite along that he would be comfortable with, but the accident of having provided a seat for that kid salved his conscience. You see, it was for the best, he told himself. I'm a good guy, after all.

When they were released onto Seventh Avenue, surrounded by the happy departing crowd, Tom turned to Fred in a determined manner (as though this was something he had been considering for a while and had made up his mind to do because he had decided it was the right thing) and said, "I told Karl I'd drop by the poker game and play for the last couple hours. Why don't we both go?"

"Uh . . ." Fred couldn't think how to put it, and found himself telling the truth: "He didn't invite me."

"I know. 'Cause of crazy Sam. Well, Karl's being stupid about it. Come along. Sam's bark is worse than his bite. He's a child. He has to be told no, or his demands just escalate endlessly."

Fred tried to refuse, but Tom insisted, and later, sitting at the game, while everybody totaled up winnings and losses, and Karl was busy writing a check to Fred for thirty dollars, Sam said to him, "You really played good poker tonight," in a tone that implied concession and acceptance.

I've won, he thought calmly, without the usual silly rush of adrenaline. He felt like tragic Ray Williams, head bowed, a champion at last, scarred to be sure, but with the home crowd finally—finally, at long last! —on *his* side.

David Bergman sipped his cold coffee. Presumably that morning its flavor had been heated and reheated away, and now it had even lost that one virtue—heat. But he liked sipping it. He was at the cover meeting, listening to a furious argument between Chico and Harpo over whether the Russian withdrawal from the Olympics was a Nation story (Chico's domain) or an International story (Harpo's bailiwick).

David listened dispassionately, enjoying, as were the other senior editors, the spectacle their supervisors were making of themselves. The effort Chico and Harpo put into disguising this battle of ego as a disagreement of substance was especially diverting. Harpo, with his longish blond hair, cheerful open face, and relaxed manner, contrasted well with Chico's dark-haired, beady-eyed controlled rage.

The majority in the room felt friendlier toward Harpo. He now occupied, and had occupied in the past, a position of less power than Chico, but only part of the good feeling toward Harpo was a result of his having fewer natural enemies. After all, Harpo was a Marx Brother. He hired and fired, he top-edited, he had to (in theory) obey the law of middle management: toady to superiors, bully inferiors. But Harpo, unlike Chico, seemed to take *Newstime* (its intrigues, its etiquette, its self-delusions) less to heart than Chico. On a week when *Weekly*'s cover clearly bested *Newstime*'s, Chico seemed hurt and baffled, a grieving man, while Harpo made jokes, sometimes gallows humor to be sure, but jokes nevertheless, which implied he had a sense of proportion, a knowledge that after all, this was simply a job, and *Newstime* merely a magazine. Chico made people feel that to point out such an obvious fact to him would be roughly equivalent to informing Genghis Khan that a battle he had just lost was insignificant, and his quest, in general, merely a transitional phase between one empire and the next. Telling Chico the truth might get you decapitated and your head stuck on top of a hot-dog stand's multicolored umbrella.

Today, however, Harpo seemed to be taking things seriously. "Look, five countries have pulled out. More will follow. There's no way LA's problems are bigger news than the international implications."

"They're national!" Chico's voice squeaked. An amusing disparity with his huge body, it brought secret smiles to the faces of the senior editors. David looked away from Mary Gould (senior editor, back-of-the-book) because her mischievously twinkling eyes threatened to crack his smile into noisy laughter. He studied the only neutral face there—Rounder's. "Who gives a shit whether Yugoslavia will come or not! This is really about Soviet-American relations, the MX, the effect on the election—"

"We've heard the list," Harpo said dryly. "I agree, no question, there are obviously important Nation implications but, my God, how you can argue that the Olympics, by definition, isn't an international story is beyond me."

"Excuse me," Rounder said. There were laughs around the room. But they were cut off by the surprised look on the editor in chief's face. Apparently he hadn't meant his polite interruption to be sarcastic. "We're not going to put this in either Nation or International, are we? It's the . . ." He hesitated, as though unsure. ". . . cover, right?"

David looked down. He had again caught the eye of Mary Gould and several of the other senior editors, and he felt himself want to laugh at their astonishment. It *was* astonishing. Surely Rounder should know what Chico and Harpo were really arguing about, namely whose writers were more qualified to cover the Soviet withdrawal, and therefore who was going to top-edit the story. Normally Chico could conduct a raid on someone else's province like this without opposition, but today Harpo had decided to put up a fight (justifiably, David thought, since it really was an international story) and it was up to Rounder (as editor in chief) to resolve the conflict. Apparently he didn't even understand its terms.

"Yes," Chico said, his voice loud and impatient, "but who's gonna write it?"

There was an uneasy silence. Rounder made the situation worse by trying to look imperious to cover what was obviously confusion. "Why don't we first decide if it is the cover?" Rounder said haughtily, implying that Chico was the one who was asking foolish questions.

"The Russians withdraw from the Olympics!" Chico said so vehemently that a stranger entering the room might think the news had just broken and Chico was a proprietor of several large Los Angeles hotels. "What else are we gonna put on the cover?"

"Robert Redford in *The Natural?*" Mary Gould suggested playfully. That had been a proposed cover before the Russians had withdrawn, but she was kidding.

Chico, however, wheeled on her. "We'd look like assholes if we did that!"

"Sell more copies than with news that's four days old," Harpo said, throwing the line away. He meant this as bitter fact, not a rationale for giving in.

Again Chico chose to attack as though the speaker was in earnest. "Oh, great! So why don't we just close up shop and let *People Magazine* handle all the news?"

"Maybe we should go with Redford," Rounder said, only he was *not* kidding or musing philosophically. He spoke in a tone of wonder while making the suggestion, as if the notion hadn't been discussed at all and he had just had a flash of inspiration.

His question hung in the air like a mysterious phenomenon of nature. They all looked incredulously at it, unable to guess at its origin, its future course, or what action could be taken. Primitive tribesmen couldn't have been more stunned by a comet than they were by this naive indecisiveness.

"Fine!" Chico said abruptly, and sat down. He stared at the table, silent, like a sullen child, intending to deprive them of any further human intercourse.

Harpo stared at Chico, amazed by his silence. He looked at the others (David met his eyes briefly and saw the desperation, with a plea implicit in their quick, darting movements. Can't somebody help me? they asked). Then he seemed to pull himself together. Harpo looked at Rounder. "I think we'd look really irresponsible."

"But *Weekly* will put the Olympics on the cover, and there won't be any way to distinguish ourselves from them."

Rounder said this in a tone of discovery, a medical researcher uncovering a previously unknown and deadly microbe.

Again Harpo looked at Chico imploringly. Chico folded his arms and sank lower in his chair, his eyes fixed on the table. Harpo despaired of him and said to Rounder, "That's always the problem. But it's inevitable that we do the Olympics anyway. There are some news events that can't be ignored, no matter how obvious or boring to our readers they will be." The surreal quality of this moment, someone explaining to the editor in chief of a national newsmagazine its most basic fact of existence, washed over David, numbing him. He began to feel he wasn't really present in the scene, that it was something he was watching or dreaming. "Sure," Harpo continued, "on Monday everybody will pass the newsstands and groan at the Olympics being on the cover, but if it wasn't . . ." Harpo stopped, as though the implied explosion of rage on the part of their readership was too horrible to imagine.

"But why?" Rounder smiled his brilliant smile, his blue eyes glistening with excitement. "We have to start questioning these assumptions we make. By Monday the Russian withdrawal will be old, old news. The magazine will sit on the stand for the next few days becoming more horribly dated with each day. I'm not saying we don't banner it inside and give it thirty columns anyway, but let's do Redford on the cover. At least we'll sell more copies and therefore more people will have the benefit of reading our excellent coverage of the Olympics." He beamed at them with the pleasant immodesty of a child topping adults at something their greater experience should have taught them.

"If we really want to surprise them," Chico said in a mumble, "let's not cover it at all. We could do a thirty-column takeout on Redford's marriage."

Several people laughed. David did not. He stiffened, a soldier ready for incoming artillery. Sarcasm at a Groucho suggestion was simply not done without consequences. Either it signaled the end of Rounder or the end of Chico, David believed, or rather felt instinctively. You don't make fun of the boss's major policy ideas. You can kid him about his tie, or the way Mrs. Thorn praised him at a general meeting, but never joke about his ideas in front of the staff—at least not when he's there to hear you. To David it was unthinkable, unbelievable, something he never thought he would see someone like Chico do. It was as if the bartender had just tossed a shot of bourbon in Jesse James's face—get away from the bar and duck behind a table, 'cause there's gonna be some shootin'.

Instead of such dramatics, Rounder turned to Mary Gould and said, "I'm sorry, I haven't seen the piece. Is there material about his marriage?"

Chico audibly groaned. He sank lower in his chair, his small eyes scrunched together, fiercely staring at the table. Mary, suddenly on the spot, dropped her cheerful attitude and answered in a hasty rush: "No, not really. Just an allusion to it. It's really about the movie and how long it's taken Redford to do one. Been four years since he's appeared in anything, and three since he directed *Ordinary People*."

"Wow," Chico said in a dull, flat voice.

"It wasn't intended as an exposé," Mary said at Chico's head, since he was still utterly absorbed by the conference table and made his comments in a tone that implied he couldn't be heard, as though they were private thoughts. "It's not controversial or newsy," she added, apparently a polite way of voting no on its superseding the Olympics.

"But it's fun? It looks good?" Rounder asked imperiously, making his question seem silly, since his attitude implied that only an affirmative answer was acceptable.

"Yes," she admitted, but with a trace of reluctance. "We have great pictures. Redford looks sensational."

"Easy, Mary, whoa, girl," Harpo said pleasantly.

She winked at him. "Say, how come senior editors don't get to do interviews?"

The room broke up, except for Chico, who seemed to have become statuary, his big body still, although in David's mind there was explosive, ominous animation implied.

"This is what I suggest," Rounder said. "Let's proceed with both the Olympics and Redford as covers. We'll see how lively the Olympics story is by the end of the week. If there's more juice in it, we'll do the Olympics and run Redford the next issue."

"Redford's a cover either way?" Mary asked.

"Definitely," Rounder said. "That's a cover or it's nothing. Don't you agree?" he asked Chico, or rather, the body of Chico.

Chico stood up. The speed of it startled those around him. For a moment he said nothing. "Yes," he announced to the wall finally. "Who's top-editing the Olympics?"

"Ray, why don't you do it?" Rounder said to Harpo, using his real name, of course. Harpo, now having won the battle he began, looked as though he considered it a Pyrrhic victory. Chico nodded knowingly at this news of his defeat and announced, "I have to go to the john," and made for the door.

"We're done," Rounder said, continuing his style thus far, namely making no acknowledgment of Chico's behavior.

They filed out slowly and quietly. That was atypical of the end of cover meetings. David caught the eyes of several others while they moved, and each time, there was an embarrassed glance away on both sides. All of them knew that they had witnessed a remarkable meeting, that they would be gossiping like mad about it soon, but right at that moment they all tried hard, far too hard, to pretend that it had been routine.

Back in his office, David tried to think it through. He needed to have a line on it for the drinks at lunch. (He regularly ate on Tuesdays with a group of other senior editors and a number of the top writers.) But his search was for a real explanation. He felt upset. And that also bothered him. Why should he?

His Power Phone buzzed. He jumped at the loud squawk. It made him react nervously. No doubt it had been designed to produce that effect. "Yes?" he called into it.

"David," Chico's voice thundered metallically, "could you come up for a few minutes?"

"Sure," he said. He tried to block out any thoughts of the meeting, assuming that Chico wanted to see him about something else and that even a hint of self-consciousness might anger Chico.

He found Chico reading blues. He nodded at David and held up a finger while he finished a paragraph. He nodded at the door. "Could you close it?"

As convinced as David had been on his way there that Chico wanted to see him about something other than the cover meeting, he was now persuaded that it was about that bizarre scene. He closed the door slowly, nervous, wishing he could delay talking with Chico until after lunch. He had had no time to think. But no matter how lightly he pushed the door, it still shut too quickly for David to have an answer to the question Chico then asked:

"What do you think that was about?"

"You mean the cover meeting?" David stalled.

Chico's eyes shut with irritation. "Of course!" he said so forcefully that the phrase was almost an expletive.

David told the truth. "I have no idea. I couldn't figure out what it was about."

Chico cocked his head, interested. "I'm surprised," he said. "I thought it was so obvious."

David sat down, relaxed. He felt tremendously relieved by his admission. He didn't know why he had felt obligated to have an answer, but now that he had failed to provide one, he felt sure of himself. "Not to me. Maybe I'm dense, but I don't know what Rounder thought he was proving. I can't believe he won't do the Olympics as a cover."

"If he does, he'll be a laughingstock." Chico shook his head no. "He won't. It was all done to keep me in my place. He knows I should have his job. He wants me and everyone else to know that I don't have it. He's in charge."

"You don't think he's trying to force you out?" David asked this so frankly because Chico's words had been naked. By *Newstime*'s standards, they were an unprecedented catharsis. If David had had time to think, he would never have asked his question.

"He can't. He wishes he could. But Mrs. Thorn wouldn't allow it. She's not prepared to trust him absolutely."

"Maybe he meant it about the cover. Maybe he's that naive."

"He's not that dumb." Chico picked up a pen on his desk and threw it down hard. It bounced up and fell to the floor. "What do you think everyone else's reaction was?"

"I'll find out at lunch," David said, again without thinking.

"Good. Call me after you come back and let me know."

David nodded and rose slowly. I've just agreed to spy for him, he thought, appalled that he had committed himself so easily to such a role. No matter how much good it might do him with Chico, wasn't it unseemly? Wouldn't it lower him even in Chico's eyes?

He left, went into the elevator, and on down to the lobby in a daze. He dreaded each step that took him closer to the Boar, the *Newstime* hangout. He had loved being in that elite circle, drinking and opening up to his peers, saying the unsayable to each other about the magazine. But now he'd have to take notes, remembering who said what, judging whether it was fit to report or not. He could alienate a rival from Chico's affections, cast himself as Chico's only defender. That simple promise was an endless ladder down into the depths of corruption: only his own will could keep him from the black depths of the bottom rung.

As he opened the dark glass doors and saw the gang already assembled, he almost felt like crossing himself or finding a clove of garlic to wear around his neck. Anything that could ward off the devil . . . and allow him to keep his soul above the slime of this opportunity.

Tony Winters waved to Lois while she turned off Sunset Boulevard. She had helped him pick the route he would take to the Valley Studios for a meeting at International Pictures, though she had laughed at his refusal to get on any freeways or to take shortcuts through the canyons. Instead, she explained he could stay on Sunset almost all the way, although a brief stint (one exit) on the Hollywood Freeway was unavoidable.

He felt a sad loneliness watching her car go. A childish, weak sensation in his belly. Maybe he was nervous about the meeting. The summons to Los Angeles had been so abrupt, and the lack of comment on his first draft of the script so puzzling and ominous. He had been sufficiently startled that he called his father—fresh from recently seeing him in New York—and asked whether the request for him to come without any comment on the script was a good or bad sign.

His father was silent for a moment or two. Then he sighed. "Neither. The odds are they neither love the script nor hate it. If they loved it, they would have said something. If they hated it, they wouldn't want you out here for a meeting. They probably want changes, and Garth is notoriously insensitive. He probably doesn't think you need to be stroked. After all, you're just a writer."

Just a writer. My God, what a universe of difference there is in the movie business between their view of writers and mine, Tony thought. He took the gentle curves of Sunset with pleasure, soothed by the silent flow of traffic and pavement, surrounded by the whoosh of his car's air conditioning. Just a writer. To Tony, to be a writer was to be royalty. A breed of humanity that could survive time. The triumphant recorders of human life. A master psychologist, a delicate historian, a great lover, loving parent, actor, set designer, director, sound technician—to be a writer, to Tony, meant being all those things, and more, much more. Priest, comic, fool, wise man. A writer must know every line and every thought. The look of things, the sound of things, the ideas of life, and its trivialities. A writer must master everything or he is nothing. Just a writer! To him, the others were the limited ones. Temporal, insignificant. Tools to help him build his monuments.

The enormity of his task, the noble vision of its demands, cheered him as he approached the Hollywood Freeway. I have mastered these things. Maybe not as well as the great geniuses, but I have written good stuff. Shakespeare, Chekhov, Shaw, they would welcome me. I'd get a round of drinks from them. I'd get some stroking. And with determination and time, one day another Garth in another century will dream of playing the roles I write!

He negotiated a terrifying crossing of the freeway within a distance of a few hundred yards from an entrance on the extreme left to an exit on the extreme right with relative ease. Soon he was descending a hill into the pancake of the Valley. The huge billboards of International's current movies loomed beside his car as he began to look for Gate Three. The low brown buildings of the studio seemed peaceful in the morning sun, like beach bungalows for a lower-middle-class resort. Only the parking lots filled with Mercedeses and BMW's suggested money.

The security guard at Gate Three, who seemed to regard him suspiciously when he announced himself and whom he had come to see, became instantly servile when he found the drive-on pass that confirmed Tony Winters had a right to be there. Probably that was all in my head, he lectured himself while finding the lot where he was supposed to park. Why can't I rid myself of this monitoring whether the world approves? I approve, dammit!

He glanced at his watch before entering the inner courtyard of the main administration building. He was on time. He found the silver-colored plaque that read WILLIAM GARTH and paused, listening to the faint steady hum of traffic outside the low buildings. Birds chirped. There was a small-town feeling to the place. This was and is the Valley Studios, Tony complained to himself. Bogey worked here. Faulkner typed away in one of those buildings. American fascism stalked these halls. And what does it look like? A small-town college.

Then the office itself was a shock. The furniture was tacky, fake wood desks, the usual plants, an ugly white shag rug. They might have been selling aluminum siding in Queens. Garth was on the phone when he was shown in. He acknowledged Tony's presence with a wave, while Foxx, whom Tony had recently seen in New York, glanced up at him (he was reading *Variety*) and said casually, "Hi, Tony," as though they were old friends accustomed to seeing each other daily.

Garth's secretary asked if he wanted coffee. Tony said yes. Foxx put *Variety* away. "How was the flight?"

This seemed to be a ritual. Tony had this conversation with everyone. "Fine."

"What do you take out here?"

"TWA."

Foxx shook his head as though Tony had answered a quiz incorrectly. "You should try Pan Am. They're really much better."

Meanwhile Garth was saying to the phone, "They say she fucks everybody on the set. Yeah!" He laughed. "Even the cameramen. No, I don't know about gofers." He laughed. "Why? Your deal is so tough you're gofering on the side? What do you mean, 'gofer' isn't a verb. Of course it's a verb. I got a writer here. I'll ask him." Garth moved his mouth away from the receiver, calling out to Tony loudly, as though they were far apart, "Isn't 'gofer' a verb?"

"I'm not sure," Tony answered gravely. " 'He gives good gofer' might be more proper."

Foxx smiled. Garth roared and repeated the line, laughing again, presumably at the laughter of his listener. "Who?" Garth said. "Tony Winters." Pause.

Tony was openly eavesdropping now, but Garth didn't mind, he was smiling at Tony.

"Yeah, he's writing a script for you and me. *Concussion*, it's called. *Concussion*, not *Curmudgeon*." Garth made a face. "Ha, ha. I gotta go. I'm not hanging up angry. I got work to do. I got a writer here. Yes, the same one. Ha, ha. Good-bye." Garth hung up and sighed, staring at the desk. "What an asshole," he decided.

"They say he's in trouble," Foxx commented, not committing himself to the opinion, merely reporting.

"He's always in trouble. But if they fire him, the fat fuck'll be president somewhere else." Garth said this as though he were a scientist accepting a gloomy fact of nature.

The secretary entered with Tony's coffee. Garth looked at her blankly and then said, "Get one for me." He looked at Tony and smiled in a weary and forced manner. "How are ya? You look good. Flight all right?"

"Yeah."

"Where you staying?"

"Beverly Hills Hotel."

Garth nodded seriously, his brows furrowed. "Hmmm," he said thoughtfully. "Has Jim"—he glanced at Foxx—"had a chance to talk to you about the script?"

"No!" Foxx said, aggrieved. "We've been listening to you on the phone."

"I was on for a second! He's only gonna be making our goddamn movie," he complained, pointing to the phone. "If only he knew we were doing it."

The secretary reappeared with Garth's coffee. Tony lit a cigarette. He had no idea what to expect. Their manner was too matter-of-fact for him to assume disaster, but it wasn't the tone of people who are delighted and ready to proceed. Garth wistfully watched Tony take a drag. "Aren't you worried about cancer?" he asked.

"No," Tony said with a smile.

Foxx laughed.

Garth nodded. "Well, we've read the script. I've read it twice." He looked at Foxx expectantly.

"So have I," Foxx said.

"I haven't," Tony said with a nervous giggle.

Garth ignored him. "I guess my feeling is that the character is there. But—"

Foxx broke in, "The structure isn't."

"It's not suspenseful," Garth said. "I always felt I was a step ahead of the picture."

"Can't have that in a thriller," Foxx said.

Tony swallowed. He thought he had braced himself for a mixed reaction (was this merely a mixed reaction?), but the tightening presence of fear in his throat belied that assumption. He felt under pressure to respond. Foxx and Garth were both looking at him quizzically. "No, you can't," Tony agreed. "I thought I . . ." He was about to argue he *had* made the story surprising, but he realized that was foolish.

"You think it is?" Garth prompted. The famous face looked timid and kindly, unsure of itself. Foxx, however, was frowning, certain of his judgment. That surprised Tony. He had expected, from the rumors of Garth's temperament, the reverse.

"Yeah," Tony said timidly. "Weren't you surprised that his brother turns out to be the FBI agent?"

Foxx shook his head no, his lips pursing with disdain. Garth glanced at his producer. "I think it's a good choice," he said. "You haven't . . ." Garth hesitated.

"You telegraph it with all those little scenes between them. They have a tone that lets you know there's more to that brother than just someone helping." Foxx said all this thoughtfully, his eyes going to a small window next to the far end of the couch. It had no view. His refusal to look at Tony while criticizing suggested that the words were harsher than they sounded.

"But that isn't a structural problem," Tony objected. But he felt his point was pedantic. "Not that that makes any difference. I just mean— you said there were structural problems, so I thought you hadn't liked that choice, making your brother the villain."

"No, I like that," Garth said eagerly, as though he were glad to have something positive to say. "There are a lot of things I like in it. I think there are terrific scenes for my character."

"Yeah," Foxx said. "But not for her. Not for Meryl's character."

"Yeah," Garth agreed. "She's, uh, she's, I don't know, kind of unpleasant, you know? You don't like her. You don't believe I would be in love with her."

You, a short twerp like you? Tony thought. In life, you'd be on your hands and knees thanking god that Meryl Streep was willing to pull her panties down for you. This bitter, and, Tony knew, wrong-headed thought cheered him up. "Okay," Tony said with an easy smile. "I'll be happy to fix her. But again, that's not a structural problem."

Foxx turned his eyes to Tony. "All right, so they're not structural. What difference does that make?" His tone was both angry and petulant. Tony felt that a whip had been cracked. Get in line, was Foxx's message. Don't try to act smarter than us.

"You're right," Tony said, looking down at the floor, a child accepting a scolding.

"This is a tough story," Garth said.

Tony felt a rush of good feeling for Garth. He had been warned by his mother, his father, Lois, his agent, and others that Garth treated writers like breakfast cereals, stocking his cabinets with a dozen varieties and switching brands every morning. But Garth seemed to be trying to soften the blows, treating Tony with unusual deference, as if Tony were a special case, not the typical Hollywood writer whom Garth could feel free to trample on.

"It's gotta be fun!" Foxx blurted, moving forward on the couch in his excitement. He got up when he reached the edge and paced across the small room in between Tony's chair and Garth's desk. "There's no fun in your script. You're a funny writer. I don't know why you've made it so dark."

"Well . . ." Tony said, again his first impulse being to argue, followed by an equally strong impulse *not* to. The result was inarticulate hesitation.

"Hitchcock wouldn't do it that way," Foxx said after a brief wait for Tony to say more. "He always kept the fun in his thrillers. Even *Psycho* is fun!"

Psycho is fun? Tony asked himself. It gave him nightmares for six months. But he nodded in agreement, looking chastened. He wanted to slow Foxx down. He feared the producer was talking himself into believing Tony's script was unsalvageable. Tony realized he had given up any notion of trying to defend what he had written; he was fighting now to stay on the project, to be allowed another chance to satisfy them. "I'll be happy to rewrite it," he said.

Garth smiled. "You have to rewrite it," he said in a gentle voice, but with a disdainful look in his eyes.

"Of course," Tony said. Somehow he had now aroused Garth, the last thing he had wanted. The harder he tried to act humble and harmless, the more aggressive they seemed to become.

"Why did you hand it in if you weren't sure of it?" Foxx asked. He put a hand in his pocket and looked down at Tony, jiggling the keys impatiently.

This question stunned Tony. He wanted to cry foul. He hadn't contested their opinions out of deference to them. It was unfair now to turn his niceness against him. He stared at Foxx, unable to respond.

"I mean, are *you* happy with this draft?" Foxx continued, seeing Tony paralyzed.

Tony looked at Garth, a plea for protection from these low blows. But Garth didn't look like a referee; rather he stared at Tony as if he were the other member of a wrestling tag team, trying to decide if he would be needed to finish Tony off.

"Uh . . ." came out of Tony, the groan of a wounded man. But resistance welled in him. He straightened in his seat—he noticed while doing so that he must have slumped quite low in the chair earlier—and banished the cautious censor that had accompanied him to the meeting. "Look, that's a silly question. Do you think I want to hand in an unsatisfactory draft? Is that something a writer would want to do? You think I want to be fired? You think I want to fail? I liked the draft. I thought it worked. Do you want me to sit here and stubbornly argue about it? Would I be able to change your minds?" He snorted and allowed himself a sardonic smile. He returned Garth's stare, challenging him to answer his questions. Foxx looked surprised, curious, studying Tony as though he had just entered the room with amazing news. "Right? If I told you you were wrong and sat here for an hour arguing and arguing, would you like that? Would you consider that professional? Helpful? My job is to give you a script *you* want. Not what I want. What *you* want. Isn't that right?"

Garth returned his daring glance, watching as though he were appreciating a performance. Foxx, however, seemed thrown. "Well," the producer said, almost stammering, "if . . . I mean, if you think we're off-base, if we're missing something, then you should argue. Your name goes on the script. Not ours."

Tony stayed on Garth. He felt contempt for Foxx. He had backed down so easily. It was Garth who got stronger as Tony fought. Garth, who had seemed so pliant, ready to compromise, was the one who had suddenly gotten firm and unyielding. Tony stared at him. After a moment of this, Tony said, "Let's go through the script. When I disagree, we'll discuss it. But if you really don't like something, I'm not gonna sit here and waste our time arguing. It's your project."

Foxx jiggled his keys. Garth continued to study Tony. Then he said quietly, "Yeah. Let's get to work." He broke his pose and leaned forward, opening a copy of Tony's draft.

Foxx crossed back to the couch and opened a soft leather carrying case, removing another copy.

"I don't have one," Tony said forlornly.

Foxx turned, surprised. "You don't have a copy of the script?"

Tony looked embarrassed. "No, I . . . uh . . ."

Garth got up. "We've got more," he said, smiling, and walked to shelves behind Tony. He handed him a script, and then, before moving on, he quickly rubbed the top of Tony's head, tousling his hair with the affection of an older brother, the way he had in the Polo Lounge almost a year before.

I won, Tony thought, opening his screenplay. I won, he told himself. I didn't know this was a fight for survival, but I won it anyway.

Patty had been keeping a secret. For the first time in her life, she had confided in no one. Usually, if Patty limited information to three or four people, that qualified as top security. Perhaps she had occasionally held it as low as two people. But this fact, that she had been writing a novel, a serious novel (or at least a nonromance book), for the past two months, was absolutely private.

The pressure was becoming unbearable.

She had written an amazing amount, nearly a hundred pages, and no matter how many times she read them over, she continued to admire and like them. As opposed to her one and a half romance novels, a rereading of which inspired nausea. She felt delighted with herself, with her newfound passion, and she ached to hand her pages to someone and get confirmation of her own good opinion. But who?

David? As a critic, he frightened her. He was the type of person who compulsively pointed out misspellings and grammatical mistakes. No doubt there were a few, but any editor could catch them, and Patty knew they would be rare and unimportant. But the presence of even one would be noted by David. And he would judge her against major writers, evaluating her novel as though she had placed it as a candidate for the Nobel Prize against Tolstoy, Joyce, and Mailer.

Betty? She would mark the misspellings and grammatical mistakes, but not mention them until she was through praising Patty. And every allowance would be made for her inexperience, her age, and the general difficulties of existence. No comparisons or impossible standards would be constructed for Patty's hundred pages to hurdle.

David would be too tough. Betty too easy.

There were other friends, but they weren't in publishing and had no expertise in judging writing other than the fact that they read books. Their response might tell her if it was good, but not how to improve it or how to finish it. The last was Patty's worry. She had gone into her story blind, without a true plan. So far that hadn't hurt her. She started each day with a shortened horizon, but somehow it moved as she moved, keeping just enough ahead of her so that she never fell off the edge into nothingness. Up until now she had been content with this daring voyage into an unknown sea, but lately she worried that without a map, without a navigator, she would never reach land.

David could certainly help her there. He was so organized, his first impulse would be to plot the rest of her novel even if she had one figured. Betty, oddly, she wasn't sure could. Theoretically, it was her job to do so. She was an editor. Her ambition was to edit novels. So far she had only worked on books that were acquired by her boss, always by established writers who either didn't need or were contemptuous of Betty's abilities. She often complained to Patty that she was no more than a copyeditor on those manuscripts. Her larger skills as an editor, helping to shape a book for example, had been limited to self-help books, at which she'd been successful. However, Betty despised that accomplishment. The truth was, it became obvious to Patty, that years of hearing Betty downgrade her career had infiltrated Patty's mind and made her think of Betty as inexperienced and insecure—not someone to go to with confidence.

How awful, Patty decided. I'm resetting the sexist trap Betty's in. Because the men don't take her seriously, I don't. Patty decided to give her the pages, and caught herself feeling she honored Betty by doing so. That astonished and embarrassed her. Honor? Being given my manuscript to read is an honor? She laughed delightedly at herself. I must be a real writer, she thought. I've developed their egomania.

She took her pages from their hiding place, buried at the bottom of a five-hundred-sheet box of typing paper, beneath two hundred or so blanks, and stored in the bottom drawer of her desk. She went out to a store to have Xerox copies made. She worried so over their safety (in contrast to her treatment of romance-novel pages) that she waited in the airless storefront despite its lack of seating and watched them process each page. She had arranged to see Betty for dinner, since Tony was in Hollywood, and David would be at *Newstime* until at least two in the morning, closing his sections of the magazine.

In the afternoon she read over her first romance novel, thinking that if Betty vetoed continuing her new novel, she would have to return to that junk. It sickened her. She barely got through the first two chapters before giving up and feeling hopeless. If Betty told her to return to that, she would have to get a job. To write that silly stuff was worse than poverty.

Over dinner, Patty listened to Betty's politely worded complaints about Tony. She spoke circuitously, joking casually about being married to a traveling salesman, but when Patty confirmed that this was only Tony's third trip to LA since first signing to write the screenplay, Betty couldn't explain why such brief and rare separations should bother her. Betty moved off the subject and returned to a more familiar bitching: about how she remained unable to find a novel she both wanted to publish and could. Agents no longer bothered to submit fiction to her because she had been thwarted so many times by the ed board (the editorial committee that decided what to publish), and without such submissions the odds she would see a terrific first novel were poor. Two other editors her age, both men, had gotten novels through the board, and a few, and one in particular, had been quite successful, so that even if an agent found himself with a new good writer and wanted to submit his work to a young editor at her house, she would be the last choice.

"Why don't you quit?"

"And do what?" Betty snapped.

"I mean, and go to another house."

"Where are the offers?" Betty said.

"I thought Caruthers offered you a job."

"Same job I have now. They wanted someone to work under Phyllis Racknell. I would have been line-editing her multigenerational sagas and acquiring more self-help books." Betty frowned at the table. "I get offers like that. No reason to take them. Wouldn't change things."

"Then leave publishing," Patty said. She was angry at Betty's whining. First, because it made her not want to give her what she had written, and second, because her attitude seemed self-defeating, more concerned with seeing herself as a victim rather than triumphing over her obstacles. Other women had made it in publishing. Escaped their domineering mentors, gone to less classy houses, taken chances on unknown writers, and eventually carved out a niche for themselves. Phyllis Racknell had, for example. Patty didn't say so, but she suspected Betty had turned down that offer because Phyllis was a woman, and if Betty couldn't gain her independence from her, no one would believe her cries of sexism. Even if they were true.

And Patty was especially, given her own situation, irritated by Betty's beef that agents didn't send her their new hot young writers. Was she only willing to put herself on the line for unknowns who were already stamped with "potential"? What was so great about signing young writers who were in demand? Any imbecile could do that. Patty would have no trouble being an editor the way most of them were: taking huge chances on novelists like Philip Roth, Norman Mailer, and the occasional new writer, like some punk who had been writing for *Esquire* for three years and knew every publishing person in town. Betty bitched because she wasn't able to break into that circuit. Well, tough shit, Patty thought, feeling bitter about her own exclusion from that world.

We're a pretty fucked-up pair, Patty said to herself, looking at Betty while a waiter poured them coffee. The thought amused her. She was pleased to think of herself as Betty's equal, even if it was a miserable peerage. She knew instinctively that Betty was no happier being married to Tony than Patty was living with David. The moaning about Tony's absence wasn't the longing of a loving wife; it sounded more like the petulance of a neglected child for whom separation only made clear how little intimacy there was normally. "What does Tony say?" Patty asked, to approach this assumption the long way.

"He doesn't know."

"He doesn't *know?*"

"He doesn't pay attention." Betty shook her head as though to rid herself of these thoughts. She didn't want to confess these problems. "He's busy. He's under pressure about this script."

"How's it going?"

"I don't know. He had a meeting today with Garth." She stared off for a moment. "He hasn't called. Maybe it went on all day. I'll call him when I get home."

"Is this a meeting where they're going to tell him if they make his movie?"

Betty shook her head. "Tony says it doesn't happen that way."

"How does it happen?"

"He says there are . . . I don't know. That a lot of people have to agree before they make the film."

"But they pay well, right? And he can still write his plays."

"He hasn't worked on a play in a year." Betty admitted this in a tragic tone, a wife of thirty years telling her friend that her husband had become an alcoholic.

"We're not worried about Tony, are we?" Patty asked.

"No." Betty smiled. "No, we're not."

"He's been getting on our nerves," Patty supplied the complaint for her. "Too obsessed with his work."

"Poor us," Betty said, laughing.

"We don't live our lives through our men, though."

"Of course not," Betty agreed, trying to keep her face straight. Patty looked so earnest, Betty couldn't even be sure how much of it was joking. "How's the torrid romance novel, by the way? Are you close to finishing?"

This was the moment. "I hate it."

Betty looked startled. "What's wrong with it?"

"I hate doing it. It's so dumb. Dumb. Dumb."

"Yeah, but it pays."

Patty nodded. She took that point to heart. Ultimately, even if Betty thought her serious novel was good, money would still be an issue. The odds against her getting a first novel published were bad enough without also needing to earn a living from it. "There has to be a better way for us to make money than publishing self-help books and writing romance novels."

"Yeah, what?"

Patty reached in her bag and brought out a manila envelope. "You should publish this and make it a bestseller. Then we'll both be fine. Tony can quit writing screenplays and return to the theater. David can leave *Newstime* and have my babies."

"What is it?" Betty said, taking the package. She seemed wary.

"It's half a novel. Next year's bestseller." Patty amazed herself with this remark. Not even in jest did she ever predict success for herself.

"David wrote it?" Betty said, barely making it a question. She spoke in a suspicious tone, as though Patty were trying to fool her.

"No!" Patty was furious. "I wrote it. You think only—"

Betty, embarrassed, tried to head her off. "I thought you said—"

"—David can try to write seriously. I can only write about these airheads who—"

"Stop! I thought from what you said that this was David's. Of course you can try to write a novel."

"Try?" Patty had never yelled at Betty and she had little reason to. But keen resentment suddenly ballooned in her mind. She felt overwhelmed by everyone's attitude toward her: the silly little blond who wasn't even permitted the delusions everyone else has. Betty can think of herself as another Maxwell Perkins, but Patty can't hope to be Fitzgerald. "I'm doing it!" she shouted at Betty, leaning over the table and shooting the words at her.

Betty held up her hands, surrendering. "Okay. That's great." She looked down at the package.

Patty, her anger spent, sat back and stared off, an exhausted shopper whose buying impulse is satisfied but now wonders if poverty will be the consequence. Had she bankrupted the friendship, or, more to the point, Betty's willingness to be a sympathetic reader?

Betty looked up. "When did you do this?"

Patty couldn't bring herself to return the glance. "Last two months," she said, sulking.

"It's the whole book?"

"No, just half. I don't know! That's why I wanted you to read it. I think it's . . . well, I just don't know where it's going." Patty had straightened and looked at Betty once again, apologizing with her tone and her wide-open pleading eyes.

"I'm really impressed," Betty said with feeling. "And not because I didn't think you could!"

"I'm sorry."

"I can't believe you said that."

"I'm awful, aren't I?"

"Yes," Betty said, exaggerating a frown of disapproval for a moment, before she relaxed into a smile. "I'll read it tonight."

"Call me when you're done. I don't care how late."

Betty smiled, confidently back to her role of the calm, mature elder sister. "I'll call you tomorrow. I might be on the phone with Tony late and have to fall asleep. So don't wait up worrying."

"You mean you're going to sleep tonight instead of reading my manuscript? You care more about talking to your husband than my work?" Patty said, making it a great joke, but keeping enough of a glint in her eye to tell Betty that in fact it was the way things should be.

"No, I don't," Betty said, playing along. "But I have to keep up appearances or you'd gossip about me."

And they laughed like girls again, playing at adulthood and giggling at the naughtiness of it. But something of Patty's angry outburst—a faint echo of distant artillery—still rang in their ears and worried their happy tones.

CHAPTER 10

Fred's life caught excitement. Fate tossed him a series of slow glamorous pitches right into a large infallible mitt.

Tom Lear befriended him with a vengeance. He took Fred to see a rough cut of the movie that had been made of his screenplay, which meant that Fred got to sit with Tom, the famous director Jay Forsch, and Sam Billings, the producer, while they discussed what changes could be made in the editing. Tom solicited Fred's opinion and he babbled away, inspired by Tom's easy manner, feeling no pressure or self-consciousness. To his astonishment, Forsch and Billings listened and— agreed! Later that night, when he told Marion that the world-famous director and producer were going to cut two scenes at his suggestion, she nodded at Fred as if he were speaking in a foreign language and she had to fight in order to understand him.

Lear, Forsch, and Billings took him to Elaine's afterward. All the important people in the restaurant—with the exception of Woody Allen —came over to their table to chat. Fred was introduced to each of them. Names that before then existed only on film credits, book jackets, magazine covers. Fred shook their actual hands and enjoyed considerable success. He frankly told the famous that he loved their work (didn't have to lie once, he told Marion), and they not only didn't despise his compliments, but seemed to enjoy them. The whole thing was unbelievable. It was as though he had merged into celluloid: after a lifetime of watching, he was up there playing the scene!

Lear took him along to a series of exclusive screenings for the movie-business crowd in New York. They usually ended up joining a variety of glamorous people for dinner afterward at Wally's, or Cafe Central, or Orso's, or Texarcana, a changing series of "hot" restaurants with subtle distinctions made over who merited what kind of table. In some, sitting in the back room was everything—in others, it was death. A few were presumably secret (like Raos, located on a Mafia-protected block in the midst of a devastated and scary section of Spanish Harlem), though in fact the chic crowd all seemed to know of those. Others, such as Elaine's, were landmarks, sacred sites that demanded pilgrimage. Because of the people he accompanied, Fred experienced service he had never heard of —entrées cooked that didn't exist on menus, complimentary drinks, waiters standing asleep on their feet at two in the morning waiting patiently for them to go home, even though they had finished eating hours before. He marveled at it. Like an astronaut viewing the surface of an alien world, he found every detail stunning.

Once he was known by these restaurants as part of the crowd, he found himself welcomed as though he were a celebrity. Sometimes he was even seated ahead of other famous people. The first time that happened he replayed the moment over and over in his mind, recalling it to memory blissfully, the way one might cherish an ecstatic night of love with an ideal mate, staring off in happy reverie for minutes on end. The way those famous faces watched him get in before them, their brows furrowing, attempting to place him. Who the hell is that fat little Jew? he imagined them thinking. I'd better smile at him, he must be important.

Only I'm not important, he would be forced to remind himself. But even that hardly depressed his elation. At least he was there. And he could talk to these people. They actually listened to him.

There was a price he had to pay for this happiness, however. Marion provided the bill. Since Tom's invitations involved screenings, permitting him only one guest, she couldn't come. She could have joined them for dinner after the movie, but she had refused on the basis of how late that would make the evening, too late for her to then get a good night's sleep. Of course once she heard the stories of whom they were meeting, she changed. Asked to come along. By then Fred didn't want her to. He didn't know why, but her switch in attitude angered him. Maybe it was that having spent a few nights without her, he realized how much more relaxed he was. He seemed to be more intelligent when she wasn't around. People liked him better. She wasn't there to forever burst his balloon.

Keeping her away was hard.

"Where are you going tonight?" she asked.

"I don't know," he said. "We're going to the Paramount screening room—you know, the one where it's all Eames chairs."

"Yeah, you told me. Where are you going later?"

"I don't know." A lie. They were going to Elaine's. "We're meeting Sam Billings, Tom's producer—"

"I know who he is. When will you know where?"

"I guess, uh . . . not until we get there. Billings is meeting us at the screening room." A lie. Billings wasn't going to the screening. Fred realized only now that if he failed to dissuade her from coming, he had just told a falsehood that might be easily exposed. "I'll call you from the restaurant."

"I'm supposed to sit at home starving until you call?"

"You want me to cancel? We'll go out to dinner."

She sneered. Looked away and sighed with irritation. Then turned back to him and said, "Yes! Call Tom and cancel."

Fred had done a good job while making the offer to cancel—spoke as though the matter was insignificant. That he'd be happy either way. And even though Fred suspected she was merely testing him, that all he'd have to do was go to the phone with a similar easy manner and start dialing Tom's number, he couldn't. The slight chance that she wouldn't tell him to hang up worried him so much it showed on his face.

Marion snorted. "Forget it. Go ahead and enjoy yourself." She spoke with hopeless disgust, the despairing resignation of a disappointed mother faced with a favorite son's betrayal.

"You can join us later," Fred said, relieved. "I'll call—"

Marion got up, walking to the coat closet. It was time for her to leave for work. "Forget it. You don't want me to."

"Come on!" Fred whined. "That's not true! I'll call you from the rest—"

"Forget it," she said, grabbing her coat, opening the front door, and going, letting the metal door swing shut behind her.

Its slam emptied the apartment. He listened to the refrigerator hum, sorrow vibrating into his crass manipulation. He didn't feel guilt—or rather, shame at his own behavior and motives was too constant a companion for it to be noticed. He felt tragic, awesome despair at the hopelessness of things ever being carefree between him and Marion. They were like siblings, thrown together involuntarily by fate, personalities that clashed, but were somehow stuck to each other with a glue that never dried to fasten them, and also never evaporated to free them.

Tom Lear, Tom Lear, Tom Lear. The name played in his mind like a pretty song. Everything the guy did seemed so perfect. He even dressed well. He had it all over someone like Tony Winters. He had Tony's connections (and he got them by merit, not by birth), he had Tony's quick wit, but he also had the common touch. There was always something snobbish in Tony's manner—he let you know he thought he was smarter than you. Not Tom. He had a frank, almost childlike innocence when he'd disagree over a book or movie with people. An earnest desire to hear the other point of view. Tony always seemed to want to win the fight, make the other person seem stupid. And Tom had a broader experience and interest in the world. He liked sports. He played poker. He pointed out women with great tits, just like a regular guy.

Tom had asked to read his novel. That was something Tony Winters would never do. Tony couldn't care less about someone else's work. Tom was really eager to see Fred's stuff. He asked about it every time they got together. Two nights ago Fred had given him the first third of the book, a hundred and fifty pages. And because Tom was such a great person, Fred felt no anxiety over Tom's possible reaction. He was confident that if Tom didn't like the pages, he would say so, make helpful comments, and continue to be as friendly as ever. That more than anything else was what made Tom different from the rest of the New York cultural scene. He was a real friend.

Fred had to deliver the first one hundred pages of *The Locker Room* soon. Both Bart and Bob Holder had been asking for them. Therefore, having someone like Tom as a first reader was lucky. Fred happily spent the morning reading over his work. Just the substantial size of his manuscript pleased him. Soon he would have a published book, a small enough achievement in the world in which he now moved, but a climax for him of six years of struggle.

He felt a slight disappointment when Tom Lear called to confirm their date and made no mention of his pages. Probably hasn't read them yet, Fred told himself, and made up excuses for Tom, not wanting to feel critical of him. He spoke to Marion at work in the late afternoon. He had given little thought to their argument so he surprised himself by saying, after hearing a sullen, clipped hello from her, "Hi. Listen, Tom called. We'll be at Elaine's at nine-thirty. Want to meet us there?"

Long pause. As though she were looking for a trick. There wasn't one, however. Fred had realized there was no reason for her not to come. Her presence wouldn't change anything for him. In fact, he now wanted her to come. To see how seriously everybody took him. Maybe she would become more respectful. "That's kind of late . . ." she said.

"What is this? You hocked me about coming and—"

"I didn't hock you. Jesus! Nine-thirty's late—"

"You can leave when you're tired. I'll put you in a cab."

"Okay," she said, suddenly. "Great. I'll see you there."

Fred thought maybe Tom had read the hundred and fifty pages and wanted to wait until he was with him in the flesh to talk about them, but when they met outside the Gulf & Western Building a few mintues before the screening, Tom said, "Fred, I haven't had a chance to read your stuff. I'm sorry, things have been crazy—"

"That's okay," Fred said. "But do you think you could by the week-end? I've got—"

"Definitely. I'll read 'em tonight."

I'll read 'em tonight. That sentence interfered with the fortunes of *Indiana Jones and the Temple of Doom* throughout the screening. Instead of groaning at the cave with insects, Fred heard Tom's casual voice, imbued with confidence. I'll read 'em tonight. While around him people squirmed and moaned uncomfortably as a heart was removed with bare hands from someone's chest, Fred envied Tom's situation. He hoped one day another writer would sit next to famous author Fred Tatter before the lights came down and be thrilled to hear that Fred would "read 'em tonight." He watched impassively as the beating heart was held high into a close-up. While the rest of the room turned to each other with disgust on their faces, he found the image peculiarly normal. Somehow a just expression of the state of his life. Beating and bleeding for everyone to see.

When the picture was over he felt constrained, back to discomfort as usual. It was a mistake giving Tom the pages, Fred said to himself. I can't take it. He thought it would be different with Tom Lear, but as they took a cab to Elaine's and entered, greeting the crowd, kissing cheeks, pumping hands, glancing about to see who was there, he knew it wasn't. He needed Tom's good opinion. Things wouldn't be the same if Tom hated the manuscript. After all, Tom might have forged the friendship, assuming Fred was a good writer—discovering otherwise could change everything. Isn't a big part of the reason I like Tom because I think he's a terrific writer? Fred asked himself.

Fred copied Tom's drink orders. By the time Marion arrived, he had had two Scotches and soda. Her appearance surprised him. It wasn't simply that he had forgotten she was coming—he stared at her amazed, as though her very existence startled him. "Hi, Marion," he said, kissing her on the cheek and sitting down. She remained standing (she looked flushed with excitement at being there, Fred noticed, but the observation meant nothing to him in his gloomy mood) behind a chair, and stared at Tom. Why is she doing that? Fred wondered.

"I'm Tom Lear," Tom finally said.

"Thanks," she said, laughing. "I'm Fred's wife, Marion."

"You haven't met!" Fred said, genuinely surprised.

"How many drinks has he had?" Marion asked Tom, and laughed.

Tom smiled at her. "He *is* out of it tonight. What's the matter with him?"

"No, really," Fred said, making it worse. "You haven't met?"

"Of course we haven't met, Freddy," Marion said. She called him Freddy when she was most contemptuous of him. "You know that. I complained about it enough, for Chrissake."

"Has he been keeping you from me?" Tom Lear asked with mock outrage. "He knew it would be magic between us. That's why."

Marion laughed and winked at Tom. Fred knew she meant to be flirtatious, but that subtle art was beyond Marion—she made it seem dirty somehow. Can't she tell he's making fun of her? he asked himself.

He found himself spending much of the evening listening to Marion with disapproval. She talked a lot. Asked briefly about *Indiana Jones* and then launched into a pompous lecture saying that scary movies damaged kids. Tom pretended to take her seriously, Fred thought, indeed he probably did consider her point well-taken, but Fred also saw the bored look in his eyes. Marion's not pretty enough to be dull, Fred could hear him think. Tom's eyes drifted to the door, probably hoping someone interesting would come in. Fred could feel, like a sympathetic itch, the restlessness in Lear's body, the desire to be free of them.

Marion was oblivious, tipsy from her two glasses of wine, asking (too loudly) who was who at the other table, and puzzled by Fred's morose air. "What's with you?" she asked Fred when another (one of many) lulls in the conversation had caused Tom to stare off toward the bar.

"Nothing," Fred said, afraid she was about to say something intimate and embarrassing.

She smiled, her eyes unfocused. "The food here sucks," she said. Loud.

Tom's eyes went to her instantly. The sentence shot through Fred like a current, startling every nerve. "Shhh," he said, his head whipping one way and the other to check whether Elaine or one of the waiters had overheard. Tom, however, was laughing.

Marion looked at him. "Right? She's got a great racket going. Lousy food, horrible decor, the worst tables made into the chicest. The woman's brilliant."

Fred spotted the owner seated only two tables away. Marion's speech, in his mind, was as loud as a PA broadcast in a public school. "Shut up," he said. "She's right over there."

Marion smiled at Tom about Fred and put a hand on his head, patting it. "Poor boy. He lives in fear of everybody."

Tom's eyes went to Fred, as though the proof of her observation was visible on Fred. The look burned through Fred. He imagined he could see Marion's statement click into place for Tom, characterizing Fred for him, belittling him.

"That's bullshit!" Fred said, desperate to discredit Marion's remark. "It's rude, that's all."

Marion looked triumphant. "See?" she said to Lear, who was watching with greater interest than he had shown all night.

"See what?" Fred said. "What the fuck does that mean?"

"Fred." She said this like a command, a confident dog owner announcing: Heel. "Come on. I was teasing."

"Fred," Tom Lear said gently. "We're all afraid."

"It was rude." Fred stared at the table. He felt hot in the face, unable to meet their eyes. Somehow he had been made into a jerk. "It was rude," he heard himself repeat petulantly. He didn't look up. He knew the shame and hurt would show too clearly on his face. There was a heavy silence before Tom said something—obviously to distract the conversation—about an article in that morning's *Times*. Lear kept that going for a while, long enough so that the suggestion they get a check wasn't placed too close to the angry exchange between Fred and Marion. It was smoothly done. The departure had no more than a trace of the embarrassment of that silence.

But during that silence, during the long moment of peering at the blue-and-white-checked tablecloth, while Lear and Marion said and did nothing to ease his wounded feelings, Fred had felt his bright new world collapse around him.

David, the faithful spy, tattled effortlessly to Chico about the senior editors' reactions to the cover-meeting argument. David had no worry that by repeating everything said he might harm anyone's reputation with Chico, because the comments had been universally disparaging about Rounder, even the remarks made by two people whom Rounder had hired. A few joked about Chico's childish manner but there was admiration for him as well for having called Rounder on his foolish naiveté. Thank God I didn't volunteer to do this for Rounder, he told himself, watching the pleased expression on Chico's face. They were having dinner together at an Italian restaurant near *Newstime* on a Thursday night that looked to be a virtual all-nighter for David. A major Midwestern bank had suddenly appeared near to collapse in midweek and they were scrambling to get a story together. David had put his best writer on it, but his early draft had been awful—the explanation of how it happened was muddled, and there was a complete absence of drama.

"But there is no drama," the writer complained. "The computers showed up with bad numbers."

"Somebody punched the numbers up on a terminal, didn't they? That person had a reaction, didn't he?" David asked. He wanted to grab the bureau reports and write the story himself. But he had done that early in his tenure as senior editor (doing a total rewrite on one of the aging hacks under him), and Harpo, figuring it out when David submitted the story—he could recognize David's touch—told him that was not being an editor. "You're supposed to help the writers write, not make it clear they don't know how." Since then he had left them to do the writing, even if that meant five or six revisions to get it right. But the frustration of standing by while someone floundered in waters he himself could easily swim never lessened. Tonight would be one of those late nights that, as a writer, he could have ended early.

Why complain? It had its advantages. He could go to dinner with Chico and do himself some good. And he could drink! He sipped his third gin and tonic (when the thermometer reached seventy-five degrees that afternoon, he decided to inaugurate his summer beverage) and enjoyed Chico's rapacious pleasure at hearing Rounder criticized. "That's all," David finished to the eager face.

"Well," Chico said. He looked off. "I wish Mrs. Thorn could have been there."

"She must know."

"Know what? How the staff feels?"

"No. What a bad job he's doing. She reads the magazine," David said, and then laughed at the thought that maybe she didn't read it.

"Presumably. But she's happy no matter what's in *Newstime*, unless her Washington friends complain."

David vividly pictured Henry Kissinger, in a tuxedo, at a fashionable Washington dinner party, holding up a copy of *Newstime* over his (what? lobster newburg?) and making faces, holding his nose maybe and saying, "Yecch," like a kid rejecting spinach. But no matter how silly he made the image, it still impressed him, as it had years ago when he joined the magazine straight out of college, just how important every word, every decision, every action that a writer or an editor of a national newsmagazine could be. Nobody notices you until you fuck up, he thought with masochistic pride. After all, it takes a pretty tough and remarkable person to withstand that pressure.

"I got to get him off my back," Chico said.

David nodded. "He's a disaster." *Is* Rounder a disaster? he wondered the moment he had said so. David always retreated from absolute statements once he had made the initial advance. An uncertain general, he preferred to marshal the troops of judgment and seek higher ground rather than commit them to the mess and chaos of battle.

Chico added to his regret by staring at him. His small eyes fixed on David. "Do you think he can last long?"

"I don't know," David said. He had no idea. The truth was he found the firing and hiring of Grouchos hard to imagine or understand. Hiring Rounder had been so obviously wrongheaded. An inexperienced outsider was sure to create ill feelings among the veterans—and, predictably, he had. "Maybe she'd be too embarrassed."

"Mrs. Thorn? Embarrassed?" Chico smiled. Apparently that was impossible, a naive remark.

"I guess not," David said.

"She has the selective memory of the rich," Chico went on. "When she fires Rounder, she'll probably also fire the president of *Newstime*, thinking, by then, that it was his fault she picked Rounder."

"We should let him sink," David said thoughtlessly. He heard himself almost slur the last word. He stared at the water glasses, and they quavered in his vision. I must be drunk, he thought, wondering if his capacity was diminishing.

"What do you mean?"

"Stop protecting his ass!" David said, aggrieved, as though he, not Chico, were the main victim of Rounder's presence. "He wants to ignore the Russian boycott and put Redford on, let him! He's the editor in chief. Let him run it."

Chico shook his head. "I can't. When she made the decision, she spoke to me privately, saying that eventually she wanted Rounder to become sort of the spokesman for the magazine, help the company formulate new projects, that I would be the editor in chief within a few years. She expects me to watch him. If he doesn't keep his nose clean, I might be blamed for not having wiped it."

"Bullshit," David said. He felt at ease with Chico: his equal. A sudden elevation of status that Chico's manner—curious, interested, even slightly abashed—confirmed. "She's suckered you. She knows she needs you to run the magazine. But if you run it for free, there's no reason to promote you. She can't ask you to do the work of Groucho without giving you the mustache."

Chico's eyes widened, and for a second David wasn't sure if he would take the use of the lower echelon's jargon in good humor. Presumably Chico had once been a lowly employee, chipping away at the awesome statuary of his bosses with like chisels, but ascending the pedestal might have made him as humorless and cold as marble. Instead, he laughed. "I haven't heard that for years!" he said, delighted. "That's still the lingo?"

"Nothing changes at *Newstime*," David said in a mock announcer's voice, "not even the childish nicknames."

But Chico had already lost his enjoyment of the slang, and was back to fretting over David's advice. "You know, you're right. I should let the fucking guy sink. Him and Ray."

Ray? That was Harpo, who, when Chico had fallen into his sullen fit at the cover meeting, had continued to explain why ignoring the Olympics would be a mistake. Rounder had humiliated Chico by finally giving the cover to Harpo to top-edit, but that wasn't Harpo's fault.

"Ray thinks he's going to kiss ass all the way to being number two," Chico went on with surprising nakedness, his big head scrunched low on his shoulders like a football player's. He looked ready to charge a running back, prepared to take a jolt and give an even worse one. "He thinks I can't take it. That I'll leave and he'll inherit."

God, David thought, I'm so naive. He's probably right. That's why Harpo kept on arguing it out with Rounder. Not to support Chico, but to appear like a responsible number two, disagreeing but not pressing the point too far.

"And he's slipped, you know that?" Chico also seemed to be slurring words. How many drinks had they had? Maybe it was four. Their glasses were suddenly full again, magically, though David remembered sucking the last drops from the ice only moments ago. "He used to be a terrific editor. The kind of editor you are now. Bold, decisive. In control of the writers. On top of the section. Now he's focused on dominating the meetings. Getting more pages for his sections whether they deserve 'em or not."

"Yeah!" David said, wanting to encourage more talk, not to agree. None of it seemed true, but it was working out well for him. However, his "Yeah" had come out too enthusiastically. He sounded like a bloodthirsty fan. Yeah! Get 'em!

Chico shut his eyes and rubbed his forehead. "You and I could do great stuff with the magazine . . ." He let it hang for a moment, opening his eyes before adding, ". . . if we were given a free hand."

David remembered from his college days, from the antiwar era, a favorite comeback used when someone would try to include another in a decision or action without actually asking for his agreement: "What do you mean, 'we', white man?" He smiled at the thought of saying this to Chico. But even with four (was it five now?) drinks in him, he didn't have the nerve.

But Chico did it for him. "You'd be perfect for Ray's job," he said.

David, surprised and delighted, said without thinking, "I agree!"

They talked around this subject for quite a while, drinking steadily. The booze seemed to hit David hard. He bumped into a table on his way out of the restaurant. Out in the night air, passing well-dressed couples walking back to their hotels from theater and dinner, he felt woozy. The faces loomed past him—big, frozen in his mind for a moment in the smiles or the pensive or laughing looks they happened to have. Chico walked with his head down, shuffling his feet on the pavement, as though he were a bored schoolboy reluctantly going back to his unhappy home. There were curious silences from the traffic, moments when the sound of David's breathing seemed to be the loudest noise in the city. He felt empty. Not depressed or sad or lonely or abandoned. He felt absent. Expected back, but not there.

Later, David sat in his office waiting for the writer to finish more changes he had felt were needed on the bank collapse. He replayed that moment when Chico offered him Harpo's job. David knew it was no trick to give someone a promotion that you're not in a position to grant. Still he felt flattered and excited. If Chico could somehow unseat Rounder and if he could dispose of Harpo and if he could fulfill his promise to David (incredible, impossible ifs, all of them), then David would become the youngest Marx Brother in the magazine's history, a surefire successor to Chico. He might even make Groucho by the age of forty. His heart didn't beat eagerly. The alcohol gave him a dispassionate eye. He regarded the prospect with quiet satisfaction. And somehow, he felt a reasonable certainty that the incredible just might happen.

"But that makes no sense!" Tony whined. Garth leaned back in his chair, staring coldly. Foxx looked in Tony's direction as though he were a weary tourist checking off a sight he was supposed to have seen because of its great reputation, but in fact found boring. Neither spoke, despite Tony's urgent voice. "I mean," Tony continued quietly, hoping to bury the tone of injury in his voice, "how could he have belonged to the movement and then become right-wing without some explanation?"

"Can't have political speeches," Foxx said, a coffee-shop waitress informing a customer that an item on the menu was unavailable.

"You don't want me to be right-wing," Garth said. "I'm turned off to politics. Not right-wing."

"That's not enough of a conflict!" Tony complained. Again, impatience showed through the veil of modesty and reasonableness he had drawn over his true nature. Lois had told him, over and over, "Writers don't have power in this town. They expect you to do the rewrites they want. No arguing. The only way you can get them to do what *you* want is to make it seem like it's what *they* want." Last night they had screwed three times and talked out this meeting. He had actually lain inside her with his sore and numbed penis while they planned strategy.

It had all been for naught. He had, at the start, mollified them by announcing he'd do what they wanted, but as they went through the script, beginning with the very first line, picking away at his stage directions, his dialogue (my dialogue! my God, I'm famous for my dialogue!), his character choices, and even, incredibly, the names he had given to one of them, rage, incredulous fury, threatened to erode his submissive mask.

Garth watched him. Tony was stuck in the middle of his desire to insultingly reject their criticisms and his desire to pleasantly persuade them they were wrong. The famous eyes seemed sadistically detached from the emotion in the room. Foxx, at least, looked wary of Tony, slightly scared by the vehemence of his voice. But Garth had a laughing quality in his glance, a gamesman coolly observing an opponent's desperate attempt to escape an inevitable defeat.

"Then your character has no conflict," Tony said after a pause, softening his tone. "You simply become someone to whom events happen and, in the end, you won't be changed by them."

"My *conflict*," Garth said, the emphasis sounding disciplinary, "my conflict is over whether I love Meryl's character."

"Meryl would never play this part," Foxx said bitterly.

Garth glanced at him. "We'll get to that. Let's stay—"

"What do you mean?" Tony asked. He was hurt by Foxx's tone.

"It's a nothing role."

"A nothing role!"

Garth interrupted. "I want to stay on my character. My character's conflict is whether I love her or not."

"You're not conflicted over whether you love her," Tony said, now not bothering to conceal his disdain. "You love her. You're conflicted over whether you can trust her."

This silenced Garth. He nodded. Interested. Not at all, apparently, wounded by the way Tony had made his point. "Isn't that, ultimately, the same thing?" Garth asked.

"No. You can love somebody you don't trust. That's a tragedy."

"Oh, great," Foxx said to the wall. "Now we're writing a tragedy!"

"No we're not! That's not what I said!" Tony whined like a boy whose parents are teasing him. "If what he wants"—Tony pointed at Garth—"was done, we'd be writing a tragedy!" My God, he thought, slumping back, exhausted, into his chair, now I've said it: "*we'd* be writing." That's what this is, all right. A collaboration. They're writing it with me. Two people who couldn't compose a witty telephone message.

"It doesn't work!" Garth said with pleasant enthusiasm. "What you say sounds fine in the abstract but it doesn't work on paper. It's unsympathetic."

"It worked in *The Maltese Falcon!*" Tony said. Lois had advised him to come up with past movie successes. Arguing by analogy, she said, was common and respected. "The whole relationship between Bogart and Astor is about whether he can trust her. Same thing in *North by Northwest*. The second half of the film is about whether she is or isn't a spy."

Sure enough, these references entranced them. Garth nodded and then peered at his desk. Foxx's head snapped up, his eyes studying the ceiling as though something had begun to crash through. Tony felt a surge of confidence. He sat up. Do I finish them off? Or, if I push, will they get stubborn and push back just for the hell of it? "Maybe I didn't execute it well," Tony said, handing them a token of self-humiliation, "but I think my concept is right. Your character has to once again make the political choice he faced in the sixties, only now it is a woman—Meryl's character—who has become, if you will, the Vietnam war, the physical embodiment of whether he will have the courage to oppose society and defend what is right."

"*North by Northwest* is fun!" Foxx said, suddenly furious. "It's not some symbolic story about the most depressing war in American history."

"Oh come on, Jim," Garth said.

"Come on, what?" Foxx pleaded, his hands spread out, begging Garth. "This project is starting to sound like *Apocalypse Now*—without the action."

"No!" Tony said. "It's a gothic thriller. Like *Marathon Man* or *Three Days of the Condor*. They were hits."

"Exactly!" Garth said to Foxx. "I'm not Cary Grant. And besides, I want to play a real character. I want this picture to have some meat to it. No one's really done a great picture about the struggles of antiwar activists. Tony's figured a way to do a contemporary thriller—which makes it commercial—but with a real theme."

"Well, then, why were you so down about this draft?" Foxx asked. Garth nervously glanced at Tony. "You said—"

Garth cut Foxx off. "I was disappointed in the execution of some things. I always liked the concepts. I think there's nice stuff here, but Tony needs to work more on the characters."

"And the action! There's not enough action!" Foxx almost hopped with annoyance.

"Yes, yes," Garth said. He looked at Tony, his expression tired and bored. "The chase at the end is no good. It's full of clichés."

"Okay," Tony said, swallowing hard. He felt abashed, a boy who has peed in his pants on the first day of school. He didn't even know if they were right, but each criticism hurt more and more, as though he were being punched repeatedly in the same spot, right on the already bruised skin. The fact that Garth was actually concealing the extent of his disappointment in the script made it all the more horrifying. Tony had felt the sting of rejection as a writer before. People who felt his work was still young, limited, too cold—usually the complaint was simply that it wasn't commercial (not Broadway), but never that he was inept, so inadequate that he had to be protected from a truthful opinion.

He listened to their dissection of his chase sequence at the end of the script. Foxx did most of the surgery, heedless of scars or of how thoroughly the patient had been anesthetized. Everything about it was bad, even down to how Tony had formatted the pages. "This reads like prose," Foxx said with disgust. "You have to give us shots and angles, some kind of pacing, so we can picture it. It's totally nonvisual." Garth suggested he read some scripts they had selected for him so he could get an idea of how, as he put it, "a professional screenplay looks."

He felt his cheeks quiver with shame. They had beaten him at last. Really finished him. He nodded passively, not as a trick, not as a social hypocrisy, but because he felt they were right. He didn't know what he was doing. He was just a kid after all, someone who had never set foot on a movie set, who had no idea of what any of it entailed. Probably the script was bad. Worse, something that could never be done. An embarrassment.

When they finished, Tony asked, "Are you sure you want me to do this rewrite?"

They both looked startled. "Well, what the hell do you think we're talking for?" Foxx said. "The fun of it? We expect you to make these changes."

"No, no," Tony said. He knew this question revealed how hurt he felt, but he had to know the answer. "Do you have confidence I can do it?"

Foxx stared at him in amazement.

Garth frowned. "Doesn't matter whether we have confidence, Tony. It matters whether you do," he said, but sadly, as though having to point this out with another example of Tony's ignorance.

Later, Tony walked back across the legendary lot, only now its mythic past had dissolved in the face of his present misery. They were only ugly low buildings with an excessive amount of parking space, a McDonald's of culture, fast food for the mind, where a decision as to whether you wanted your burger medium or rare was irrelevant since they all came out well-done. But even that thought, he realized, was a cliché, a well-worn fact of American life that looked even drabber on him, since he had volunteered to wear the uniform.

Back in the car, he drove slowly, uncertain where to go. He had planned on visiting his mother's set (Lois would be there) and having lunch with them all. He was expected there, no doubt in triumph, to report that Garth was planning on shooting his script. To admit the truth to them, even to his mother, was beyond imagining. In New York (perhaps), little would be thought of it. He could say blithely, "Oh, the assholes want a lot of stupid changes," and the result might even reflect well on him. Writing for the movies in New York was almost a sure thing. If you succeeded you were considered clever, if you failed you were considered too refined a talent. In LA, failure had no subtleties. It was just pitied. The answer, of course, was to lie. Behave as though the changes were minor, that Garth and Foxx had been enthusiastic. But to will himself to that deception seemed almost as staggering as to will himself to tell the truth.

He returned to his hotel. In the middle of the day, the halls occupied only by cleaning women and their carts, the choice felt lonely. His room had been straightened. It looked anonymous, his presence erased. He stared at the phone. For a moment his mind (always talking at him, never resting) went blank, relaxed. He felt tired. He wished he could move out of his life, like a hotel, out of his elegant but standard room, and find an eccentric villa, or even a dreary cave, but leave certainly. He picked up the phone and dialed Betty in New York. He had made no decision to, his hand seemed to have developed the desire.

When he got her, her voice happy, pleased to hear from him, he had nothing to say.

"Did you have your meeting?" she asked.

"Yes." And he had no energy to continue.

"What happened?" she asked, fear creeping into her tone.

"They didn't like it." He couldn't say more, and thinking about it, he really didn't have to. That's what it amounted to, pure and simple: they didn't like it.

"So they don't want to go on?" Betty asked, gently, very gently, testing a hair-trigger spring.

"Oh yeah." Tony was surprised that she would think—even for a second—that it might be that bad. "No, they're not firing me. They just want a total rewrite."

"Oh," she said with relief. "Oh, I'm sorry," but with pleasure returning to her voice.

"Well, it's kind of insulting," Tony said, angry she found this situation relatively comforting. "I'm a . . ." for a second, he was going to say: I'm a genius. He caught himself with that monumental word of self-praise (and delusion!) right in his mouth, ready to sing out uncensored. Like his mad mother, capable of the most outrageous statements of egomania. I'm a genius? he asked himself. Since when?

Am I losing my mind? Like her, when she met defeat? But that wasn't defeat. That was political oppression. *He* had met defeat. And his mother *was* a genius.

"What?" Betty asked into his uncompleted sentence.

"They wouldn't fire me, Betty," Tony said darkly, furious at her, angrier at her than he felt toward Garth and Foxx. That was nuts too. He was falling apart.

"All right," she said. "Okay. Calm down. I didn't say anything."

Now there was a silence. A silence he could fill with a thousand speeches. All of them words of regret. What had happened to him? To his youth of sheer promise, of bold confidence? Who or what had blocked off his clear view of the horizon? He had failed. As a playwright. As a screenwriter. And as a husband. The image of himself that he carried like an icon, that he was a handsome, happily married, brilliant young playwright in the early stages of a long, glamorous career, had been revealed as a stupid object of worship, a childish understanding of life. He was none of those things. He was an unsuccessful writer with a fucked-up marriage in the midst of a tacky affair. How he had become that was a mystery still, but the truth of it was no longer a revelation.

"I love you," he said in a low, cracked, despairing voice.

"I love you," Betty said back.

"I'm tired. I'll call you later, okay?" He thought of Lois. "Or maybe tomorrow morning. All right?"

"Sure. Don't feel bad!"

"I won't," he said, hanging up, and feeling the weight of his sorrow crush him down onto the bedspread, forcing his legs up to a fetal position. He lay there, still, afraid to move, watching the afternoon California sun light up the curtains into a white neon glow, while he passed into a sleep of numb despair.

Patty couldn't say why, but once she gave her pages to Betty, joy flooded her being. She went home, put an old Stones album on the stereo—loud—and danced wildly to it, using the cast-iron columns as her partners and the long smooth wood floors as a vast stage for a solo that could rival Mick Jagger's for exuberance. She was alone. Late at night. And happy. There was no longing for someone to be there, creating a personality for her. She didn't miss David—still working late at the office—as she had in the first months of living with him. She could bear to be there without watching television. Without calling a friend. Without going to sleep. To be awake and alone had become possible.

She exhausted herself dancing, and sat sweating, on the couch thinking all this. But soon she was drawn to the new manuscipt, to read the pages—she hoped—along with Betty. They were good. They excited her. She found herself mentally writing more when she reached the end, and soon she was drawn back to the typewriter. Concentration, always hard for her, had become automatic. She could break into the surface of her book as easily as diving into clear calm water and there was no effort in staying below, no need to come up for air. Nothing had ever been so completely her own.

The phone rang. She stared at it for a moment, unconscious of what it was. She answered it abstractedly.

"Hello, hello," a male voice said with excessive cheerfulness. "Thank God it's you. I didn't know what I'd do if he answered."

Patty, still picturing her characters frozen in position, unspoken words in her mouth, had no idea who this was. "Well, that's lucky," she said.

"I know it's late. I'm sorry. Can you talk?"

"Yeah," she said, puzzled. And then she recognized the voice. It was Jerry Gelb! Her old boss, the villain who had shattered her self-esteem. He sounded so odd.

"What? He's asleep?"

"You mean David?"

"If that's your boyfriend."

"No, he's at work. Is this you, Jerry?"

"Yeah!" he said with a combination of bravado and sheepishness.

"I'm bombed. I'm snookered. I've been thinking about you. I had to call."

"It's one o'clock in the morning," Patty said, but she knew, with a clarity that had utterly escaped her when she worked for him, why he was phoning.

"I know, I know," he said, again with a mix of shame and pride. "I'm cracking up. I can't forget you. Your beautiful big eyes. How are you? I miss you."

"I miss you too," she said with a sarcastic lilt.

"You do?"

"Sure. I always miss men who reduce me to tears on a daily basis."

"Oh, come on. Surely I wasn't that bad."

"No. I was."

He laughed. "Touché. You sound great. Any chance we could meet for lunch tomorrow?"

Patty wondered if she could have asked for a better revenge than this drunken call. She had control of him now. Sex had put him out of control, and being fired had put her out of his control. She could so easily torture him now, without any fear. "What do you want to have lunch for?" she asked sweetly. Too sweetly for it to be meant honestly.

But Gelb didn't seem to notice. "My God." He sighed. "You know."

"No, I don't." Again, she almost sang the words. A siren luring him to disaster.

"Don't make me say it. I've made enough of a fool of myself. I have to see you. You sound great. You sound beautiful!" he added.

This ceaseless flattery and boyish confession of adoration began to intrigue her. She tried to summon up her image of him as a middle-aged man, but the youthful voice on the phone interfered. "I am," she heard herself say. "I've gotten thin and beautiful."

"You were always thin and beautiful!" he protested.

I could get him to say anything. She marveled at this power, relished it. "I can't have lunch with you," she said.

"Why not?" That sounded more like the old Gelb. Demanding, arrogant, controlling.

"My boyfriend wouldn't like it."

"So don't tell him." Gelb laughed.

"That would be dishonest." Patty cooed. I'm mean, I'm mean, she thought, delighted.

"Come on! Say yes. Go ahead and tell him. Tell him you're having lunch with your old boss. Nothing strange about that."

"He would think it was strange. Having lunch with the man who fired me. He would want to know what you wanted."

"I need your advice," Gelb said.

"My advice? What about?"

"It's a secret."

"How are you going to get my advice if it's a secret?"

"I can't talk about it on the phone. But . . ." He hesitated. "I may have a job for you."

"You want to hire me?" Patty said, flabbergasted. Would he really go that far just to get laid? Hire somebody he believed was incompetent? Wouldn't a whore be cheaper and less of a fuss?

"Come to lunch. I'll tell you about it."

"You can tell me now."

"No." He was firm. "Come to lunch. You have nothing to worry about. I'm not going to assault you in a restaurant."

"Where are we going?"

"How about the Four Seasons? You love that place."

"Okay," she said, without considering it. She could cancel. She didn't care how rudely she treated him.

"Great! See you there at twelve, all right?"

"Okay."

"Love you. 'Bye." And he hung up before she could refuse to accept so intimate a statement. He had managed to leave her feeling furious. He had gotten her to agree to see him. And he had insulted her by sneaking that farewell—the good-bye of an accepted lover—in at the end. She looked at the pages in her typewriter, unseeing, back in her past, living again as a confused and scared young woman battered by embarrassments. She wished she could have it all back to replay her stupid responses. Maybe at lunch she could do that. Desert Gelb, leave him with his erection at the table, laugh at his unsatisfied desire for her.

The heavy lock on the door to the hallway turned. David was home. Patty moved hastily, guiltily, putting away her manuscript and her thoughts. Both felt like betrayals of David.

David found her standing awkwardly in the middle of the room waiting for him. She felt like a teenager who has frantically put out the illicit cigarette and desperately fanned at the residual odor and smoke.

"Hey! You're up!" he said with the exuberance of a drunk. Were all the men in the world loaded tonight? she wondered. He went to her unsteadily and hugged her. She didn't want the embrace and moved quickly out of it.

"Did you close the section?"

"I have to go in tomorrow for a while. Check on a few things. Basically it's done."

"What happened? The world blow up?"

"No. . . . What did you . . . ? Oh, you had a dinner with Tony's wife."

"Betty. Her name is Betty."

"My, my." David looked amused at Patty's seriousness. "I'm sorry. I didn't mean to be sexist."

"I was just telling you her name. God, am I in a foul mood," she said, by way of apology. In fact, she had been in a great mood until Gelb called.

"Why? Did she say something?"

"Who?" Patty, thinking of Gelb, couldn't imagine what woman he meant.

David smiled. "Tony's wife," he said pointedly.

Patty smiled back. It was this, his wit, that she had once been so fond of. Still was fond of. "No."

"Well . . ." He moved to her, gently putting an arm around her. "What is it?"

Patty felt a sudden revulsion at her behavior, at her distrust of David. "I gave something to Betty to read."

"Something?"

"A novel I've been writing."

"You mean, not the romance novel?"

"No, a serious . . . Something of my own."

"No kidding!" David looked startled. "How long have you been working on it?"

"A month. A few weeks."

"Why didn't you tell me?"

"I'm sorry. I wasn't sure I could keep it up. I wanted to wait until I was really into it. Am I terrible?"

"No. I understand. I would be the same way."

"You mean to say you wouldn't tell me if you were working on a novel?"

David laughed. "Just like you."

"But that's terrible!" Patty insisted, her face a perfect mask of shock and outrage. "Don't you trust me?"

David smiled. "I never know when you're kidding."

"Good," Patty answered. "Don't you want to read what I've written?"

"Sure." But he looked doubtful, his eyes red, his feet unsteady.

"You're too tired."

"No!" he said firmly, but then sagged. "Is there any coffee?"

"You can read it tomorrow."

"Oh, for Chrissakes. You want me to read it now."

"I don't want you to die."

"Get me the pages and some coffee."

Patty hustled over to the desk, pulling the manuscript out of its grave, buried under several hundred sheets of blank typing paper in the bottom drawer.

David laughed. "You really didn't want me to know."

She smiled and gave him the pages, rushing out of the room to the kitchen, relieved to have something to do.

The coffee took forever to heat up. She couldn't hear anything while she waited—no paper rustling, no laughter, no groans—and she became convinced he had fallen asleep. But no. He was sitting up reading attentively. As she approached with the coffee, she got a view of his profile. His lips were pressed tight, his chin up. He looked prissy and dissatisfied. She knew it. He was going to hate her novel, probably spoil her desire to go on. She should never have succumbed to her hungry vanity. She handed him the coffee.

He looked up. His eyes looked funny. Patty thought for a moment that his wide and confused eyes were due to drunkenness, but when he took the cup and stared longer at her, she knew it was the writing. "They're good," he said, his tone surprised.

"You haven't read very much. Maybe you won't like the rest."

David's eyes slowly returned to her pages. "They're good," he said again slowly, a man in shock, repeating unbelievable news to himself. "They're good," he mumbled once more.

CHAPTER 11

I'm gonna give it to her, Fred thought furiously. He looked at the shadowed figure of Marion in the taxi. The seat made her look small, a fat little girl, her head barely reaching above the window. I'm gonna let her have it, he thought again, the excitement of his resolution pumping through him. She thinks I'll take it quietly like I always do, but I won't. I'm gonna call her bluff. She can't get away with making a fool of me anymore.

The Plexiglas partition between Fred and the driver was frosty with dust and scratches, the side windows covered with stickers that warned or cajoled the customer with New York City Taxi Commission regulations. The seat seemed to be sliding down through the bottom of the car. There was nothing to look at but the shrinking form of his wife. His anger welled in his chest. But he couldn't begin, frightened that once out, the flood of his rage would never subside and would end only by drowning them both.

No, no, he told himself. I won't show fury. She'd like that. Prove to her how she got to me. I'll give it to her cold. Aloof. Marion, as far as I'm concerned, our marriage is over. I don't want you to accompany me on any social occasions, I can no longer promise to be faithful, I don't give a shit about shopping for dinner. We can continue to live together but—

It made no sense.

If I hate her, I should leave her.

The taxi dropped into a pothole hard.

"Jesus," Marion exclaimed.

The driver mumbled something.

"Watch where you're going," Marion called out.

Fred forgot his problem and felt dread that the taxi driver would get angry and start fighting. This driver looked insane. He had hair growing all over his body, he looked sooty, and his eyes were bloodshot. Fred had noticed all that when the cab stopped for them in front of Elaine's, and

227

had even considered waving him on, but didn't, only because he was frightened that the driver, cheated of a fare, would get out and punch him.

The driver shouted something back, Fred couldn't hear what, and now his heart beat rapidly again, this time with terror. "Shhh," he said to Marion.

"He nearly broke my spine!" she said loudly.

"I know, I know," he whispered back. "He's crazy. We'll be there soon."

They relapsed into silence. I'm soothing her. I wanna blow her head off and I'm soothing her. It was like being a teenager living with his mother. He'd want to scream at his mother, tell her she was a whining, unattractive, bitter woman, ungrateful to his father (always tired, exhausted from work) for providing her with a life of ease. A maid to clean daily, caterers for parties, expensive trips, all the clothes she wanted (though she continued to look drab, no matter what her hairdo or the style of her dress), and all the power in making family decisions. And yet, like Marion, there was no end to her complaints that she was neglected, ignored; no action or comment his father could make that she failed to deride or despise. How his father had had the will and courage to build his business in the fog of complaints and meanness his mother exhaled at home . . . No more remarkable, he imagined, than his own ability to persevere in his ambition to be a novelist despite Marion's poorly concealed skepticism.

They arrived home. Fred gave the driver a big tip, knowing that would guarantee he wouldn't say anything. To his surprise, the driver said, "Thanks. Sorry about the bump. They oughta fix the fuckin' streets."

"Yeah," Fred said cheerfully, ecstatic that the guy was reasonable and decent. Marion had gotten out and gone ahead.

"It's that fuckin' fag we got for a mayor," the driver said out his window while Fred closed the door.

"Yeah," Fred said, not so cheerfully. He's probably an anti-Semite, he thought to himself, convinced that anyone who disliked Mayor Koch had to be. An anti-Semite and stoned, he decided after another glance at the driver's angry red eyes. Fred hurried to catch up with Marion.

She greeted him with: "What the hell did you give him a big tip for?"

"Oh, shut the fuck up," he answered with thorough bitterness. He almost covered his mouth, embarrassed by the release, but he forced that feeling away and strode into the elevator. Then he felt good. Not happy, but vigorous. No longer constipated by a little boy's timidity.

Marion stood outside the elevator and stared at him. For a moment he thought she wasn't going to get in. "You're such a baby," she said, and then finally entered, moving to the other side of the elevator as though they were strangers riding to different floors, different lives. He wished they were. He kept his glance downward until they got to their floor, looking up when Marion moved to get out. He watched her behind move while he followed her to the door. Although there was nothing exciting about either its shape or its motion, he felt horny for her. If only he could get her to bed without all the bullshit—if only he knew for sure what made her want to fuck. Other than his pressing her for so many days in a row that she eventually ran out of excuses, he couldn't say what did make her want to have sex. Years ago, when they were kids in college, he didn't remember that either of them had to initiate making love. They were both so thrilled to be doing it, it was automatic as soon as they were alone together. They would kiss immediately and soon . . .

There was an empty feeling to the apartment. The place was jammed with their things, eight years of living together, but their footsteps seemed to echo as though it were bare. Fred turned on the television to rid the place of the silence. Marion disappeared into the hallways. Probably gonna take a bath, Fred thought to himself bitterly. Well, I'm not going in there to apologize and whine just because I want some nooky. I'll find someone else. She doesn't think I'd ever do that, doesn't think I'd have the nerve to have an affair. Maybe she doesn't think anyone would have an affair with me, Fred thought, furious. She doesn't want to fuck me, so she probably thinks no one else does.

There was a moment, a moment of nameless dread and despair, when he feared she was right.

Patty would! Fred thought, blessed by the aburpt recall of their kiss at that dinner party, the party that had firmed up his relationship with Bart and led to his book contract. Yes, that was another time Marion had whined. Just because he needed her help to throw a party, one little party in eight years to advance his career. She had made him feel like a piece of shit that night. He remembered his erection, surging madly when he met Patty's gaping wet mouth. He had felt firm breasts against his chest. He knew her ass would also be a shape, a definite shape, not floating in a sea of blobby formless flesh like Marion's. Yes, Patty would have fucked him and Marion was a joke compared to Patty, hardly part of the same gender. Patty would do it. Or she would have before she had a boyfriend.

If only he had the nerve to march into the bathroom (since Marion no doubt expected him to come in like a penitent dog wagging his tail, head down, eyes up balefully, hoping to be forgiven) and say, "Patty wanted to fuck me."

What? He burst out laughing. Marion wouldn't have the faintest idea that was meant as an answer to her behavior. He laughed again.

"What's so funny?" Marion asked.

He gasped, turned to find her, as though he were a potential victim in a horror movie, his enemy having sprung from the grave. "You startled me."

"I'm sorry," she said. She was trying to be pleasant. "What's so funny? I heard you laughing. I thought it was something on TV."

Fred glanced at the set. He hadn't been paying attention to it. "No," he said, and offered no explanation.

"Why did you get so angry?" she asked. She squinted at him as if he were a distant object.

He made a sound, a disgusted laugh.

"I was just teasing at Elaine's," she said.

"Bullshit." He stared at the television, afraid to meet her glance. It would be amused and tolerant, contemptuously forgiving. When she treated him like a child, he always became one: more interested in winning back her love than winning the fight. Even now part of him wanted to make up, knowing that to continue the hostility meant weeks of sexual deprivation.

"You're right," she said.

Her tone was firm, settled. He looked at her out of curiosity.

"You were being an asshole," she said, again in a definite way, a telephone operator repeating a number. "You didn't want me to come, and then everything I did, everything I said, you acted like it embarrassed you. You acted like I was a slob who doesn't know how to behave. I have news for you. You were the one who behaved like a fool. Tom Lear thought you were the asshole, not me." She put her hands on her hips, an outraged landlady, a middle-aged shrew. Fred felt ancient, cowed. He imagined he had communed with his father's life: he understood, as he never had before, what that man felt while he sat in his Barca lounger, staring ahead at Monday Night Football, silently absorbing his wife's verbal abuse. Had Dad also kept quiet, fearing he would never get laid again if he fought back?

No, impossible. His father would have gone out and fucked someone else. He must have stayed for the sake of the kids.

Then why the hell am I still here? he asked himself. "You're pathetic," he said at last in a weak voice, almost paralyzed by despair. He meant her delusion that he was the one who had been embarrassing. She was incapable of seeing herself truthfully.

"Get out!" Her chin quivered.

"What?" he said, almost with a laugh.

"Get out of my house!" she screamed, her face red, her shoulders shaking.

Fred got out of the chair, his legs trembling. She seemed insane, terrifying.

"I don't want you here! Understand?" She moved at him, her hands clenched as though she meant to physically get rid of him.

"I live here," he said inanely, pleading.

"I can't stand looking at you! You make me sick! Get out of here!" She was screaming, her voice tearing her throat, the last words rasping from the exertion. She took a breath, put out a hand on the couch to steady herself, and then said in an exhausted whisper, "If you don't get out of here now, I'll have to leave. I don't know what I'm gonna do . . ." She closed her eyes and shuddered.

He moved toward the door, taking a wide route around her. At the closet he stopped. "Where am I gonna go?" he said plaintively.

"Oh, God," she moaned, as though stabbed, her knees buckling so that she was not totally supported by the couch. "Please go," she said in a whine, sounding so weak, so desperate, that her life seemed to be at stake.

He stood there indecisively. He could soften her if he went back, pleading an apology. He wanted to—walking out into the night with nowhere to go felt forlorn. He took a step toward her. "Marion . . ." he began.

"Go!" she said, and then, after a breath, "Please. Just go."

"Well, when do I . . ."

"Call me at the office tomorrow. We'll talk then."

She's gonna divorce me, he realized with disbelief. Tomorrow she'll tell me she thinks we should spend some time apart, but really she knows now she means to be rid of me. He was appalled. Divorce had seemed to be *his* option, *his* threat. He wanted to call foul, summon the umpire and have the rules read. He was sure this wasn't allowed. It infuriated him to contemplate her high-handedness: throwing him out, "we'll talk tomorrow," the whole uppity fake sophistication of it.

"Fuck you," he said with relish, opened the door, stepped into the hall, and turned back to make sure that when he gripped the door handle and slammed it shut, he did a good job of it. "Fuck you," he said again from the hallway and then pulled the door closed with every ounce of strength he could muster.

In the silence that followed, he waited, expecting to hear something from inside the apartment. What, he didn't know. Tears? Cries of apology? Derisive laughter?

He heard nothing. The hall hummed with lights, the starts and stops of the elevators, faint sounds of televisions and stereos, but nothing from Marion.

He walked away, rang for the elevator, and considered his choices. Whom could he call? His oldest friend lived in Long Island. His parents were out of the question. His brother was in California, his sister in Vermont. To go to Karl or one of the other of his writing friends meant spreading the story among all their friends. And what was the story? Were they breaking up?

Yes, I'm never going back.

Then why avoid their New York friends? They would have to know eventually.

He rode in the elevator, walked out into the street. It was too late to go to a movie, except at Times Square, where he wouldn't dare go at that hour. He could walk around for a while and then sneak back in and sleep in his office or on the living-room couch. Unless she bolted the chain. He hadn't heard her do that. She might later. He could telephone and insist on returning . . .

My God, Tom Lear is probably gonna call tomorrow morning to talk about the manuscript, he remembered. Humiliation at his situation washed over him. Then he realized he could call Tom first and eliminate that danger of discovery. But where would he sleep? Her behavior was a fucking outrage. And his acceptance of it! Incredible. He just left. He could have planted himself in that chair. What the hell could she have done about it?

An image of her screaming at him answered. She had looked so furious, so insane and out of control, that maybe she would have attacked him, poured gasoline on him while he watched late-night television and burned him to a crisp. And on top of everything, the really fucking outrageous thing, was that if she did incinerate him, she'd probably become a hero, celebrated in a novel by a feminist writer, played on the big screen by Meryl Streep or Jane Fonda. His part would probably go to Dabney Coleman or Richard Benjamin. The villain as jerk, or the jerk as villain.

He couldn't cheer himself up with this line of thought. It was humiliating. It was painful. It was stupid. And above all, baffling.

He stood out on Third Avenue, looking across its broad length, hating the fucking city. Huge and empty. Small and crowded. Too cold or too hot. Too lonely and without privacy.

When Norman Mailer got a new wife or stabbed an old one, it sounded romantic. People spoke with breathless excitement about famous writers getting bounced by their wives. Fuck it, he thought, heading for a phone, I'll tell all of them. I'll get them out of their fucking beds and tell all of them.

David Bergman listened to Patty typing. There were long periods of silence in between her bursts, unlike the steady flow when she had worked on the romance novels. With this writing, she was either quiet or frantic.

He punched another button on the cable-television box and got a scroll that told him the time, the weather, closing stock prices. He punched another, the sports channel, where they were showing a billiards championship.

She didn't seem to know, but she had made him a character in her book. Sure, he was disguised. Indeed, she had romanticized him physically (just another insult), making him taller, his features handsome. But the heroine's attitude, the male's responses—they were portraits of the inner truth of their relationship. In a court of law you could never establish a similarity, but she had captured the real nature of their feelings. It was impressive.

He punched a button for a movie channel and groaned that *Gandhi* was being shown again.

And insulting. She was a good writer. Oh, she needed to learn some grammar, to be sure, her craft could stand more work, but the essential, the absolutely necessary ingredient of being a good novelist she possessed —her characters lived, they inhabited the reader's skin, benign parasites mingling with the reader's own feelings and prejudices until they seemed inseparable. She was much more honest as a writer than she was in real life. The heroine stayed with her lover out of inertia, fear of being loose in a big city, mollifying his ego, stroking his personality as effectively as she pleased his cock.

He punched another button and a tall red-haired woman was on screen saying, "Kneel, slave!" The camera, obviously a hand-held video one, awkwardly pulled back, revealing that she was dressed in a skintight leather outfit that exaggerated the curves of her ample body. At her feet was a pathetic-looking middle-aged man—fat, bald, his skin pasty, his ass hairy.

"Yes," he said.

She struck him sharply on the back with a riding crop. It left a faint red stripe. "Yes, what?" she said, her tone also sharp, like a whip.

"Yes, mistress," he said in an abject whisper.

"Good," she said, tapping him lightly on the back with the whip. "Lick," she said in a bored tone.

The camera bounced and jerked as it moved to show the man put his face near her black leather boot and tentatively touch the tip of his tongue to it.

David had an erection. He looked down at his pants, outraged. He had an astonishing hard-on. He guiltily looked across the loft at Patty's back to make sure she hadn't noticed. She couldn't, of course, but his physical response to the screen implied things that horrified him and he dreaded her knowing. He could never convince her it couldn't mean anything.

The redhead brought the crop down on his back, lower this time, striking part of his buttock. "Faster," she said.

"Yes, mistress," he answered.

The sexual excitement David felt amazed him. He knew of course what he was watching. He had never seen anything like it, had only seen such scenes done in brief burlesques in movies, a joke shot to make fun of a macho character. He had read the Marquis de Sade in college. He didn't remember . . .

The image jumped. The tall woman was now standing next to a long black leather table. The man was strapped down, facedown. She raised the riding crop. "You want to be fucked up the ass, don't you, slave?"

"No," he cried in horror.

She whipped him on the ass twice. She was really hitting him, David realized, flabbergasted, noting the red marks the blows left.

"Yes you do. Tell your mistress you want to be fucked up the ass."

The image jumped again. The man was now standing, his wrists and ankles bound so that he was spread-eagled. She stood in front of him, her riding crop slowly stroking one side of him. With her other hand she brushed a nipple. He moaned. "Sensitive, aren't you?" she said, mocking. She took the nipple between her index finger and thumb and squeezed.

"Oh!" he yelped, his body trying to arch away from her.

She flicked her crop against his flank. "Don't move! How dare you move while I punish you!"

The screen went black and silent. David swallowed. His throat was dry. He stared at the blank image, angry. He desperately wanted to see more. It blipped and a telephone number appeared. "Call now, slave! And get the punishment you deserve!" a husky woman's voice said, recognizable as belonging to the redhead he had seen. The telephone number stayed on while he heard the man's voice say in a penitent whisper, "Yes, mistress."

It was replaced by another advertisement, this time for an escort service, a euphemism for prostitution. He knew there were explicit sex programs on cable television, but he hadn't heard or read of what he was now seeing, a program which consisted of a series of commercials for various sex services. There was an ad for a massage parlor, but most were for the escort services, which David assumed were used by traveling businessmen, since the commercials stressed they served all Manhattan hotels. He sat through fifteen minutes of them (usually they showed a girl dancing, doing a strip-tease, or putting something—a lollipop, a banana—in and out of her mouth while a telephone number was superimposed), waiting for a recurrence of the redhead's spot.

He kept a good check on Patty, who, to his annoyance, seemed to be getting ready to quit. She was leaning back reading pages, her typewriter off.

The erection he had while watching the redhead's ad dwindled the moment it was off, and, to his amazement, no amount of girls, in bikinis, topless, or totally nude, with or without banana in mouth, stirred him. The implication was clear. He judged himself quickly, the defense having no evidence. He wondered how he could have had this sexual longing, or perversion (he reminded himself), without a hint or a prelude of it until that night. If he were a henpecked husband or a clumsy fool who pursued women that rejected him repeatedly, then it might make sense.

And then she returned in a close-up. Her face was angular, her eyes black, her thin lips painted a vivid red. "Do you have a secret desire to be punished?" she asked contemptuously, as though she knew the answer was yes. "Mistress Regina will force you to admit your submissive desires. Call now for a consultation, worthless"—she made a solo of the word, drawing it out, chopping it into extra syllables, pausing both before and after it and then finishing with a hiss—"slave!"

His throat was dry again, he was hard. His absorption was so complete that he hadn't noticed his penis become stiff and large. But he felt it yearn against his pants for freedom. He had been struck a blow, deadening his brain, making him dumb with fascination.

"How do you spell . . . ?" Patty's voice said, sounding nearby. David leaned forward to hit the off button so abruptly that he lost his balance and had to grab the set to prevent himself from pitching forward onto the floor.

"What?" he said, breathless, his face feeling hot. She stared at him. Damn, I'm blushing, he though with horror. He spoke through it. "I didn't hear what you said. What do you need to spell?"

She looked at his cheeks, then at the television, and then back to David.

Why is she so fucking smart? he thought furiously. "I was watching a girl strip-tease on cable," he said with a sheepish laugh. "When you startled me, I turned into a teenager. Hiding *Playboy* under the sheets."

Patty smiled, satisfied. "Is she still on?" she said, reaching for the television.

"No!" David cried out, but to no avail. The set was still tuned to the channel David had been watching, but what appeared was simply a crawl listing the schedule of programs. David glanced at the clock. It was past the half-hour. The show he had seen was over.

"Oh," Patty said, disappointed. She smiled at David. "You don't have to be embarrassed you like watching naked women."

"Thanks. That's big of you."

"You pig," she added with mock coolness.

"Maybe you should punish me for it," he said, his voice casual. He was horrified that he had said this, contemplating quickly that if he revealed this interest in sadomasochism she would be sure to put it in her novel. Even if she went along with it. Nothing she exposed about herself in her writing seemed to worry her.

"My, my, we are getting kinky," she said, walking away, staring at the pages she had brought with her. "Oh," she said, turning back. "How do you spell 'prosthesis'?"

"P-r-o-s-thesis. What's happening? You introduced a dentist to the story?"

"Sort of," she mumbled, walking off, back to her typewriter.

He watched her back, disgusted. He wished they lived in an apartment rather than the open loft space, so he could go into a room and slam the door behind him. Then at least he could masturbate. He made that casual joke (maybe you should punish me for it), and she knew right away. Not all of her, but her instinct for the truth behind every casual statement was infallible. Both real privacy and real intimacy were impossible with her. She could penetrate any defense, and if you didn't have one, she considered you contemptible and boring.

He was nervous. Between the sexual excitement and the rush of horror at being caught, his body was confused. He paced into the kitchen, opened the refrigerator, seeing not food but the leather-clad redhead holding her long crop, her face an unforgiving mask of ironic disdain. He was appalled and excited, afraid of his thoughts and obsessed with them. He wondered about a slew of practical matters. Was she really a prostitute? Of course. Presumably, if you wanted, after a nice spanking you could ball her, or whatever. What if she really liked beating men? Maybe she wouldn't stop if she really hurt you. That possibility terrified him, but strangely caused his erection to return. So the danger excites me too, he observed clinically. There seemed to be no bottom to the depravity of his perversion. David had always thought of himself as a shrewd survivor, someone who looked out for himself thoroughly, perhaps even too cautious, unable to take the kind of risk great men needed for a final boost to attain an orbit of success. What could explain this thirst for harm? He didn't ski or cross in the middle of the street, take any chances with his body. He always pointed the knife away from his body when slicing a bagel. How could he want to put himself at the mercy of a stranger, tied up, whipped, with no guarantee that it would stop short of real damage?

Impossible. His thrill came from the security of voyeurism. Surely he would find being a participant disgusting and unpleasant. His erection would certainly disappear quickly when that crop left marks on his behind and not someone else's. Maybe that was it. Maybe he was sadistic. Maybe he wanted to punish others.

Oddly, this perspective comforted him. He wondered about that too. How despicable that being the tormentor seemed more respectable than being the victim.

But another image of her, tall, scornful, her charms encased in seamless impenetrable leather, seduced his imagination and argued against the notion that watching the beating was the cause. He believed in that vision, the punishing unyielding woman. Is that the true nature of my mother? His stubborn, solicitous, small, overweight mother? Sure she had demanded a lot from him and his brother. They had to be successes, but there was no punishment, no going to bed without meals, certainly no physical discipline. Apparently amateur psychology couldn't help him.

I should see a psychiatrist, he thought without enthusiasm. He'd rather see the redhead. Or at least know more about her . . . it. To that end he was furious with himself for not having written or remembered the telephone number that had appeared at the end of the commercial.

He looked at the cable-television guide to see whether what he had seen had a title and was a regular show. It was called *HotSpots* and seemed to be on almost every night of the week, its time varying from midnight to one in the morning. I'll watch it tomorrow night, he thought, and write down the phone number.

But this decision seemed insane moments later. What was he going to do? Call that number and make an appointment? Waltz to some address—God knows in what kind of neighborhood—and let that woman chain his hands and feet . . . It was insane. Yet a part of him didn't believe she existed, that a real person would answer the phone. He wanted to call, if for nothing else than to confirm that all of it, from the images on the screen to his erotic response, was simply a mist of a tired imagination, briefly clouding his sound, clear mind. A harmless fog, easy to forget, and sure to evaporate under the heat of investigation.

The farewell at the airport had been agony. Sadder and more hopeless than any good-bye Tony had ever spoken before. His affair with Lois, born of vanity, sustained by sexual appetite, had become, on this trip, painful and tragic. He wondered, closing his eyelids, hot from fatigue, and feeling the cool air from overhead his seat in first class, whether he had ever really been in love before. Didn't the anguish of holding Lois in his arms—feeling her tears on his neck, this empty depression in his spirit that made the colors, tastes, and sounds of the world dull, metallic, and tinny—didn't that represent true longing, and therefore true love?

He was always glad to leave Betty. But, of course, he knew he would be coming back. It wasn't a fair comparison. This was the first time in his life that he had been prevented from seeing as much as he liked of a woman he loved.

And was he now? Couldn't he go home and tell Betty their marriage was over? Get on the next plane back and return to the delighted, wise, and adoring embrace of Lois? After all, he didn't require dispensation from the Church, there were no children who would be scarred forever, his parents certainly wouldn't be in a position to disapprove. In fact, no one would give it a second thought. Other than Betty, of course.

What a monstrous betrayal of her! She was faithful, endured all his moods, had been solicitous of his work and ambitions—no more trouble to him than a faithful dog. God, where did all this contempt for her come from? There had been no inkling of it until he slept with another woman. Was it merely a way of justifying himself? Belittling what he had and had had with Betty to lessen his guilt?

He was seated next to an executive who made the coast-to-coast trips often. Tony had had a brief conversation with him after takeoff, ending it (pleading fatigue) when the man began to brag about the number of women he had slept with on his trips. The executive, while claiming how great his emotionally nomadic life was, how it had helped maintain his marriage, was downing drink after drink, his language deteriorating along with his motor skills. Tony worried that that man's first indiscretion had seemed to him as romantic and grand as Tony's now did and that one day Tony would be slurring his words at some young man, talking of pussy and happy marriages.

He wanted to avoid cliché in his life as desperately as he wanted to avoid it in his plays. The screenwriter who breaks up the marriage of his youth as he makes it in Hollywood seemed to Tony too obvious a dramatic choice. Besides, he wasn't making it, he had flopped. He had a chance to redeem himself with the set of revisions (which would really end up being a complete rewrite, given Garth's and Foxx's objections), and he now felt that how well he met this challenge would determine the course of his career for years to come, perhaps for the rest of his life. For the great artist, life should be an unbroken series of success; anything else, he thought, implied mediocrity. At thirty, Shakespeare had written *Hamlet*, Tennessee Williams had *Streetcar* making Brando's reputation (he too was under thirty), Arthur Miller had earned the right to compete with presidents of the United States to screw Marilyn Monroe because of *Death of a Salesman*, Stoppard had *Rosencrantz and Guildenstern* running on Broadway, Mamet had already been hailed for *American Buffalo*—there simply wasn't much of a tradition in the theater for undiscovered genius. After all, in the end, it was still show business, which made the phrase "undiscovered genius" oxymoronic. Nobody went around looking for unproduced plays of fifty years ago, there are no art dealers finding genius in the manuscripts of obscure writers of the last century, no academics demanding productions of unknown nineteenth-century playwrights. The famous of today may not be the famous of tomorrow in the theater, but the unknown were sure to remain rotting in the ground.

And he was rotting. Inside, strapped into a seat on a plastic bullet speeding through the air, maggots eating at his confidence, his energy, his will to continue. Five years ago, no woman, no love, no emotion would have distracted him from concentrating on his work. Every time he closed his eyes, Lois was on his body, kissing his penis, holding him in her tight desperate embrace. She listened to his every word, weighed each anxiety as though it were gold, studied his moods, picked him up at the airport on arrival, and drove him there on departure, a precious package of happiness for her that she protected with the fierce will of a mother. She loved him, apparently without any restraint, irony, or condescension. She loved him hopelessly, knowing she would be hurt, expecting to be discarded, exposing her heart to the sword of betrayal. He could run her through, cut her aorta in half, splatter the floor with her gushing blood, and still her eyes would look at him with unblinking adoration.

He was despicable. It was terrible being on the plane alone, unable to escape from this conclusion. He had two women who loved him and he was betraying them both without a single legitimate complaint against either one.

The trip took too long. He squirmed in his seat, the boredom relieved only by occasional premonitions that their plane was about to explode. Over and over an image of his charred body, still strapped into the red-white-and-blue design of the seat, perhaps clutching his wineglass, projected onto his mind a horrible internal slide show. He tried to sleep during the movie, but he would start awake the moment his body relaxed, convinced they were abruptly falling out of the sky. Finally he gave up trying, asking the stewardess for coffee, and stared forward at the low plastic ceiling. He wondered if he could make a play out of his observations of the behind-the-scenes actions on his mother's sitcom. He tried to imagine it onstage, how he could get their inner lives out during scenes of them at work, but he decided it would be false and melodramatic. Besides, he could think of three plays running off-Broadway that used Hollywood as a setting. Then there were all those musicals that were really about show business. Playwrights had nothing to write about but their attempts to make money in tinseltown, and now he was becoming one of them. He remembered making this point about those three off-Broadway plays last year when they were in the works. He had bitterly ripped them apart at every social occasion, usually to everyone's approval, accusing the authors of having no subject other than their own greed. And now he was one of them.

The plane began its descent. He could feel the subtle pitch forward, the shift in engine noise. Soon it would be worse, his ears would pop, the seat-belt sign would come on. A vivid picture of his plane lancing into another jet filled his mind—he saw his limbs fly off, his head roll into a stranger's lap. And he would be nothing. Dead, he would be forgotten in weeks, talked of occasionally as a tragic case of a young artist whose chance was robbed by cruel fate, killed not only figuratively but also literally by the movie business.

He sat rigid during the landing, closing his eyes when the wheels touched down and the ferocious roar of the engines crashed over him like the ocean's surf. He saw himself skipping, flying through the air amid wreckage, a bright ball of fire, his life consumed.

During the long moment of his imagined death, he remembered arching into Lois, her body sighing with pleasure, and then she opened her eyes, saying, "I love your penis inside me," in a rushed whisper.

He was met by a limousine, a prerequisite he had forgone after his first trip to LA, but Lois had insisted he take it this time: "Cheer you up for the rewrite," she said. When they weren't screwing—it was screwing, all right, done casually, in the middle of breakfast, or desperately, tragically, at dawn, a lovemaking that transited from ordinary conversation to naked embrace with the fluidness of a movie—Lois kept encouraging him, telling stories of famous screenwriters doing draft after draft of scripts, reviled throughout by the studio, director, and star, only to triumph in the end with the ultimate rewards, a hit and an Oscar. People in LA finished stories with "And he won the Academy Award," or more often, "And it grossed a hundred million," the way a Christian might finish a tale of someone's life by saying, "And he went to heaven."

He made fun of her, belittling her values, and she went on undaunted, without anger at his resistance. She knew, unlike Betty, how much he really wanted all of it, the money, the stupid award, the interview on *Entertainment Tonight*, and she persisted in her whisper of ambition, "You can do this rewrite. You didn't really concentrate on the first draft. You know what they want. Your ideas are brilliant. You'll knock 'em dead with a new draft. Garth wouldn't have flown you out and spent all that time meeting with you unless he had confidence in you." And so on, her energy for feeding his ego rivaling a doting grandmother's. She told him he was a genius. Handsome. Kind. A great lover. There was no virtue he didn't possess, according to Lois, and he believed her, cherishing some of her more outrageous compliments, especially the sexual ones. She claimed he moved inside her so well that foreplay was either unnecessary or overkill.

He started each conversation skeptically, convinced her view of him was too good to be true, watching patiently for a giveaway of her true feeling. She wants me to leave Betty and knows she can't afford to criticize me, he thought, feeling quite sympathetic with her circumstance. In her position he would also try this tactic.

But two of her friends had told Tony, during brief private conversations, that they had never seen her happier, and she did seem different than when they first met. Her thin glum face had relaxed, her unsmiling expression becoming wistful and soft. She laughed easily, had boundless energy, and, according to his mother (when he asked, as a preliminary to confessing the affair, which he then abandoned), had become so good at supervising scripts that offers for other series were coming in at a regular flow, forcing the executive producer to sweeten her deal.

"Listen to any advice she gives you about the business," his mother had said in her guttural, slightly drunk voice (warmly cynical, a critic had called it). "She's got the Midas touch." The last said so that you knew she both admired and despised such a gift. But it was the best she could ever say about someone who "is absolutely without talent, who wouldn't know a Ming vase from a Tupperware container," a contemptuous phrase Maureen Winters had been using since her nervous breakdown about anyone who wasn't an artist and yet had succeeded in show business. But Tony didn't feel contemptuous of Lois—the confidence with which she moved in the Hollywood world dazzled him.

It was ten o'clock at night when he arrived in New York. The city, unlike LA, was alive at that hour. In the pale faces of the pedestrians Tony saw weariness, anger, forced gaiety—as opposed to the tanned, rested, self-assured countenances of the LA movie people. But there was something much more daunting in the eyes of the New Yorkers, something much more difficult for him to match than the breezy confidence of the West Coast. There was the fierce will to succeed: eyes assuming each passerby was hostile; the walk brisk, as though stillness meant vulnerability. They moved, amid the cars, the drunks, the pickpockets, the drug dealers, they moved armored, bubbled in little worlds, smiling only for their companions, and turning masks to the outside world. In LA, people wanted to win; in New York, they had to. In LA, people did win; in New York, they were more often crushed. In LA, failure was death; in New York, it was merely a pause before another round of fighting. He didn't want to struggle anymore—the armor weighed too much.

Tomorrow the friends would call, wanting to know if he was getting a movie made, expecting stories of how he had been lionized. The writers would phone one by one, asking how it had gone, but really wanting to know if he had stepped up in class, out of the range of their punches, or whether he had taken a cut on the eye and would miss the next few events against them. I'm gonna write another play, he thought as the limo approached his apartment building. He had come home, the cold anger of the struggle infiltrating his sun-warmed West Coast heart. "I'll write another play," he said, nodding to himself, pumping his muscles for strength.

The doorman hustled out of the lobby, almost wrestling with the chauffeur over his bag. Tony noted the difference in the doorman's attitude between his arrival in a limo as opposed to a taxi. That a man who saw him every day changed his attitude over such a detail of success made the fierce blizzard of his soul complete.

He put his key in the lock in a rage.

Betty pulled it open before he was finished. She was dressed in a black silk nightgown (new to him) and holding a glass of champagne, smiling gleefully. "Darling!" she said, her thin voice vainly attempting to sound throaty and seductive. "Back from the Coast so soon?" She shook her red curls.

He stared at her dully. The man who had always been too quick with an answer. On their first date she had been scared to talk much, afraid he would cut her to pieces over a naive comment. Her silence had seemed to him mysterious, a hint at profound secrets and knowledge. Now he stood stupidly, dumbstruck, not getting the joke, like a dullard from the Midwest flabbergasted by some arch, obscene New York play.

"Come in, darling!" she continued bravely, sweeping her arm dramatically to welcome an entrance. "The caviar is on ice, the champagne on little pieces of funny brown bread with the crusts missing. Or vice versa."

"Hi," he said, his voice tired. "That's beautiful," he added without enthusiasm, nodding at her nightgown. "When did you buy it?"

"Buy it? Buy it? I didn't buy it. Someone left it here last night—with his hat." She broke herself up with this one, laughing so hard that her little breasts trembled against the lace frill at the top of her low-cut gown, bobbing into and out of view like buoys on a stormy sea. They were pretty—impertinent, cheerful, like her little girl's face, her nipples smiling brilliantly, eager to please and yet sure of their ultimate distance and superiority. Laughing, she put the glass of champagne down and moved into his arms, holding him tight (the only suggestion that there was more to her mood than gaiety), and holding her mouth up to be kissed, closing her eyes before the contact. He watched himself kiss her, his hands sliding on the silk that made the curves of her body like a sculpture's, flowing and smooth.

"I missed you," he said, interrupting the kiss, and then continuing it, her arms squeezing tighter. The fight, his body's stiff resistance to the cold world, sagged, and he held her wearily, hopelessly, feeling her body, tasting her mouth, the sensations mingling dissonantly with Lois' now more familiar shape and smell.

She led him silently into the bedroom, apparently not resenting his reluctant manner. Why doesn't she know there's something wrong? he wondered as she pulled his shirt out of his pants and unbuckled his belt.

He stood passively like a little boy, too tired to undress. Because she thinks I'm depressed over the script, he reminded himself. He took over and unbuttoned his shirt.

I am, he told himself. Maybe that's all it is. Maybe I've confused myself over Lois and Betty to avoid facing the enormity of the danger I'm in. I don't want this, he said to himself angrily, naked, moving toward his wife's now nude body on the bed. I want to be a genius, he thought over and over as he jammed his penis inside her, roughly moving in and out, grunting with the effort as he pushed himself so hard it seemed he wanted to ram right through her body. I want to be a genius, he thought —I don't want to be in love with anybody.

Gelb began right away, getting up from the table, pulling Patty toward him when she extended a hand, kissing her on the mouth, his lips slightly open, enough to make it more than a greeting and just less than serious foreplay, a hand encompassing a buttock and squeezing, again with slightly more emphasis than friendliness and less than open seduction. "It's great to see you. You look great," he said in a breathless rush, Antony reunited with Cleopatra.

"So do you," she said, not resisting his embrace. She knew, here, visible in the Four Seasons, that he would never have the nerve to go too far, that he was counting on her playing the stammering, shocked, reluctant ingenue. She wanted to call his bluff, convinced he was acting out a fantasy he would never actually realize. Sure enough, he withdrew quickly, glancing nervously at the other tables and moving to his chair. She meant her compliment. He was tan and trim, looked younger than she remembered, probably because a year and a half had made no difference in his age, but had changed her perspective of how old that old was. David, despite his fifteen-year advantage on Gelb, seemed no younger in manner or energy. Less so, in fact. But he's still an old man to me, she argued to herself. I'm not attracted to him.

"I feel good," he said. "Things are going well."

"They always went well for you," she answered. The waiter interrupted. When she ordered a Perrier, Gelb insisted she have it with white wine, and the waiter ignored her protests, outraging her.

"I can't believe it," she said.

"They know who's boss," Gelb said, laughing, as though it were a joke, but it wasn't, and they both knew it.

"You're not my boss anymore," she said, not scoring on him, but a pleasant reminder, a stewardess stating an airline rule.

"I want to be. Not your boss," he added. "I want you to work with me."

"That's nuts."

"No, it's not."

"You fired me. You told me I was incompetent. Suggested—"

"No, no—"

"—I go into advertising or selling shoes, I forget—"

"I was lying!" he said in an angry, embarrassed tone. Patty paused. "I was lying," he repeated, his eyes lowering apologetically.

The drinks were brought. He took a sip and she did as well, feeling, even with the first taste of wine, the light-headedness that hit her instantly with alcohol. The desire to run through every red light would soon follow. Don't take another sip of it, she told herself, reaching for the water glass.

"What do you mean?" she said at last.

"Let's order. Then I'll make my confession." Patty tried to order light, but he wouldn't accept that, and once again she was left with no choice. He told the waiter to bring her shrimp in mustard sauce to start, and then a steak and salad—the kind of lunch she could never put down. To her horror he ordered an expensive bottle of red wine.

"No matter how much I drink, I'm not going to bed with you," she said, whispering the last part. Gelb opened his eyes wide, startled. "I'd only throw up anyway."

Gelb laughed, delighted. "You're terrific," he said, beaming at her.

"Yeah. A terrific piece of ass, you mean." She sneered at him, her eyes daring him to contradict her.

"Amazing," he said. "I don't know how I could have been such a fool."

"You fired me because I wouldn't go to bed with you," Patty said, knowing, for the first time, that it was true, really true. Along with it came the exhilaration of being unshackled from almost two years of self-doubt, of failure. She had told no one, not David, nor Betty, that she believed Gelb's frustrated lust had been the cause of the debacle of her editorial career, partly because she didn't think they'd think it credible and partly because she had never been able to accept it herself. Now she knew, looking at him, drinking her in, watching her as a consumer does a display of expensive goods he can't afford, that it was yet another example of sexism, of the patina that had been glossed over the old rules. She looked at the restaurant, at the so-called power lunches that surrounded her, and they were dominated by men. Men, men, men with their blind hairy cocks that wanted warmth and shelter anywhere it could be found, who would sacrifice any promise, years of struggle, any principle, for their moment of sweaty release. What was in that white stuff anyway that they wanted so badly to be rid of it?

"I fired you because I was falling in love," he said quietly, his tan face solemn. He looked down at his ironed cuff and touched it.

Patty stared at him. He must be kidding. She felt nervous. This was not going right, the map had misled her, the scenery missing the proper landmarks.

Gelb looked up at her, his eyes serious. "I thought I just wanted an affair—God knows, I've had enough of them—but I couldn't pursue it well, kept getting too aggressive, making mistakes because I wanted you so badly. I'd get furious at you, think of you on the weekends, the way you say things—I don't know. I haven't felt like this since I was a kid. I'm totally in your power. It's been a year and a half and I can't get you out of my head. You're so beautiful . . ."

"You want to sleep with me. That's all it ever was. You want to sleep with me." She pleaded this as though arguing with a recalcitrant bureaucrat for a passport renewal.

"Sure. Of course it looks like that. And that's part of it," he said, laughing. "But you get over wanting to sleep with someone in less than a year. Look, I'm going about this wrong. I was in trouble that year. My job was on the line, I hated my marriage and couldn't face it. Things have changed. I'm going to tell you something, something you can't tell anyone—"

"You're getting a divorce," Patty said wearily, stunned by his confidence in her gullibility.

"No," he said, surprised. "No. I wish I were. I've been offered the job of publisher at Garlands."

"No!" Patty said, appalled. Her bad luck stunned her. That morning she had discussed in detail with Betty, an excited and nervous Betty, how they would approach Betty's publisher (Garlands) about switching Patty's contract for a second romance novel to a contract with her to do Patty's new novel. It would be hard for lots of reasons, even apart from the difficulty of being forgiven for the romance novel. Betty had no track record acquiring fiction, Patty obviously had no experience writing it, and so on and so on in the infuriating tautology of publishing logic: they don't trust you unless you've been successful in the past, but how can you become so without someone trusting you? The plan was predicated on Betty's belief that Patty's partial manuscript was terrific and the strength of her own solid relationship with the editor in chief of Garlands. And now this meant that was all irrelevant, that Gelb would become the hurdle, that once again he was her boss.

Her horror at his announcement was misunderstood by Gelb. He interpreted it as surprise that Garlands would move him—a man with a violently commercial reputation—into a house better known for publishing quality books. "Look," he said in a sales-conference tone, "there are business realities in publishing that now even Garlands can't afford to ignore."

"Are you going to accept?" Patty asked.

"Yes, and I want to hire you."

"To do what? Go to bed with you?"

Gelb smiled, shaking his head, astonished and delighted by her frankness. "I'm not hiring you to go to bed with me. I want you to go to bed with me, but I also want you to work for me. I got rid of you because I was so angry at the feelings I was developing for you—"

"You never said anything—all you ever did was yell!"

"No—"

"Yes, you yelled," she teased, "you criticized, you never said a kind word—"

"Oh, come on, Patty! Nonsense!" Gelb leaned back, a hand pulling his jacket closed, armoring himself. "What about all those lunches and dinners to console you over the end of one relationship or another? You think it was easy?" He pushed his face at her, his body bumping the table so that the glasses trembled, their liquids shimmering. "Listening to you catalogue your sexual adventures? I'll never forget that look you had on your face when you were dating the carpenter—"

Patty laughed, as much to relieve the pressure of his assault as at his absurb claims to unrequited passion. No amount of protest could convince her that this man, whose dark eyes glistened invulnerably, reflecting back any searchlight into his soul, was capable of sustaining love for anything, unless . . . unless he couldn't have it. Maybe, incredible though it may seem, he had never been frustrated before. "Carpenter?" she said, and laughed again.

"Yes, the carpenter who you said was so damn good in bed? What the hell was he so good at anyway? You refused to tell me, as though it was something astonishing. What the hell was it? His penis was ten inches long?"

"Shhhh!" Patty said, convinced his voice was amplified, that the whole restaurant had interrupted their plots of power, their schemes for success, to listen to this verbal rape.

"Damn!" he said, sagging back and rubbing his forehead feverishly.

"It was torture. And this past year, thinking you might get married any day. I found out what I could about David—"

"You did?" She was intimidated enough by him to be frightened by this. Maybe there was some harm he could do David. He was capable of anything, and the limits of his power were a mystery to her.

"Couldn't sleep the night I was told by Rounder that David is the brightest star of the magazine. Thinks he'll have his job one day."

Patty looked off, away from his energetic body, from his insistent eyes, and considered how thrilled David would be to hear this. She wondered if David (secretly) would love the whole story: this powerful man of publishing taking David's girl to the Four Seasons to seduce her, losing the battle, and speaking angrily, enviously of David's future. If she wanted marriage from David, going home and telling the story would be the perfect cattle prod. She felt regret that a union with David wasn't her ambition. She could have it so easily now. A free ride on David's trolley to the top. David would love the story all right, he wouldn't even bother to conceal his pleasure. She knew, from her experience of living with a victim of the virus of success, that to men like David, and like Gelb, the praise of the powerful was a keener and more lasting medicine than the love of a woman.

"Are you going to marry him?" Gelb's voice said sadly.

Patty returned to him, to the world, to the fine linen of the table, the ruins of their expensive lunch. What a sickening fraud it all was. Wasn't it possible for everybody to satisfy lust, whether for power or sex, without all this elaborate finery and fakery? "No, I'm not going to get married. Not to anyone. Men are disgusting," she said with conviction. "Why the heck would I want to marry any of 'em?"

"You don't mean that," Gelb said, made hopeful by a denial of betrothal. He smiled at her, grinning like a child who was confident that after a few more months of hinting, he would get the Christmas present he coveted. "Will you take the job?" he said, whispering the question as though it were a murmur of seduction.

"I feel like I'm a prostitute and we're negotiating."

"No," Gelb protested. "I love how there are no games with you. No, I want to sleep with you whether you take the job or not, and I want you to take the job whether you sleep with me or not."

"You mean you think I'd make a good editor, that everything you told me about how incompe—"

"Yes, it was all a lie. I'm a shit. I admit it. I'll offer you forty thousand a year, that's at least ten thousand more than someone of your experience should get. That'll make up for it."

"And what's my job, exactly? Blow-jobs every afternoon? What are we talking about? I feel like I'm going crazy—"

Gelb laughed, shaking his head, his eyes on her, ravenous. "You'd be *my* editor. I'd give you major authors, let you acquire one or two novels in the first year. Don't worry about the blow-jobs," he added, and then giggled.

"I don't believe you. You wouldn't do any of those things—"

"Yes I would!" he whined.

"No, you wouldn't. You're not a fool. There's nothing in the world you care more about than business. You wouldn't trust me with anything that might affect your job."

"You're wrong," he said solemnly.

She paused, looking into his unyielding eyes, daring him to maintain his pose. He did, regarding her unflinchingly. "Why are you still married to Elaine? If you're so damn unhappy? Dump her. You can have all the little girls of publishing at your feet."

"Honey, I can have them at my feet anyway. I want you," he said in a dramatic, ominous tone. "You want me to leave her? Before you'll start anything with me?"

"No!" she exclaimed, horrified that he seemed to think she was taking him seriously. "I'm just babbling, you know—"

"Will you leave David for me? I'd leave Elaine if that's the only way I can have you. But then I want all of you. I'm not sharing you with a *Newstime* wunderkind."

Patty gripped the soft cushion of her chair, feeling herself loosened from the surface of reality. Any moment, she feared, she might spin off into the madness of space, with no up or down, no gravity to restore balance. "I have to go," she said. She needed distance from his baffling presence, fast, before she made a fatal error in responding to his outrageous and incredible proposals. "Please," she begged, almost crying. "Please, I have to go."

"Okay, okay," he said. "But you have to promise you'll call."

"I will."

"Soon."

She had to breathe deeply to speak. "I will. Okay? I really have to go." She moved to get up.

"Wait," he said, signaling for the waiter. "I'll get you a cab."

"You have to eat your lunch," she pleaded.

"Fuck it," he said, and asked for the check.

She couldn't protest, afraid of another round of losing to his insistence on doing things his way. She sagged against the chair weakly and waited patiently until he finished, allowing him to take her by the elbow on the way outside.

On the street, the city was too bright—the sunlight shimmering on the blank rising towers of glass, harshly iluminating every curb and gutter, examining all the crumpled papers and trails of urine, nakedly exposing each suit's wrinkle, every stocking's tear. The wan pale faces of harried passersby seemed bleached, cruelly open to the flooding rays. Gelb moved her through it all without any cooperation on her part, as though he had levitated her above the sidewalk and could push her like a store mannequin, face frozen in expression, legs stiff, eyes blank and lifeless.

When he got in the taxi with her, she made no protest, although it was unexpected and made little sense. He was only a few blocks from his office, she thought; walking it would be much quicker. But her mind's observations were heard only faintly: she was still in shock from the awful bad luck of her life. Only that morning she had had the book and a way to get it published and now these prizes were being snatched from her with terrible precision, as though a malicious intelligence was against her.

Gelb gave the two addresses and, when he leaned back, put his arm around her. She didn't look up at him, or away; she kept her eyes down, seeing the flowing line of his pants leg, the big, very adult shoes straddling either side of the transmission's hump. After some moments of dreadful heavy silence, she felt his head move near hers, his lips brush her ear, and then a whisper, "I've missed you." He kissed her neck. Shivers ran down one side of her body—the rest of her was numb. "I've wanted to do this for so many years," he whispered again, his voice breathy, his tone desperate.

Now, rapidly, as though he had to quickly finish the ice cream before it melted, he kissed her cheek, just next to her mouth, her eyes (she closed them dutifully, like a toy doll), and then her lips, his wine-hot mouth busy and angry.

She didn't respond.

She didn't fight it, either.

He would get out soon, she knew. She needed time and freedom from his presence to escape this trap fate had baited, to stop the steel jaws from snapping her in two. He said more things, more wildly romantic things, before getting out. She nodded and managed to croak out, " 'Bye," to satisfy him so that he would shut the door and let her go.

CHAPTER

12

Fred enjoyed sleeping on the couches of his friends. He liked waking up in other households, whether bachelor or married. With the single men he had the fun of sloppiness and adolescent talk. With the couples there were the pleasures of studying the wife in T-shirt and panties or nightgown at the breakfast table and receiving her sweetly feminine attentions. Having been thrown out by Marion turned out to be an enhancement of his image. People seemed to like him all of a sudden, especially the more he talked of his regret over his failed marriage, the difficulty he had talking openly with Marion. As soon as Fred noticed that the more he blamed himself for not being receptive to Marion's feelings, not giving her room for her desires, the more he portrayed himself as a man chained by the traditions of male chauvinism, trying to break free but discovering new bonds with each success; the more he attacked himself, excusing Marion, the more people believed the opposite, felt sorry for him, and seemed to enjoy his company.

He stayed with Karl for a few days, and then Tom Lear, and then he began to be passed about among their set, like an adorable puppy whom everybody wants to cuddle and hold, but finds, after a few days, that walking him every night is too much of a bother.

Fred understood that he could wear out his welcome quickly, and he made sure to be scrupulous in leaving money for groceries and the telephone, as well as an expensive bottle of wine or something the house needed, on departure. When he felt guilty that he was deceiving these people, pretending to tragic emotions, assuming an air of melancholy and loneliness that in fact was nonexistent, he reminded himself of how they had lied to him. He discovered, as a by-product of living in these so-called friends' apartments, that they all had active and intertwined social lives from which he and Marion had been excluded. He also discovered a lot of contempt for Marion. The talk about her—begun in an effort to convince him he wasn't all to blame, but continuing with an unseemly relish—the disdain for her intellect, her lack of style, her provincial background, and so on, were things that Fred, in his heart, knew could also be said about him. He smiled and accepted the criticism of his wife as though it pleased. He did nothing to stop them, indeed he often provoked more, but he loathed them for it, and felt sorry for her. And, ultimately, for himself.

They were terrible snobs, just as Marion had always said. Because she wasn't pretty, because she didn't know how to dress, because she wasn't glib or flattering, because she didn't apologize for editing cookbooks, and claimed no desire to be more than a hack editor, she was disdained. The truth, it seemed to him, was that she possessed a realism they were incapable of. She knew that they were all less than they thought they were—she had listened to their fantasies of becoming major writers or whatever, without the proper amount of awe and seriousness. It was a bargain they had all made with each other: I'll pretend you're great, and you pretend I am too.

People are never who they say they are, Marion had once complained about them. It was true. Every journalist was really a novelist, every editor really a writer, every art director really a painter, every graduate student really a professional. And they combined this fantasy life with an astonishing arrogance toward the famous. Philip Roth was a narcissistic bore, Meryl Streep was too technical and unemotional, the New York *Times* critics were always wrong, successful books always bad, hit plays always trivial, and so on, in a joyless competition with the greats of their day, the whole discussion conducted in a tone as though they were equals, people whose obscurity was only a temporary condition and certainly unmerited.

He lied so much about the drama of his marriage, he exaggerated it into such a complicated and difficult problem that the reality bored him. When he phoned Marion at the office the day after she threw him out, she suggested they go to a marriage counselor and live separately for a while. He agreed, furious at her, but after a few nights of his journeying among friends, he was glad for the arrangement. It took more than two weeks before they saw each other at all, meeting for a cup of coffee half an hour before an appointment with a therapist that Marion had arranged.

The session with the psychologist was dull. Mostly they each covered the facts of their relationship and made their complaints about the marriage in formal, almost sociological terms. Fred made much of the fifty minutes when telling his friends, saying it was good to air the feelings and have a referee to prevent the conversation from turning into meaningless shouting. Actually there had never been such a danger. At one point Marion began to cry while attempting to say that she thought Fred considered her unattractive and then Fred *was* glad for the presence of the psychologist since that complaint had always presented him with insuperable difficulties. Instead of Fred's having to deny the truth of her charge, the psychologist was there to ask Marion solemnly, "Do you think you're unattractive?" Fred guessed immediately that the therapist wouldn't ask him if she was right (psychology has a wonderful way of ignoring the obvious, Fred thought) and stay focused on Marion's low self-esteem. The whole thing seemed overdramatic to him. Not that he didn't believe in psychiatry, or felt the counseling wouldn't work, simply that it seemed of a piece with the overcrowding of the New York world. Two people couldn't even fall in and out of love by themselves.

He tried not to think of the future. He assumed they would get back together, that his current condition was temporary and therefore should be enjoyed rather than wasted in melancholic solitude. He went out every night, spent a fortune on dinners and entertainment (he went to four Broadway shows those first two weeks, swallowing the forty-five-dollar ticket prices without a hard gulp, much less choking), and sublet a one-room office from a friend of Karl's for four hundred dollars a month, picking up his typewriter and papers while Marion was at work. He spent as though the money he was withdrawing from his and Marion's joint account was a college allowance from his parents and the consequence was going to be a scolding, not bankruptcy.

In the grand explosion of this drama, Tom Lear reading his pages and telling him they were good, but making some suggestions for changes (which Fred executed in a few days, not showing the revisions to Tom), made only a small noise. Tom spoke casually about the writing, seeming neither too impressed nor too dismayed. And he socialized with Fred just as frequently, even putting him up for a few days.

Bart called him daily when he heard the news, took him to lunch, offered his guest room either to sleep or work in, and asked for the one hundred pages with increasing insistence. After the meeting with the therapist, Fred decided (see, he told himself, *my* self-esteem is okay) to hand them in.

"They're pretty good, Fred," Bart said on the phone, with a lack of enthusiasm or despair similar to Tom Lear's. "They need some work of course, but they're ready for Bob to see."

Fred worried during the weekend that Holder was reading his manuscript, but not intensely. He felt a general sense of safety in the world now that Marion had thrown him out. The peculiar rise in his self-confidence puzzled him, made him wonder if he should make any attempt to reconcile with her, whether the marriage was somehow debilitating and dangerous. But even that seemed to be out of his hands, since Marion had all the momentum with her, though why that should be also baffled him. Everything in his life, whether he was married or not, whether he had a place to live or not, whether he had a viable book contract or an income for the year, whether he could stay in the race with his circle of writing friends—everything was in other people's hands: Marion's and Bob Holder's. And yet this absolute lack of control, instead of corrupting his mood and invading his sleep, kept him lighthearted, interested in each day with its surprises and dangers, and let him fall asleep soundly, happily exhausted by the complicated arrangements and busy social life of a tourist in a big city loaded with friends.

Bob Holder phoned Monday morning. "Hi, Fred. How are you?" His voice was pleasant, casual.

"Good. How are you?" Fred asked, feeling more than ever the person he wanted to be.

"Fine, fine. Listen, I think you should come in, maybe this afternoon, and talk about the book."

"Okay."

"See if we both feel like continuing with it. I think it may be getting away from us."

"Un-huh." Fred was in a stranger's kitchen, and when, at Fred's shocked tone, his hosts looked up from their coffee, he smiled bravely at them.

"Can you come in today at three?"

"Sure."

"Great. See you then."

"Is everything all right?" he was asked while he returned the phone to the cradle with the slow motions of an accident victim. If the worst were about to happen—a total rejection, a canceling of the contract— everyone would have to be told, but Fred wasn't sure of the disaster, and if it wasn't, he wouldn't want anyone to know that Holder had ever been critical of his work.

He lied, saying that Holder had praised the pages and simply wanted to discuss what lay ahead. Within a half-hour he invented a reason to go out, and called Bart from a phone booth. During the past few months their relationship had progressed to intimacy. Bart got right on. "What's up, Fred?"

"I heard from Holder. Sounds like he's dumping the book."

"What?"

At the surprise in Bart's tone, Fred already felt relieved. "Well, he said I should come in today to see whether it's worth continuing with the book at all."

"What the fuck does that mean?"

"He said we . . . he said we should discuss if we want to continue with the book."

"Well, we do!"

Fred laughed. "Damn right we do."

"I'll call him." Bart spoke as though that would take care of it, a President announcing he was in charge.

"Maybe you shouldn't. Maybe I'm making too much of it. I don't know. It may just be the way he talks."

"I'll feel my way around. I have to call him about another project anyway, and I'll casually bring up your book."

"That won't fool him. He'll know."

Bart snorted. "You overestimate him. He won't. When are you meeting him?"

"Three."

"Okay. Where are you gonna be?"

"I don't know."

"All right. Call in at two . . . or, no, call between two and two-thirty."

"Okay."

"Don't worry. Relax."

"Okay," Fred said obediently. He wanted to marry Bart after this conversation. The terrible demons that Holder's conversation had summoned were gone in an instant, their damp invasion of his soul burned off by the heat of Bart's energy. For a few hours he went about his business without more than a ripple of worry. But as two o'clock approached he began to get a clear image of what it would mean if Holder didn't proceed with the contract. He would have no immediate income, and unless Marion was willing to take him back, the expense of finding an apartment in New York would be prohibitive without the guarantee of some money. Of course he could probably return to *American Sport* (the newsstand sales hadn't collapsed on his departure, but still he was pretty sure . . .) or some other publication, but that was failure. There would be no more Elaine's, screenings with Tom, poker games at Karl's, and so on. Sure, supposedly they were all friends now, but he knew, he just knew, that his standing within the circle he now moved would be compromised. And even if he could keep his new social position, would he enjoy it without the right to it? He had loved being a novelist. Working privately at this great project, being asked about its progress by everyone as though it were a public work, a bridge whose completion was eagerly awaited. That would be gone. The independence, the pride in his achievement, all of it removed from the table of life by a hasty waiter, carrying off plates that still had plenty of nourishment on them.

He called Bart at two. His secretary said he was still out at lunch and would call back. "That's no good," Fred said. "He can't reach me. I'll phone again in ten minutes." He decided to get uptown for the meeting and try Bart from there. He took a cab, got stuck in traffic, and wasn't able to find a telephone until two-twenty-five.

"He just got on a long-distance call to London," she told him. "Call back in ten minutes."

He waited six.

"Bart said I should tell you he hasn't heard back from Holder," she said this time. "He'll keep trying. Call back in ten minutes."

Fred's confidence in Bart, damning up the stormy waters of fear, broke, washed over him, and smashed him against midtown. The busy streets quavered in his vision. The itemized list of his troubles passed before him, wrapping around the buildings like a stock-market ticker tape recording a crash.

When he phoned again at two-fifty, knowing this would be his last chance, he was sure of defeat. "Hold on, Fred," the secretary said. Even her tone had become urgent and fearful.

"Fred," Bart said, anxious, a general pinned by enemy fire, trained to fight off panic, "I've tried Bob three times. He hasn't called me back. I don't think that means anything. Your meeting's—what?—in a couple of minutes?"

"Yeah." The sound of his own voice appalled Fred. It was hoarse with dread.

"Call me after you're done."

"But . . ." he began, and then fell silent. Fred breathed hard, as though he could suck in words and thoughts from the air to fill the vacuum that nervousness had made of his brain.

"Yes?" Bart said after a few moments of silence.

"I don't know."

"Look, you'd better get to the meeting. Just don't commit yourself to anything. Listen to me. Report it to me. We'll discuss it. You don't have to make any decisions on the spot. Okay?"

"He's gonna reject the book."

"You don't know that. I don't think he will. He would have called me first. Don't assume that. Now, come on. Relax. Get going."

"Okay," he said, hanging up without a good-bye, like a doctor on call rushing to an emergency. He hustled across the street and into the lobby. At the reception area he was sweating, relieved that he had gotten there a minute before three.

Then Holder kept him waiting a half-hour. During the slow agony of the minutes passing, Fred passed into a state of hopeless resignation. He considered begging Holder for a chance to do a complete rewrite, but he doubted if even that would be accepted.

Finally he was brought in. Holder got up energetically, saying, "Sorry I kept you waiting. There's been a disaster here today with a manuscript. It was delivered to the wrong . . ." He waved his hand at the air, dismissing it. "Sorry. Anyway, I won't have a chance to talk to you, because I've got a meeting in a half-hour and I have to return calls . . . I'm way behind." He picked up Fred's manuscript from his desk, revealing a sweater with the elbow eaten through by the moth of his nervous manner. The first page of Fred's one hundred pages was marked in numerous places and there were so many yellow flags sticking out (markers placed on the edge of the pages to indicate places where Holder had made changes or queried something) that it looked like a badly made paper duck. "I found a lot of things I didn't like. I still love the basic idea. I've showed where I think things go wrong and what you should do about them. Obviously, you may not agree and want to drop the contract. But read it over, take your time, and let me know if you can make the changes. Then we'll meet again and I'll make sure I have plenty of time to talk." Holder held out the tattered object with a touch of regret, as though he were surrendering something he wanted to hold on to.

Fred stared at it for a second, a skeptical pedestrian peering at a flier thrust at him. He reached for it slowly, took it gingerly, afraid to bend the yellow stickers—there was hardly room to grasp his pages without bending one of them. He looked into Holder's eyes and said, "I'll make any changes you want."

Holder nodded, seeming neither surprised nor confirmed in his expectation. "Good boy," he said.

In Chico's siege of Rounder's job, David Bergman played the role of a keeper of secrets, an overzealous agent of the usurped prince, working to return the just to power. David's intense dislike of Rounder, this stupid blue-eyed blond who had smiled and blundered his way into a job that rightfully belonged to men who had come up the ladder that David was now climbing, seemed at times greater than Chico's. David stirred the already churning envy in Chico's soul on a daily basis. He kept a precise inventory of the institutional injustice that was Chico's lot and waved it in his face to cnrage him further. In return, he learned the last remaining intimacies of Animal Crackers, and was told the status and presumptive fate of every employee, each time sworn to silence.

And though this made him a great friend of Chico's, his distance from his peers widened. He could not cheerfully drink and joke with men above whom the sword of *Newstime*'s wrath hung, no matter how invisible its presence to the victim. Nor could he resist, through slow hints and comments to Chico, corrupting the good opinion the Marx Brothers held of his rivals, whether their judgments were correct or not. In the dim light of morning, feeling lonely and repentant, David would swear to stop his machinations, but like an addict, he was seduced by Chico's eager face, promising rewards of power and information and he let the drug flow freely between them.

He was using Chico. Ironically, Chico no doubt believed the reverse was true, that he had made an ally of a bright young talent. Thus even David's one remaining intimate relationship at the magazine was founded on a lie, that he was a soldier in Chico's battle to defeat Rounder, while in fact he used his position to keep his rivals down. He didn't admit any of this to Patty, and lived in the loft, skulking among its painted columns and soaring walls, alone with his loathing for himself.

Nor did he dare tell anyone of his sexual obsession. During late nights at the magazine, he carefully arranged things to be free when the show with the pornographic ads came on, closing his door and turning on his television (a perk of senior editors), watching it with his face only inches from the screen so that he could switch channels instantly if someone knocked on the door.

He began to notice at newsstands that there were magazines with photos of women in leather outfits, standing over chained men who writhed in mock abject pain. He would see words blazoned across the COVERS: BONDAGE, SEX, SLAVE, DISCIPLINE. They had magic for him, stunning his brain into dumbfounded stares, drying his mouth, awakening his otherwise dulled genitals. He looked for newsstands that carried such magazines and tried to calculate the likelihood that someone he knew might walk in if he were to attempt a purchase. There simply was no way to know. The only measure of safety he could give himself was to do the buying out of both his loft's and *Newstime*'s neighborhoods. His other temptation was to call Mistress Regina as she ordered her slaves to do. He wanted to laugh at it, the stupid name, the bad camerawork, the lamely delivered lines, but there was no comedy in his desire, no objective higher ground for his mind to climb. He was stuck, transfixed by the secret lust, and paralyzed by its equally covert twin, his self-disgust at giving in.

His job, the actual editing of the sections under him, became increasingly easy in its challenge, and increasingly elaborate and tedious in its execution. He had eased the task of getting story ideas approved by the Marx Brothers because of his intimacy with Chico, but handling the writers got harder. He fought for three weeks to get a story in on the economics of Disney's amusement parks (it was a growing problem since Walt's death and the eighty-two recession, and David wanted to do it before national attention was focused by a takeover), and won, largely because Chico backed him, only to be handed a story by a writer under him, Jeff Nelson, that missed the point and was impossibly dull.

Nelson was a middle-aged man, a corporate retainer, just above a level of incompetence that would provoke firing, but well below true value. He was joked about regularly, "floated" from section to section, usually dumped on the newest senior editor, the least able to defend himself from being given an albatross. David had liked Nelson (his relentless pleasantness was an essential reason for his long survival) and did nothing to remove him from his sections because David could assign Nelson stories David himself cared about and then freely rewrite them in his own style without the fuss and hurt feelings that caused the writers who had vestiges of self-respect and ambition still in them.

But this time Nelson didn't even do a good job of culling the bureau reports. David couldn't make a landscape out of the flatly written facts because even they were absent. Besides, the story had come in late, leaving little time for David to request the files himself and go through them, if he also hoped to edit his other sections. "I'll have to kill the piece," he said aloud, staring at Nelson's blues. He thought of how that was going to sound to the Marx Brothers. They had said all along that Disney having problems which hadn't really surfaced was going to read dull or, worse, incomprehensible, and Nelson's story was both. But David knew it could be wonderful. People didn't think of Disney as a business, few knew how white-bread and religious its organization was, what an anomaly it was in the modern world, a feudal empire built by a bizarre man whose death had left it bewildered, an immensely profitable institution whose inner workings were at once silly and spooky. It was the kind of stuff that made him want to be a journalist, revealing the odd and weird nature of things that people took for granted. It was "soft" reporting, despised somewhat, certainly not respected in the way "hard-nosed investigative reporting" is, but it was the kind of writing that it seemed to David was more likely to say something worthwhile, precisely because the information wasn't startling. Had America really learned anything from Watergate? Hadn't its monstrous excesses allowed people to take it out of the realm of politics-as-usual and escape its implications about the real nature of government?

His Power Phone buzzed. "How we doing?" Chico's voice blared into the room.

"I got a problem," David said. Talking to this device on his desk was like speaking to a deity, as though Chico's spirit inhabited the walls and David was on a mountain pleading for guidance.

"Come up."

David's relationship with Chico had become so relaxed that he prepared no speech, nor made any attempt at gloss. "Nelson's story on Disney is a mess. I could redo it—I want to redo it—but it won't make this issue."

"Let's kill it. Nation can use the space."

"I don't want to kill it forever—"

"David, it's a boring story. Don't aggravate yourself. Lose it."

"It's not. Nelson is a hack. I don't know what he's doing here. What the hell *is* he doing here? Why hasn't he been fired?"

"Costs too much. Fucking Guild. Too much bother. Anyway, he's all right—"

"He's totally incompetent! What do you mean? I have to rewrite *every* word."

"Not *every* word," Chico said with a smile, amused by David's anger.

"*Every* fucking word!"

Chico frowned. He cleared his throat, swiveled his chair away from the desk, and leaned back thoughtfully. David sighed wearily and sat down. "We'll move him out of your section," Chico said at last.

"Yeah? Who'll take him?"

Chico laughed. "Somebody'll take him."

"I don't want to lose the story."

"We'll see if it fits next issue," Chico said in a dismissive tone and then shifted to his favorite topic: Rounder's ineptitude. The effects of the new editor in chief's indecisiveness about cover stories was beginning to be noticed by Mrs. Thorn. The business side had showed her the escalating costs since the new administration took over, overruns caused by closing the magazine late. "The profit margin for the last quarter is a disaster," Chico said in a hushed voice.

"Want me to do a story on it?" David asked with a smile.

"I hear the *Journal*'s preparing one," Chico answered, gloating. "It won't be long now," he concluded.

That vision, of their coup d'état's approaching culmination, soothed David's dismay at losing the Disney story. He let out some of his anger by calling Nelson on the phone—a trip down the hall would have been the polite way—and saying curtly, "Jeff? We've killed the Disney story. It's dull."

"Oh." Nelson's fear and shock were palpable in the one word, despite the relative anonymity of the phone. "You don't want me to try a rewrite?" It was barely a question, and not at all a protest.

"No. Gotta run," David said quickly, embarrassed by Nelson's lack of spunk. He hung up and closed his eyes. He felt so old and inhuman, as though he were a decorative angel on the *Newstime* building, his smooth white face now lidded by New York's dirt, the disembodied head yearning for mobility.

One of the pornographic magazine covers he saw on the way to work came clearly to mind: a tall dark-skinned woman, her long black hair shining, pulling back a kneeling young man's hair and holding a whip in front of his mouth. Her teeth were gritted, almost in a snarl. The young man's face was calm, patient, and raputurous, staring into her angry face with the baleful eyes of a faithful dog.

The memory aroused him. No image or picture of naked women had that effect anymore. He knew it was only a matter of time before the grip of this perverse fascination tightened on the throat of his timidity and strangled it. He flipped his *Newstime* appointment book to the last page, where he had scrawled Mistress Regina's phone number. Why wait? Why pretend he could defeat this lust?

He got up to close the door to his office and moved quickly back to the phone, punching the numbers in fast, hoping to outrun his fear. But his hand froze after the sixth number. Couldn't his secretary accidentally pick up in the middle of the call? True, he could call on his private line, but the capability for her to listen in still existed. He could wait until she went to lunch.

His heart was pounding, his face felt hot, the last number on the phone stared at him, challenging. Finally, out of fatigue of balancing on this high-wire of indecision and terror, he let his finger fall, as though gravity made the choice, on the final button.

He put his finger on the cradle knob to leave himself the option of cutting off the connection instantly while it rang. By the third ring, he relaxed, convinced there would be no answer (always in the back of his mind he had the conviction that Mistress Regina didn't actually exist), and then she picked up.

"Hello," the unmistakable voice said, throaty and angry.

He swallowed. He had no idea what to say.

She sighed, irritated. "Well, are you going to talk?"

Scared out of his wits, he pressed the knob down and then dropped the phone on the cradle like a hot coal. He breathed deeply, a man surfacing from underwater, gasping at life. He must have been holding his breath because he inhaled air quickly, as though he had been severely deprived.

He carried the sound of her voice home with him. He heard her contemptuous challenge over and over: "Well, are you going to talk?" Was he? He sat silently throughout the dinner Patty had arranged with Tony and Betty. David's morose condition matched Tony's sullen mood. The women did most of the talking—a lot of it, to David's annoyance, about Patty's novel.

He managed to ask Tony about his movie project, and though the answer sounded optimistic—("They're happy with it. But of course they want changes and I'm doing them.")—David knew something was wrong. A few months ago he would have been happy to see Tony get his hair mussed and take a fall. But his own disgust and obsession were too powerful.

He took a kind of pride in his desperation and sorrow. The worries of these people seemed so trivial compared to his. They were like children still, worrying over their grades in school. He was in a battle for his soul.

Over the weekend, he thought constantly of her, but he stopped watching the cable show and never attempted another call. The moment of real contact had at once deepened his curiosity and increased his timidity.

On Monday, Rounder asked him to drop by his office after lunch. A private meeting with Rounder was rare and David had no clue as to what it might be about. He tried to reach Chico, but couldn't. When he arrived at the appointed hour, he was surprised to find Chico also present.

"Hi, David," Rounder said cheerfully. "We've been discussing your problem with Nelson and, uh . . . uh, we've decided you can replace him. It'll be expensive, but it's time to make a change, bring in a new face."

"But—" David stopped himself. It had never occurred to him that Chico might act on his complaints. *Newstime* never took decisive action so quickly. He was appalled that something had been done.

"That's what you wanted," Chico said, frowning at him. He had been beaming before, as though he were presenting a Christmas gift.

"Yes," David said. "I was . . . surprised, that's all."

"My advice is to tell him quickly," Chico said. "Get the figures from Hal Bunting, you know, his profit-sharing and all of that, to soften the blow."

"You mean *I* tell him?"

The two Marx Brothers both laughed, not spitefully, but with elderly sympathy. "Welcome to the joys of responsibility," Rounder said.

"Yeah, you tell him," Chico said. "Don't feel bad. Remember, later on you get to tell some hopeful out there that he's got his big break—a job at *Newstime.*"

Back in his office, once he had the information from Bunting about the compensations for being fired after fifteen years at *Newstime*—they were considerable—David knew that if he delayed the confrontation, it would become harder. He asked Nelson to come in right away.

Nelson was a small man anyway, but he looked more shrunken than usual. He came in apologizing: "Sorry about the Disney story. I couldn't get a fix on it."

David nodded. Now that he had the human being in front of him, he had no idea how to announce the facts.

"There wasn't a real peg," Nelson went on, encouraged by David's silence. "I'm not sure—"

"Uh, I didn't want to talk about that," David blurted out to stop him from continuing a conversation that implied an ongoing presence at *Newstime.* "I have bad news," he said, the only line he had prepared in advance.

Nelson tensed, his eyes scared. "Oh," he said, and folded his hands in front of him, his mouth closed, his shoulders hunched, like a flower closing.

David starting talking, speaking vaguely at first about how valuable a change can be for someone who's worked for many years at one place. Nelson looked away immediately, staring at David's radiator. David said that he had been satisfied with Nelson's work, but wanted to bring in someone new. "Maybe I'm insecure," he said with a laugh, starting to feel comfortable, "and need to have only people I've hired working for me." This like everything else, got no response. He started going over the details, how long Nelson could take before leaving, the fact that David and Chico would both provide excellent references, and he began to give the current status of his profit-sharing.

"I know what's in there," Nelson said. "Can I go now?" he asked, his tone angry, but his body, like his choice of words, sullenly childish.

"Sure. I'm sorry—"

"Un-huh," Nelson said, and walked out.

Chico phoned later in the day to ask if he'd spoken with Nelson. "I'm impressed, very impressed, you did it so quickly," Chico told him after David recounted the story. "Well, you've made your bones," he continued, and let out a grim chuckle.

"It wasn't too bad," David said. "But I sure hope I don't ever have to fire somebody again."

"For your sake," Chico said, laughing, "I sure hope you do."

Tony made two resolutions when he awoke in New York the first day back. He acted on them immediately, first calling Gloria Fowler and frankly reporting how badly the script conference had gone.

She listened, interrupting him only to call out (probably to impress him with her concern) to her secretary to hold all her calls. When he was done, she said, "Do you want to refuse to do the rewrite?"

Tony hesitated. "I have that option?"

"Well, you wouldn't be paid the outstanding amount on the contract."

"Would I have to return what I have been paid?"

"Uh, not if it's handled properly. You might . . . The worst that would happen is, the studio might ask you to write a different script. Move you to some other project."

"Without getting additional money?"

"Right. but I think I could get around that. Do you want me to try?"

"Do you think I should?"

"No," she said. "I think you should knock their socks off with a terrific rewrite. You know, people hating first drafts is very common. They give you a few suggestions, you add the little things they want, and suddenly your script is a work of genius."

Tony laughed. "They can't be that stupid, Gloria. They'd know I hadn't made real changes. Garth really wants a complete rewrite."

"Well, do you think you can give him what he wants? Did he give you good notes?"

"Yeah, I know what he wants. He wants his character to stand on a street corner in the pouring rain, the gutter swamped with water, and no matter how many Mack trucks pass by, not a drop can splatter him." Tony laughed with pleasure at his metaphor of the star's desire to have an unblemished character in the most dubious of circumstances. Just to have conceived of such an image restored his sense of power and control.

But from Gloria there was a puzzled silence. "I . . . It's a clever sentence, but I don't know what you mean."

That his verbal picture hadn't been clear reminded him of his lack of popular success. "Just that he wants his character to have been in the movement, in fact to have been in the underground making bombs, and somehow be somebody who can never be perceived by the audience as a terrorist. Well, to some people he's going to be a terrorist, to some he'll be a hero. No audience sees a character, a real character, the same way. People bring their prejudices with them to the theater, like their raincoats, but they don't fold them on the seat and sit on them. The prejudices stay in their heads and you can't be afraid to confront them. Not if you want to make exciting drama."

"He doesn't want to make exciting drama, Tony. He wants to make a hit movie."

"Yeah, you're right. I'm being a child about this. This isn't my Sistine Chapel, this is his next World's Fair."

Gloria laughed. "Right, exactly. You don't have to do it if you don't want to. But then I think you're going to have to reconsider writing for Hollywood. Because though you might have an easier time working with other people in the business, this kind of rewrite is going to confront you over and over. If you want the money and the glory, you have to pay your dues."

Somehow, after he had spoken with her, he felt better. Nothing she had said altered anything, but the sting of his humiliation was salved. She had made him feel it was less personal, not a bullet aimed at him, Tony Winters, but rather at writers, any writer.

His next resolution was harder, both to bear and to execute. He had arranged with Lois that she would call him when she woke in the morning, since the three-hour time difference would mean that by then Betty would be out of the house.

Only moments after his conversation with Gloria, Lois phoned. "Hi," she said in a sleepy voice, relaxed and inviting, broadcasting in its tone her circumstances—he could see the rumpled blue pastel bedsheets, the California sun bleaching the tiled windowsill, the white phone cord stretching from the night table across her breasts.

He had showered first thing to wash off the residues of last night's copulation with Betty. He couldn't bear speaking to Lois with his wife's liquids still on him. "Are you in bed?"

"No, I'm in the kitchen," she said, still in that dreamy tone. "I miss you so much already, it's sick."

Tony sighed. He hadn't expected it to be easy, but the way she spoke to him made it impossible. "We have to talk," he said sharply.

"Oh?" She was alert almost instantly. "I knew it!" she added with surprising energy and command. "I had a feeling last night it was going to happen—Judy said it was paranoia. But I was right! You went home and you got scared, right?"

"Well, don't say it like I'm a wimp. Not scared, no. It's just . . . this isn't right."

"What isn't right?"

"Doing this. To you. To Betty. To me. It's too much pain—it's too hard. I don't know who I am. I don't know who I'm living with—I spend every minute with Betty scared I'm going to call her Lois."

"And do you spend every minute with me scared you're going—"

"No! God, no." He sighed. He felt put upon, cast in a role he didn't want to play. He wanted a rewrite, something more in a star's part, where all the sympathy would be with him. Make his wife a bitch, or Lois a scheming homewrecker, at least give him a tragic past so that there would be something to take the curse off his treating these two women so badly. "I have to make a decision—"

"Then decide to move out here. Live with me, Tony. I'm good for you. How much writing have you done since you married Betty?"

He frowned at the phone, irritated by her question. It didn't bother him that it insulted his marriage—he was annoyed that it was something he had never thought about. "I don't think Betty's responsible for my not writing."

"Okay. I love you, you schmuck. No one could love you more than I do. If you don't appreciate that, you're an asshole." She hung up. All he heard was the click, but he knew she must have slammed the receiver down. He dialed her number immediately, but got no answer. He tried to imagine whether she was standing there weeping at the ringing phone or whether she had stormed out, driving to work furious. The latter, he thought admiringly.

He estimated how long it would be before Lois reached work, but when the time came, he didn't call. Speaking to her weakened his resolve to say that they should not see each other for a while (something that was likely to occur in any event) and that a good test of the seriousness of their relationship would also be to maintain a silence of letters and telephones. She had guessed correctly at his mealymouthed introduction anyway; perhaps more talk was redundant. He reasoned this way all day, explanations for his cowardly silence evolving by afternoon into a monologue that minimized how intimate he and Lois had been.

Altogether they had had only twenty days of physical contact. And though they had spoken on the phone almost daily (Tony had praised the fates that Betty never looked at New York Telephone's itemized list of long-distance calls), most of their talk was no different from conversations with friends. (Even Tony, in the throes of rationalization, knew that this particular diminishment of his relationship with Lois was specious—the warm, gossipy conversations they had were what made him fall in love with her. The sex was great, but her absorption in his career and life was what had made him feel she was superior to Betty, who seemed slightly bored and depressed when hearing his anxieties and hopes.) But he told himself these lies over and over, masking the real face of their love, dressing it up in shabby cloth, and by nightfall the costume had become convincing, the ugly nose he had put on the face of their romance had made the loss seem unimportant and easy to bear.

He watched his wife when they went out to dinner, observed how many other men looked at her (there were plenty, he discovered, to his shock and irritation), and checked item by item Betty's physical advantages. His wife was prettier. Any man would think him a fool to trade Betty for Lois. And, oddly, Betty seemed sexier, her perfect posture holding the breasts high, impertinently, exposing her long white neck, her eyes always on you, her mouth in a smirk of mild amusement. Lois was sincere, her thin body energetic, not sensual, her eyes guarded, often distracted, her flat breasts unimportant and undisplayed. Yet, in bed, Betty was dull, perfunctory, almost embarrassed, with none of the energy she displayed in conversation, while Lois was high-spirited, her tight body flowingly loose and embracing, her eyes sparkling from pleasure, her throat laughing with ecstasy. Maybe I'm responsible for the distinction, bored with Betty, and so making her boring.

For a week he thought of nothing else, and yet told himself how surprising it was that breaking up with Lois didn't seem to bother him. He went to bed each night mildly outraged that Lois hadn't phoned. He opened his mailbox with a little rush of anticipation, mounting as the days went by, that there would be something from her in there. She's so damn proud, he thought to himself, imagining (somewhat hopefully) how miserable she must be.

He looked at the screenplay each morning, but couldn't begin on the rewrite. The words themselves seemed drab and lonely on the page, as though they were uncollected orphans walking the streets aimlessly with runny noses and tattered shoes. It depressed him to meet their eyes and take them to the institution, to be washed with cold dirty water, dressed in uniforms, and left to the surveillance of coldhearted taskmasters.

He did begin work on a play, as he had promised himself on arrival in New York. And although those words seemed cheerful, the bright

students of an expensive school, clean faces pushing eagerly to the fore
to be noticed—they still seemed like children. His plays didn't have the
stern power of an army assaulting the world with confidence and pomp,
their mission profound, their audience cheering with ecstatic liberation.

He resumed his attendance at the Uptown Theater Company's
weekly readings. He hadn't gone in more than a year and, to his surprise
and delight, he was greeted like a brother returning from war: they asked
awed questions about Hollywood, as if the experience was not only exciting, but deadly as well. Hearing the works in progress of fellow playwrights cheered him. Nobody was writing really well. Most were unable
to execute even the simplest of structures, their characters frequently
were unformed or their motivations inconsistent. The few whose skills at
the craft of drama were sharp had no subject matter other than, usually,
the story of their families. If they reached middle age, sometimes it was
the story of their marriages instead. Tony had the same problem, and to
be reminded that it was a universal condition made his illness seem less
serious and easier to bear, though it also made him less patient with his
own work, less eager to do it. The dialogue on his page the morning after
a reading too often sounded like another's, the story merely a rewrite of
everything he had heard, in some ways more dramatic, often funnier,
but never more profound.

He drifted through the days. Reading the paper, watching game
shows, going to movies in the afternoon, writing a page of the screenplay
once a week, discarding the play he had begun about his mother's show,
starting one on his summer visits to his father's house, dropping that
after a mere two scenes, and then taking out a draft of an old work, an
ambitious drama about the three civil-rights workers who were killed in
the South by Klansmen. He tried to rid it of its sixties "social-conscious-
ness" tone, its obeisance to liberal principles, and focus it more on the
questionable psychology of these middle-class kids who put themselves
in jeopardy for a people and a life that, in truth, were no more their fault
or responsibility than apartheid. But after a few weeks he concluded that
the effect of his revisions was merely to diminish their heroism with
obvious Freudian insights about middle-class family life; that he had
managed, by a circuitous route, to take this story of the birth of social
activism in the baby-boomer generation, an activism that he in fact
believed had forever altered the terms of political debate, and turn it into
just another play about how hard it is to fulfill the expectations of a
Jewish mother without getting yourself lynched.

Then his ideas all turned to farcical satires, the desperate resort (he
knew) of all young writers without new stories to tell, or new insights into

old ones. He briefly considered using his knowledge of being a Hollywood child to write a black comedy based on the circumstances of Ronald Reagan's son—he could easily imagine offending everybody with that one. Might even be a hit. He started it, but the sour tone of his dialogue, the grotesque prospect of yukking it up about a senile opportunist who was in fact making fools of the American people, killed his desire to make fun. It really wasn't amusing. He would agree with the outraged responses: to josh about the horrible is to eat without paying the bill. Art might not be as important as he believed, but it had to have some objective beyond tickling the funny bone of sophomores and leaving the dull-witted with their mouths open.

He began to regard himself as having a terminal illness. He was dying as an artist. He had no faith that the cold engine of his imagination could be started, no matter how many times he replaced the batteries or friendly passersby brought out cables to jump-start it. The feeling wasn't dramatic or desperate. It was the sure knowledge that came each morning when he stared at the typewriter, sipping his coffee, that every word in his mind, every character, every story, every setting, every theme that drifted out of the misty chill in his brain turned out to be a bore. A cliché, a character he knew nothing of, or a circumstance that had been done and done and done. The muscles were dying, paralyzed by dismay and hopelessness. He no longer believed that time would rescue him, that the inevitable accumulation of experience and writing would lead him to a final victory.

And if he turned to the screenplay, this numbness of creation was made worse, because after all, that wasn't even art. If he couldn't be a hack either, what was to become of him? He had to earn a living. He had to have something to say at dinner parties when asked what he did.

He started having trouble falling asleep, perhaps because his days were so lethargic. Often evening came without his having been more venturesome than going from his study to the kitchen. He watched television as though afraid of silence, keeping it on from the moment Betty left, turning it off only when they had dinner. The effort of conversing when, on his side, there was nothing to report other than despair, drove him to turn the TV back on after clearing the dishes, this time to create silence.

After a while Betty stopped asking if he had written that day, her studious avoidance adding to the sense that he was a victim of a fatal illness, that his condition was too terrible even to be mentioned. She took to reading in the bedroom and he stared stupidly at the set, excited only when a favorite movie was on, though even that would remind him of how miserably he had failed with his screenplay. For the first time in his life, he regularly watched his mother's show, perversely waiting through the credits to watch Lois' name scroll by. He began to play a sick little game, imagining a moment from their lovemaking at the instant the letters appeared—her head bobbing on his cock, the look of her cunt as he approached it with his lips.

When he tried to fall asleep, the long dreary day of inactivity and repressed thought would make his brain feverish. In the dark of the bedroom, incidents from his life were replayed each time he closed his eyes, startling him awake with their horror and pain. His mother screaming, his father greeting him at the airport with dulled eyes and perfunctory hellos, images of falling out of windows, the world detonating in the white blast of nuclear death, and he would be up, out again in the living room, watching late movies and all-night news programs, falling asleep only when fatigue was so great that no coherent thought could be formed to scare him.

Finally Betty couldn't stand his mood. She appeared at three in the morning. Tony hadn't shaved or showered for two days. He was sullenly eating a bag of potato chips and watching sitcom reruns. Betty stood in the doorway in her pin-striped nightshirt, squinting slightly from the bright light, but with no sleepiness in her eyes, though she had gone to bed hours before.

"Hi," he said, worried. "I thought you were asleep."

"What's the matter with you?" she asked sternly.

"I can't sleep."

"Why not?" she snapped.

"I don't know."

"Sure you do. Do you want to tell me or not? Because if you don't want to tell me, then maybe you shouldn't be living here."

Tony smiled. "Come on," he said.

"Come on, what? You're like a zombie. You think it's fun living with you?"

"No, I guess it isn't."

"You can't write because they didn't like your script?"

"I guess," he answered. He was glad that she was interrogating him, relieved that she was angry, but still not wanting her to know exactly how he felt.

"Well, then don't do it. Why the hell did you want to write for them anyway? You're a playwright. Why do you want to write screenplays?"

"I don't know. I don't think I do. Not anymore."

She sighed, the stiffness in her body collapsing. She walked in and sat down, staring at him wearily. "Then why don't you just drop it? Can't you do that? Can't you tell them you don't want to do it?"

"Yeah, I can. I asked Gloria. She said I could. It means I won't get the rest of the money."

"I don't care about that. Do you?"

"No."

"Then tell them you're not going to do it."

Tony gazed off for a moment. "Okay," he said.

"Good," she said, and stood up. "You'll tell them tomorrow morning?" He nodded yes. "Now come to bed. I'm tired."

"You go ahead—"

"No! I want you in bed next to me. I didn't get married to fall asleep alone."

He laughed, delighted by her fury, and followed her to bed. As she fell asleep, snuggling into his arms, she said, "Shave tomorrow."

"Okay," he answered and slept also.

Patty couldn't decide whether to tell Betty about the situation with Gelb, to stop her from submitting the manuscript as they had arranged. If it were not for this single thing, that her best chance to get a contract for her novel was at a publishing house where Gelb was soon to become the publisher, she would have no difficulties. She could have tossed the Four Seasons' shrimp in mustard sauce in his face and gone home to put the scene in her novel while awaiting the good news from Betty that Garlands was willing to publish it.

Instead she went home and threw up her mostly empty stomach and took a sweaty restless nap. Betty called at five o'clock, excited, speaking in a whisper: "I think they're gonna let us do it. I spoke to Jeffries before lunch. He said I should have Ann Wilson read it and if she liked it as much as I did, we could transfer the contract from Shadow. That means you won't get any more than five thousand."

Patty had pulled herself up and leaned against the pillows. Her mouth tasted of both alcohol and vomit.

"Patty! You there?"

"Yeah. That's great," she said listlessly, despite her desire to feign pleasure.

"What's the matter? You worried about Ann? Don't. I gave her the manuscript a couple of minutes ago, told her all about it. She was excited."

"She was excited? What's she got to be excited about?"

"My opinion!" Betty said, not kidding. "This is the first novel I've given anyone here with this kind of hype, Patty."

She wants me to thank her. "I really appreciate it."

"Well, it deserves it. I read it again last night, Patty, and it's terrific."

"Thanks."

"Are you okay? What's wrong?" Before Patty could answer, Betty rushed on. "Oh, today was the big lunch! What did he say?"

"Nothing. Just apologies."

"For firing you?"

"Yep."

"Well, that's nice. The bastard. I can't imagine what it must be like to work for him."

"I feel a little sick from the lunch. Let me . . . can I call you back?" She hung up the moment Betty said okay, her mind reeling from the irony of Betty's last statement. What could she do? She was trapped. There was absolutely no guarantee that she could get a book contract from another publisher. She knew how hard it was to get them to gamble on a first novelist. She didn't even have an agent. She would have to accept Betty's offer—assuming it came through—and then sleep with Gelb. In fact she'd probably have to start spreading her legs even before the public announcement of his hiring, judging from how eager he was in the cab. He had fired her because she refused once—what would he do to her book? She had been ruined once by her prudery, her reluctance to use sex as a career move. She wouldn't allow a repetition, she couldn't permit her book to be destroyed by naiveté. A year of screwing him and she might even get a big print run and a major advertising campaign. A year of saying no and her book would be screwed once and for all.

She hadn't told David about the lunch, thank God, so she was spared having to make up a lie to him about how it went. She suggested they go to the movies, and after considerable coaxing, he agreed to go. Afterwards she pleaded illness and got into bed, lying there listening to the faint sound of the television in the other room. I could do it, she told herself, if only Gelb attracted me. But his stubble had felt scratchy, his thick neck and cold eyes weren't sexy, and the terms of the sexual exchange—her body for a successful career—didn't turn her on either. She didn't entirely mind the possessiveness of it, or even its evil tone—it simply didn't seem to have anything to do with lust, with the physical.

She had controlled men with sex before, tamed their demands, seduced them into usefulness. While writing the novel she had recognized the pattern of her behavior with men, observed how even with David she didn't give her real self to him, that her assumption (often reinforced by people like Gelb) that her only power over men, the granting or denial of sexual satisfaction, was not only immoral but also ultimately self-defeating.

She had vowed not to do it again, had stopped stroking David's penis to get him out of his grumpy self-obsessed moods—though she had to admit the new approach didn't seem to be working. But this was different in one important respect. Her novel was at stake, the promise of a long interesting career, the establishment of a beachhead on the continent she wanted to conquer. To use sex for herself, to gain an identity and a presence in the world, was that self-defeating? Sure, it was immoral—but harmful to her?

She tried to imagine fucking Gelb. She could probably just lie there and let him drool over her breasts and hump her quickly—she tagged him, from his breathy nervous kissing, an early ejaculator. And she worried whether he would keep to the bargain, whether she could handle a manipulation of him. She suspected that Gelb, despite his frantic pleas, his apparent lack of negotiating skill, would manhandle her once she took the edge off his horniness.

He called at ten the next morning. "So, are you going to take the job?"

"No," she said, still without a plan.

"Why not?"

"Because I don't want to be an editor. In fact, I don't want to have a job."

There was a silence from Gelb's end and then an abrupt snort of contemptuous laughter. "You don't expect me to believe you want to write that romance shit."

"No, I don't want to do that either."

"Well, what? You want to stay home and have kids? What is it?"

"What difference does it make to you? You only—"

"I love you," he said gruffly, as though he were complaining about being mischarged on a bill. "That's why."

Patty shook her head, truly baffled by him. This attempt to portray himself as a romantic suitor was so preposterous, so obviously a lie, that she couldn't believe he was attempting it. Did he really have that much contempt for her, to think she would buy his shabby goods?

"I don't love you," she said without thought, simply telling the truth. The moment it was out, she realized it was the perfect answer.

"Of course you don't. Why should you? I've behaved like an asshole.

But I want the chance to reform. To change your mind." Again his tone was matter-of-fact, a salesman soothing a difficult client, exuding enough confidence to let you know he expected to succeed, without containing sufficient arrogance to make you want to balk just to show him up.

"I'm in love with David," she said, this time coming up with an answer she had planned.

"No, you're not," he said quickly, stating a fact, not arguing.

"How can you say that? You've never met him, you've—"

"I accept that you don't love me, even maybe that you don't like me, but when a woman is in love she doesn't discuss it like this. She doesn't come to lunch like you did and sit in a cab like you did."

"I'm intimidated by you. That's all. I'm scared of you."

"Really?" His voice sounded surprised and delighted. He chuckled. "That's hard to believe."

"It true," she said with convincing earnestness, because, after all, it *was* true.

"I'm just a scared little kid like everybody else, Patty."

"Oh no you're not," she said, and he began to laugh, and then she joined him, relaxing into the conversation for the first time. "You're a tough guy," she added, controlling her laughter. "And you scare the shit out of everybody."

"That's sad," he answered. "Help me change. Give me some of your sweetness."

Patty laughed. "This is ridiculous. I feel like you're ordering take-out sex. Do you want me delivered in a white cardboard box?"

"No," Gelb answered, chuckling. "Wrapped in silk, dear. And no chopsticks."

"Let me call you. Give me some time."

"Okay," Gelb said breezily. "I'll give you until the afternoon." And he rang off without a good-bye. She sat at the typewriter all morning unable to write. To work on the book seemed irrelevant now, since its future hung in the balance. She expected Gelb to phone right after lunch, but Betty did instead.

"Feeling better?"

"Oh, yes. I'm sorry I didn't call you back."

"I hope our working together isn't going to make things weird between us," Betty said hastily, as though this were something she had planned to say and felt nervous about.

"Me too," Patty said, thinking of how it would be, sleeping with Betty's boss, turning down a job for more money and with more authority

than Betty had. Even now she was keeping secret from Betty the imped-
ing fact of Gelb's arrival at Garlands, fearing that it might somehow stop
Betty from continuing with her efforts to get Patty a contract.

Meanwhile, Betty laughed. "I wanted you to reassure me it
wouldn't."

"Well, we'll do our best, won't we?"

"We'll always be honest with each other," Betty said, again in a tone
that implied a prepared speech. "If you get pissed off at something I do
as an editor, I want you to tell me."

"And vice versa."

"And vice versa. We have to keep the air clear."

"Anyway, we don't know. Ann might hate the book, and we won't
have to worry."

"That's why I'm calling. She read it last night. She's willing to recommend we transfer the contract from Shadow."

Patty stared at the polyurethaned floor.

"Hello?" Betty said.

"That's it? It's over?"

"Well, I've got to handle Shadow, make sure they don't make a fuss.
It'll probably take until next week to make it official and start on the
contract, but there should be no problem."

"That's great," Patty said in a slow, astonished voice. "Thank you."

"You're welcome," Betty answered with sly pride. "I'm really excited, Patty."

"I'd better call David. He won't believe it."

"Sure. But call me back later, okay? We should go to a fancy lunch
next week to celebrate. Maybe I'll bring Ann along. We can go to the
Four Seasons! Won't that be fun?"

"Oh yeah," Patty said. "That'll be a real hoot." She hung up and
dialed right away, only she called Gelb. He got on instantly.

"Hello, beautiful," he said.

"Lighten up," she answered. "I want to tell you something. You
know my friend Betty Winters?"

"Sure. Don't worry. She can keep her job," he said.

"I'm not worried about that. She's recommended that a novel I'm
writing, a serious novel, be published by Garlands. She says she'll have
a contract by next week."

"That's great," he said, a little startled, but easily covering it. "Congratulations. What's the book about?"

"Me."

He laughed. "I like it already. Sounds like a big book."

"If I see you, it's only going to be because of this insane situation. I want you to know that. If that doesn't bother you, okay, I'll meet you in some seedy hotel. If that's what you want."

There was a pause. She heard nothing. No breathing. No chuckle. Then, solemnly, carefully considered, he said: "Okay."

"You don't care. It doesn't make any difference to you why I'm doing it."

"Of course it does, Patty," he said in a hurt tone, but still very much in command. "But beggars can't be choosers. I'll take you on whatever terms I can."

"Then it's a deal," she said, and hung up the receiver with a bang.

GARLANDS PROJECTS REPORT—
BOB HOLDER

[Excerpt]

Initial hundred-page submission Fred Tatter
novel, *The Locker Room*, being revised. Second
part of advance released.

NEWSLIFE

[Excerpt from in-house *Newstime* publication]

The climax of Retreat Weekend was the hotly
contested Editors versus Writers softball game.
David Bergman, recently promoted to senior
editor, hit a two-run homer in the bottom
of the ninth to squeak out the 15–14 victory for
the Editors.

GARLANDS DEAL MEMO

Shadow Books contract, *Dark Dream*,
transferred to trade division for untitled novel.
$5,000 advance. Author, Patty Lane. Editor,
Betty Winters.

INTERNATIONAL PICTURES
PROJECT MEMO

[Excerpt]

Tony Winters' contract for *Concussion*
canceled. Financial obligations are satisfied.

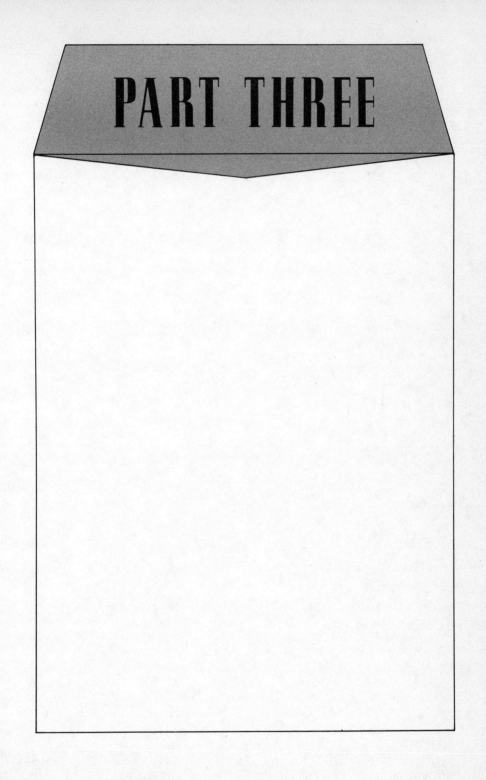

PART THREE

CHAPTER

13

"*He* has no self-esteem! Why are you bothering me? *He's* the one! He doesn't even know what to eat unless he checks with his fancy friends!" Marion didn't look in Fred's direction or acknowledge in any way that he was present. She argued her case to the psychologist eagerly—a debating student scoring points. "It's pathetic. Do you know what it's like? To know that your husband will only like you if he gets permission from *Town* magazine?"

"This is such bullshit," Fred said, and though he got a glance from Dr. Feldman, it was merely cursory.

"What about *your* friends?" Feldman asked.

"What?" Marion looked blank, almost frightened, as though caught in class not having read the assigned material.

"What do your friends think of Fred?" the doctor asked.

Marion stared at him, blinked her eyes, and swallowed hard.

"She doesn't have any friends," Fred said with a triumphant guffaw, a mean sibling tattling to the parents.

"That's not true!" Marion snapped at him, really stung by the remark, her brows scrunching up in pain, her furious tone barely covering the hurt.

"Why do you think Fred says that?" Feldman said with his mild, abstracted voice, a slightly bored questioner.

"Because he likes to hurt me, that's why," she said, and then dissolved. Fred was amazed. Tears flowed down her face, her chest heaved, her hands covered her eyes. Feldman looked at him. Fred felt reproved by the doctor's glance.

"It's just the truth!" Fred squeaked. "I'm just telling the truth." He leaned toward Marion, almost pleading for help. "Name one friend." She sobbed louder, turning from him with horror and loathing. "I don't know one! That's all! Name one!" he cried, an innocent man being sentenced unjustly.

"You don't let me . . ." she choked out between the sobs.

"What!" Fred spread his arms out in incredulous outrage, looking at Feldman for rescue. "Come on," he said to the doctor with weary disgust, crying for the referee to stop these low blows.

"You don't let me have any. All my old girlfriends were stupid. The people we used to know from college, losers."

"This is fuckin' ridiculous!" Fred said, turning to the wall, in the absence of a sensible person to look at.

Marion cried for a while, Feldman looked impassive, Fred stared off. When she quieted, Fred grumbled, "I don't know what this is accomplishing."

Feldman immediately spoke to Marion, almost squashing Fred's words: "Why do you let Fred decide who your friends are?"

"She doesn't! It's bullshit!" Fred said.

"Is there anything Marion has said that you think is true?" Feldman asked, without his tone containing the challenge inherent in the sentence.

"About this?" Fred said, scrambling, knowing he was in trouble, caught in the backfield without a receiver to throw to.

"About anything," Feldman said. "Do any of her criticisms ring true?"

"I don't know—I can't remember them all. There are so many! Everything that's wrong with her life is my fault. Nothing is her fault! Her fucking job, our sex life, every fucking thing is my fault!"

Feldman looked at his clock and then back at Fred, somewhat balefully. "We have five more minutes and I want to talk a little about what we're doing." Marion and Fred both looked at him, surprised, so used to his role as questioner that declarative sentences were a shock. "This has been helpful, both of you coming in as a couple. But I think it's getting . . ." He struggled for a word.

"Stupid," Marion said, and laughed happily, wiping away the tears from her cheek.

"No," Feldman said, but there was a trace of a smile that quickly disappeared. " 'Bogged down,' I was going to say. A lot of the problems in any relationship really begin with the individual and can only be resolved through individual therapy. I'd like to suggest that you both start coming separately."

Marion looked at Fred. She seemed to be asking a question. He had no idea what it was. He could think of only one thing. "You mean," he said to the doctor, "we each take a separate hour?"

"Yes," Feldman said with a puzzled tone.

"But that's . . ." Fred couldn't say it.

"That's gonna get expensive," Marion said.

"Right," Fred agreed. Who said they weren't a team?

Feldman seemed unfazed. "These joint sessions have made some progress, but I think from now on they'll be unproductive. However, if you wish to continue them, that's fine."

Again Marion looked to Fred, as though he had the power to make a decision. Fred's leg began to hop impatiently. "But . . . but . . . excuse me, doctor, that's bullshit, isn't it? I mean, you say the sessions aren't going to work, and then say continue them?"

"I could be wrong," Feldman said, as though right and wrong were both somewhat boring and unimportant distinctions. "We could experiment. Marion could come in alone next week, and you the following week. That wouldn't increase your costs."

"Oh, that's a good idea," Marion said cheerfully. Fred noticed that in these sessions she seemed to go from despair to gaiety at supersonic speed. He always felt the same: nervous, disgruntled, bored, and harassed, much like sitting with an accountant and doing taxes.

"But then that means we never see each other," Fred said to Marion.

"I think that seeing each other outside of this office is something you should be doing," Feldman said.

They both looked at him openmouthed. The judge had blurted out to the jury in mid-trial that he thought the defendant was innocent. The umpire had been caught wearing a partisan T-shirt under his neutral uniform.

"So?" Feldman said after several moments of their astonishment had passed. He looked at Marion. "You'll come in next week?" He glanced at the clock. "Because I'm afraid our time is up."

Marion agreed in a daze and they walked out to the elevator and looked at each other with amazement. Six months had passed since she tossed him out, and these weekly sessions were all that was left of their marriage—apart from its history, which had come alive for them during the intervening days, their minds casting back for fish to fry on Dr. Feldman's stove. "Well!" she said, smiling at Fred.

"Heavy shit," he answered. "You wanna go on a date?"

She cocked her head at him, her eyes, which only minutes before had been manufacturing tears, now clear and sparkling. "Sure," she said with a smile.

The rumors flounced down *Newstime*'s halls, an ingenue seducing everyone from his work, peeking in doors to mock the dull with laughter, the quick with worrisome teasing. David was often asked to confirm, deny, or amplify the various stories. But he couldn't enjoy his position, since he knew the truth. He was obliged to be silent, and knowing the reality, he couldn't enjoy speculation.

Chico told him that Rounder was out of favor with the queen about a week before the news buzzed in the lower honeycombs of the hive. The focus of the complaints were the cost overruns due to the editor in chief's indecisiveness and his penchant for running "soft-news" covers during hot-news weeks. It only added to Chico's and David's amusement that the latter grievance of Mrs. Thorn's—Rounder's love of features— was the reason she hired him in the first place, preferring a man with commercial instincts rather than Chico, whose background was in hard news.

"It won't be long now," Chico told him. "One more fuck-up and he's gone." Chico's strategy during the last six months had been to do nothing to restrain Rounder's desire to run soft stories, and to put no pressure on the editor in chief to make decisions quickly. Chico credited David with the conception of this plan, and praised him repeatedly for it. "I would've kept doing his job for him," Chico said gratefully, "if it weren't for your advice."

Although David was encouraged by these words, he also noticed, now that the moment of Chico's mating flight, alone—in joyous ecstasy above the hive with the queen—was imminent, that the promises earlier made about promoting David to Marx Brotherhood weren't repeated.

Whether it was tension over this or the wait for the expected great event, David felt irritable all the time, scratching against the stubbly surface of the unkempt world. It was obvious to everyone at the magazine, David felt sure, that Chico deserved to be Groucho, and that he would also be elevated. Yet it had not happened—they were still stuck in this temporary and unsatisfactory universe.

And then one Wednesday morning the buzz grew fierce with the news that Mrs. Thorn had flown in from Washington unannounced and was headed upstairs for a conference with Chico and Rounder. It was confirmed moments later over the phone when David picked up his line, to be greeted by Chico saying without a hello, "This is it! This is it!"

"You think?"

"Definitely. Gotta go."

David closed his door to keep out gossips, knowing he couldn't successfully pretend he wasn't excited, and somehow feeling that to reveal his expectations would jinx them. He tried to imagine the scene taking place above him. He couldn't. The real face of power at *Newstime*, despite his intimacy with Chico, despite his presence at all the cover and run-through meetings, remained in shadow, as difficult to picture as what Mrs. Thorn was like undressed in bed.

For a few unbearable minutes he sat and waited. Then he flipped to the back of his appointment book where the telephone number he had called so often was scribbled. He gently lifted the receiver and got an outside line, pausing, a man at the edge of cold water, wanting its refreshment but squeamish at its first shock. He pressed the numbers and let it ring. She answered, as always, in an angry tone:

"Yes?"

"Is this the mistress?" he asked, surprised at his husky voice, so choked the words were barely escaping the constriction of his throat.

"Yes?" Even more irritated and impatient.

"I saw your ad," he said, and felt a burst of sweat release from his underarms. At last he had done it! He hadn't hung up in a panic like all the other times.

"Your age and occupation?" she snapped instantly.

He hadn't been ready for this. It panicked him. "What?" he said, flabbergasted.

"Your age and occupation," she repeated, bored.

"Uh, I'm thirty-one. I, uh, I'm an executive."

"I offer dominance and submission. I have a completely equipped dungeon located in Chelsea. It's a hundred for the hour and it's a full hour. Do you want to make an appointment?"

"Uh . . ." He swallowed hard. His breath was so short, his heart's percussion resounding so frighteningly throughout his body that he almost felt too weak to remain conscious. "I've never done this . . . can I ask some questions?"

"You'll have a consultation with the mistress to discuss your limitations before the session begins. It's important you understand, however, that this is dominance and submission. There's no sex."

"What does that mean?" he asked, his surprise at this statement overcoming his shy terror.

For the first time, she sounded startled, surprised by his return of serve. "Well, it means slavery, basically." She recovered her stern tone and went on: "Do you have a particular fetish?"

"Uh, I don't know. I thought I might like to be forced to . . ." Overwhelming embarrassment flooded his consciousness, followed by incredulity at the fact that he was actually having this conversation. He cleared his throat. "To worship you."

"You mean body worship?"

"Uh, yes."

"Anal worship is permitted. Pussy worship is not."

He loved her saying that—the flat tone, so matter-of-fact that she could have been someone ordering a large orange juice with the breakfast special. Now he wanted to provoke more discussion of her rules. "Uh . . . can I worship your breasts?"

"No!" Now she was furious, speaking rapidly, the words clipped. "That's not dominance. That's sex. You go to a prostitute for that!" And she hung up.

David stared at the phone, abashed. And amazed. Could she really mean it? She wasn't a prostitute? She could afford to turn down someone willing to pay a hundred dollars an hour just to lick her breasts?

He imagined kneeling behind her as she lowered her ass onto his mouth, and felt hard. He replayed in his mind her controlled dull voice: "Anal worship is permitted. Pussy worship is not." He rubbed himself through the pants, his penis straining against his underpants, and wanted desperately to speak to her again.

He picked up the phone to call back—without noticing that the line light was on. Through the receiver he heard the media writer Charlie Huddleston saying to his secretary:

"You mean *Little* Chico isn't up there with them for the beheading?"

His secretary was laughing, which covered the sound of David picking up the receiver.

"Do you think he'll take you up to Animal Crackers with him?" Huddleston went on.

"God forbid," she said, still giggling.

"Is he really bad to work for?" Huddleston said.

"No. But he's no fun. Spends most of the time in there with the door closed. I don't know what he's doing."

"Probably drinking," Huddleston said. "He's bombed every Friday night. I guess its tough being a prodigy. Well, you better buzz me through."

"Okay," she said, and instantly David's intercom rasped.

He felt no rage. He flipped the button.

"Charlie Huddleston on two," she said.

"Okay," he said, and got on again. He noticed with interest that Huddleston's tone with him had the same casualness and ease, maintaining a respectful friendliness with no effort. "Hi! I'm hearing wild rumors. Should I be preparing a transfer-of-power story?"

"Gee, Charlie, I don't know. Hey, you know there was something I wanted to ask you. Get confirmation."

"What's that?" Huddleston said.

"I heard from somebody that I've got a nickname at the magazine."

"Oh," Charlie said, nervousness creeping in.

Let's make him wonder, David thought. "Yeah. Have you heard it? Little Chico."

"No kidding," Charlie said, now definitely shaky and confused. "I haven't heard that."

"Oh, good. It's kind of insulting."

"Yeah, it is. Oh, there's my other phone. I'd better—"

"Sure," David said with a smile. "'Bye." He hung up, feeling good. Feeling lucky. In control.

Tony stretched forward in his chair to relieve the dull ache in his back. The last lines were being said. He noticed with pleasure that they had the right tone of finality. The audience at this reading of his new play—the other members of the Uptown Theater and, especially important, its artistic director. Hilary Bright—were rapt, their expressions concentrated. There had been a lot of laughs, not quite as many as he had hoped, a few sounded automatic, polite, but the "heavy" scenes had played even better than he had expected. The success of this reading was important: Hilary Bright had arranged it to help her determine whether his play was ready for the Uptown Theater to do a production of it this fall.

Now came the applause. There would have been clapping no matter what they thought of the play—after all, everyone there had to suffer the same sort of evaluation at one time or another, and between compassion and fear there was never an insulting response at a reading. But this applause was loud, enthusiastic, and genuine. Tony had heard enough of the other kind to know the difference.

Hilary, while clapping, got up and moved in front of the actors seated on chairs, and turned to face the audience. "Well, that was delightful," she said, smiling.

Delightful? Tony thought. It's supposed to be either shattering or funny, but delightful? Sounds like a description of a magic act, not a good play.

"Tony," she said, looking at him. "How can we be of help to you?"

She always asked this preposterous question, this fastball begging to be banged out of the park with a bat of sarcasm. And, predictably, Tony took his cut: "Got an empty theater?"

Laughter. Hilary smiled. "Not if we get plays like this," she said, but hurried on, as though frightened by the commitment it implied. "Is there anything that surprised you about the play—hearing it read?"

"I thought it would be funnier," Tony said. "But I don't really want to talk about what I think. I'm sick to death of what I think. First I'd like to hear from the actors—who did a wonderful job," he added, and began to clap, joined immediately by the audience.

When the applause died down, Hilary gestured to the row of performers seated on folding chairs, their copies of the play on their laps like prayer books. During the last six months, since he had dropped the screenplay, he had worked madly, joyously reworking his old play about the three civil-rights workers who were killed by the Klan, feeling younger, stronger, and happier with each day. Nearing the end, his confidence in the future had returned in earnest. He really believed this time it would happen, this time he would win the honors so long expected for him, so long taken for granted, and now so desperately needed for survival. He had broken free of the small autobiographical limitations of his early plays, he had forced his head through the birth canal and observed a world other than his own.

The actors began. Tony liked listening to their opinions and he sometimes changed things because of them, but never because of the content of their criticisms. Performers always believed their parts should be bigger, their motivations less selfish and explicated in greater detail. They were forever forgetting that their job was to tour the audience through a walk in the woods, not stop and discuss the bark of one tree endlessly. This time they were unusually content: they praised "the structure" (something they knew nothing about) and then talked about how much they "liked" their characters (the highest possible encomium). Then the audience of playwrights and directors began to comment. The toughest remarks at these readings were commonly from other writers, and that held true again, although the major criticism wasn't posed aggressively.

"I didn't think, Tony . . ." said Hal Turner, the most successful of the Uptown Theater playwrights, a likely candidate for that year's Pulitzer Prize for his off-Broadway success, *The Evening*, a grim two-character play about a confrontation between a rapist and the husband of his victim. "I didn't think," he repeated, his eyes wandering to the ceiling musingly. Everyone fell silent, respectfully. "Though I loved many, many things, I didn't feel, at the end, that you had really taken it far enough. I don't think the ending is sufficiently dramatic."

"You mean because the killing is offstage?" Tony said, his worst fear confirmed. He too had felt the ending was anticlimactic, but so far no one else had said anything.

"Uh . . . I'm not sure. I think your instinct to stay away from the killing is right. It wouldn't really end the play, it would just kill the characters."

"That's an ending!" someone called out. Everyone laughed.

"You've raised terrific questions about these characters," Turner went on. "You need to answer some of them."

"Oh, but he does!" Hilary protested. "When—"

"He does answer some of them!" Turner quickly modified. "But I mean decisively, dramatically. I certainly wouldn't want a talky finish, with everyone wrapping up their lives as though they know they're about to die. I love the effect of the casualness just before they go off to be killed, the sense, the eerie sense, of them naturally assuming they will be back later and do this and that—it's a powerful effect. But it leaves some of the play's questions unanswered. Not unasked. But unanswered."

"I don't know that I *can* answer them," Tony admitted. He glanced at Hilary and briefly worried that a frank discussion on his part might scare her off doing the play that fall—she seemed ready to commit. But when he returned his glance to Turner, a bright man whose talent he admired, an experienced playwright who was obviously sympathetic to Tony's work, he wanted to continue. "I've asked myself over and over. Were these characters sincere? Were they risking their lives—sometimes I'm not even sure they really believed the threats—were they risking their lives out of pure altruism, or was it some kind of neurotic calling of their parents' political bluff?"

"What do you mean by that?" Turned asked with the enthusiasm of a lonely soul discovering a kindred spirit. The others stayed quiet, fading into the background, as though they were medical students observing two surgeons conduct a dangerous and experimental operation.

"I guess this may come from my past," Tony said, "but when one is raised by people who put a high value on dangerous political action, there's a tendency to do what they want, carry it so far that it almost becomes a kind of rebellion . . ."

Turner smiled. "Yes, that's what you mean by the funny scene with Stein's mother."

"Right, right."

Turned frowned. "I'm not sure your point there was clear to the audience. It's a funny scene. Maybe it's too funny, makes everybody think it's only there for the laughs, and they don't realize it carries the real point of the play."

There were murmurs of agreement from the others. Tony had almost forgotten they were there. He suppressed a surge of anger at them, convinced they were too dumb to have noticed such a subtlety whether he was right or wrong to have put it in the play. They were merely parroting the influential playwright's opinion. "You all feel that?" Tony asked, to be polite.

"Yes," said Polly Howells, the resident feminist whom Tony had been told despised his work. Someone quoted her as saying, "He's just another one of those Yuppie playwrights who writes plays complaining his parents didn't encourage him enough," a remark that hurt all the more for its potential accuracy. "Yes, I missed that," Polly said, obviously glad to have something to say. She always seemed so eager to give opinions. Tony had been surprised by how long she had stayed silent. "I like the play a lot, Tony. I really think its a big step forward for you . . ."

Tony smiled at her, narrowing his eyes. He hoped she'd realize he was close to murdering her and stop talking in such a condescending fashion.

On the contrary, she warmed to her words. "But I felt, in the end, that you kept going for the easy one-liners just when you were about to break through to the heart of the theme."

"That's putting it strongly," Turner said in a hurt tone, as though she were attacking him. "And, you know, it ain't so easy to write funny one-liners like Tony's. I can't do it. I've tried. And I think I'd be a better writer if I could. Tony keeps a good balance in this play between heavy drama and social satire. It ends up being very real precisely because he touched both extremes."

"Yes, yes, yes," Polly said quickly. Tony smiled at her panicky withdrawal. She sucked up to Hal Turner constantly, always praised his work to excess, and it amused Tony to see how she didn't even dare to question his opinions. "I think he has a wonderful play here. But, like you, I felt Tony buried some of his more serious questions—what is real political commitment? can we ever escape our parents' expectations, no matter how far from home we go?—that he lost some of these in trying to be funny. Maybe you were a little scared to explore the pain involved here," she added directly to Tony.

He had to admit she might be right in her dull sociological way. He knew this subject was a way for him to explore the challenge of his mother's and father's political past. Perhaps he made comedy out of the family scenes not because it was accurate or a good choice dramatically, but because he couldn't look at the ugly face of his family without turning to stone.

He nodded after a pause, and that seemed to open the floodgates. Suddenly everyone, including those who had previously spoken only with praise of the play, found the same weakness, and hammered away with growing enthusiasm, like kids imitating each other.

Hilary cut it off at last. "All right, I think we've made our point to Tony." There was self-conscious laughter. "I think we're agreed we've got a good play here that needs some work at developing its theme."

Tony got up wearily, and merely nodded yes to Hilary when she said he should call tomorrow to discuss the next step. He knew that the muck and the mire had risen once again—rewrite, discussion, compromise. He would have to struggle again: to get the play right, to get Hilary to put it on. He was tired of spinning his wheels in the snow, making what was once white, pure, and beautiful into brown sludge. Get me out, he asked New York's night sky while walking home, after refusing Hal Turner's invitation to have a drink. Get me out of this muddy ditch.

Because Patty wanted Gelb's support for her novel to seem objective, she had insisted on absolute discretion. She demanded that he not gossip, that their meetings take place at an anonymous location, such as a hotel, rather than at the apartment of a friend who would have to be let in on the secret.

Thus she was infuriated when, on the day she went up to Garlands to deliver to Betty the final chapter of her novel, Gelb "happened" to drop by, feigning (badly, Patty thought) surprise at her presence.

"What are you here for?" he boomed.

"Her novel's finished!" Betty announced with a wide smile, as though it were the accomplishment of a precocious child. "She's a big girl and goes in the potty now," was her tone. Patty loathed them both. She felt rage at being at their mercies, an anger redoubled by the fact that she had to pretend intimacy with them. Her child was in their care: its health in the hands of a lech and a coward. Why the hell doesn't Betty have the sense to screw him, Patty thought, and really make sure of a big print run?

"When can I read it?" Gelb asked.

This is hopeless, Patty thought, noticing the look of astonishment on Betty's face. Betty still thought of Gelb's arrival at Garlands as a

disaster, assuming that Gelb bore ill will toward Patty—a notion Patty
encouraged—and now the big bozo was blowing it. "I'll give it to you
right away," Betty said.

"I have to go," Patty said.

"We're having lunch!" Betty said.

"Oh, that's right," Patty admitted.

"You are? I don't have a lunch. I'll join you," Gelb said. Patty was
so disgusted, she almost stuck her tongue out at him. He wants everybody to know, she decided. Pride of ownership.

Betty looked seasick. "Great," she said.

The three of them stood there for a moment. Betty opened her
drawer, coming out with the bathroom key. "But Patty and I had better
freshen up first."

"Okay," Gelb said.

"I'm fresh enough," Patty said, not wanting to have to answer Betty's
questions yet.

So now Betty was stuck, the ladies' room key in hand. "I'll be right
back," she said, and walked out, turning her head away from Gelb and
signaling violently with her eyes at Patty. Betty's attitude toward Gelb
was what Patty's once was—a schoolgirl's toward the principal—but having seen his lumpy buttocks while he stood at the bathroom sink angling
his head to see if he had trimmed all his nostril hairs had altered Patty's
perspective.

Gelb moved at her the instant Betty was gone, his hands out. "How
dare you!" Patty said, outraged, as he took possession, his hands reaching
for her ass, his lips kissing her neck. "You're making it so fucking obvious! You might as well come in with my panties in your teeth!"

He laughed into her hair and then murmured, "You're so beautiful
—I got a hard-on in the cab just thinking of you."

"Fabulous," Patty said, and pushed at his chest. "Anyone can see!
Will you stop!"

He moved away. "Who cares if they find out?"

"I do! Everyone will think it's the only reason I'm being published."

"Nonsense," he answered with a devilish smile. "Everybody knows
I'm not that nice." And then he laughed, delighted.

"Hilarious. I can't trust you. The affair's over."

"Bullshit," he said confidently, but his eyes were worried. "Your
orgasms are too good. Last time you almost shattered the chandelier."

"Don't flatter yourself. If a dog licked my clit that long I'd come."

Betty breezed in, her face set in a wide smile. Patty and Gelb both looked at the floor like guilty children. "All set?" Betty said with an even brighter smile.

On his way to see Holder for his weekly meeting, Fred passed Patty, Betty, and Gelb in the hall. His routine for the last six months had been to submit rewritten pages each Friday and meet with Holder on Monday and be given changes. This was to be the last of their conferences, since Fred was handing in the final ten pages.

"What are you doing here?" Fred asked Patty without even a hello. "Returning to editing?"

"Patty's just handed in her novel. We're publishing it in the fall," Betty said triumphantly and—Fred thought—as though it were somehow a slap in the face. It did worry him.

"You've written a novel?" he asked Patty.

"Amazing, isn't it?" Patty said in a sarcastic and disgusted tone that also smacked of confidence and control. "I walk and talk too—I'm a real bargain."

"Oh, stop," Betty said. "Fred, you know Jerry Gelb? This is Fred Tatter. We're publishing him also. When, Fred?"

"I guess in the fall," he answered, terrified, now that he knew for sure that Gelb was Gelb, the man himself. Patty used to work for him, Fred remembered, and now felt better, assuming that's why she had gotten a contract. Sure, and Betty, her best friend, is her editor. He regained his balance. "We'll be on the same list. We should have a joint pub party."

"I'm not gonna have a party," Patty said. "I'm gonna stab the *Times Book Review* editor in the stomach and get some decent publicity."

Fred frowned. Betty and Gelb laughed. They said good-bye to him and he felt keen resentment toward them while he walked to Holder's office. He had been worked to the bone by Holder, had had to rewrite every page, while his advance was drained by the studio apartment he had sublet, his expensive social life, and his share of the couple's therapy. Increasingly he felt financial pressure to return to Marion, which would automatically reduce his costs and restore access to her income. Life seemed so easy for these women. If they got into trouble, like Patty had a couple years ago, they banded together, found a man, a place to live, and even a career. He had struggled his whole life to get a novel published and Patty just got one handed to her on a feminist platter.

For once, Holder was wearing a sweater with no holes in the elbows. "I'm real excited, Fred. This book is terrific. I love the story . . ."

Fred nodded, smiling sheepishly while Holder went into this now familiar litany. The plot was Holder's, and it seemed to bear a remarkable similarity to the progress of Holder's life, with a few exaggerations, which were probably fantasies—mostly the hero's sexual prowess. It was awkward and embarrassing to listen to his editor praise what were basically his editor's ideas as though they had originated with Fred. If he accepted the compliments he would be a fraud, to refuse them might seem ungracious and resentful of Holder's editing.

Instead, he changed the subject. "I just met your boss, Gelb, out in the hall. With two friends of mine."

"Oh yeah?" The mention of the publisher's name had Holder on the alert. "With who?"

"Betty Winters and Patty Lane."

"Oh, yeah, yeah," Holder said. Whatever had worried him was gone. "Yeah, Betty's nice. She's doing her first novel with Patty. It's exciting for her."

"Patty? Or Betty?" Fred asked, not archly, but out of confusion.

"Both, I guess. I mean for Betty. Gelb has helped open things up around here—used to be so uptight, so scared to take risks. I really like him. Do you know him?"

"No," Fred said, unable to conceal his irritation that Holder didn't listen carefully. "I told you, I just met him." Holder made Fred feel he was barely in the room, his words merely a string interlude between Holder's orchestral crescendos.

"Oh. Yeah, he's a great guy."

"They were going to lunch together," Fred mumbled.

Holder looked at him curiously. "That bother you?"

"What?" Fred maneuvered in his chair nervously. "No, no. Patty used to work for Gelb."

"Oh!" Holder drew the word out, leaning back with a smirk on his face. "So that's why she got a book contract."

"I don't know, I don't know," Fred said, frightened somehow to admit to his opinion.

"Going to lunch with him doesn't mean a thing, you know." Holder leaned forward and raised his hand high in the air, his index finger pointed down, swooping through the air and landing on the title page of Fred's manuscript. "*This* is going to be a big book. I haven't started lobbying in the house. I was waiting for the whole book. But you've done great work. And this book is going to be big." Holder fixed Fred with his eyes and nodded solemnly. "Believe me," he said.

"You're not gonna believe this," Chico said, feverishly pulling David into his office and closing the door. After a wait of two hours David had been summoned by the Power Phone to Animal Crackers, Chico's voice rasping anxiously, so that David guessed the news wasn't good.

"What?" David asked, the word spoken in dread—though of what, he couldn't imagine.

"You know why Thorn came here? Because of him! This is the most diabolically brilliant maneuver, or he's an idiot, I don't know which. What difference does it make?" Chico cried to the ceiling. "Either way, he's saved himself."

"What did he do?" David asked, panicked, the suspense unbearable.

"He resigned!" Chico spread his arms out, laying out for David his incredulity like a map. "Can you believe it? She's ready to fire him and he resigns! Says he's wrong for the job. Doesn't like it!" Chico grabbed the sides of his skull as though to close in the bursting fury of his mind.

"But . . . but . . ."

"She said no! She's so arrogant—she can't allow him to resign! *She* has to fire him! The minute he said it, she was against it! It's an abrogation of her power. Brilliant! Fucking brilliant! The guy's an idiot savant!"

"Maybe she wasn't ready to fire him."

"Oh, she was ready. Came in dressed like the Black Widow Spider —ready to suck his brains out. Then he comes up with that he-doesn't-want-the-job! No fun eating a prey that's already dead. She ended up wooing him, begging him to stay, and she appeals to me to back her up—"

"Why were you there, anyway?"

"*He* asked for me!" Chico almost shrieked this. "He's so brilliant! We're amateurs! Amateurs!" He flung himself into his desk chair and leaned his head back to stare at the ceiling.

David waited, hoping Chico's silence would lead to a more articulate explanation. He felt relieved, to his surprise. There was something comforting about the lack of change, especially since it didn't mean a true reversal. His position hadn't become precarious, it was unchanged.

"We ended up," Chico said, his voice hoarse. He paused to clear it. "We ended up asking him to stay for another year. She said she'd allow him to experiment some more with the magazine."

"It's just a delay," David said with confidence. "Your insight is exactly correct—she wants to do the firing herself. She'll wait till he's back into the job and then yank the rug out."

Chico brought his small infuriated eyes to David and nodded at him, a lost soul wanting to believe in the prophet. "I keep telling myself that."

"There's no doubt. One incident will break his back."

"All right." Chico sat up. "We'd better go back to normal operations."

David smiled. "Right, chief," he said, and saluted with mock formality before leaving.

Tony met Hilary for a late breakfast the day after his reading. She had called first thing in the morning to suggest the meeting, her voice cheerful and encouraging. The long night he had spent worrying over the play—he had read it through twice, hating it—had left him weak and willing to concede that it wasn't ready.

Hilary began by chatting, complaining about the recent cutback in funding from the National Endowment for the Arts, saying that it would mean two fewer productions in the next season. To Tony this sounded like a preliminary of backing out of her partial commitment to putting him on the schedule.

He was too tired to wait. He interrupted. "So I suppose you won't be able to do my play."

She looked surprised. "Why do you say that?"

"Well, the funding being lost and so on—I thought . . ."

"I wouldn't tell you like that!" she said.

"I'm sorry," he said, and felt rage at her, because he knew he was correct.

"We want to do your play. I've told you that all along. But I do think the questions about the thematic content raised last night have to be considered." Tony nodded. "Didn't you feel some of what was said was helpful?" she pressed when he stayed silent.

"You want me to be honest?" Tony asked in a tone that implied she sure shouldn't.

Hilary seemed startled, but she answered, "Of course."

"Until Hal brought it up, no one mentioned that they thought I had left deeper questions unanswered. I took what he said very seriously. I think I made that clear. *Then* everybody jumped on the bandwagon."

Hilary frowned. Despite the fact that his comment wasn't overtly insulting, in truth it was. She had been consistently complimentary until Turner's comments. "Well, it often does take an experienced playwright —I mean, we are talking about one of the major writers of our time— to express for an audience an uneasiness that they can't articulate. I know I didn't mention my reservations until last night, but I felt when reading the play—and it's one of the reasons having a play read is so important—"

Tony lost it. Whatever brake he had on his speeding fury at the world lost its resilience: his foot slammed to the floor and his heart raced as caution flew by the window. "Come on, this is bullshit. I've heard this over and over. Sure Turner's questions are valid. I have valid criticisms of *Hamlet!* My play probably isn't one of the great works of art of this century, but frankly, Hilary, if that's the standard you use before mounting a production, then your theater should have been dark for the last twenty years!"

'Tony"—her thin face seemed to squeeze itself, narrowing—"all I'm suggesting—"

But his vehicle was racing on, the freedom of releasing his contempt and rage like a sexual liberation: "I've been coming to readings for four months regularly. Not one can compare to mine! Not one!" he shouted, and noticed the movement of heads at nearby tables.

She did too and looked down at the table while putting her right hand up, like a traffic cop. "Please," she said. "There's no need for us to quarrel."

"Why is telling the truth a quarrel? I could bullshit you. I've done it well enough in the past. I knew that I could've gone out for a drink with you and Hal last night and beat my breast and then worked for two weeks adding a couple of scenes like he writes, everybody announcing what the fuck their motivation is, get you to commit, and then dilute it during the rehearsals. And maybe I will!" Again he saw people glance at them. He felt as though he must be screaming. Hilary's downward glance was becoming more severe; her body seemed to be trying to merge with the table. "Maybe I will rewrite it! But I don't want you making that decision for me. I want a director. I want actors. I want a date. Then I'll go into rehearsal and find out for myself. And decide myself! I may not be a great playwright, Hilary, I'm not sure how good I am, but one thing, one goddamn thing for sure, no one else around me is either! I haven't met anyone in my entire life who knows more than I do about what works and what doesn't. I understood what Hal Turner thought better than he did! It's my problem! It's my fucking play! Let me fix it or *not!*"

She raised her head when he paused. The tearful look in her eyes, and the wounded, trembling movement of her chin and mouth, surprised him. He really didn't know her very well—she had seemed no different from the dozen or so artistic directors he had dealt with over the years. They were obstacles, abstractions, infuriating people because he never understood why they took the jobs they held. Off-Broadway theater didn't pay well; their role wasn't really a creative one, despite the title; they had all the disadvantages of being put in a business posture in charge of artists, with few or none of the monetary rewards. Because of their lack of financial prestige, there was a kind of unspoken understanding that one didn't treat people like Hilary as though they were Broadway producers or movie-studio executives. They were in the same leaky rusted boat with the starving character actors and the unwashed playwrights. Tony had torn up his part of the agreement and treated her like a boss, a philistine wearing the sackcloth and ashes of the holy.

"I came here . . ." she said, and the tremors of her lips made the words sound weepy. It flashed through Tony's mind that to the others in the restaurant this scene probably looked like a romance breaking up. ". . . to suggest you work with a director on a rewrite . . ." She stood up, breaking off abruptly. "I can't continue this . . ." She opened her purse, her hands shaky, and pulled out a mangled ten-dollar bill and let it drop on the table. "I'm sorry," she added, and walked out on wobbly legs.

He looked straight ahead to avoid the glances of the waiters and customers. He remembered vividly, as though it had happened yesterday, going to lunch with his mother at the Russian Tea Room twenty years before, something he had loved to do because the waiters in their red tunics treated him like a young prince (indeed then he *was* a member of New York's royal family: the child of a Broadway star), and enjoying the special dishes they brought for him while she talked with . . . whom? her agent? was it a producer? He was eating a dessert when he first noticed the shift in tone and heard the harsh sound his mother would make when the craziness began. The nonstop talking at someone, sentences looping out of her like snakes entwining their insults on the victim, slithering so quickly out of her mouth that there was little chance to escape and no hope for defense. She was always so charming, had won the affections of her eventual victims so completely, that they would be in shock as the long bodies of her rage wrapped around them and squeezed. The betrayal of her hatred, the utter lack of any hint prior to its release, was what so stung them. Whoever it was had walked out. Her yelling had caught everyone's attention, and they were so well-known there, so many people were in business with her, that the embarrassment was profound. Indeed, they never went back. That night she got drunk. In his bed staring at a Superman comic by the weak light of the streetlamp outside his window, he had heard her retching. The choked gasping sounds weren't that different from the noise her rage made at lunch. That was exactly the look her victims had—horror—as though she had vomited bile on their laps.

Sweat broke out all over his body. He felt a cold eye from the heavens turn his way and freeze him. He heard a deep voice intone: You are going mad. Just like your mother. Mad, mad, mad.

Patty listened to David tell his story. He was excited about this one. She marveled, when he was done, at the fact that nothing had happened. He was steeled for battle, talking angrily, vehemently, but nothing had happened. Mrs. Thorn had had a talk with his two bosses, and they decided nothing would change. And there David was, knowing this, and yet feeling it was all so thrilling, so important. She wondered if he would really make it in that world. Gelb wasn't so foolish. She had learned from him that most things in business were much more simple and pure than someone like David imagined. What is, is. If Mrs. Thorn wanted to fire Rounder, she would have accepted the resignation. She didn't want to. That she would someday was no daring insight on David's or Chico's part. Everybody at the top is eventually fired. And once a person reached the zenith, failure no longer existed. Rounder would go on to other jobs, either as well paid or better, his so-called failure at *Newstime* just last week's snicker, not forever's shame.

She hadn't slept with David for weeks. When she began the affair with Gelb, she had resisted enjoying the sex. Her lack of orgasm had piqued Gelb: he worked extraordinarily hard at the task of breaking her attempt at passive coolness; however, when she stopped fighting him, she was, now to her considerable annoyance, unable to come. Her loins would ache, her hard nipples plead in the air for liberation, but nothing could seem to push her over the plateau of mounting excitement into the blissful free-fall of release.

Finally, after two months of this agony, Gelb accused her of being afraid to give in to the final pleasure of sex because she equated that with love. She laughed at him, told him he was truly from another generation to believe that orgasm depended on emotion. He answered that he didn't, but she obviously did. She mocked him. But that afternoon, she came, and had ever since. Often Gelb, thrilled at the breakthrough, would continue the lovemaking beyond his penis' interest, to watch her groan again in his arms, relishing her surrender. Since then, she had been unable to enjoy sex with David, something she had not admitted to Gelb, knowing that he, armed with that information, would claim he had been right—orgasm equals love.

She felt guilt about her lack of desire to make love to David the most keenly of all the specific betrayals her affair involved. That she was fucking this man to insure her career made her hate herself (and certainly the world) but gave her a sense of justification in relation to David. He was so ambitious that she knew, in her spot, he would do the same. But the transfer of her lust to Gelb—an occurrence that she found incredible, despite the ferocious, almost voracious energy he applied to making love, because he was neither handsome nor sexy—*was* something to abhor and regret. Why was she such a nitwit? Why did she have to convince herself that her screwing Gelb was anything other than ambition? Part of her was attempting to conceal the opportunism behind sentiment. She knew her orgasms were lies. They had to be. Gelb was a contemptible, unscrupulous man—no amount of clitoral stimulation should convince her to feel passion for him.

David finished his monologue on the day, asked her perfunctory questions about her lunch with Betty, showing no interest at the appearance of Gelb. When she complained about his showing up (to be consistent with what she thought he knew of her relationship to him, namely that he had fired her), she discovered, to her disgust, that David had forgotten the story of her dismissal from Goodson Books.

"It was two years ago," he said when she remarked on it. Shortly afterward he buried himself with business magazines in front of the television, responding only with grunts to her comments on the shows.

Betty phoned late. "I love it," she said without a hello. "I love it."

"Really?" Patty asked, pleased, and then wondered why she cared. Since the contract, Betty hadn't made any criticisms of her pages, which she submitted chapter by chapter.

"You know what I've been thinking?" Betty said, her tone full of serious calculation. "I'm going to give it to Gelb right away. I think there's some cutting we might do, but I don't want to wait. He made that offer to read it at lunch—he probably wasn't too serious, so I want to take him up on it before he has a chance to back out."

"Cutting?" Patty asked, ignoring the rest. It was simply too absurd. Betty thinking herself brilliant, believing Gelb was simply being polite, missing the whole drama like a silly minor character in a farce.

Betty laughed. "God, you writers are all the same. Can't touch a precious word."

"I didn't say that," Patty snapped. "I merely wanted to know what we were cutting."

"Nothing. Just little things. We'll meet later in the week." She lowered her voice. "I can't really talk long. Tony's in a mood. Just wanted you to know I love it."

Patty hung up and looked at David, his nose in *Forbes*. "I'm going to bed," she said, thinking that if he wanted to make love, he'd go too.

"Okay," he mumbled.

I said it too coldly. She softened her tone and smiled. "Sure you don't want to come too?"

He looked up, his glasses off for reading, and squinted at her. "What?"

"Sure you don't want to come to bed?" she asked with a broad wink.

"Oh," he said, as though she had proposed having dinner with her parents. "I'm too . . ." He paused.

Dull, she decided for him. "Okay," she interrupted breezily, and walked away, thinking: He doesn't deserve me.

By nightfall, Fred was excited. His goddamn book was gonna be published. Tom Lear had invited him to a screening, and when Fred announced Holder's praising reception, which Tom took to be an event that had been in suspense, since no one knew, not even Marion, that Fred had been writing the book virtually in collaboration with Holder, Fred could see in Lear's response how much fun might lie ahead for him.

"Oh, you know who's going to be at the screening? A lot of New York *Times* people. I bet Harry Reynolds will be there. Don't let me forget to introduce you."

Reynolds, being one of the *Times*'s daily book critics, would be a great prize if Fred could impress him enough to get a review. Lear pointed him out when they sat down. He was at the other end of the room. Since the screening was about to begin, Lear whispered, "We'll get him on the way out."

His faith in Tom had been borne out. He had stuck by Fred even after reading the original one hundred pages—which Fred now believed had been so bad that the thought of Tom reading them sometimes startled him awake when falling asleep, as though it was a war veteran's memory of a terrible scrape with death.

While the film credits rolled at the end of the movie (traditionally at screenings everyone remained seated until the last name of the third assistant gaffer rolled by), Fred repeatedly rubbed his right palm against his pants, trying to dry it in anticipation of shaking hands with Reynolds. He closed his eyes to try to relax: he saw an image of Harold Reynolds printed in New York *Times* type loom and obliterate everything. He sat up and whispered to Lear, "Let's go, I'm starving."

"No, I want to introduce you to Reynolds."

"It won't do me any good," Fred said.

"Sure it will," Tom said, giving him a big wink. "Name recognition. Very important."

The lights came up moments later. Lear dawdled on their aisle, allowing others to pass them, and surged forward when Harold Reynolds' row conjoined with the flow out. "Harold!" Lear said as though he had just spotted him.

To Fred's horror, Reynolds looked balefully at Tom and said in a low voice, "Hi," in the way one might address a doorman, someone to whom a hello is necessary but certainly not fervently desired.

Lear stepped next to the book critic, walking out shoulder to shoulder. Fred hustled to get himself behind, momentarily relieved by his being out of sight. "I loved your review of Heller's book. Hilarious."

This seemed to warm Reynolds. "Piece of junk," he mumbled.

"Gutsy of you to say so."

"I don't care if they fire me. Been here too long anyway." All this in a whisper so that even Fred, who was standing directly behind them, had to strain to hear.

"Well, it needed to be said," Lear answered in a solemn tone. They arrived at the elevator bank and Fred found himself facing them. "Oh," Tom said, looking at Fred as though just discovering him. "Do you know my friend Fred Tatter? This is Harold Reynolds."

Fred stuck his hand out.

"Hello," Reynolds said with a nod, his eyes barely lighting on Fred and missing the fact that his hand was out. Fred quickly withdrew it and didn't hear the conversation continue as he tried to calculate whether or not Harold Reynolds had done it intentionally, cleverly disguising the insult as distraction.

They got into the elevator and everybody fell into the typical post-screening silence, no one daring to make a remark lest it offend someone whose connections or power were unknown to him. Lear, Fred noticed admiringly, made sure he stayed near Reynolds without seeming to. Once out on the street, the three of them broke off from the crowd, Reynolds glancing at the avenue and commenting, "Terrible time for a cab."

"I think if we head over to Sixth . . ." Lear pointed, and, to Fred's surprise, given Reynolds' aloof attitude, he marched with them. "We're headed uptown," Lear said while they walked. "Can we drop you?"

"I'm all the way east on Seventy-second. East River Drive. It's probably out of your way—"

"No, not at all," Tom said.

"Oh good," Reynolds mumbled, and glanced at Fred as though he were an obligation. "Did you like the movie?"

Now Fred wished he had listened more carefully at the elevator bank. He didn't know what their opinion was. "I can't say why," Fred said, "but somehow I didn't really get involved."

"Yes," Reynolds agreed. "I didn't care whether they were together or not. I feel as though I've seen movies like that all my life. Guess I'm tired of them too. Are you in the movie business?"

Here it comes, Fred thought, and swallowed. "No, I'm a . . ." He wanted to say "novelist," but in this situation somehow it seemed so bold as to be almost be rude. ". . . a writer."

"Journalist?" Reynolds asked.

"I was . . ." And Fred paused, unable to admit his condition, afraid of how obvious it would then become that he wanted Reynolds to know and remember him.

Tom broke in, his voice tense. "Fred's publishing his first novel in the fall."

"Oh," Reynolds said, utterly without self-consciousness. "Congratulations. Who's your publisher?"

"Garlands."

"Good house," the critic said with a nod, a personnel man checking off items on a résumé. "What's the title?"

The Locker Room."

"About sports?"

"No . . ." This, more than anything, was the moment he had dreaded. He would now describe the idea and if Reynolds made fun of it, life might simply become too terrible to face. "It's kind of a response to *The Women's Room.*"

"Well," Reynolds said, smiling, "certainly time for that, isn't it?"

Fred guffawed, laughing harder than he meant to because of the relief. He noticed that Reynolds glanced at him quizzically, and he cut off the amusement. They had reached Sixth, and to cover the awkwardness, Fred, without looking, stepped out with his hand up, signaling for a cab.

He heard Tom laugh behind him and say, "There are no cars, Fred."

Now that he really looked at the avenue, he saw that for at least five blocks the avenue was empty. He pulled his hand in. "Gotta start early in this town," he said, and guffawed again.

Reynolds smiled at him gently, almost mercifully. "That's true enough." He turned to Lear and began to question him about his current book. Lear answered the questions effortlessly, joking about his mixed reviews, bitching about his publisher, his manner natural and at ease, speaking no differently than he would to an intimate.

His performance made Fred conscious of how badly he had handled his interrogation. He took out a cigarette to calm himself, but in the curious swirling wind of the city, his first three matches all went out. Reynolds, out of the corner of his eyes, noticed his trouble and brought out a lighter, flicking it on and offering the flame.

"Thanks," Fred said, humiliated. He brought the end of his cigarette into the fire, inhaling, and in an effort to loosen up, swept his arm away from the light.

For a brief, brief second the gesture had just the right dash and casualness . . .

. . . but then, like a victim in a fatal crash, he watched in slow horror as his hand and cigarette went directly into the left sleeve of Harold Reynolds' pin-striped jacket, the bright red embers scattering in brilliant firefly sparks as they burned a small but quite irrevocable hole into the clothes of one of the country's most powerful and influential book critics.

CHAPTER 14

Patty looked down at Gelb. He had his hands on her breasts, reaching up for them like a baby wanting succor, his eyes closed in blind, pleading ecstasy.

"I love you," he said almost in a shout.

She held herself up, supporting herself by pressing down with her palms on his hips, clinging to the tip of his penis. He yearned upward, pathetically raising his buttocks, begging for more of her warmth: "I love you I love you I love you."

Her arms trembled from the effort and she let herself down on his shaft, to his relieved groans, feeling him fill her, the penetration soothing but not exciting. She felt above both him and the experience, the pleasure coming from her possession of his genitals. She vacuumed him up, nothing touching but the most intimate parts of their bodies. She loved watching him from this distance. Looking down at that usually self-absorbed face and seeing him at her mercy, rolling in a blissful dream, seemed a perfect metaphor for their relationship. She had dominated this man with what had always seemed to be her weakness: sex.

He opened his eyes and saw the smirk of satisfaction on her face. He looked glazed, delirious. He moved a hand to her trimmed bush and searched inside with his finger for her magic button of instant orgasm.

"Don't bother," she said contemptuously but gently: not with anger, with knowing patience.

"You bitch," he said weakly, and his eyes rolled in their sockets. "Ohhhh," he moaned as she moved up, his butt bucking to stay completely inside.

"Lie still," she suggested.

"I can't I can't," he said, and then, from his stomach, loud groaning. She felt his penis swell suddenly and then jerk. "No no no no," he sang, writhing so violently that she had to drop all the way down to prevent being thrown off. She bent forward, running her hands up his hairy, big chest while she felt herself get wet inside from him. The publisher of

Garlands squeezed her right nipple hard and whispered over and over: "I love you I love you I love you," while she, his former assistant, said back in a seductive whisper: "No you don't no you don't no you don't."

David dialed the numbers. They had become as familiar to him as his own. He must have telephoned her a hundred times, although they had had only two real conversations.

She always answered the same way: "Yes . . .?" as though irritated by the interruption.

"Hello, I've called you before—"

"Age and occupation?"

"I'm thirty-one. I'm an executive."

"Name?"

"Bill," he said quickly, having decided to tell this lie, though he really didn't see what safety it provided.

"Do you want to make an appointment?"

"Yes," he said. This time there was no rush of panic, of coursing adrenaline.

"It's important for you to understand that I offer dominance and submission. There's no sex."

"I understand," he said.

He could hear a smile in her voice. "My sessions are on Monday, Wednesday, and Friday. I don't have anything open until next week unless you can come today at eleven o'clock."

Now the pressure began, powerfully present in his system. "Okay," he said dully, automatically, unable to cry out his fear, his dreadful fear of giving in to this obsession.

"Come to Twenty-third Street and Eighth Avenue. There are phone booths on the corner. Call this number from there at eleven. I'll give you the address then. I'm a minute away. All right, Bill?"

"Yes," he hissed like a creature from the dark, from the muddy swirling slime of the underworld.

"See you then."

His hand trembled while putting the phone back, an addict suffering withdrawal. It was nine-thirty in the morning. He had only an hour to decide if he was going through with it. He had told himself he would make an appointment, because, after all, he didn't have to keep it. There would be no penalty—except, of course, that if he changed his mind later and wanted to see her she might remember his voice and refuse to give him another chance. He was convinced she already recognized him from their two conversations, both of which ended with her hanging up on him. Each time he had tried to get an assurance that the experience would be pleasurable, that he could control what she would or wouldn't do. Despite all his cynicism about the world, no matter how often he told himself that she must be a whore who would do what the customer wanted, he couldn't rid himself of wild and terrible fantasies. That she might be mad and actually beat him mercilessly, perhaps cut off his penis, maybe kill him. How did he know? There would be no Better Business Bureau, no other employees to stop her, nothing, no restraint. It was an illegal act—and at that, an unusual one. Not a visit to a traditional whorehouse with bouncers, a madam, a clientele. This would be in some room, isolated, no one knowing where he had gone. Who would hear his last cry, his final whimper of agony?

He could disappear completely. One of those mysteries that haunt American cities. Perhaps, like a character in a *Twilight Zone* episode, he had found the answer to all the missing persons in the world, only to reject the answer as paranoia and then at the fadeout become one himself. A victim of some diabolical group picking off those who are vulnerable to perversion.

He got such a clear image of being chopped to bits by gruff hooded men, his money stuffed away, his clothes and identification burned. How could he be traced? Naturally they would assume he'd make every effort to get there unobserved and alone, with no record of the appointment or location left behind.

But, ultimately, it couldn't be. She had ads on television, for God's sake. If her clients were all being murdered, someone would put it together. Anyway, this was big money. Someone, probably the Mafia, was making a ton off the pathetic obsessions of people like himself. Why kill the golden goose? No, the truth, like always, was probably much duller than he imagined. Just a service, provided gruffly and sloppily, like all the other services to the middle class in New York.

But that was what the character in the *Twilight Zone* episode would tell himself, and then walk in confidently, a lamb to the slaughter.

He looked at the clock. Nine-forty. He'd have to leave in fifty minutes to be sure that he'd be at the phone booth on time. Why a phone booth? Why didn't she give him the address right away? Probably some screening procedure. But if you were going to murder people and wanted to reduce the chance they'd write down the address somewhere, somewhere that the police . . . He'd have to cut this out. It was stupid. Paralyzing. An excuse to avoid what he knew, sooner or later, he would inevitably do: go and find out if these fantasies were something he wanted to be real.

He stood up. His feet almost gave out from weakness. "I can't do it," he said to the empty loft, a bent figure alongside the straight ridged columns, aloof with dignity. "I can't do it," he pleaded.

Fred walked into his apartment, his old apartment, the one he had lived in with Marion for years, but hadn't seen for over seven months. "This is weird," he said to her.

She laughed. Her mood was light, girlish. She seemed tipsy to him, not because they had had champagne at dinner, but generally in a state of amusement, giggles bubbling throughout her, sparkling in her eyes, lifting her shoulders, opening her heart. He kept having flashes of worry that this was some sort of practical joke. In the couples therapy everything that she said had been bitter—complaints about him, his treatment of her, and then of the world in general. More than ever Fred had realized that her gloomy existence with him, the frowns, the rushing off to bed to read alone, the sudden fits of irritation about trivialities, had all been little eruptions of a buried, boiling volcano of disgust, hatred, and resentment.

Months ago he had given up on the marriage. And even begun dating, not simply to get laid, but with a view toward the future. But the therapy had made it hard for him to see new women, he thought. Hearing the endless list of Marion's fault-finding left with him a dim view of his own attractions. He almost felt at times that he should warn women that he was, apparently, a colossal bore to live with. Finding himself convinced that Marion's criticisms were valid, he became enraged. Within the last few sessions he had lashed back, fighting for himself, advocating his good qualities with a passion and conviction he never guessed were in him. Then the doctor said they should see him individually and see each other socially if they wanted.

They had had two dates, quick things, going to a movie, out to dinner, chatting about their lives superficially—the therapy was always about the past, about ugly feelings, and so they had a lot to catch up on. Tonight had been the same at first, but then she began to flirt with him, getting high on the champagne (she had suggested they order it), and now, asking him back to the apartment. For Marion such behavior was wild, wanton. He liked her for this girlish happiness, remembered dimly that in college she was like that, but still he wasn't comfortable with it either. She simply wasn't the woman he had lived with for eight years, and that made him wary.

She settled on the couch, kicking her shoes off and putting her feet beneath her, her oval face dreamy. "Your book was accepted."

"Yeah." He didn't know how to comport himself. Should he sit on the couch and begin necking (this sense that he was in a virgin sexual circumstance with Marion was really weird, silly, and embarrassing), or sit in one of the armchairs, more formal, like a meeting of super-powers?

"How come you didn't tell me?"

He grunted. "Come on, you said over and over in the therapy that all I did was talk about my work constantly. As long as I live, I'm never telling you another thing about what I do." He sat down in an armchair.

She pouted. She made a big show of it, but it was real. "Oh, that's terrible. You don't mean that."

Fred looked down. She was trying hard. He wasn't. He felt ashamed of himself. "No, I'm sorry. They accepted it about a month ago. Who told you?"

"I heard from somebody who knows Bob Holder that he's wild about it. Getting everybody in the house to read it, talking to book-club people—"

"Really?" Fred said, looking up, surprised. He had assumed for so long that Holder's talk was merely bluster that this came as a pleasant surprise.

"Yeah. Sounds like it's gonna be a big book."

"No," Fred answered. "He hypes everything. You told me that yourself."

"Did I?" she said, looking at the ceiling in wonderment.

"Oh yeah. Told me I was a fool to believe him."

"Can't believe I said that."

"You did—"

"No, no," she said, laughing at him. "I mean, what a bitch I was. I believe you. Just what an incredibly bitchy thing to say. Holder hypes books, but when he does, they sell."

Fred smiled at her. She was great—he loved her like this. "I want to go to bed with you," he said.

"Great," she answered. And smiled, sitting there like a cheerful doll eager to be played with but helpless to initiate anything. "I thought maybe you'd found somebody else."

"What?" Fred asked, puzzled.

"You never said whether you were dating anybody," she said, shyly now, lowering her eyes, her smile fading.

"Well . . ." he huffed, shifting uncomfortably. He didn't want to admit that his sex life had been at best dull, at worst dormant, but on the other hand, he didn't want to enrage her with a portrait of promiscuity. "I *have* gone out."

"With anybody serious?" she asked, suddenly hoarse.

He sighed. He shook his head. "I been doing the book. It took everything I had. It was a bitch, Marion. I went out a couple times, but . . ." He trailed off.

She nodded. Not triumphantly, not smugly, not with confirmation. She nodded in acceptance of how hard, how tediously grim their lives had been. He felt, too, that the stupidity of their marriage, its begrudgement of love, might have been dreary and disgusting . . . but it was the only real content in their lives.

Tony lay in bed. The day was bright. And loud. Nearby a brownstone was being gutted. He heard its insides landing in a dumpster. He looked at the clock. Noon. He still didn't want to start the day and it was half over. Betty usually made coffee before leaving for work. He should get up and heat it. The *Times* would be in there, the business section untouched, still ironed flat by neglect. But the C section with its reviews (not of his plays) and its Broadway column, full of plans for future work (none of it his) and gossip about those now working (none of it about him), would be on the kitchen table, wrinkled, open to the last article she had read. *All* of them read it, even the fucking stockbrokers who read the business section. Less than ten percent of New Yorkers actually went to the theater, but by God every one of them knew who was hot and who was not on Broadway—because of the accursed, the horrible, the infuriating goddamn cultural pages of the *Times*. It was better to do without coffee.

And he was dead for years, by that standard. Now, when a review made reference to the promising young playwrights, his name was no longer listed. A few more years like the last two and he would no longer be able to complain that he should be mentioned in a young-playwrights roundup.

A month had passed since he threw his fit at the artistic director of the Uptown Theater. He hadn't returned Hilary's calls. He had skipped the regular readings since then as well as the meetings of the Playwrights' Lab. Indeed, he had done nothing other than attend a few publishing cocktail parties for Betty's sake. He had spoken to a friend from college about seeing a shrink, frightened by his exhibition of rage in the restaurant, but hadn't called the names suggested.

He sat up in bed and thought about Proust. He felt he understood his work habits today—the bedroom was cozy, protected. Still can't read him, he thought, and laughed. The sound felt lonely in the empty apartment. Outside they worked on, the whole city, memorizing the New York *Times*, working, and not knowing his name.

Tony picked up the phone and dialed. He had to think for a moment about the number—disuse had made what was once automatic unfamiliar. It rang only once before she answered, brightly, energetically:

"Hello!"

"Hello," he said. And there was silence, a shocked silence.

Then, tentatively, incredulously, Lois asked, "Tony?"

"Yep," he said. "How are you?"

"Fine," she said, sounding uneasy, as though she were constrained by the presence of someone. Could that be? "I'm fine. I'm really surprised to hear from you."

"Why? Am I supposed to be dead or something?"

"No," she said in good humor. "I thought you . . ." Again the hesitation.

"Thought I was out of your life?"

"Yeah," she admitted, and laughed quickly. "So what's new?"

"What's new! What kind of question is that? I expected rage or tears of happiness or something! What's new indeed!"

She was laughing while he spoke. "Well, I'm sorry, I can't provide any of those things. They happened long ago."

"What long ago? A few months."

Her voice was gentle, solemn. "It's been seven months at least, Tony."

"I didn't realize it was like a visa. What happened? I didn't renew it in time and now it's canceled?"

"Sort of," she said. "Listen, I really can't talk now. Can I call you back in an hour? Will you be home?"

"Yeah." She's got somebody there, he realized, shocked. It had never occurred to him that she wouldn't remain frozen, unchanged, awaiting his defrosting presence, the warm light of her life.

"Talk to you soon."

Who the hell was it? Who was she fucking? Some TV writer? A producer? Maybe she was fucking a TV star. Maybe she was a lesbian. He was furious. He got out of bed and turned on the shower in a rage. He stepped in without checking the temperature and scalded himself, jumping away and hurting his back against the towel rack.

"I don't even want to take a goddamn shower!" he yelled at himself, and stood there panting, aching, his skin red, half of his head wet. After a moment the fury passed, and he washed himself quickly, shaving and dressing in a rush, as though late for an appointment.

Later he got to the kitchen. He picked up the New York *Times* and threw it across the room. It lay on the floor humpbacked, like a broken umbrella. He heated the coffee and sat down to drink it, staring at the kitchen phone, waiting for it to ring, waiting, as he had his whole life, for an explanation of why he had lost something he wanted.

Gelb lay between her legs, his head moving up and down while he worked his mouth over her clitoris. The warmth spread from there, radiating into her belly, down her thighs, her breasts feeling the heat wave over her like a rising tide. She felt gentle on the sea of sensation, floating there blissfully, basking in the sun of its relaxation. She could rest in the midst of its excitement forever, she felt, without the surf picking her up to crash on the shore.

She glanced down at him. His cold eyes were staring at her from under his eyebrows while he licked, checking on her progress. He was so achievement-oriented that he never seemed to relax, to let any experience simply be itself, a man forever tugging at the sleeves, straightening the tie, tucking in the shirt of life; always dressing for a job interview, desperate to make a good impression, or at least an impression. A-for-effort Gelb, she thought, and he began to move his tongue rapidly sideways, pushing her knob one way, then the other, and suddenly she *was* riding a wave, cresting up in the air, the sky spinning, her arms reaching for an anchor to hug. . . .

When she was done, he moved up to her navel and kissed it, smiling like a prankster. "Good, huh?" he asked.

"Yep," she answered. "We're getting better."

"Oh, you're so full of shit. I got you and you know it."

"Oh, shut up." She sighed. "What am I going to do about David?"

"Leave him," he said, and put a hand around a breast, squeezing it, staring at the effect on her nipple.

"I just pack and say 'bye?"

"Yeah!"

"Is that how you're going to do it with Elaine?"

Gelb looked at her angrily. "I have kids!" he claimed.

"Oh, please. You don't give a shit about your kids."

He sat up, staring furiously. She smiled sweetly. He frowned at his lack of effect. "You don't know what you're talking about."

"Yes I do. You've got a great life. You're the most important man in your field, your wife is beautiful and she loves you—"

"Bull—"

"—*she* loves you, your kids adore you, and you have a beautiful mistress who writes brilliantly. You don't care what you feel about people, you only care what they feel about you, and you're the center of everyone's attention, which is the closest you can come to happiness."

"You didn't say you love me."

"I don't. I'm attracted to you. I like power-hungry greedy bastards like you. David's just like you—only younger and not as mean."

"You like talking tough, don't you? But you're whistling in the dark. You're conventional. You want the three kids and the station wagon—"

"And a big fluffy dog to slobber on the upholstery."

"Right," Gelb said, smirking. This kind of exchange had become a game with them. She liked it, the saying of horribly selfish unsayable things. The abandon of it was thrilling, like their sex, heightened by the constant knowledge of the taboos they were breaking.

"So what I want to know," Patty said, "is when you dump me? When does a mistress get too old? Forty?"

"Thirty-five," Gelb said matter-of-factly.

"You mean it, don't you?" Patty said aloud as it occurred to her. "You're really not kidding."

"Of course I'm kidding, love," he said tenderly, but he moved off the bed toward the dresser, fumbling in a pocket for cigarettes. "You're the one who doesn't love me, remember? You're going to bed with me so your book'll do well." Gelb puffed furiously on the cigarette once, glanced at his wristwatch stretched out on the dresser like a sunbather, and said, reaching for his pants, "I've gotta get back to the office."

She stayed in bed until long after he was gone. She stared down at her naked body. Small, white, young. There was some tiring in the skin, the beginnings of looseness—but she was beautiful. She looked too small, however, her belly button innocent and lonely, hovering quizzically above the center of all the fuss—asking her unanswerable questions about all the grief of love and men.

David looked them in their eyes, searching for a hint that they knew. He paced up and down the broad, crowded, messy street, his legs so weak from dreadful anticipation that he had to stop every twenty paces or so and lean against a building or sit on a stoop. He had arrived on the corner of Eighth and Twenty-third fifteen minutes early, located the phone booths she mentioned, and now watched them anxiously, terrified to make the final call and equally worried that somehow, impossibly, all the phones would be busy at the appointed hour and stay so for too long. In fact, they were rarely in use so far, but he kept his eyes on them, vowing to take possession of one if he saw a rush to use them.

In between his starts and stops he looked up at the buildings, many of them lofts or brownstones, their shades drawn, wondering in which one she was located. He stared at the blank, dirty windows, the traffic groaning and roaring beside him, and thought: No one would hear the screams. They were anonymous, these buildings, all the entrances desolate, monitored by intercoms, no doormen, no happy tenants with busy comings and goings. Maybe they were all whorehouses, each room occupied by sex: Perverts Row.

He walked himself toward the phone booths, grabbing on to the parking meters for support. He had prayed that the booth next to his would be empty, but the moment after he had situated himself, quarter ready to put in, a man got into the one next to him, able to overhear. But that was silly: his end of the conversation wasn't worth eavesdropping on. "Do it," he said to himself, and dialed. It rang three, four times, and he began to relax. She wasn't there, he wouldn't have to go through—

"Hello?"

"This is . . . this is Bill."

"You're early," she said. "Call back in five minutes."

He hung up. They hadn't finished chopping up the last one, he thought, but this time the fear really did seem ridiculous. In her hello there was the harried tone of a shopkeeper juggling customers, bored with the work—despite all the rhetoric, he knew she was just a whore. She'd do what he wanted. In any event, she certainly wouldn't really hurt him.

Now the wait was unbearable because he was eager. He called back in three minutes. She was in control now. "I'm in 684 West Twenty-Third, next to the florist behind you about twenty feet." He had noticed the building, suspected it of being likely. "I'm in three A. See you in a minute."

He hung up and walked quickly, not meeting anyone's eyes, into the building and stood in its tiny vestibule, looked at the intercom system, none of the apartment buzzers supplied with names, and rang three A. The buzz back was instantaneous. He moved quickly to open the locked door and bumped into a man with a horrendously guilty look in his eyes who quickly brushed by him and out.

That was her last customer, he thought, and, getting into the small elevator that was right there, having left off the guilty man, he recalled what he could of his face: pale, unshaven, the eyes worriedly not meeting his, a miserable, hunted look. It made him feel better. And as he rode up, he wondered why. All his reactions were the opposite of what they should be. But nothing about this obsession, and his pursuit of it, had ever made sense. Except now, walking down the narrow hallway, past, to his surprise, a laundry room (what the hell was it doing in a common hallway on the third floor?) and up to a quite ordinary door, at last he felt it was over. He would know now, and even if his fate were to be a terrible one, the awful wondering, the constant doubts would be gone. He rang the bell gladly.

Fred sat up in the bed, feeling foolish. He had finally moved toward Marion on the couch and started to kiss her. He had tried to put a lot of movement and passion into it, but it felt fake, and Marion saved the moment by smiling. "I think we'd better just get into bed," she said. "We're not strangers."

He had undressed in the bedroom, their old bedroom, unchanged from when he had last slept there, while Marion disappeared into the bathroom. He wondered whether she was planning something, going to come out in some sort of sexy nightgown. He hoped not. It would seem pathetic, just like his maneuver on the couch. Whatever their situation, they certainly weren't courting.

She didn't. She came out in her robe, naked underneath, walking to the bed and shedding it before quickly crawling under the covers and snuggling into his arms. "What were you doing in there?"

"Putting in my diaphragm," she said. "I didn't want to stop to do it later."

He had always complained about the effects of breaking off foreplay for the sake of contraception, so this too was another sweet attempt on her part to make things between them amicable. To improve on the past. It was their enemy. All the things they had done and the way they had done them were to be avoided. He felt the weight of her head on his chest heavily. The task semed too great.

He shook off this feeling, moved her head away, and again began kissing with mock passion. She went along this time, brushing a leg against his penis while he pressed his upper thigh against her groin. After a while the self-consciousness passed, he felt aroused, and she seemed to be also. He began to hope again that it might work.

He threw the covers off them. The lights were still on—she had usually insisted they be turned off and he realized that the fact they weren't was another concession to him. He looked at her body. She kept her eyes closed, her hands urging him to return. He looked at her belly, her flabby maternal stomach, her thick bush of hair. It was the body of a real woman, not the models of magazines, but the real comfortable female form of nature. He loved it. Staring at it in the bright light, leaning down to kiss it, moving his hands under her soft substantial buttock, feeling the warmth and give and pliancy of her fat felt good.

She was tensing against his investigations, embarrassed (he realized for the first time) by her body, assuming he didn't want it. But he did! He kissed and moved back to look, seeing things he had never noticed, feeling her sex, utterly different. Soft and warm. Home. He wanted to be inside her. Kept safe inside. No longer fighting the hard ungiving world.

She seemed relieved when he entered her. She hugged him to her gratefully. The ease of her body seemed designed for him, from the glove of her wet vagina to the soft pillows of her breasts. To be inside her forever in this blissful peace was all he wanted, all he wanted from life and the world; acceptance and comfort; a place to be, nothing more, just be, without effort or pain.

Marion urged him with her hips. He began to move. He felt reproved by her movement, assumed she had been displeased by his stillness, his willingness to remain parked inside. He moved. Withdrew and pressed back in hard. She liked that. For all her gentleness, she liked him to move hard and fast. Had said so in therapy in fact, complained (to his astonishment) that he liked foreplay too much, that she liked to screw vigorously.

She had tried so hard—shouldn't he? He pushed himself, pulling out and then slamming back in, each time harder, surprised that she liked the force, and never reacted with pain, even though it felt to him that their pelvic bones must be bruised and battered by now.

And the itch had begun. The restless tickling yearning of his penis, desperate for more and more sensation while he felt its liquids gather and hope for escape. He tried somehow to restrain it despite the powerful tease of moving out and then quickly into the softest, most desirable home in the world. When he felt the cool air on his balls and most of the length of his penis, only the head peeking inside at the warm fires, the longing to return was overwhelming. And then the relief, after the collision of their privates, the sweet relief of complete docking in the harbor was so quickly taken away by her desire for more and more and more . . .

He started to come without warning. He tried to cut it off, freezing his movements, but she pulled at him, and the liquid dribbled out of him guiltily, guests skulking out early from a party, hiding their escape from the host.

The fuel was gone but she wanted to continue. He pushed in and out, praying he would stay hard. Suddenly everything felt uncomfortable. Her substantial thighs pressing against him were hot and irritating. Her big belly and wide hips seemed too crowded to penetrate. Each time he tried to press farther in, they seemed to frustrate him, the goal of her pelvic bone receding. I'm losing it, he thought, listening to her breathing to judge if she was near climax. He reached down with a hand to infiltrate it in the traffic jam below and speed things up, but she angrily grabbed his hand and moved it away, putting her hands on his ass and pushing him in at her, irritably.

He pushed. He pushed. There was no goddamn way past all the flesh and hair. Everything was awkward. No place to rest his head: having to hold the upper part of his body up, as though he were exercising, not making love.

She began to moan. They were choked sounds—coughs repressed at a concert. Quick, short sounds increasing in frequency. He gathered himself for a final effort and pushed in hard—feeling nothing, the bottom half of his body numb—but she did let out one long last satisfied moan. The tension in her body evaporated and it was over. Thank God.

By the time Lois called back, he knew. After her hello, he made the accusation immediately: "You're in love with somebody else," he said coldly.

"Uh . . . yeah," she agreed,

"All right," he said. "Good-bye."

"Wait a minute," she said, and laughed. "You've gotta be kidding."

"I'm not hanging up. But I'm not kidding."

"You can't blame me!"

"I'm not blaming you."

"You dumped me. You didn't even call to say you were dumping me!"

"I didn't dump you. Jesus Christ, what a phrase! I needed time to think. I told you that."

"Oh, I see," she answered sarcastically, challenging him. "And now you've figured it out?"

Well, she had him there. He was dead wrong, as wrong as a human being could be: his position was illogical, arrogant, deceitful, probably insincere, certainly selfish. "Who is he?" Tony asked. "How serious is this?"

"Uh . . . what do you mean? What do you—I'm not gonna report to you. What's the matter with you? I really expected you to have . . ." She stopped.

"What? Have more class?"

"Yeah, exactly."

"Guess again, honey. I'm just as stupid and mean as everybody else."

"Yeah, I noticed," she answered.

This was a mistake. Probably she had just begun a romance. It could fall apart, fail to move beyond dating, he might even be able to break it up—there were lots of possibilities. The nicer he acted about it, the more points he would have racked up for the day, the inevitable day, when she would seek more adventure, and he would be back in the game. It happened to everybody, to every relationship, to every marriage, it would happen to her and this guy. How could he be a major writer and be so inept at dealing with people? He knew them inside and out. "I'm jealous," he said quietly, convinced this was a lie, a manipulation. The silence on the other end told him he had finally come up with the right approach. "I'm still in love with you."

"No you're not," she said, but there was a lot of emotion in the voice, what sounded like relief and pleasure.

"Yes I am," he answered very softly. "I'm glad you're happy, though. Are you getting married?"

"We've only been dating for two months, Tony," she answered self-deprecatingly. How amusing this game was—now she was minimizing the seriousness of her commitment, just as he had once played down his marriage with Betty. "Life is a performance," his mother had said countless times, only moments before entering a party. Standing gloriously in her fluffy white mink, Tony dressed neatly and conservatively in gray flannel pants, a white shirt, a gray cashmere sweater, a red tie, and a cute little blue blazer, his hair a little long the way she liked it, just before ringing another door to enter another show-business party. Squeezing his hand and smiling brilliantly, "Life is a performance," she'd say, her rich voice making music of the words, the syllables stretching and moaning like a lover in ecstasy. When he was very young the phrase was magic, an incantation that summoned up a mother he loved and admired. Her gloomy and scary moods were gone at those parties, she was funny, a little dangerous sometimes, but fast, fast, fast, catching people with their ideas down, showing up the pompous and the self-righteous. Later, in adolescence, he realized the sentence was desperate, a tiring athlete hoping to have one last good game. Indeed, the quick wit had slowed, the years of drinking slurring more than simply the words: the new faces blurred into the old, the politics of the sixties merging oddly with positions of the fifties, attacks and defenses losing their accuracy and cleverness, the fast talk now merely garrulousness. That made her seem more right than ever: life *was* a performance. People began to have less patience with her acting, and the invitations came less frequently, and then so did the parts. The same loss of muscle tone and quick reactions were happening to him, witness the blunder at lunch with Hilary Bright and this conversation with Lois. And he didn't have his mother's valid excuses: the blacklist, a monster for a husband, a career crippled, an addiction to drink. The truth was he didn't have his parents' virtues: his father's ability to command, his mother's brilliant talent; he only possessed their faults: his father's arrogance and impatience, his mother's vanity and weak nerves.

"I love you," he said.

"Then why the hell did you stop seeing me?"

"I was scared."

"Of what, for God's sake? Hurting Betty? How do you know she'd even miss you?" Lois groaned at herself. "Oh God, it's starting." She sounded wounded. "I hated this the most about our affair. It turned me into a shit. I don't even know Betty. She's probably a wonderful woman. I've got somebody else now, Tony. And I'm glad. God! Am I glad!"

"I'm happy for you too." He swallowed. Something about this defeat was appalling. It was so fucking unexpected. Lois was an option for him, not a human being capable of hurting him. "I'm sorry I called," he said.

"You haven't left her, have you?" she asked, blurting it out, scared and excited.

For the first time he felt better. She still wanted him. She had given up, gotten involved to reassure herself, probably by now almost convinced the new relationship was more than mere compensation.

"I guess you haven't," she said after a pause.

"I don't love her," he said. His stomach contracted on the words, like a poison hitting his system, shriveling his strength and well-being. "I know that now. I love you."

"Well—" she began, and there was a choking noise. "It's too late," she let out, and now there were tears. "Too late," she mumbled through them, and hung up.

Betty looked energetic and concentrated as she flipped through the rack of dresses. She stopped at one, frowned, pulled it out partially, and angled it so Patty could see.

"Are we getting that old?" Patty asked.

Betty smiled and let it go. "There's nothing here."

They walked outside into a glittering day. After the dark, cool interior of the store, the sun was blinding. Betty turned from it suddenly and stumbled into Patty. "Whoa," Patty said, holding her up.

Betty looked at her and smiled. "Can you imagine spending your life doing this?"

"Who does?"

"Our mothers."

"They didn't shop their whole lives."

"No?"

"They changed diapers, remember?"

Betty laughed. "No, somehow I don't think my mother did." They walked on. Patty wanted to confess to her: get rid of this damn secret, talk it out, find an exit from the ridiculous mess she was in. Betty seemed happy these days, carefree. Patty was glad. She had grown much fonder of Betty, despite her wariness of the business situation they now faced.

"Things are going well with Tony," Patty said.

"Oh?" Betty said, surprised. She glanced at Patty. "I'm glad to hear it."

"Aren't they?" Patty asked. She was used to Betty's moods shifting with the ups and downs of Tony's life.

"Not for him. I feel good. I'm happy to be publishing your book. I got a good novel last week from Paul Yarmouth—"

"He's a good agent."

"—yeah, I think you should talk to him about representing you. Anyway, it's a terrific, not very commercial novel by a journalist in Seattle, a reporter. Autobiographical novel about his sister's nervous breakdown and his attempt to help her through it. Really moving book. I think I can get a contract for it."

"Great." Patty studied her. "That's why we're so happy."

"That's right, nurse. I've decided Tony's life is his problem. I can't give him what he wants."

"What does he want? What do any of them want?"

"He wants to be famous. Sometimes I think he wants to be famous without having to do anything." She brought a hand to her mouth, actually covering it for a moment. "I shouldn't say that." She checked with Patty. "That's a horrible thing to say, isn't it?"

"Not if it's true." This was her friend, she realized. This was the person who had done something for her only because she cared to help. Betty was cowardly, she was too prim, she was often abstracted, but she had given Patty advice, support, and a contract without even asking for a kiss, much less a blow-job. "Let's get a cup of coffee."

"Oh, no. I've gotta keep going. This is the last day I can shop for two weeks. And everything will be gone by then."

"I have to talk to you about something."

"No . . ." Betty said, looking at Patty with dread. "You're not having an affair, are you?"

Patty smiled at her, amazed. "How did you know? Am I that transparent?"

"Yeah," Betty said. "You've been acting weird for months. First I thought it was because I was editing you. But I figured it out two weeks ago. You've been very hard to pin down for midday dates, and when I called yesterday and got David, he made a joke about how often we've been seeing each other. I haven't seen you that much."

"I'm sorry. I didn't mean to drag you into it."

"It's okay." She put an arm through Patty's. "We have to stick together." Amazing. A year ago Betty would have been disgusted and offended to have been used as part of an adulterous lie. "Who is it?"

"That's why I haven't told you. Who. You have to promise you're not going to be furious—"

Betty looked funny suddenly, her eyes going blank, her jaw slackening, like someone shocked and fearful. "Maybe . . ." she mumbled.

"Maybe? No, you have to promise."

She pulled her arm out. "I can't promise!" she said furiously.

"What's the matter?"

Betty stopped walking, put her hands in her pockets, and looked composed, though her eyes were dark with challenge. "Who is it?"

"Oh God," Patty said, convinced she had made a mistake. After all, her affair with Gelb might affect Betty's career, and Betty had so much prudery in her anyway that the likelihood she would disapprove was great. "I shouldn't have said anything."

"You can't stop now," Betty answered. "Tell me."

"Gelb. You have to understand. He propositioned me the week you were going to the ed board to transfer my contract. He told—"

"Gelb!" Betty finally said, squinting with disbelief. "Gelb?"

"Yeah, I know it's disgusting. But he told me . . ." She babbled on about his telling her of his coming move to Garlands, her decision that she couldn't make the same mistake twice, her conviction that it would help her book. Betty looked baffled and then bemused—unexpected reactions. She seemed relieved. Patty left out of her account that she felt herself becoming emotionally dependent on Gelb, drawn to his evil in spite of her better instincts, fascinated now with what used to disgust her.

"What's he like?" Betty finally interrupted.

"He's disgusting. He lords it over me, his power, how he can help the book."

"No, I . . ." Betty looked embarrassed, smiling to herself. "I shouldn't ask."

"You mean, what's he like in bed?"

Betty nodded.

"Compulsive workaholic, like everything else. It's kinda great."

Betty smiled. "We're getting old," she said, looking earnestly into Patty's eyes.

"I am. I'm having this disgraceful affair with an old man. Not you."

"No," Betty said, and put her arm through Patty's, resuming their walk. "Because I'm thinking while you talk: This is awful. How can I talk Patty into breaking it off—"

"I'll end it," Patty pleaded.

But Betty hugged her arm tighter. "No, listen. I'm thinking. She's got to get out of it. David's a great guy—she's gonna ruin her writing by thinking the book's success is due to the affair, she's—" Betty stopped and smiled slyly. "And all the time I'm worried about saying anything to you *now*, because I'm also thinking: She's got to break this off—but not before the paperback auction."

Patty looked at her, searching for a hint that Betty was kidding. "No," Patty said tentatively.

Betty nodded. "Oh yeah." She looked away, up at the rows of glass buildings awash with sunlight, blinking. "I'm old too," Betty said, and squeezed Patty's arm as though it were a life preserver. "I'm old too."

"Make yourself comfortable," she said, holding a black dog—barking at David, but not ferociously—by its collar and leading it into another room. "Put your clothes on that chair"—she pointed to a small white round table with a single chair.

"Here," he said, holding out the two fifties he had gotten from the bank.

"Make yourself comfortable first," she said, and disappeared into the other room with the dog.

He was in a box of a room, the windows cut off by a wooden platform set six and a half feet off the ground. Behind him, facing the front door, was a black leather table with stainless-steel legs that seemed adjustable.

Hanging toward the upper half on each side were leather bracelets attached to the table by chains, supposedly for binding the wrists. He got out of his clothes quickly. He was eager for her return. She was dressed, as in the commercial, in a black leather skirt, binding her ass and thighs tight, a row of steel snaps running up to her crotch. Her top was more demure than in the ads: a simple black silk blouse. Her hair was long, and a fierce dark red, her face big, angular, her hands large, her fingernails long and painted crimson. She wore high heels and black net stockings which, combined with the tight skirt, made her walk slow and arrogant.

She appeared from behind the closed door, peering out, seeing him naked, and then entering briskly, taking the two fifties from him. "Sit on the couch," she said, gesturing toward a small white couch against the rear wall below the windows and underneath the wooden platform.

He moved there dutifully and she disappeared again into the back room with the money. He looked to his left at an extension of the wood platform that came down one wall with wood pegs on which hung a variety of S/M devices—long riding crops, studded leather collars, whips, handcuffs—a complete collection. He took a breath and felt it cool and uneasy in his chest. He was timidly excited, wanting more and fearing it all. Seated nude on the couch he felt like a boy in an examining room, assured that nothing painful would happen, but suspecting everything.

She entered again, her heels slowly and firmly sounding harsh on the floor. "This is our first experience," she said, barely making it a question.

"Yes."

"But not your first experience with dominance?"

"Yes."

She raised an expressively painted eyebrow and smiled. "Oh, a virgin! How delightful!" She gestured to a bottle of brandy on the small white table. "Would you like some brandy?"

"No thanks," he said. He wanted to make sure he went through this without any other stimulation. Already, from her rapacious approval of his status as a neophyte, he felt a tingle of excitement.

She went to the bottle, opened it, and poured herself a glass. "Do you have any particular fetishes or repulsions?"

David cleared his throat. "I, uh . . ." He tried to unblock his voice again. "I want to be aroused, and then punished for it. I have a fantasy that I'm being stroked, my penis is being stroked with one hand, and with the other I'm being spanked for enjoying—"

"Oh, that's hot," she said, again with a witch's relish of evil. He assumed she approved of any program a client laid out, that this wasn't true pleasure, but he was excited anyway, immensely relieved that she would fulfill his desire.

"Not hard, though," he hurried to say. "I don't think I'm into any real pain. It's all pretty psychological."

"Of course," she said. "I wouldn't expect you to be into pain." She sipped her brandy. She smiled, a thin, bitter, mocking sneer. "Yet," she snapped. "Have you ever fantasized about anal penetration or worship?"

"No," he said very quickly, scared.

"All right," she said soothingly. "Anything else?"

He shook his head. She put her glass down and spoke in a clipped voice: "Stand up there"—she pointed to a spot in front of the wall of devices. He did so and noticed two metal cuffs attached to the bottom of the wooden platform above him, and then saw two round metal "eyes" bolted to the floor below them, presumably for spread-eagling. "Look straight ahead at all times," she said, moving in front of him and fiddling in a drawer at a table he hadn't noticed that was underneath the wall of objects. "You will address me as mistress. You will speak only when spoken to, except to tell me if something is too painful. If you feel you are about to come . . ." She turned back to him and suddenly he felt her touch his balls, and then there was a mild tug. He looked down and saw she was tying a white rope around his testicles and the base of his already semierect penis. "Tell me if this is too tight,". she commented as she knotted it. The effect was to bunch his genitals together, keeping the penis thrust forward. "If you are about to come, say, 'Mistress, I am going to come,' so that we can stop that. Orgasm is boring," she finished, speaking right into his face. He felt the warm stale breath of brandy, and smelled her perfume: sweet, overpowering, infiltrating his nostrils. "Put your hands behind your back." He did, imitating the man he had seen on television. "Good," she said. "Do you understand everything I told you?"

"Yes . . ." he said in a whisper.

"Yes what?"

"Yes, Mistress."

"Good. Don't force me to punish you." She moved at him, pressing her body absolutely flat against his, running her hands down his back— he felt the sharp edges of her nails just barely, enough to know they were there without any hurt—and then squeezed his buttocks, pushing his groin at her. "Today we don't want to punish. We're going to play the

Queen Spider and the Fly. The queen is going to suck all your liquid. She wants all of you. And you're going to give her everything." A pause.

She smacked him on the ass.

"Yes, Mistress," he answered quickly.

"Good," she purred. "I don't want you to enjoy this. If you become aroused, I'll have to spank you." She moved away and her fingers lightly held his penis. "You would look pretty in women's clothes. Have you ever fantasized about dressing up?"

"No."

She pressed against him, reaching behind, and smacked him on a buttock. "No what?"

"No, Mistress."

"That's better. You have to learn to please me, slave. That's what you're here for. For my pleasure. Do you understand?" She was hugging him, her long hair in his face, the perfume smothering him, her hands running over his back, her nails possessing him as they lighted on his body. He was an object. A helpless thing.

"Yes, Mistress."

A smack. "Say it with a little enthusiasm, slave."

"Yes! Mistress." The slaps on his ass didn't hurt at all.

"You want to worship me, don't you?" she insinuated in his ear.

"Yes, Mistress," he heard a strange version of his voice. "You are beautiful, Mistress. I want to worship your ass, mistress."

She stepped back and he felt his whole groin pulled. She had him by the ridge of hair above his penis. He stood on his tiptoes to reduce the tension. She spat her words at his face, an inch from his mouth: "You don't tell me what you want! That's for before we begin. If you do that again, I'll slap you across the face and beat your ass until it's bloody. I enjoy doing that. Do you understand me?"

"Yes, Mistress," he babbled. "I'm sorry. I understand, Mistress."

She let his pubic hair go. She looked pleased. "Good." She sat down on the couch. "Put yourself across my knees. I'm going to have to spank you."

So it was real—she really did rule. He was hard down there, evidently enjoying it. He laid himself over her lap.

"Keep your legs spread," she said, a finger touching the base of his testicles, "so I can stroke your balls if you deserve it."

She slapped one buttock. He didn't feel it. "You're hard! You're not enjoying this, are you?" She slapped his other buttock. "Answer me!"

"No, Mistress."

"No?" She slapped each buttock in rapid succession. And then ran her cool fingernails on the underside of his balls. His prick flexed with excitement. "You should be flattered I deign to punish you, slave! Thank me for each spank!"

Smack. "Thank you, mistress." Stroke, Smack! "Thank you, Mistress." Stroke. "Get up." He did quickly, surprised that he was sorry the spanking was over so soon. "Get on your knees. Put your head on the floor and beg to worship my ass."

He spoke to the floor, his lips almost kissing it. "Please let me worship your ass, Mistress."

"A little more enthusiasm, slave!"

"Please, please let me worship your glorious ass, I beg you."

"Why?"

For the first time he knew his line: "For your pleasure, Mistress."

"Very, very good. You're going to make a good slave."

Slowly, but surely, he lost any sense of himself. He became a series of sensations. He heard his voice saying unreservedly what she wanted, his sexual longing sustained by the slaps and by the passivity. She had him press his face into her ass, raising her skirt to reveal black leather panties. She held and stroked his penis a lot, lecturing him, running her fingernails down his chest, once bending to lick his nipples and tug very lightly at them with her teeth. She had him stand facing her back and press his penis against her, his hands behind him, ordering him to make fucking motions, the desire for her growing, but never becoming a true want. He didn't really want anything to change, but to say his lines and let her move him around, always sure, no matter how many reproving slaps on his ass were delivered, that he remained hard.

Finally she grabbed his prick and started to walk, as though it were a leash. He stumbled behind her to the leather-cushioned table. "Lie down facing up," she said.

He did. He watched her fasten his wrists into the cuffs, trustingly, not afraid anymore.

"Spread your legs," she said, a hand touching his inner thigh. "So I still have this to punish." She reached for something. He glanced down and saw a tube of ointment. She put a dollop on his hot sore yearning penis. The small area it touched felt cool and delicious. "Maybe I'll just leave it there," she said with a giggle. "Should I leave it there, slave?"

"Oh God," he heard a voice wrench with agony. "God no, please, Mistress!"

"Do you want me to spread it on, slut?"

"Yes, Mistress, please, I need you to."

"Need!" she shouted. Her hand came down on his thigh with a hard smack that stung. "You don't need! I don't care what you need! You only do things for my pleasure!" And her hand smacked him over and over, really smarting, until she finally stopped and then he could hear what the deep male voice was saying:

"Please, no, Mistress . . . please, no, Mistress. For your pleasure, Mistress . . . for your pleasure, Mistress—" He stopped the devastated fragmented sound of himself.

He felt a coolness at the very tip of his penis. "Push!" she said.

He looked down and saw her thumb and index finger curved together to form a narrow circle above the head of his member. His thigh was pink from the blows. He pushed up, his penis moving through the hoop she had made for it, and the sweet ooze bathed his overheated sex in comfort.

"Push! Work for it, you slut!" Now, for what seemed an eternity, she kept at him, pausing whenever he warned her that he was about to come. She lectured him tirelessly on the superiority of women: how their beautiful sex was hidden, their climaxes dainty, not the sloppy disgusting mess men make. He babbled senselessly in agreement, pleading for more pleasure, until finally she said:

"You may come, you slut!" And she held her hoop for him to jump through, thanking her as he splattered all over himself, hearing her laugh at it, saying, "You shot right up to your chin, slave."

Afterward he stared up dutifully, adoringly at her.

"It's good to surrender to a dominant woman, isn't it?"

"I loved it, Mistress."

She nodded at him seriously. "You're going to make an excellent slave."

"Thank you, Mistress," he said.

He left happy—spent. Free from all the stupid dreary constipated fantasies: his body loose with unabashed power. I loved it, he said to himself, and flagged a cab to report in at *Newstime*.

CHAPTER

15

Fred moved back in with Marion a few months later. Many of his friends were surprised. His career seemed to be in the second stage of a stellar flight: the Book-of-the-Month Club and the Literary Guild were both interested in his novel; *Town* magazine had hired him, on Tom Lear's recommendation, to write a monthly interview with a sports personality; and Bob Holder had proposed an idea to him for another novel. He had lifted off, it seemed to Fred's friends, and had a clear trajectory to a new planet; why head back for the tedium of Earth?

"I've grown a lot," Fred answered them, looking shyly away from his interrogators. "Marion and I have been through too much stuff not to give it another try. First I discovered how much resentment I felt toward her—then I learned how much I loved and needed her." He appeared more fragile than anyone had suspected. He grew more modest, almost timid, as the publication of *The Locker Room* neared.

In the summer he and Marion rented a house in East Hampton with Tom Lear. She came out on the weekends; Fred stayed at the beach, palling around with Tom, playing in the chic softball game where his skills as a pitcher and clutch singles hitter were highly prized. He went everywhere with Tom: the pleasant friend who smiled a lot, spoke little, made self-deprecating comments about his work, and was always available for favors or chores.

In late August they held a barbecue to repay others for all the parties they had gone to. Fred found himself the center of everyone's attention when Bob Holder arrived beaming with news—Book-of-the-Month had bought Fred's novel as a featured alternate for a guarantee of thirty thousand dollars. To his bitter surprise, he was asked all over again by everyone the subject of his book, although he had explained it all before —as though the sale had somehow made it a real novel. He saw something he had never seen before in the eyes of the other well-known writers—a flicker of worry and envy. He drank a lot, consciously asked about their work, and kept Marion at least within view, if not actually close by. Despite these precautions, he still managed to make a fool of himself.

"What are you gonna do with your first million, Fred?" Holder shouted at him when they were all quiet for a moment after serving themselves dessert and coffee.

"Think it's gonna be that big?" a senior editor of *Town* magazine asked Holder.

"*The* book of the season. This year's *Garp*."

"Give him a break," Marion called out cheerfully. Fred was grateful, but he worried anyway that her comment was wrong. He shook his head at her.

"Have you started on your next book?" Paula Kramer asked. She was one of the hottest writers in the country, successful as a journalist, screenwriter, and novelist. Her personal life was as famous as her written words, she had been married to two powerful and influential men, her life had been as glamorous as Fred's had been dreary. During the course of the summer he had been in her presence a dozen times; he had nodded pleasantly at many of her observations, but this was the first question she had ever addressed to him.

And he blew it. He stared at her for a moment. Her black eyes seemed alive with intelligence, her long narrow face with its full lips and strong chin loomed at him in the red glow of sunset. He was drunk. He had trouble keeping her in focus. He looked down at his paper plate resting unevenly on the grass. "I don't know," he mumbled.

There was explosive laugher from the crowd. Someone, away from his area, said to Holder, "Haven't you told him yet, Bob?" And there was another round of guffaws.

Fred looked up, shocked, at all of them. There was foreknowledge in their reaction to the joke that Fred wouldn't know if he was writing unless his editor told him. Holder shook his head at the laughter, his eyes closed, his head shaking, a parent irritated by misbehaving children —but a parent who seemed to confess they were right, that their fault was tactlessness, not stupidity. Is that what he had told them? That he had created the book, not Fred?

"I meant . . ." Fred stammered and most of them suppressed their amusement, looking with exaggerated solemnity at him. He was frozen by the horrible feeling that he had been naked all along and everyone had been too polite to say so.

"I know exactly what you meant," Paula Kramer said in a kindly soft voice. She addressed the crowd. "It's the worst feeling in the world. You worry so much about what you're going to do next." She returned her glance to Fred and put out a hand sympathetically, touching his knee. "My worst depressions are right after finishing a book. Now you know what postpartum feels like."

She had covered for him, rewritten everyone's motivation by mis-identifying his confusion. He assumed she had done so consciously, that it was an example of the skillful manipulation of people that the success-ful always seemed capable of. God, he wished he had that talent. He knew that Paula Kramer would somehow make Holder's bragging (ob-viously his editor must be telling everyone he wrote Fred's book) seem like self-aggrandizement, whereas everything Fred tried, such as his summer tactic of being self-effacing, worked against him. He had aban-doned his previous habit of talking about his work to every stranger (having learned that unless you are famous, no one really cares) just when he should have begun such narcissistic ramblings—just when the world would feel he was justified. Now his modesty seemed like incom-petence. The summer had been hell, an endless suppression of natural urges, and now it seemed it had been for nothing.

He let his ice cream melt while Holder went on about the idea he had suggested to Fred to write. "Fred's great at doing contemporary stories. And he's done great sportswriting. You know," he said, gesturing to the *Town* editor for whom Fred was supposed to do his interviews, "I want to get inside the head of a top woman tennis player. Do a novel about, say, Billy Jean King's life. What a great story!" Holder slapped his leg as though these thoughts were just now coming to him.

There were murmurs of agreement, again the rumble of worry and envy from people who once wouldn't even have known Fred was there.

"You should do it," the wife of a bestselling novelist said to Fred. He nodded back at her. Now it was established that it was Holder's idea. If Fred did it, no matter how well, it would forever be Bob Holder they'd think of as the force that made him. The news brought to him before the party, the utterly amazing information that the Book-of-the-Month Club had picked his novel, that in one swoop his advance had been paid back, that obviously not only would his novel have an ad campaign, but it would be big, all of the various implications that added up to the fact that *The Locker Room* would make money, guarantee him another con-tract, probably many more, that he had a real chance to have a bestseller, that he was there at last, out of the dark waters onto the main deck of the luxury liner, strolling in first class—this great moment in his life was sickening, churning in the stomach like rich food wolfed down by a starving peasant.

"He's hard to take," Paula Kramer whispered to Fred over the sound of Holder listing the new idea's commercial potential.

Fred nodded at her stupidly. He couldn't open his mouth to complain about Holder, afraid somehow he would be caught at it. He felt so grateful to her, that she paid attention to him, that she seemed to be on his side.

"I'd love to read your book," she said.

"Really?" he blurted out.

"Yes," she said with a smile. "Do you have a copy you can spare?"

He nodded at the house. "Inside."

"Great. May I take it before I go?"

"Sure," he said, and glanced guiltily in Holder's direction—as though by agreeing he was cuckolding his editor.

"Terrific," she said, and winked at him like a conspirator.

Fred straightened and breathed deeply, glancing at the purple rays of the dying sun. He felt someone watching him and turned his head away from Paul to meet Marion's eyes. She was staring at him like a stranger—an enraged, murderous stranger.

Tony laughed. Every few minutes he'd burst out laughing. He prowled the apartment with more and more energy, fed by pleasure at contemplating the wonderful farcical payoff to his life. First Garth had called. Tony had been seated sullenly in his study staring at the last scene of his play, hating it, hating it fiercely. His life, for months, had been nothing. He sent Betty off alone to the publishing cocktail parties she now attended with increasing frequency. He spent virtually all his time in the apartment trying to work on the play, taking out comic scenes and replacing them with hard drama. He hated it, he thought it read like a television movie, but he was furious at the world, convinced no one had any taste and that this sort of obvious, heavy-handed dialogue would be praised. He read Sherlock Holmes mysteries over and over, delighted by their comfortable predictability. He watched the television talk shows faithfully, staring at the parade of second-rate actors and pompous authors with slow-burning rage. Into this well of lonely despair Garth phoned, and the first sign of a rope to lift him up and out into the blue sky appeared: "Tony? How ya doin'?"

"Hi . . ." He had been slumped in his chair, glowering at the words on the page stuck in the typewriter. He sat up, at attention, as though the principal had walked into the classroom.

"I'm sorry I haven't called," Garth on. His voice was excessively cheerful, hurried. "Guess I was too upset that you didn't want to continue with the project."

"Uh, that's okay. How's it going?"

"Not going at all. That's why I'm calling. I reread your draft last week—been meaning to call. There's a lot of great stuff in it, Tony. I think we underrated it."

"*I* didn't. I overrated it."

Garth laughed, a quick, studied chuckle, and then hastened on: "I mean Jimmy and me. I'd really like ya to come back on—do a rewrite. Do it your way. Just give me a little more resonance, try to play down the politics. Maybe give me a friend in the script that I can play off— express some of my confusion about Meryl's character."

God, they were still talking about Streep, as though she would ever play this part now that she had become a box-office star on her own. She'd never play second fiddle to this shrimp. "Uh, I . . . I haven't thought about it. I really thought you hated the script—"

"No, no! Look, I'm famous for being a scumbag to writers. Ask anybody." Garth laughed. No doubt he suffered from the delusion that admission of a fault meant it wasn't a serious one. "Your draft is better than anything we've gotten. By a long shot. It's just a tough story to get right, but the great ones always are. You have to understand this business is a collaboration. Maybe you were a little too sensitive about taking notes. You gotta consider that possibility too. We'll try harder—both of us—this time to communicate more and argue less."

"What about Foxx? Does he want me back on?"

"Uh. It doesn't . . . well, Jimmy is—"

Tony laughed. "You don't sound too sure."

"Yeah, well, I don't think that's important. Jimmy's a producer. He wants the project to work. He wants a go. He doesn't care who he steps on in the process."

"Yeah, but . . ." Tony sighed. "Look, I don't want to work in a situation where one of my bosses—"

"We're not your bosses, Tony. We're your partners."

"Bill, my mommy taught me that when somebody can hire and fire, that makes him a boss."

"How is your mom? Do you think there's a part for her in this?"

"You mean if Meryl doesn't accept?"

Garth really laughed at that one. His first relaxed, genuine laugh. "I was just thinking it would be great if we could fit her into a great cameo."

"Maybe. It's an idea."

"Will you help me out, Tony? There's nobody else who can pull this

off for me. I'd love to fly you out, talk some, and maybe you can stay at
my house in Malibu. Do the rewrites there. We can talk out the pages
each night. I've already discussed this with Gloria—I'm sure International will renegotiate your contract to give you some more money. What
do you say?"

Tony smiled. He could feel the oppressive madness of the last nine
months lifting. At last, someone had admitted to being wrong, that he
did have talent, that he did know what made a good story and what
didn't. "Let me think about it, okay?"

"Sure, sure. I really hope you do it. This movie can really work. For
both of us, it can be a breakout project."

Gloria Fowler called minutes later. Tony's relief had become exhilaration. "I can't get over it, Gloria. He's practically begging me."

"I know," she purred. "It's wonderful. So you're going to do it."

"I'd love to tell him to go fuck himself. He put me through hell. My
confidence has been shot for almost a year!"

"Well, that shouldn't have happened. I wish you had called me.
Writers have trouble on movie projects all the time—they're fired, they
have to rewrite. It's nothing to beat yourself up over."

"I know. I was a fool. But this is a great payback. Garth on the
phone asking me to stay at his house! Incredible!"

"I think you should say yes. He'll be a pussycat about this rewrite.
He wants to do this picture desperately. He's got nothing on the boards,
everything else has collapsed, and you know he hasn't been up there on
the big screen in three years. They could be shooting this in the late
fall."

"All right. Fuck it. I'll say yes—I mean to the deal. About staying in
his house in Malibu, I don't know."

"Garth's serious about that."

"Really?"

"Really—and frankly, it's a good career move."

Gloria asked about his play. He had told her, when he declined to
do the first-draft rewrite, that he would be busy on a play for a while,
and though she hadn't sounded enthusiastic then, she now seemed genuinely interested in his progress. Finally she asked an odd question:

"How are your folks?"

"I guess they're okay. I spoke to Mom last week—she was her usual
self. Complaining about her scripts."

"And your father?" Goria said, her tone strangely loaded with significance.

He hesitated for a moment, wondering if he should admit the truth, but caution didn't suit his temperament. "I almost never talk to my father. I see him maybe twice a year when he comes through New York."

"Oh . . ." Gloria said in a voice that suggested this was surprising. "I heard he was in town last week."

"Really? Well, he didn't call. But the coolness between us is because of me. I . . . you know, he wasn't very good to my mother and I think he senses my disapproval of him."

"Oh. I see."

Tony laughed. "Gloria, you sound absolutely crushed."

"I'm sorry, I got a little distracted by something on my desk . . . uh, but you don't hate each other?"

"Hate? No, no. I don't like to see him—I think he would love to change that."

"Ah," she said, sounding quite relieved. "Well, I'd better get back to Garth—he's quite hot about closing this. Speak to you soon."

Tony wondered about her interest in his family relations, but not for long. The sheer joy of replaying his conversation with Garth had transported him. He called Betty to chortle over it, spoke to several theater friends, mentioning it casually, saying it was another example of the movie business's foolishness and that he would play along just for fun. But the dark truth was not hidden from him: he knew, no matter how embarrassing it might be to admit, that this single flattering phone call from a vain actor was enough to restore his self-portrait and repair all the chips, tears, and fading of the last year.

David nodded at Rounder's secretary as she said, "Go on in," and opened the closed door to the office. Chico, Harpo, and Rounder paused in mid-sentence. They looked concentrated, their eyes blankly taking him in. "Close the door," Chico said, unnecessarily, for David was already doing so. "Is your passport in order?" Chico asked like a border guard in a thriller.

David smiled. "Yes. The cover's so bad we're fleeing the country?"

Harpo laughed, but Chico and Rounder had no humor in them today. Rounder looked pale and tired. He had been on a seemingly endless tour of events with Mrs. Thorn, from Washington dinners to visits to far-flung bureaus, supposedly to boost morale. Chico had been left to run the magazine, deserted, so that he had to do a good job of it. Indeed, the commonly held theory within *Newstime* was that Mrs. Thorn, in her mind, had already fired Rounder and elevated Chico to Groucho. Naturally this muddy earth upon which both men stood made them irritable and insecure, Chico's feet sticking unpleasantly as he tried to move to higher ground, Rounder nervously unsure as to whether the glop beneath him would harden or suck him under to drown.

"No bullshit," Chico said. "Is your passport in order?"

"Yes, sir," David said. "I'm compulsive about those things. Haven't been anywhere in five years but I renew my pass—"

"Good," Chico cut him off. "You may have to fly to Brazil tomorrow."

"Really?" David consciously showed no excitement. It had become automatic not to respond with the predictable gee-whiz that was typical of young staffers. Although it seemed silly, he believed a substantial portion of his success was due to surface behavior of this sort. He sat down and looked interested—in a mild way.

"We may have our hands on a big story—" Rounder began.

"Exclusively. We have to keep this totally buttoned up," Chico interrupted, though he spoke not as if he had talked over his boss, but rather as if no one had been talking. David noticed Rounder bow his head and lower his eyes when it happened, like a farmer patiently suffering the stubbornness of an animal he needed to reap a harvest, but wished he could instead slaughter for food. "So no gossiping, no sign that you might have to go somewhere. If you leave, we'll simply tell people you're out sick."

"Okay. This sounds exciting," David remarked. "What's up?"

"We may have found Josef Mengele's chief assistant—Hans Gott. He's—" Rounder began.

"—willing to give us an exclusive interview!" Chico finished. "He was Mengele's right-hand man. Stood there with a clipboard charting the experiments. Apparently he escaped with Mengele. He may have the whole inside story from gas chambers to drowning. Here are the files on Gott." Chico handed David a folder. "You're our choice to do the interview."

"Uh . . ." David felt scared. He had a vision of himself seated in a jungle facing an ominous old man surrounded by savage bodyguards, a Jew facing a fiendish Nazi, armed only with a notebook. "Alone?" he asked.

"No," Chico answered. "I'll go with you."

Rounder looked gravely at David. "He can't know you're Jewish."

"What?" David said, stuttering with amazement and nerves.

"Because if he finds out, you'll be carted off to Auschwitz," Harpo said in a low sarcastic tone.

"That's hilarious," Chico said, frowning.

Rounder ignored their exchange, staying on David. "He specified no Jews."

"Then why risk blowing the interview?" David asked, feeling a desperate desire (to his shock) to escape being assigned to this story, though no doubt it would be stunning—a spectacular that would make him: a news event with which he would always be linked.

"Because of the hook!" Chico shouted. He spoke quickly, thrilled by his vision of the magazine: "We want you to write what it's like—as a Jew —to listen to this man talk about his experiments on your people. We'll run a Q-and-A and then a personal essay from you on your reactions."

"How come no one else has this?" David asked.

"He's chosen us," Rounder said.

"For a big fee," Chico added.

"If it's him," Harpo said.

David looked sharply at Harpo. "You mean there's some doubt?"

"A lot," Harpo said.

"Come off it already!" Chico shouted.

"Settle down," Rounder said, and looked expectantly at David.

"What evidence is there?" David asked, feeling he had to say something.

He was shown copies of wartime photos of Gott (alongside Mengele) that bore a similarity to the picture of the old man now, shown standing with the Brazil *Newstime* stringer. There were signatures and a string of false identity papers to compare as well, and their appearance created another fuss between Harpo and Chico. "They look alike," David had commented about them.

"But we haven't had them compared by an expert," Harpo mumbled.

"We can't risk it!" Chico shouted. "Besides, they always disagree. Gott refuses to give the definite proof until the interview."

"Until he sees the money, you mean," Harpo said.

"We're paying him the money before the interview?" David asked, incredulous.

"Part of it," Harpo said.

"A small part," Rounder added.

"Ten thousand bucks. It's nothing!"

"How much will he get if he's really Gott?" David asked.

There was a reluctance to answer. Each of the powerful men glanced at the others, silently handing around the duty of response. Chico finally looked at David. "That must remain a secret."

"Understood," David said impatiently. Who the hell did Chico think he was talking to? A stranger?

"Hundred thousand," Chico said, and glanced quickly away, looking out the window, giving David the impression he expected to see it fluttering down on Madison Avenue.

"What happens after the interview?" David asked.

They blinked at him. "What do you mean?" Rounder asked.

"What happens to Gott?"

"I don't know," Rounder said, looking at Chico inquisitively.

"He crawls back under another rock," Harpo said.

"But . . ." David shut his eyes, uncertain how to put this so it seemed calm and rational, not the reaction of a participant, an interested party, but rather a cool and pleasant observation of disinterest. Instead he saw his father, now an old man of seventy, sitting in the Florida sun screaming into a phone. David opened his eyes. "If we do an interview with Gott—he did the work of the most hated of the Nazis . . ." He paused, feeling the tone of tension in his words, and waited until it subsided.

"You're not about to suggest we kidnap him and hand him over to the Israelis?" Harpo said with aloof sarcasm.

"Let David talk," Rounder said. "His is a point of view we haven't considered." He folded his arms and leaned back, his cool blue eyes glistening with challenge. "Go ahead."

"I think we're going to be criticized. For paying him, for doing nothing to alert the authorities, and even for writing about him in a way that tends to glamorize him."

Chico moved behind Rounder and shook his head no at David. Harpo looked at the signal and laughed. Rounder glanced at him. "What's so funny?"

"Nothing," Harpo said with a sneering smile. "My mind was wandering. Go on, David, I'm sorry."

"I've said it. I don't think you can get around it. We'll be accused, and it will be hard to answer, of abetting the escape of one of the great criminals in history."

"I can answer it!" Chico said. "David, I'm surprised at you. We're a news organization. Someone offers us a story, no matter who they are, we aren't police officials. You know that—"

"This is a little different," David said quietly.

"No it's not!"

"And what happens if he's a phony?" Harpo asked. "Then we get all the heat and we don't even have a story."

"Sure we have a story!" Chico shouted. David looked at the floor. Rounder closed his eyes at the sound, pained. Harpo went on looking at Chico with an air of amusement. "We have an imposter story!" Chico insisted, his tone aggrieved. "People love that."

Harpo laughed. "Terrific," he said to no one in particular.

"What the hell do you suggest we do?" Chico said, leaning in toward Harpo oppressively, his face thrust at him like a kid making a dare. "You having fun shooting down all the suggestions? What the fuck do you want us to do?"

"Pass on the story," Harpo said angrily. "Just a nice, simple polite no, we're not interested."

Chico's mouth opened, his eyes wide. He looked comically baffled, a cartoon caricature of a man flabbergasted. "You gotta be kidding."

"If we had a real guarantee that it is Gott, I'd say do it—"

"Oh, that's very courageous! Gee whiz, I'm impressed!" Chico's sarcasm shuddered through his body. Harpo looked away in disgust. Rounder seemed to be elsewhere now, staring off at some point beyond David.

"We're supposed to cover news, not make it," Harpo said.

"Oh, that's original," Chico answered.

"Look, if all you have to offer is sarcasm—"

"Have you ever heard of investigative reporting?" Chico demanded.

"This isn't investigative reporting," Harpo shot back. "This is buying a pig in a poke."

"If he's a phony, we won't run any story, all right?" Chico argued, sure now that he had this disagreement won. "What does it cost to find out? Ten thousand dollars, three plane tickets, and a couple nights in a hotel. If he's real, then we've got a story you just said you would run."

Harpo nodded reluctantly. "That's true," he said. He looked suspicious about his agreement, though, as if he'd been mugged by his own words.

"Mrs. Thorn will be the one to make the final decision. But I'm prepared to recommend it," Rounder said suddenly. Chico and Harpo both seemed startled by the reminder that he was in the room—and in charge to boot. "All right, then, we're set. Except for your decision whether you want to do the interview," he added, staring at David.

"Of course he's going to do the story," Chico blurted. "My God, David, this is a once-in-a-lifetime piece for you. This is what being a newsman is all about."

David wanted to turn it off. Change the channel. Type over the page. Remove himself from the moment and contemplate it distantly, like an interesting tableau that didn't require movement or participation. In a way it didn't. He had to say yes. It was the logic of his position, the only sensible climax to his life. He'd been handed his chance. All the years of service were paying off. To refuse would have meant making nonsense of his life. He nodded slowly at first. Chico smiled encouragingly.

"You'll do a great job," he urged. "You're perfect for it."

"Thank you," David said.

"I'm going to leave my wife." Gelb pursed his lips. He stared off at the Hudson River, squinting at the gray water, the hard impenetrable surface looking like liquid steel boiling beside Manhattan. They were meeting in Riverside Park in the late afternoon at his request. She hadn't seen him for two months. She had called off their affair at the worst possible time (from the point of view of her novel's success). Indeed, she assumed it had hurt her book already. Fred Tatter had gotten a book-club deal, his first printing was four times the size of hers—obviously it was Garlands big first-novel of the season. Betty hadn't even gotten an assurance of a single dollar to run an ad for Patty's novel, though she claimed Patty had had just as good a shot at the book clubs.

"They make an objective choice, Patty," Betty argued. "They read the books. The publisher doesn't get to pick who's a book-club selection."

"Come on! If they know the publisher is pushing a book, they pay attention. Who are you kidding? I was Gelb's assistant! He had those people hopping for weeks ahead of time! One word from him and I'd be dead, and you know it."

"I don't think he'd do that. He's not angry at you. He under—"

"Have you talked to him about it?"

"Of course not!"

"Then how do you know whether he's angry!"

Betty lectured her then, saying that she had to calm down or she'd be dead by the time her novel came out. "It's not going to be a bestseller, Patty. You have to face that."

"And Fred's is? That piece of shit!"

"You've read it?" Betty sounded surprised.

"Of course I haven't read it," Patty said, laughing. "But it has to be a piece of shit."

Betty laughed. "It is," she said, and laughed harder. "But it's shit that moves," she added.

"Really," Patty said, dismayed. "I can't believe Fred Tatter is going to have a bestselling novel."

"I didn't say it was going to be a bestseller, for God's sake," Betty protested. "It'll do well. Anyway, what do you care? What's the point?"

"I should have had an affair with *him!*" Patty cried out. "He at least would give me a blurb."

Betty roared with laughter. "You're terrible."

"Why can't I do anything right!" she screamed, only half-serious.

"Your book is wonderful. You have a great career ahead of you. What are you so desperate about?"

She didn't want to explain herself to Betty, tell her that she couldn't go on living with David. She apologized for her hysterics and went on feeling desperate. She had broken up with Gelb so she could give their relationship a chance. But it seemed dead. David never fucked her. Indeed, on some days he shrank from her touch guiltily. She wondered at times whether he was having an affair, his manner was so distant and worried. But he had no time to: he worked at the magazine sixty hours a week (she knew he was really there); and the rest of the time he sulked in the loft reading and watching television. She wanted out of their life together. But if her novel didn't make money, she couldn't afford to leave without getting a job, and that meant the end of her writing. She loathed herself for her weakness, her dread of being alone in the world, but she couldn't break free of it. So when Gelb called and begged, literally, to see her for an hour, she agreed.

"I'm going to leave my wife," he said. She watched his profile after this opening shot. He had his chin in the air, bravely, his full cheeks darkening with stubble—he looked like a weary victorious general gazing over the cost of his triumph. He glanced at her after a long silence. "Well?" he said.

"How come?" she asked.

He snorted. "You know why."

"Because of me?"

"Yes."

"We haven't seen each other for two months," Patty protested. "You hate my guts."

"No I don't."

"You said you did."

"I was angry! You broke up with me. Don't tease it out of me. I love you. I've missed you horribly. I tried to hate you. I can't. I tried to convince myself you were just an opportunistic bitch—"

"I am," she interrupted.

"I don't care. That's what I've come up with. I don't care what your motives are. I want you. If I"—he nodded toward the monolithic River-side Drive buildings that stood like mute gods frowning down on the dull oppressed river—"have to divorce and lose my kids, I will."

"Jesus!" Patty turned away. She felt tears in her eyes. "Great! If we destroy your children's lives I can have you." She began to walk, the broad space of the sky scaring her. The river's motion nauseated her. She walked quickly away. She heard him run behind her. She expected him to grab her, but he only moved in front, blocking her path.

"I don't mean it that way. I don't like admitting I'm beaten—that I need you. I'll see my kids as much as I ever have. Even if you say no, I'll leave her. I can't stand living there. She's miserable, and I've gone from being bored by her to hating her. I have to get out. It has nothing to do with you."

She was crying. The damn tears were coming out of her and she had no idea why. She felt acutely nervous. Her breath was short. Gelb seemed so big and awkward, looming over her as though he were another of Riverside Drive's buildings, his words cold and restless like the river: she skidded on its slick surface waiting to drown. She couldn't love him —being with him never felt wholesome; sometimes thrilling, often mor-ally disgusting, but never simple and pleasant.

Gelb tentatively put his arms out, coaxing her to him. "You're so beautiful. You're so great to be with. I can't stop thinking about you— you have to say yes. I love you. I don't think I've ever been in love before—"

"Shut up," Patty said while blubbering into his chest. "I can't take this. I'm not strong enough." She tried to pull away, but he stopped her, effortlessly, with one hand. She felt so weak pulling against him. She was stuck out there in deep water, helpless against his invisible relentless undertow. The memory of the peace of the shore had faded—there was only this water rising up to choke her, while below she was steadily seduced out into the overwhelming ocean.

She wanted fame. She wanted money. She wanted power: to strengthen her, to allow her to break the iron grip of his fingers with an easy gesture. Either that—or surrender: to stop the pathetic flailing of her arms and let the drowning come, fill her ears and nose and mouth with their oppressive demands and possession. "What do you want me to say?" she pleaded, sobbing. "What am I supposed to say? I love you! I love you!" she shouted. "Is that enough?"

She saw a face clearly. It belonged to a middle-aged woman, twenty feet away, walking a white terrier. She looked at Patty with horror and longing in her eyes, as though she were empathically feeling each of her emotions. When they made contact with their eyes, the woman looked down at the dog.

Gelb suddenly became yielding. He hugged her, whispering, "It's all right, it's all right. You don't have to say anything. I'm sorry. I've put too much pressure on you. I just wanted to tell you how I felt. You don't have to respond."

She trembled in his arms. He held her for a while, rubbing her shoulders and back as though drying her after a dip in the ocean. When she stopped shivering she leaned her head against his chest and felt sleepy. She could close her eyes and rest there, let him make the decisions and move her through life, abandoning thought, effort, and will.

"I have to go," he whispered finally in her ear.

"Okay," she said weakly, beginning to move.

"I'm going to tell her tonight," he said.

"I know," she said, not wanting to hear it. All the fuss and fury had been a waste.

"I really am going to leave her," he insisted.

A waste. There they were, back at the beginning. All the upheaval was merely noise and nonsense. Nothing had been settled.

Paula Kramer answered the door herself. The apartment was huge, decorated sparsely—to Fred's mind, like a museum. A few superb antiques were in each room, set far apart from each other, the enormous Oriental rug stretching across the living-room floor with only a single object on it—a coffee table that seemed to be some sort of chest—the beautiful Victorian couches way off, beyond the border of the rug. Paula greeted him warmly. She was thin and energetic, her long frizzy hair sprouting off her head as though her brain were electrifying it, her wide mouth flashing big bright teeth in a cheerful, welcoming smile.

Life had been dreamily successful since the end of summer and his return to New York. Holder was on the phone almost every other day with more talk of how hot Fred's book was becoming. Using the hook that *The Locker Room* was a statement of the "new man's" sexuality, Holder seemed to have created the possibility of a book tour (making the rounds of television and radio talk shows), a common promotional technique with nonfiction, but rare or nonexistent with novels. In the midst of these bulletins, Paula Kramer had phoned to say she loved his book, was fascinated by its frank revelation of the male response to feminism. She had talked to *New York Times Book Review* about doing a piece on the emerging novelists under thirty-five, had gotten approval for the piece, and she wanted to use Fred as the central focus, since she felt his book was the most dynamic and important of the first-novels of the season.

Holder's reaction to this news was unrestrained: "*Un*believable! *Un*-believable! *Un*-fucking-believable! Do you know how much free publicity that is! Fred, I've got to tell the people here now! Right away! This is going to affect the entire campaign."

Paula asked him if he wanted coffee and went to get him some when he said yes. He felt intimidated by her and her living room. He also had no idea what to say about his book. Obviously she expected some sort of intellectual discussion, that his novel had a point to make. Did it? Men aren't monogamous, women are. That had been his original idea. But Holder's changes had occupied him during the writing, alterations that concentrated on keeping the story lively and sexy, with surprising twists and turns of fortune.

"My husband," she said, entering with the coffee in a large china cup and saucer, "is a fan of your sportswriting." Her husband, Brian Stoppard, was one of the most famous criminal lawyers in the country. "So many good American novelists began as sportswriters—why do you think that is?"

She was so charming and friendly that he forgot his nervousness. " 'Cause it pays steady," he answered.

She laughed, a quick ringing chime. He guffawed back at her. "I thought it was an interesting arena—pardon the pun—for you to come out of, given *The Locker Room*'s theme. You know, the machismo of sports, modern male sexuality."

"You know, the athletes aren't really macho. They're little boys putting it on. 'Mine is bigger than yours.' The biggest shock you get when you first meet a team, first time you meet an athlete face to face, is that they're kids!" She nodded eagerly at this observation, her eyes opening with surprise. "You know, twenty, twenty-one. Babies. And they stay babies, 'cause their life is playing."

"Fascinating," she said. "Do you mind if I use a tape recorder?"

"No, I always use one."

Paula walked to built-in shelves (they were so discreet, painted the same white as the walls, that he hadn't noticed them) and brought out a machine, turning it on and placing it on the table between them. "Is your book autobiographical?"

Fred smiled worriedly. He had expected this question, but still hadn't settled on a satisfactory answer.

Paula smiled back. "Terrible question. I hate it when I'm asked. I know that all characters, in a way, are autobiographical, but some are more than others, if you know what I mean. I feel a lot of you in this book. It's very honest. I really admire that kind of courage."

"Thank you. You gotta put a lot of yourself into something to make it real and meaningful, don't you think?"

"Oh, absolutely." She nodded. "How does your wife feel about it?" she said in a mild wondering tone.

"She loves the book," Fred answered, telling the truth insofar as he knew it. He suspected Marion thought it was too sensational, but she had made no criticisms.

"I'm sure. It's wonderful. But . . . I know that Brian sometimes is sensitive about my work. Does she feel at all exposed—the affairs the character has and so on."

"Oh, none of that's true!" Fred said quickly, horrified. "I didn't mean it was autobiographical that way. I've never had any affairs."

"Your fans will be so disappointed," Paula answered, smiling. "Sure you're not being modest?"

"No, no. Honest."

"So how is it autobiographical? The affairs are a substantial portion of the narrative."

"The feelings. You know, I . . . uh . . . uh . . ."

"Extrapolated?"

"Yeah, I extrapolated fantasies into reality."

"Hmmmm." She looked let-down. Almost cool to him now. Maybe she had been hot for him, he suddenly thought. The sex scenes were pretty steamy. Maybe she figured he was a good lay and this was all a prelude to . . . No, impossible. She looked up at him quickly, as though she had made a decision, and turned off the tape recorder. My God, she's gonna end the interview, throw me out, Fred thought. "Off the record, Fred—I don't want to screw up your marriage. But just for my own curiosity—it's not all fantasies, is it? The whole book is about faithfulness, how difficult it is for a man to sustain. Why would somebody who's managed to do it write about its being impossible? If it's possible for you, doesn't that make nonsense of the whole book?"

Fred felt caught. Obviously she had believed, from reading his book, that he was a serious and talented man. Such a reaction was so unexpected that he hadn't considered that the effect of meeting him might be a letdown. Of course he couldn't tell her that Holder's infidelities had driven the narrative. It was Bob who insisted on the restless sexuality of the hero. Fred's original intention had been to have only one instance of adultery; he hadn't considered—

"I don't want to put you in a funny position," she went on. "I understand about privacy—"

"I'll explain, I'll explain. You see, writing the book made me very aware of this . . . uh . . . problem. And Marion and I split up for a while —separated for six months."

Paula looked relieved. "I see. Over this point?"

"Yes," Fred answered, knowing it was a complete lie, but gambling that Marion, if it ever got out, wouldn't bother to contradict him. Anyway, Paula had turned the tape off.

"And you worked it out openly?" Paula prompted, now energetic again.

"Yeah, uh-huh. See, I don't consider that being unfaithful."

"Of course not." She nodded admiringly at him. "You know, Fred, I'll be sensitive about it, but I can't keep that out of the interview without its being pretty bland."

"What part of it?" he asked nervously.

"Just the fact of the separation. Not the fact that you saw other people then. But this open way of handling the monogamy crisis you went through—without it, I don't have a piece the *Times* would run."

There was now in the room a heavy, heavy silence. Paula looked at him gently, considerately. He couldn't blame her. She was right. He thought of Holder, bouncing up and down the halls of Garlands, lobbying for more ads and bigger print runs.

"Okay," Fred said. "Carefully, though."

She turned on the recorder. "Don't worry. Trust me—women will love you for your honesty."

A little thrill went through him at that. He began to talk. . . .

Tony Winters, his black hair shining, his face pink from the air, emerged from the swivel doors into the warm and smoky gold-and-red Russian Tea Room, unbuttoning his camel's-hair greatcoat and meeting the apparently casual but supervisory glances of the famous, near-famous, and companions of the famous seated at the semicircle booths opposite and beside the bar. He handed his coat through the cloakroom's half-door to the woman. She handed him a plastic check. "Hi," he said to the wave of Donald Binns, the now ancient and quite mad Broadway producer seated with his chorus-girl wife and faggy assistant.

"How's your mother?" Binns croaked out.

The glances returned, this time as puzzling stares. "Rich and famous in Hollywood," Tony answered.

"That's good." Binns groaned when he spoke, as though the flattering lies and blustering rages of a half-century had corroded his vocal cords. "You still writing?"

Tony nodded with an indulgent smile, giving the impression that he was humoring a senile uncle. In a way, he was.

"Send me something!" Binns almost shouted. The stares were now mixed with speculative whispers. "What's the matter? Broadway's not good enough for you?"

"I will," Tony answered, and moved on. "Good to see you," he said. The heads returned to their companions as he passed. He saw himself in the mirror out of the corner of his eye. He looked great. Life is a performance, assholes, he thought to himself. No one knew Binns had rejected all three of Tony's plays—probably even Binns himself had forgotten. All that mattered was Tony's crisp walk, his clear bold eyes, the slight witty smile wavering on his lips. "I'm meeting Gloria Fowler for lunch," he said.

"Of course, Mr. Winters. How are you?"

"I'm fine," Tony said, acknowledging the hostess, now that he had been recognized.

Gloria rated a booth on the left (number seven, Tony guessed, remembering from his childhood the station numbers; explained to him by the waiters with whom he would play while his mother got progressively drunker), and she was already there—her expensive haircut, her creamy silk blouse, and her simple (but unbelievably costly) rope of pearls leavened by the modest pair of blue jeans hidden beneath the pink tablecloth.

"You look lovely," Tony said, kissing her on the cheek and then sliding in.

"Deal's made," she said.

"You're kidding."

"No, when Garth wants somebody, it's done. Want something to drink?" He ordered and then she went on, "He wants you to call him tonight—the afternoon out there—at his home. I'll give you the number. He's very hot about you staying with him in Malibu to do the rewrites."

"Really?" Tony looked around the room with mastery, owning it. Mom must have felt like this when a hit was running, he thought to himself. "Well, I guess if I do it, the movie'll get made."

"It'll keep his attention and make him feel he's part of the writing of the script. Would Betty be a problem? Can she get time off?"

"She can't leave now—or rather, she doesn't want to. She's got a

. . ." It sounded so trivial and small-time, Tony hesitated. "She's got a book coming out—"

"She's written a book?"

"No, no. I mean a novel she's edited. But she wouldn't make a fuss about my going. I've been so moody, she'd probably feel relieved."

"I'm sure she'd miss you terribly. Garth says it'll only take a few weeks—"

"They always say that—then it goes on for months."

"You could stay with your father if Garth gets to be too much."

"God, I'd rather stay at a hotel."

Gloria frowned at her glass and lifted it to her lips, sipping. When she put it down she smiled and put her hand on Tony's shoulder. "It's just a rumor, Tony, but I think you should know . . ." She paused and smiled encouragingly.

He was baffled. "Yes . . .?"

"Your father—they say—is probably going to be named CEO of International Pictures."

Tony swallowed. "CEO?"

"Chief executive officer. The head of the company, overseeing television and features."

He looked away from the band of mirrored glass—reflecting the glittering hairstyles, sparkling glasses, and open laughing mouths—down at the brilliant red leather of the booth. He closed his eyes as the humiliation fell over him like a shroud. Don't show it! Life is a performance. "I see. That's why Garth wanted me back."

"No!" Gloria said, like someone commanding a dog not to pee on the rug. "That's why I wanted to warn you about it. I knew you'd think that. But Garth has no idea of—"

"Gloria, that town is worse than high school. Somebody pops a pimple out there and everybody knows how much pus came out. If you've heard the rumor, he's heard it."

"Not true. I know it and I'm the only one who does, because of my association with someone—I can't explain. I know that no one else knows. Have you heard anything about it?"

"No, of course—"

"You see!"

"But that—"

"Listen to me, Tony. Garth has had two other writers do drafts since yours."

"You're kidding me. Two?"

"Yes. They're awful. Whatever problems your draft has, at least there's a movie there. These other drafts are unusable. *He* wants you back. I was afraid that the rumor might come true and be announced while you're out there and you'd get paranoid and pissed off and walk off. I don't want that to happen."

Tony stared into her eyes. "Forget it, Gloria. Don't bother with the speech. I don't care why I've gotten the job back. I was going crazy. I'm just glad I'm working. Garth wants me to live at his house—I'll live at his house. He wants me to do the dishes, I'll do the dishes. I don't care." He straightened his shoulders and smiled. Life is a performance, his mother's ringing youthful voice spoke through time in his head. "To a *go* picture," he said, raising his glass.

Patty entered the loft grimly. She had discussed it thoroughly with Betty at lunch. She had to get away from these men. She couldn't think clearly about her life while living with Grumpy David and seeing Demanding Gelb. Tony was going to Los Angeles for at least a month and Betty had offered to put Patty up for as long as he was gone. Four weeks of male abstinence, both sexual and emotional, might clear her head.

She had decided to blurt it out—her desire for a temporary separation was the story she planned to tell David—the moment she entered, afraid that any hesitation would end up in cowardly silence. She walked to the bed area, where she saw light, and stopped, amazed: David was packing a suitcase. It stunned her. How did he know?

"Hi," he said. His voice sounded rushed. "Where were you? Believe it or not, I have to fly to Brazil."

"What?"

"You can't say a word to anybody. This has to be absolutely secret. I'm flying to Brazil to interview, or possibly interview, Hans Gott."

"Who?"

David looked up from folding his pants and smiled. "You wouldn't know. He's on the hit parade of Nazis. He was Mengele's favorite helper. Decided who would live and who would die in the ovens. Also performed experiments on twins, dwarfs. Shot blue dye into the eyes of children, and so on . . . lovely man."

"Oh. Yeah," she mumbled, baffled by this turn of events. "I thought he was dead."

"You're thinking of Mengele. This one might be, too. The guy I'm supposed to meet could be a fraud."

"Isn't this dangerous?"

"We're supposed to meet in a public place—I sure as hell am not going to meet him in a dark alley."

"How long will you be gone?"

"Don't know. A few days?"

"Oh." Patty sat on the bed and stared off, nonplussed. She felt deflated, and, oddly, sad to be left alone in the loft. She had wanted to walk out on him and be with Betty. Not wait in solitude for the return of a man she didn't want anymore. And he looked so appealing right now —his cheeks flushed with excitement, his tone energetic and funny.

"You'll be all right," he said.

She nodded.

"Won't you?"

"I want to move out," she said. The words floated out of her, levitating from her inner thoughts mystically, in violation of her mind's censuring gravity.

"You're that scared to be alone?" David asked, almost laughing with amazement.

"I'm sorry . . ." she said, and got up, wanting to walk away to shut herself up, but she couldn't move, unable to figure out where to go.

David studied her back. She had taken to hunching her shoulders more, it seemed to him, since she had become a novelist. Was it bending over the typewriter?

Now he understood what she meant: she was leaving him, he thought dully. It didn't surprise him, though it was unexpected. Since his regular visits to the Mistress, he had lived side by side with her, passengers on a subway, sharing noise and light and movement, but not speaking or knowing each other. Strangers seated together on a dull trip.

Patty turned back. "Can I help?"

"You want to move out," David said. "Break up, you mean."

She stared at him like a frightened little girl. Her eyes wondered at him. What will you do? Don't be angry. What will you do? Don't hate me. "I'm sorry, I shouldn't—"

"My flight isn't until tonight. Everything's ready. I was just nervously packing." He paused and cocked his head, asking calmly, "You're going for good?"

Tears formed in her eyes: a deserted child, shrinking from the big horrible world. "I don't know, I don't know," she said, weeping between the words. "I feel like I'm going crazy. I shouldn't be saying this now . . ." She hunched over, moving toward the bed as if she were collapsing uncontrollably and needed to cushion her fall.

He watched her coldly. He felt heartbroken for her: she lay on the bed like a broken doll. He was convinced that if he hugged her now, spoke of his love, she would reverse her decision to go. But the effort, both physical and emotional, of feeling and giving, the whole boring mess of vomiting up the truth, repelled him. He didn't want to smell and look at his innards, to regurgitate his perversions, inadequacies, and failed hopes. "Is it anything in particular?" he asked.

"What?" she said, her voice muffled by the bed and her tears.

"Are you upset about something I can fix?" he answered in a grudging tone.

"No, it's not you—I'm fucked up," she said, and rolled over onto her back, her arms resting outward, crucified on a soft mattress. "I love you," she said.

"I love you too," he answered perfunctorily. "So why are you moving out?"

"Kiss me," she said, looking like a centerfold—yearning for an unseen lover, her body defenseless, the gates open to any violation.

David shook his head. He felt like laughing. "You're crazy. What kind of breakup is this? If you're walking out on somebody, you don't interrupt it for a seduction."

"I'm not walking out. I need some time—"

"Come on, Patty. I'm not a fool. That's never the truth. You don't have the guts to do it straight."

She sat up, raised the drawbridge, filled the turret with guns, and unsheathed her sword. "I'm trying to be honest, I'm trying to talk about it. You're the one who never says a damn thing. You're so closed off and cold."

"Right. You're walking out—I'm the bad guy. That's what this is about. Getting rid of your guilt. You want to leave and be a saint. You got it. Don't bother to even argue for it. I concede it to you." He walked away, propelled by his anger.

"You have to win every argument," she shouted at his back. "Even when winning it means you lose."

"God, you're a real phrase-maker!" he answered, talking up to the ceiling. "I don't know what the fuck that means!"

"It means, all I felt coming in here was confused. I wanted time to think things out. The way you're behaving *does* make me want to leave!"

"That's gotta be bullshit!" he yelled, his hands out in a furious plea. "Confused about what?" he said, turning on her. He walked at her angrily. She stood up, startled, as though his movement were threatening. "What? What is there to think about?"

"Uh, us . . ." she stammered. "We haven't been having a good time together." She gained confidence. "We haven't fucked in two months."

"I've been busy!" he cried out.

"Oh, the magazine! The magazine, the magazine, the magazine. It's your answer to everything. You're like some terrible cliché on a soap opera. What the hell are you working so hard for? You're thirty-one years old—you act like a fifty-year-old man!"

"All right, all right. I'll stop working so hard. I was scared," he pleaded, lying, though it sounded very honest, to his surprise. "I got this big job—I didn't think I could do it." Tears formed at his eyes.

Patty looked amazed. "Oh," she said, touching his arm with her hand. "I'm sorry."

"What are you sorry for?" he said, laughing and sobbing at once.

"I'm sorry," she repeated, and moved into his arms, hugging him.

"I kept thinking they were going to knock on the door and tell me it had all been a mistake." he said, elaborating on this successful theme. It sounded so authentic, so convincing. He had reached for this explanation to avoid confessing about the prostitution—not to have to reveal the tableau of him wearing a collar and licking a woman's boots.

"It's not a mistake," she whispered in his ear. "You're brilliant."

"Thanks," he answered shyly.

They held each other for a while. For both, it was relief to be holding and loving anyone. "Where are you going to go?" he asked, meaning really: Are you still going?

"I'm going to stay with Betty. Tony's got to go to LA for a month."

David eased himself out of the embrace. "Oh. Well, that'll be good for your book."

"That's not why I'm doing it," she argued, a teenager complaining she had to stay out past eleven.

"I didn't mean anything," he answered. "I meant, you can keep her working on it. I know that's not why you're doing it."

"Oh," she said, feeling embarrassed. "I may not do it. I don't know."

"I . . ." His voice broke. He cleared his throat. "I hope you don't." His chin quavered.

She looked ashamed and hugged him again.

"I love you," she said.

"I love you too," he answered.

CHAPTER

16

Tony watched them talk on Malibu beach. He stood above them on a wide deck supported by thirty-foot-high wooden stilts that looked inadequate to the task. The surf, which seemed gentle and casual as it approached the shore, broke abruptly and angrily at its finish: a horse rearing in horror at the row of two-million-dollar houses. Garth and Redburn, two of the most famous faces in America, stood in profile, elegant in their casual clothes, tranquil faces, and perfect hairdos, their words drowned by the Pacific's noisy disgust at encountering land. The scene looked like a movie. An obvious thing to think, but fascinating nonetheless. Tony could make up the dialogue in his head—his eyes were the cameras.

"I hear the script's going well," Helen, Garth's wife, said from behind him.

She was lying on a green-and-white-cushioned deck chair, wearing a black bikini on a body so spectacular that to be aroused by it was almost too passive a response. Hurling oneself on Garth and strangling him immediately, tossing diamonds at her, instantly swearing love and running off to the Crimean War—even they might be responses not commensurate with her beauty. And to make her more infuriating, she was pleasant, intelligent, modest, and kind. "We're almost done," Tony said.

"You sound relieved."

"I am."

"Has it been very hard on you? Staying here and working?"

Below, Garth gestured toward him. Redburn looked at Tony, his eyes squinting as he concentrated on the sight. The look was almost a product's logo—the distance glance of a hero regarding the future fearlessly, or the past with brave regret. Garth dramatically held his arms out at full length and applauded Tony. Redburn smiled. Tony nodded and held his glass up in acknowledgment.

"He loves you," Helen said. "He told me last night, he'll miss you terribly when you go. Made me feel jealous."

Tony turned her way, his eyes drawn (despite the constant warning lights he flashed them) to her firm full breasts, languidly arrogant in repose. He forced them up with effort, like pulling away from a magnet (it could be done, but it required steady pressure), and looked at her wonderful face. Her green eyes were bright and cheerful. "He's been very nice to me," Tony answered in the tone of an ancient retainer speaking of his master.

"He said he thinks you could make a great director. Says you really understand actors."

Tony ignored the compliment. Hollywood prophesied future success only slightly less casually than it offered absolute predictions of utter failure. "It must have been hard on you to have a houseguest for two months. You've been very patient."

"Aren't we both wonderful?" she said.

Tony smiled. "I mean it."

"You don't really like us," she said. Not argumentatively, accusingly, but not stating a fact, either.

"Oh, no, no," Tony said, startled by her comment.

"Don't feel you have to—"

"I don't. If I've behaved distantly, it's only because of my problems. He's a great star—you are a great beauty. For someone like me—vain, greedy, childish—it's pretty hard to take."

This little speech was the first time he had spoken informally, intimately. She sat up—Tony's eyes slipped their leash for a moment and looked at her crotch, barely covered, the surrounding skin of her hips and thighs unblemished, without a ripple of fat or looseness—and looked at him eagerly. "You don't seem anything like that. You're self-confident, you're very at home with yourself."

Tony giggled. He couldn't believe she meant that about him—he felt so uncomfortable with himself, as though his ego was infested by fleas: he was scratched raw from the restless itch of its countless wounds. "You're kidding," he said, and giggled again.

"No," she said. "Both of us have talked about it. We wondered if it was our life here." She nodded at the beach and the house. "Everybody here is conscious of being judged, talked about . . . you seem to be sure of your value, no matter how things are going."

"God, I wish that were true. Thank you. But all I've felt since I came here is envy." Tony looked out at the dynamic duo below. "He's got everything. Fame, money, talent, power." Tony looked at her, letting all his lust and longing show. "And you. He even has you."

She showed neither encouragement nor dislike. She simply seemed to accept his comment as a fact.

"I'm sorry to talk about you like that," Tony said, now nervous that he had said something which was both offensive and possibly untrue. He barely knew this woman. She was stunning, but he felt no love for her. He had spoken, as always, exaggerating a momentary feeling into a dramatic speech. It was his curse, his addiction to taking center stage no matter what, even if it cost him respect and love. He wanted to be interesting to her. He had played the part of modest, patient servitude to her husband for eight weeks of the run. Now he wanted the lead. "I know you're not a possession of his. That makes it even more irritating. If he had your love simply because he's famous, then I could be contemptuous. I'm fond of being contemptuous. But I can't. You really love him."

Now she was the one to laugh, pause, and then laugh again. "You really mean that to be a question. If you want to go to bed with me, why don't you just say so?"

"No, no," Tony pleaded. He felt terror. He had blundered his way into a mess, trying to show off. He put his glass down and put his hands out to plead. "I didn't mean that. Going to bed with you wouldn't make me envy him less. I meant simply that being with the two of you is hard. You have everything. I'm just here for a while. Then I'll go back—to what? To the absence of all this." He pointed to the house like a magician indicating the objects he was soon to make disappear. "What you both have is a constant reminder of my . . ." What? What was so terrible about his life? ". . . my . . . my mediocrity."

She had resumed her normal manner: calm, interested, welcoming. "You're not a mediocrity," she said sharply, as though someone had insulted a close friend of hers.

"Well," Tony said, wanting out of this conversation, turning back to look at the tableau under him, more than ten million in talent chatting against the surf, "I feel like one here." He felt his chest tremble. He breathed out slowly to rid himself of it. At last he had spoken the truth. To an almost a total stranger, he had confessed what he dreaded about Hollywood. Not Joe McCarthy or his father's coldness. Not his mother's smothering insanity or Garth's narcissism. Here, he was insignificant— an amoeba in an ocean of whales. He expected at any moment to be swallowed whole—a tasty hors d'oeuvre for the giant mammals.

The flight to Brazil seemed to take forever. Chico accepted all the drinks that were offered, from the champagne before takeoff to the pre-lunch cocktail, to the wine during the meal, straight on through to the cordial. David matched him sip for sip, although he was quite drunk just from the cocktail. Chico passed out near the end, his head sliding off the seat and resting against the window. David felt sick during descent but he fought the nausea off by calling to mind the Mistress and her punishments—guaranteed to arouse him and prove a distraction.

On the ground they were met by the *Newstime* stringer, Ken Michaelson. Their condition was obvious. "First class is murder, isn't it?" he said, laughing, taking Chico's carry-on.

"It's hot here," was all the bleary-eyed Chico said.

It was. And humid. The strange land passed by David soundlessly in the air-conditioned car—because of the cars, architecture, and old-fashioned neon signs, Rio looked as though it were existing in a time zone ten years in the past. He felt like a vulgar American. It seemed as though everyone who looked at them knew exactly who they were—American businessmen loaded with dough and prissy assumptions. But I'm not, David wanted to answer. I'm a writer.

"You guys better get some sleep," Ken said as he pulled into the Hilton. "Our man may want to meet tonight."

"Where?"

"He didn't want to talk about that until you arrived."

They checked in. The Hilton seemed to be trying to fool its customers into believing they were really in the United States. There was barely an accent in the staff's talk, the technology all looked up-to-date, and there was an absence of Latin decor—the only false note was the excessive deference added to the usual respect with which they were treated. There was a distinctly un-American servility to it—a subservience that made David nervous again. The gross Americans who have to be placated or they bomb the hell out of you, he imagined them thinking. Chico's reaction was the opposite. Once in their undistinguished two-bedroom suite (Chico thought they should be accessible to each other at all times), he commented: "I love it here! They're so friendly."

Yeah, Chico thinks abject slobbering is friendship, David thought, his eyes burning from drunkenness and fatigue. He had a foul metallic taste in his mouth and every swallow brought up an aftertaste of the wine, the gin, the soggy meat, the sweet Drambuie. "I'll let you guys nap and get in touch with our man," Ken said before going.

Chico rang the desk and asked them to put all calls through and keep ringing no matter how long it took. "See you," he said to David, and disappeared into his bedroom. David considered unpacking and then fell on the bed—he toppled onto it like a statue falling, the way he used to as a kid. The room shifted in his vision when his head settled on the pillow. "I'm gonna be sick," he said to himself, and clutched the bedspread to hold on, squeezing his eyes tight. A thought, playing clearly above all this nausea, came into his mind: I could kill him. I could get a knife from dinner and kill Gott. He tried to laugh. But whether it was the booze or his seriousness, he couldn't. His mind winked out on a vivid picture of him plunging a silver hotel knife into a rather small old man's belly. Just as he passed out, the blood pouring over his fantasy hand, Chico stood up outraged, yelling: "Wait until after the interview, you idiot!"

Fred stood still and the world gathered speed, whirling faster and faster about him, a tornado forming to elevate him above all he had known, beyond anything he had ever dreamt. Bob Holder made up a story about a woman tennis star, discussed it with Gelb, offered Bart a hundred-thousand-dollar hardcover contract for Fred to write it, and besides the rather tentative "Yeah, okay" that he spoke in acceptance, that ended his participation in the incredible event. When he told Tom Lear the news, Tom's reaction was almost as astonishing: "I think Bart may have sold you cheap. After your book comes out, maybe you could have gotten a quarter-million."

His phone rang each day with new people and more surprises. The publicist from Garlands called daily with new requests for TV appearances, newspaper and magazine interviews, laughing when Fred confessed, "What am I gonna say?"

"Just tell them what the book's about," she answered breezily. "You'll be great."

Four weeks before publication, Longacre Books, the largest paperback publisher in the country, made a floor bid for *The Locker Room* of two hundred thousand dollars in exchange for a ten-percent topping privilege. It meant simply that if no other house made an offer, they were obliged to buy it for that amount; and if there were higher bids, they had the right to top them by coming up with ten percent more.

Fred hung up, returning to the dinner table (Marion and he were eating fish sticks), and told her the news. "Tom was right!" she cried out. "Bart undersold you on the tennis book."

"Marion!" Fred shouted. "Last year I earned twenty thousand dollars."

"I know," she said, smiling. "We'd better talk to somebody about the money."

"You mean, like taxes?"

"I mean, like, what to do with it."

"Yeah," he mumbled, worried. He sat up late, adding the figures. He would get fifty percent of the paperback sale: a hundred thousand, less Bart's commission, making it ninety. There would be another ninety from the tennis novel. A hundred and eighty thousand so far, and not a single copy of his book had yet been sold, had yet been put in a box and shipped to a bookstore. And he reflected that Marion had a point: Garlands, with this paperback floor, in essence now owned his next novel for free. He wondered if Bart was such a good agent. That Holder was a brilliant editor was obvious—perhaps Bart was living off Fred's and Holder's efforts here.

The money was more than he had ever expected, and now he wanted more. If his novel hit the bestseller list, the paperback sale would be higher—other houses would come in and the auction could end up at a million.

The next morning, Bart called. "Congratulations."

"It's incredible, isn't it?"

"It's not over yet. Listen, do you have an accountant?"

"Just my father's. You know, my—"

"Is he experienced at handling writers?"

"No, he's just a little old guy who—"

"I think you're going to need special care now. Probably you should be incorporating. You've got close to two hundred thousand already for this year—and it could be a great deal more. Hollywood is now interested. I've been at work on them for months, whetting their appetite. Now with the book club, the promo tour, the paperback floor, they're hot. I hadn't wanted to get your hopes up—but four producers have now asked studios to buy the book."

"You're kidding." That was all Fred seemed to be able to say these days.

"I always had good feelings about this book. It's a lightning rod and you're lighting up the sky. I think Bob's right when he says it'll be *the* big book of the season." There was a buzz from his intercom. "I told you to hold the calls while I'm talking to Fred," Bart shouted, irritated.

Fred smiled to himself. He wanted a cigarette. "Bart, could you hold on for a second? I want to get a cigarette."

"Sure."

Fred strolled across the living room, picked up his pack, lit one, returning slowly. He didn't know why, but this pause in the talk made him feel strong and adult. It was amazing how a little success draped a new confidence over him. He felt dressed in kingly robes. "Bart," he said casually, but as though talking to someone he controlled, "I wonder if we made a mistake, signing the new deal with Bob. If we'd waited, we might have gotten a lot more."

There was a silence. Whether it was ominous, or shocked, or wounded, Fred didn't know. To his surprise, he didn't care. He wanted to hear Bart's answer, no matter how Bart felt about being questioned. "Well, it's worked out that way. Maybe it wouldn't have if we hadn't made the deal."

There was an edge to Bart's calm tone—as though suggesting Fred not continue, not probe below the surface of his tranquil pond. He might find monsters swirling in the deep. "I don't understand. There'd still have been a paperback—"

"You don't know. You know, how Garlands feels about you is important. Now they stand to make a lot of money by promoting the hell out of *Locker Room*. They own your next book. If they succeed with this one, they've got another bestseller for a mere hundred thousand—"

"But that's why I think—"

"They've been hyping you to death, which sends a message to the industry, to the book clubs, to the paperback houses. They know Garlands is gonna promote your novel. So they can pick you as an alternate, make a floor bid, with confidence. Right now, Fred, the agents I work with in Europe are collecting offers for *Locker Room*. We've turned down, *turned down*, mind you, a quarter of a million dollars in foreign advances."

"Without even telling me?"

"Hey, Fred. Make up your mind. You felt we had been premature in selling your next novel. Now you're worried we're taking chances? The offers are pouring in, Fred. The foreign publishers haven't even read your book and they're making offers."

"Come on, that's impossible."

"Maybe a few have read it, but I doubt it. All they know is, if it's happening here, they should be in on it. A hot book has a logic of its own. The tennis book is a great idea. It isn't your idea, Fred. If we didn't make the deal, we couldn't sell it elsewhere. We'd have been slapping Holder, and therefore all of Garlands, in the face just before a critical time. You know right after the book-club deal was a crucial moment. Garlands could have brought out your book nicely, nothing spectacular, gotten a little profit on it, and gotten out. Holder came to me with the offer then. Right or wrong, he felt you owed it to him. He did work very hard on *The Locker Room*. Maybe I was wrong, but I felt saying no could have cut off your success before it had a chance to blossom. Besides, you and Bob make a good team. I don't believe in breaking up winning combinations."

Fred needed an ashtray. There wasn't one nearby. He didn't want to break off to find one. "Bart, I . . . are you saying that I'm stuck with Bob—I mean, I like Bob, but—"

"Of course not. You're a very talented writer. Once this book is on the list, I'm sure the tennis novel will be great, then we can make our move. Collect a million up front. Maybe more. Come on, Fred. Right now you should be thinking of organizing things so you can handle this money, *and* getting ready for the book tour." There was the harsh noise of his intercom. Fred heard his secretary's voice in the background: "Bob Holder on two."

"Well, speak of the devil. It's Bob on the line. Do you want to hold? Or should I call you back?"

"No, you can call me back," Fred answered in a desultory tone. The long ash from his cigarette fell and smashed itself against his pants leg, disintegrating in graceful silence.

"Cheer up, Fred! You're rich and you're going to be famous," Bart said, and hung up.

Fred stood with the phone in his hand. The cigarette's ember was burning into the filter, the red glow shrinking into a shell like a frightened turtle. "Fuck you," he said to the dead phone.

Patty spent an uneasy night in the loft. The streets of SoHo—its buildings painted in neon pastels, mobbed by tourists and flea markets— at night reverted to their past: dark warehouse alleys, their wobbly hump-backed gutters glistening with puddles, the occasional drunken voice echoing in the cast-iron tunnels. To be sure, she knew there were expensive restaurants within a block or two—if she looked out the window long enough, the long dark bodies of the limos would pass: restless city sharks on the prowl. But walking in giant space, sensing her small body alone under the high ceiling, was creepy. She kept the television on for company. Gelb had phoned twice. He had told his wife he wanted a divorce, denying there was another woman involved.

"Good," Patty had said. "Because there isn't."

"You've changed your mind again."

"I didn't promise anything. You bullied me. I need time to think. I don't want to see you and get confused."

He acted as though she didn't mean it. Called back to say so point-blank. She wanted to ask him why he wasn't doing anything for her book, but she feared he would think he could buy her body with an ad budget —and she knew now that wasn't true. She could tell him it would, but she would never keep the bargain. Not because of principle, because of vanity. She didn't want to succeed as a writer that way—she wanted the accomplishment to be real, to fill her with confidence, not turn into the mush everything else in life had become: every relationship compromised, every achievement diluted. She had always gotten by through the goodwill of men, or friends, or her winning manner. The novel was stripped of these advantages, naked but for her mind and will and talent. The reader could only be seduced by those beauties—her tits, her wondering eyes, her smooth skin would make no difference. The politics of feminism were meaningless to her; its abstractions plastic weapons when in combat with the real world, but this understanding of it, that at last there was something of her own to protect, not simply ideas, was a flag to rally under. No matter how hard or scary, with her novel she was going to do without the men, without the coy plea of helplessness. She had given up the illusion that she could change her dealings with men about sex or love—but about her work, yes. If Gelb didn't want to advertise her book because it was good, then let it not sell. If she needed him, it would be because of sexual weakness, not the fear of poverty or obscurity.

Earlier that day she demanded the truth from Betty about her novel's future, now only a month from publication. Unfortunately, Betty answered her: her book had a ten-thousand-copy printing, but there would be only one shared ad in the *Times Book Review*, and without a book club, unless the reviews were sensational, a paperback sale was unlikely. "People like it," Betty said sadly. "But they feel it's a quiet book, too similar to so many others that have come out to be a big seller."

"You mean it's not thrilling like Fred Tatter's book?"

"Right now Fred's book is controversial—it wouldn't have been fifty years ago. It's totally retro—it says men are biologically unfaithful. Just harmless hormones, not sexism. People want to hear that, even just to get angry at it. I hear some of the feminists like it because they think it shows that men are still disgusting. They say: we can use this as something to attack. That's why all the talk shows want him. He's getting on the Phil Donahue show 'cause Sara Farleigh wants to be on with him and tear him to shreds. He'll be humiliated but his novel will sell thousands."

"Not a bad bargain," Patty said.

"I think it is," Betty said, frowning. "Sure Fred'll make money, but he'll feel like a piece of shit."

"No." Patty shook her head. "His book will be read. That's really all that matters to a writer."

"Oh!" Betty sat up, an impatient governess. "That's disgusting. Don't say it."

"You're not a writer, Betty," Patty said. Her friend looked startled at Patty's tone and demeanor: a trace of pity, of condescension. "You can't understand. They may yell and scream at him, but they're *paying attention*. That's all that matters."

"You make writing sound like it's being a spoiled brat."

"Maybe it is."

Betty looked at her for a while, solemnly. "You're upset about your novel. I understand."

"No, you don't. I'm not. I was lucky to get it published. If it weren't for you, it wouldn't have been."

"That's not true—it's a terrific book."

"Thanks. But the next time I'll submit my manuscript to strangers —then even the failures will feel good."

Betty no more believed this termination of their work relationship than Gelb accepted the end of their sexual one. Betty changed subjects nervously, asking how things with David were going, implying it was failed romance that had put Patty in such a bad mood. Betty immediately offered to put her up while Tony was away. These favors she would accept. But David's sudden—and bizarre—trip had left her in limbo, wandering in a neighborhood half-changed with her life half-altered.

The phone rang. Gelb again, she thought, reaching for it wearily. She almost didn't pick it up. "Patty?" Betty was breathless. "I just got off the phone with Paula Kramer. She called to ask my feelings about Garlands publishing Fred's novel . . ."

Patty closed her eyes in despair, hearing Fred's name mentioned again.

". . . I couldn't say anything—*except* I talked about your novel. Said that was the sort of thing I felt analyzed modern relationships in a way I understood them. She got quite excited about the contrast between your novel and his—you know, given the hook that you're both at the same house, both first novels, both being published the same month. She wants to interview you. I gave her your number. There's a possibility she'll include you in the piece she's doing for the *Times* on young novelists."

"That's great," Patty said, unsure it was. Paula Kramer worried her. Her pieces, even when flattering, had an edge of smart-ass condescension that Patty enjoyed only when it was about people she disliked. "Has she read my book?"

"Read it? She'd never heard of it until I told her about it. I'm pretty proud of myself. I really did a selling job."

She wants to be thanked again. Oh thank you thank you for helping sweet little me. Gelb was the same. When he had shown her the book-jacket cover, he boasted: "I insisted they hire Golum, best cover man in the business. Cost an extra five hundred." She tried to forgive Betty for doing it—hers was the self-praise of insecurity; his, an itemized bill. "That's great, Betty. Thank you."

"Listen, you sound lonely. Don't you want to come and stay with me?"

"I don't want to miss Paula's call," Patty answered.

"Oh, right! I better hang up."

For an hour she waited, expecting it to ring. When it did, it was Betty. "Did she call?"

"No."

"I called to warn she might not for a few days. She asked me to messenger a copy of your novel over tomorrow. She might intend to read it first."

"Oh," was all Patty said. But it changed everything. No one had yet read her book and flipped over it. If Paula Kramer was looking for a counterargument to Fred, Patty's slim sardonic observations of the conflicts arising in a young woman raised to be Doris Day in a world that wanted Superwoman wouldn't have sufficient clarity or stridency. Her story didn't come to a definite conclusion like Fred's—she simply wanted the reader to ride her heroine's roller coaster and, at the end, know only what she knew: there were other rides, but that was the only one she had a ticket for. Maybe her book was boring. At least, unlike Fred's, it had the virtue of truth.

"So you can stay over," Betty said. "You sound terrible."

"I'm just tired," Patty answered, telling the truth. She was tired of being helped. Tired of all the little lies everybody told each other. Tired of this stupid city, with its expensive slums and overpaid egotists. "I'll be fine here," she said.

Tony reached out of the car window and pressed the button. He glanced at the fifteen-foot-high gate, half-expecting it to open automatically. A voice squawked at him, sounding like a parody of a Japanese houseboy: "Yes? Who is?"

"It's Tony. Tony Winters."

"Please close behind you."

There was a buzz and the gate unlocked, the doors separating a few inches. He got out to open them wider, drove in, and then got out again to close them. The wide sweeping driveway curved around to an entrance with white columns that supported a structural awning. He glanced up at the place. It looked huge: the plantation home of a wealthy Southern family. "Here I am at Mom's," he said to himself.

The Japanese who had buzzed him in opened the door as he approached. "Did you lock gate?"

"Yes."

"Tony!" his mother called from inside the house. He wandered toward the voice, entering a large living room crowded with couches. There were four of them forming a square in the center of the room, leaving only a foot or so between them to squeeze through. The rest of the room seemed to be taken up by end tables, except for one forlorn low Victorian chair in a corner.

"Is your security gate supposed to work that way?" Tony asked, approaching the couches. He then noticed, buried in one of them, a smallish woman with a sharp chin, a long thin nose, and small clever eyes accented by arching sarcastic eyebrows, smoking a long thin cigar.

"It's there to encourage burglars and discourage guests," the stranger said.

Maureen laughed. "You're too clever," she answered the woman. "It's broken, darling," she said to Tony, draping an arm over the back of the couch, reaching for his hand. He took it and she pulled him toward her. He almost flipped over the couch. She kissed him (her breath smelled of wine; there was an open bottle on the glass coffee table) on the lips. "You look marvelous."

"Malibu tan," said the small lady, putting her cigar gently onto an ashtray.

"This is my dear friend Andrea Warren." Maureen squeezed Tony's face. "My beautiful brilliant boy."

"Hello," Andrea said in a deep voice. Everything she said seemed sly and sarcastic.

"Hi," Tony said. He hated all his mother's friends on sight. Experience had taught him they were invariably flatterers.

"Do you remember Andrea?" Maureen asked.

"Of course he doesn't," she said. He looked at her closely. Her pageboy haircut and smooth skin had fooled him: though at first glance she looked ten years younger, the graying streaks and crow's-feet betrayed that she was his mother's age. "He was a baby."

"We lived through the dark ages together out here before you were born and—"

"He couldn't have been more than two or three," Andrea said to Maureen.

"My dear, that whole decade is a fog to me." She drank from her glass. "Everything is a fog. When I glance at the news and see Ronald Reagan, part of me thinks: 'Is he still working?' "

"No!" Andrea snapped. "He's just renting the White House to take naps."

"I bet it is a good place to nap," Maureen said. She patted the couch. "Jump in."

Tony smiled. "I practically have to."

"Kyoto!" Maureen yelled. "Bring a glass for my son!"

They sat while the sun went down, drinking and talking. Tony felt drunk after only a few glasses, but soon that passed, and it seemed no amount of alcohol could influence the languid sense that time was passing very slowly, if at all, in the mountainous couches. Food was never mentioned, although he had been invited to dinner. With the second bottle of wine, cheese and crackers appeared, but only Tony partook. Maureen and Andrea seemed content to merely drink and smoke. They had him talk about living and working with Garth—he made the obvious jokes about a star's egomania. "Oh, we actors are terrible!" his mother would comment periodically, more, Tony thought, to imply that she wasn't that way than to acknowledge that she was. Andrea, he found out, had been the wife of a blacklisted writer who died in the sixties from a heart attack ("from a condition Joe McCarthy gave him," Maureen said; "from booze and red meat," Andrea answered), and had turned to producing herself. "She's a great success," Maureen commented. "She did *The Last Dinosaurs*." Namely a TV movie about nuclear war ending all human life. "We sit and talk," Maureen went on. "Talk and sit. About the old days. Right?"

Andrea raised her glass, her mouth twisted in a smile of celebration and a frown of regret.

"Before we knew the world was full of bastards," Maureen concluded. There was a heavy pause. The moment of silence for all the wounded of the blacklist, Tony had long ago named it for himself. She looked at him coldly. "Like your father," she said.

"Maureen," Andrea said sadly, the way one might react to a hopelessly spoiled child: scolding having given way to a perfunctory acknowledgment.

"Don't count on him to help you out," Maureen went on. "If you agreed to go back to work on this script because you assume Daddy, being the big cheese at International, will give it a go, you're sadly mistaken."

"I don't count on him," Tony said, looking away from her: everything else seemed to blur, however, until he returned to focus on her face. I'm very drunk, he realized.

"Bullshit, you don't. You should have stuck to writing plays. Not let them get their filthy hands on your art."

"Now, now," Andrea interrupted. "The only people who haven't sold out are the ones who haven't been asked."

"That's not true! You didn't sell out," Maureen said.

"I had nothing to sell out," Andrea answered.

"What about you, Mom?" Tony said, unable to restrain his anger. "What the hell are you doing in *I Love Lucy II?*"

"That's not selling out, honey," Maureen answered, saying "honey" as though it was an obscene word. "That's staying employed."

"Well, that goes for me too, Mom. I haven't turned down Broadway —they turned me down."

"You didn't try very hard," she answered, looking lofty, though her consonants had become soft from drink. "You quit after three plays at the age of thirty."

"Let's go out for dinner," Andrea said casually.

"And now," Maureen concluded, closing her case, "you're counting on Daddy to hand success to you like a Christmas present."

Tony held his breath: he teetered on the edge of his rage, frightened by its limitless horizon.

"I'm sorry, darling," Maureen added, implying not apology but pride. "I can't stop myself from telling the truth. I have no tact. It's my curse. *And* my blessing."

"Fuck you, Mom," Tony answered. The sentence was complete, said with plenty of clarity and gusto, unhurried by fear, enunciated with conviction. "I'm sorry there's no McCarthy for me to blame my failures on. He's a convenient partner for you—I wish I had one." He felt quite triumphant with this construction of his retaliation. Glancing at Andrea to measure her shock, he saw instead a sympathetic face utterly unlike her look up till then.

Maureen blinked at him. The liquor seemed to have just hit her.

She put both hands down, steadying herself on the couch. "What the fuck does that mean?"

"You know damn well what it means." Tony thrust the words at her. She had hurt him all her life: he meant to give it back. But Andrea's sorrowful eyes worried him.

"I see," Maureen concluded. She tried to stand, but lost her balance halfway up and sagged back. "You think my career wouldn't have been any different."

"If you were so goddamn committed to your art, what the hell were you doing here in the first place? You came out here before the McCarthy—"

"I came out here because of your father!" Her great voice lost its resonance. She was squawking from her throat, like an ordinary person in pain, and her face was squeezed from repressed tears, unlike the graceful slow flow that she could release on cue for the final close-up.

"Oh come on," Andrea said, trying to be light, but almost yelling. "We all came out here for the weather—let's admit it."

"Even then he thought nothing of sacrificing anything for his career! You should have seen him, wooing me to do it!" She laughed—a mad stage laugh that almost dissolved into tears. "Said it would help me. Guaranteed stardom!" She had been speaking to the past, faces and voices long gone but still alive for her. She returned to Tony: "And now he's fooled you with the same lies. Maybe you're right, Tony. Maybe I would have cracked up anyway." She brushed her graying hair off one ear, a trademark maneuver from her TV show. "Lord knows I was always fragile. And maybe you're really *my* son: vain, facile, and in the end, weak. Too goddamned weak to ever really be anything but a mass of regrets." She struck him with her eyes, glittering with clever anger. "Yes. Maybe this is just the town for you. Probably you didn't give anything up. You never had it."

He felt hot. Around his throat and in his eyes there seemed to be a fire burning, the air superheated and unbreathable. He tried to fight the suffocation, to remember she was a frightened old woman, furious with ghosts, not him . . . but the room pulsed with fire, the scene from another world, its colors distorted, the faces inhuman. Who was he? A little boy? An old man? He felt his legs shrink. The couches were giants with long arms that entwined and mocked him to move. He could hear the voices from all those parties: "Look how handsome he is! He has your beautiful voice!" A famous writer, his old face unwrinkling with pleasure, saying: "You are a born writer, don't let them destroy you." The Japanese was in the room: had he bombed Pearl Harbor? He carried whiteness in his hand: a towel? Andrea was holding him: something spattered from his mouth—blood! He was spewing blood on his mother's glass table. Chunks of his intestines spilling out also, bobbing helplessly in the thin red river. I must be dying, he thought sadly. Well, all great artists die young, he told himself gently, and watched more of his heart and stomach vomit out. . . .

Hans Gott looked like his photo. "There is little of the arrogant Nazi left, after years of being hunted," David found himself writing mentally. The eyes glared at everything, as though each little evidence of life—a buzzing fly, the warm breeze rustling leaves—was an outrage. The world was disobedient, his face seemed to scold.

The arrangements had tortured them all. In the end there was simply no way to guarantee Gott that they weren't really Nazi-hunters or hadn't sold him out in one fashion or another; just as there was no long-distance way for him to prove definitively that he really *was* Gott. Finally, however, he must have wanted the money for the interview desperately, because after they met all of his precautions, driving to two different locations (presumably so he could watch them to see if they were followed), one a public park, the other a café, they were instructed (from a phone booth, just like in a movie thriller) that they could find him in the Hilton coffee shop. The voice on the telephone warned them that there were armed men hidden to deal with any surprises.

This was the first of the possibilities that arose for David to do the right thing. He could excuse himself abruptly (Chico would hardly risk blowing the interview by wasting time to argue that David must come along) and go up to his room rather than to the coffee shop. From there he could phone—what? the Israeli consulate? the local revenge group? the police? Gott, after all, had fled from Argentina fearful of extradition, and was in Brazil illegally. But David doubted any of those actions would succeed. Besides, he didn't want to miss seeing Gott. And there was the suspicion that it was all some sort of practical joke. That there would be no one in the last booth of the Hilton coffee shop.

But the old man was there. He looked very similar to the file photos of Gott at his glory: starving children to death, injecting dye into their eyes, cutting off limbs without anesthetic to see how long it would take to bleed to death, and on and on in a list of horrors that boggled the mind, not simply because they were so brutal, but because they were done by a man in power, not by a serial killer in a plastic American suburb, not by a gurgling homicidal psychopath, but by a distinguished figure in a society that enthusiastically sanctioned his actions. Gott didn't kill and torture from afar, phoning his orders for the millions to be gassed; he was there every day, hearing his victims' screams, watching their bodies be mangled, looking into their faces while picking and choosing death or agony. Yes, the old man looked like the black-and-white photos, only now the eyes seemed disgusted by the rude world—the black fire of arrogance was gone.

There were knives on the table. Not sharp, but David could plunge one in quite thoroughly. He was a frail old man, and David would have time to strike his chest over and over, looking into his eyes to tell him: "I am a Jew, monster. I am a Jew. And I have paid you for all my brothers."

He would be arrested. Or perhaps Gott's threat wasn't a bluff, and hidden supporters would appear, gunning David down, his body sagging, collapsing onto the knife handle only to drive it farther into the villain's chest. There would be death or jail, but he would have triumphed, willed himself through the moral cheesecloth, free of the stale smell and gauzy fog. One pure simple action, ending everything. The nights of guilt would not come: for once, he would never have to wonder what he *should* have done.

Chico began the questions that were intended to help amplify the bona fides *Newstime* had insisted on. It was a shock to hear Gott's German accent, his halting attempts to form grammatical sentences in English: he sounded a little bit like a Jewish immigrant. David couldn't take his eyes off Gott. He peered at each liver spot, noted the constant slight tremble in his right hand, observed the gnarled swollen look of his knuckles, and stared into those eyes—the enraged middle-class man furious at the world for its bad manners and sloppy plumbing. He saw no fear or regret in them. The exchange of money and identification material took place. Gott let go of his folder filled with various passports and other private papers reluctantly, but he took the envelope with the bank check eagerly. He glanced at it and then held his hand up in the air— the thumb up in a signal of victory.

A middle-aged man dressed in a drab summer raincoat appeared next to the table seconds later. Gott handed him the check. David felt scared. He swallowed hard and began to worry that this Gott was more than merely a hunted old man—that he could still do harm. "He will dispose of the check as we talk," Gott said while his associate walked away. "Until he returns I won't be reassured enough to discuss important matters."

Chico asked if he had had plastic surgery.

"I am myself," Gott said. David wrote it down: good quote for an ironic last line. He began to feel some of the excitement that Chico had been full of—this was going to be a knockout story. The entire journalistic world would envy him his seat at the coffee table. Later he would come down and take notes on the decor—the details of its mediocrity would contrast nicely. "No one glancing into the hotel coffee shop and seeing three gentlemen hunched over their coffee would suspect that one of the great criminals in . . ."

"I don't want to give details—dates and so on—of my recent movements," Gott said. "Is this man your secretary?" he asked, nodding at David as though he were mute and couldn't answer for himself.

"No," Chico answered. They were both nervous that Gott would find out David was Jewish. It had been decided not to introduce themselves beyond first names, to let Chico ask all the prepared questions (David was to come in only if he felt Chico had missed an opportunity), and not to explain their positions at the magazine. "Why have you decided to tell your story now?"

"To get rid of the lies about me and Mengele!" Gott's attempt to yell came out as a rasp of irritation. "They become more fantastic every day —the things they say we did. Ridiculous."

"I thought the accusations had been consistent," Chico said.

"Ah!" Gott said, waving his hand in disgust.

"In our files, we haven't come across anything new."

"The victors write history, my friend," Gott said. "Files can be altered. Made to look consistent. Everybody does it. It is so easy, when a man is silent, to say what you like about him. But there is no proof! Everything is exaggerated."

So it would be garbage, David thought, looking down, ashamed. His eyes fell on the partially serrated stainless-steel knife resting nude on the Formica table. Unable to question Gott at length, it was obvious they would be left with an interview that would consist of denials. Other than the pure sensation of having an interview with him, there would be no news in this story—nothing of real benefit to history. The fact of the event would be news, not what David contributed. I was there, he could say, and go on pompously about his feelings. The knife was there. In a moment it could be in the old man's heart. That would be real news. History. Justice. Fulfillment.

But the knife was flimsy—probably it would bend comically, or its dull tip would fail to penetrate, and if he plunged hard enough, it might rebound and take out Chico's eye.

He could decline to write the piece.

He could—

"Gott?" a woman's voice asked. David glanced up and saw Gott's small head turn to the side. Chico's large body, leaning forward to ask questions, had cut off David's view of her, but in her hand, emerging from a coat, he saw the long black nozzle of a gun.

"No," he heard the rasping voice say.

She spoke in the language of the holidays, softly, like his mother reciting a prayer while she lit Hanukkah candles.

And then the world ended. Something splashed on his face. The noise was ghastly, screeching at the world, filling it with sound. The Formica table was streaked with elegant lines of blood. Gott's head seemed to move on its own, trailing goo like a jet's tailstream, disappearing under the table's horizon.

Horror roared in David's brain—he leapt up, his thighs banging hard against the table. Crowds shouted at him, and in his brain he was screaming for mercy. Chico seemed stuck in place. David pulled himself up onto the booth. She stood at the edge of the table, sweet and demure, and pointed the gun down at the fallen old man, firing into his already lifeless body. She spoke again, screaming this time, in Hebrew.

"I'm a Jew!" David shouted, crying to her like a frightened baby. "Don't shoot me! I'm a Jew!"

Marion frowned at Fred. "What's bothering you?"

"I told you. I'm making these guys a fortune!" He paused to see if this astonishing fact registered. She stared back stupidly. "A fucking fortune! And Bart turns down offers without telling me, sets up my next book with Bob and I'm barely consulted—"

"Why did you sign the contract, then?" She shook her head. "I don't get it. You just got angry about this?"

"He doesn't think I can write a book without Bob," Fred said, admitting this to himself fully for the first time.

"Bart? Oh, come on."

"He doesn't. Because of the rewrite." Fred closed his mouth, kneading his lips in and out. He wanted to shut himself off, stop talking about it. He was rich. Soon he would be famous. Shut up already.

"Everybody makes changes for their editor. I'm sure Bart thinks Holder is useful because of the marketing. He's done a great job selling your novel—you have to give him that."

"Goddammit. Can't *you*, my wife, at least give me credit for writing a good book—"

"Fred!" Marion stood up. "I can't take this. You're not happy when you can't sell a book. You're not happy when you *do* sell a book. You're not happy when you can't write. You're not happy when you *can*. You're scared the book won't succeed. And now you're not happy when the book is a success? It's insane!"

Fred laughed. She was right. "You know me so well."

"That's right. And you're damn lucky to have me. 'Cause from now on no one's gonna tell you when you act like an idiot. You're too successful to criticize."

He carried her statement with him into the world, like a photo in his wallet, to remind him of home. Now when he went to Karl's poker game, he was greeted enthusiastically. Karl, Tom, and even Sam Wasserman (who had once threatened to leave the game if Fred continued to attend) all asked him to read their works in progress. They stopped the game to listen to his account of having lunch with the Book-of-the-Month Club people, they asked if he planned to adapt his novel to the screen, and hooted down his honest reaction—that he doubted he would be asked to.

He took out Marion's sentence and looked at it: they once despised me, he repeated over and over. Their performance of admiration and deference was so convincing, so seductive, that he found himself wondering: maybe when they read the book (he had had advance copies sent to them) they realized how wrong they were.

After the game, Sam Wasserman asked him if he wanted to share a cab since they were both going in the same direction. That had been true for the last two years, but Sam mentioned this geographical marvel as though it had only now occurred to him. Fred agreed and also accepted Sam's invitation to come upstairs for a drink. They tiptoed past the bedroom (Sam's second wife was asleep in there; his first now lived in Great Neck) into the study, where Sam poured cognac.

"Writers are so competitive," Sam commented, staring at his snifter.

"Yeah—the game gets pretty loud."

"No, I wasn't thinking of the game." Sam drained his glass in a quick motion. "I was thinking of Tom Lear. You have to watch out for him. He fights dirty in the clinches."

"Really? Tom's always been great to me. Very supportive of my book before anybody else." That was the closest Fred had come to chiding Sam for his earlier rejections.

Sam shook his head. "He's smooth. You should be careful what you say to him."

"Like what? You mean, ideas?"

"No, no. He's not a thief. Tom hates other people's success. I don't know why. We writers aren't in competition, right? I mean, it's not like batting averages—there's no such thing as somebody leading the league in writing. Just because *Anna Karenina* is a masterpiece, it doesn't mean we don't want to read *Crime and Punishment*."

"That's true," Fred said. It sounded all right, but it wasn't true nevertheless. No doubt Dostoevsky had been sick and tired of hearing about how great Tolstoy was: he probably compared how many full-page spreads he got in the *Moscow Times Book Review* and fumed if Raskolnikov came up shy of Anna's ad budget.

Sam nodded at Fred with great significance. "I don't know why Tom feels another writer's success has to be diminished for him to feel good about his work."

Fred felt a headache coming on. Sitting in the stuffy room playing cards had wearied him, and the cognac seemed to go to his head. The lamp lights glared harshly. "I . . . I don't see that in Tom. He's . . . I've never heard him put down another writer's work. I mean, he kids around with you—but that's to your face."

"He's not kidding." Sam stood up. "Do you want some more?"

"No thanks. I'd better be going." Fred felt uneasy, almost trapped.

Sam picked up the bottle on his desk and started pouring more into his snifter. "Maybe he isn't backbiting when he talks about your book. I just assumed he was lying."

This is bullshit, Fred told himself. Sam was an asshole, he'd known that from the moment he met him. He couldn't trust anything Sam might have to say about Tom—Sam was jealous of Tom's more glamorous reputation and was often stung by his wit. "Lying about what?" Fred asked, emphasizing "what" in a challenging and skeptical way.

Sam shrugged. "He talks as if Bob Holder wrote the book." He sucked on his teeth and went on casually: "Says he had you rewrite it almost page by page." Now he looked Fred straight in the eyes. "Told me you gave him the first hundred pages to read before you submitted them to Holder. He says not one word of those pages is now in the book."

Fred's confidence that these must be lies constricted: he *had* given his original hundred pages to Lear; they were completely different now. Sam could have known about the pages only from Tom. There had to be some truth to this story. In a moment, all of Tom's recent praise, social invitations, jokes about the careers of other writers—things he cherished, the one close friendship he had formed with a talented writer before success—they decayed in his heart, like the memory of an adulterous lover's kisses and protestations of love, mocking him for his gullibility. To be unloved was enough of a burden—to be made a fool of as well seemed unendurably cruel.

He cleared his throat after looking down, away from Sam's eyes. "I gotta go," he said.

"Don't let it bother ya," Sam said. "Being lied about is a measure of how successful you are. Tom wouldn't bother if he weren't jealous."

Fred got up and walked quickly to the door. He didn't want to embarrass himself further by showing how hurt he felt. He brushed past Sam, who got up, saying, "Don't tell him I—"

"He has nothing to be jealous of," Fred said in a gasp, an almost tearful gasp.

For a moment Sam looked into his eyes. He must have seen how effective his gossip had been—he looked away, ashamed. "Forget it," Sam said.

Patty told herself over and over that Paula Kramer wasn't going to call once it was past eleven o'clock. She tried to put out of her mind both the fantasy and the nightmare that assaulted her: Paula raving her novel into the surprise hit of the year while castigating Fred's book; Paula patronizing her novel as slight and unimportant and enthusiastically rewarding Fred for his honesty and clarity of vision. She played out an imaginary interview and found herself pretending that Paula would spring the fact of her affair with Gelb as a surprise. Even in this make-believe, Patty had no defense for her act of opportunism—incompetent and unsuccessful opportunism at that.

The worst of her imaginings was that Paula would never call, that reading her novel wouldn't cause a desire to interview her. Neglect seemed the most horrible of fates.

Patty tried to sleep, but the empty loft, dark, absorbing the passing guttural noise of trucks and off-key drunken songs, kept triggering new paranoid scenarios. She tried to remember what her novel was like: would it defuse the canon of criticism, or were there passages that might light Paula Kramer's fuse to fire devastating salvos?

She got up to get her copy, given to her by Betty last week. The light blue cover with its feminine, girlish title print—*Surburban Dreams*—had filled her with despair. While David oohed and aahed (unconvincingly), Patty had decided to put it away and forget it. Now she sat up in bed like an ordinary reader and opened it.

She felt the pride of authorship. There was real paper, real typeface, real words. She tried to put her mind away from itself, from its expectations and knowledge of the book. She hoped to be a stranger while she read. But she couldn't. She told herself (reading and laughing, reading

and being impressed) that her story was ordinary, her language merely
serviceable, but the truth was that, like a doting mother, the simplest
accomplishments of her child, the pure beauty of its very existence, were
thrilling. She was in love with her work, charmed by its wooing tone,
and moved by its tragedies. She could no more dislike or separate herself
from it than she could loath or divorce herself.

Patty read her whole novel straight through, enchanted, occasionally surprised by an awkward sentence, a transition made too abruptly, a
narrative moment whose dramatic force seemed diffused by timidity, but
generally impressed by her own intelligence, style, and imagination. She
was a good writer. The novel probably would have been published even
without Betty. Maybe another editor, a more influential editor, would
have pushed it harder, believed in its commercial possibilities more, and
have been more persuasive within the house.

When she finished, it was four in the morning. She felt exhilarated.
She felt strong. She was going to leave David. Stick to her resolve not to
resume her affair with Gelb, even if he did leave his wife. She'd get
herself an agent and sell her next novel to a stranger. She held her slim
volume in her hands like a prayer book and told herself: I am going to
rely on this. I'm a writer. That will make sense of my life.

She went to the closets and began to pack clothes that she would
need immediately: she didn't have enough suitcases of her own for everything. She tried to think of an alternative to staying with Betty while she
searched for a place to live. Other than going home to Philadelphia,
there wasn't one.

She had a favorite black cashmere turtleneck that she couldn't find
in her drawers, so she resorted to opening David's drawers. In the bottom
one, underneath some of his sweaters, she found a pile of pornographic
magazines.

She stared at them uncomprehendingly for a moment. She closed
the drawer at first, staring at it angrily. She laughed at herself. "What a
prude," she said out loud, and then reopened it. It was then that she
noticed the top cover: it was an S/M magazine. She took out the pile and
went through all of them; without exception, they were leather and whips
—fierce women and penitent men.

There was a noise from the street. She guiltily dropped the magazines and looked at the door until she realized the sound's origin. She
was scared. Maybe there was an innocent explanation—research for a
story, and he was embarrassed to have . . . But that was hopeless. Was
this what he wanted? To be tied up and whipped until there were red
stripes on his ass? Did that explain the collapse of their sex life? She felt

like a fool. She thought she understood David so well, had blamed herself for the poverty of their romantic life, charging it to her affair. She called herself a novelist and yet she had lived with a man for almost two years and didn't know what was going on in his head.

Impassioned and angry, she went through all the drawers. She found a studded leather collar and a Polaroid photograph of a red-haired woman in a complete outfit, brandishing a riding crop. She didn't understand exactly what that meant, but she knew it implied some sort of contact. He had obviously gone beyond masturbatory fantasies.

Was he having an affair with some bizarre sadistic woman? The images that flooded her mind were appalling, humiliating. The thought of him coming home to bed from some hole in the wall where he had let a pervert whip him was sickening.

She finished packing, not bothering now whether she had enough things. She wanted to get out. She made sure she had her copy of her manuscript and book. She waited until it was seven o'clock in the morning before phoning Betty. She still woke her up.

"I'm coming over right away."

"Okay," said a sleepy voice. "Are you all right?"

"I'll be over right away." She hung up and looked at the magazines, the collar, the Polaroid lying on the coffee table where she had examined them.

Sooner or later she'd have to tell him. She'd rather do it without having to see his face.

She picked up her suitcase and walked out. She left them behind, exposed grotesque fossils of their now extinct relationship. That would suffice as her Dear John letter.

CHAPTER 17

After Tony had been cleaned up, Andrea Warren drove him back to Malibu in her car. He could remember only a few blurry moments of the drive, his face buried in the soft upholstery of the Mercedes. He woke up when he felt stillness: he saw Andrea's small body at the door to Garth's house, talking to two figures, who peered out at him. They came toward him eventually—he tried to get himself up, but his body had a mule's stubbornness, moving only when forced to.

"Hey, man," Garth's face said to him. He felt arms reaching under him.

Helen, looking beautiful, her eyes sympathetic, her long hair falling on tanned shoulders like an innocent Tahitian girl's, smiled sweetly: "We'll get you to bed."

They put his arms around their shoulders and became his crutches. Andrea held the wooden gate open. Tony's head flopped from side to side, a helpless newborn. He rested on Helen's shoulder and found himself looking straight down her nightshirt at those remarkable breasts, full and long, big nipples, standing with languid elegance, erect, but not arrogant. He kissed the top of her chest, his lips smacking. "God, they're beautiful!" he shouted.

She laughed. A deep, throaty, amused noise, unselfconscious and welcoming. He heard Garth say: "He'll be fine," to someone, and then time skipped, a needle dancing across the record surface, making nonsense of the music.

Without Tony knowing how, he was in a bedroom. Garth stood a few feet away, naked except for bright blue underpants.

There was hot liquid in him. He forced his eyes open and saw a large mug at his lips, a light green pool lapping at his mouth, its gentle tide infiltrating, warming him, his head clearing. He heard the pleased chuckle again.

"He's turning me on," a voice at his side said.

"I don't mind, if you don't," Garth answered, squinting with concentration.

Like a picture coming into focus, he could now see. His eyes must have been closed before. He was lying in their bed, naked. His right thumb was rubbing Helen's nipple, while his palm caressed its underside. But she wasn't looking at that, her eyes were on his genitals. Tony glanced down and saw he had an erection, so complete in its yearning that it arched above his belly, a missile angling for launch. She was holding a mug of tea to his mouth.

"I thought booze made you boys impotent," she commented pleasantly to her husband. They spoke as if he weren't conscious.

"He's young," Garth said with his patented ironic smile, almost a sneer, one corner of his mouth furrowing. Tony closed his eyes again. "And horny. It's been two months. Told you we should have gotten him a girl."

"Shouldn't we let him sleep?" she asked in a halfhearted tone.

"This'll deal with tomorrow's hangover."

"I'm not out," Tony heard himself say. He wanted to shut up, continue pretending unconsciousness, but he was still too drunk to dissemble. He spoke the words together, all soft vowel sounds.

"What?" Helen asked, moving the cup away.

Tony opened his eyes. At first he couldn't focus on anything. "I'm awake!" he shouted, so his words would be clear. He stared at her, seeing that she was also nude. He told himself to let go of her breast, but his hand held on. Looking into her eyes, he forgot everything else. They were all that existed in the universe. Again, he wasn't sure who he was —he felt very young, lying in bed with a beautiful motherly woman smiling lovingly at him. "I'm only pretending to be drunk!" he yelled again, slurring his words so badly that "drunk" came out "drugged."

He heard Garth laugh. "It's a very good performance," he said.

"I'm sorry," Tony said in his direction, but when he swung his head that way, he felt his stomach swish and slosh sickeningly, a bag full of water precariously connecting his torso to his legs. He groaned.

"Easy," she said, and he felt her arms, very warm, come around him. He closed his eyes. Her breasts pressed against his tired, tired face. Her heat swelled over him, a mother bear protecting her cold child.

"I'm asleep," he mumbled and let go of the world.

The rest is silence, David Bergman repeated to himself, hearing Richard Burton's long hiss of sorrow from his high-school drama-class days, the sour-faced teacher standing rapturously beside the big box of a turntable. David moved through the nightmare with a still mind, becalmed of anxiety. The rest is silence, a dead actor's voice told him.

Chico had taken it hard. He shouted and pleaded with the Brazilian police, switching from nervous pleas for understanding to arrogant demands for freedom from questioning. He had made a brief feint at pretending they didn't know who the dead man was—but he soon gave that up and began shouting for the right to communicate with *Newstime*. Not only to have this story explode in their face but also to be scooped on it was the cause of Chico's agony.

He hasn't realized yet, David coolly observed, that our careers are over. Neither of them would ever be Groucho.

After twelve hours they were freed and permitted to leave the country, *Newstime* having agreed to release and in fact surrendering all the information they had on Gott. In a brief phone conversation with Rounder, Chico had been told that *Newstime* was making a completely open response to the event.

On the flight home, they had in hand the first burst of world news coverage. The pertinent embarrassment, that *Newstime* had been in the process of paying Hans Gott for his story, was mentioned only in passing —David knew it would take until the second editions for the criticisms to begin. The simple facts were that his killer, Tamar Gurion, arrested at the scene peacefully, was the descendant of a Jewish family—most of whom, she claimed, had been victimized in the camps by Mengele and Gott. Whether the dead man was in fact Gott was still in question, and it was this problem that obsessed Chico throughout the flight.

"I think we owe it to Mrs. Thorn to make no comment until we've talked it out with her and Richard," Chico said, knowing they would be mobbed by reporters at the airport. David noticed Chico was now calling Rounder by his first name—usually he contemptuously referred to him as Rounder, sometimes as Round Robin.

"I thought he said we should be open," David said. "Doesn't that mean answering all questions?"

"We have to talk it all out and then hold a news conference. We're going to be making appearances anyway."

"Appearances?"

"*Nightline*, the *Today Show*, they're all gonna talk to us—but you have to do your piece on the killing first."

David stared off. So he would have to preside over this indignity. Report his own stupidity, cowardice, and avarice as though they were merely the virtues of being an innocent bystander. What platitudes would he have to invent about the young woman, whose eyes seemed so calm and happy as she killed? Predictably, he would have to take the attitude she wasn't a hero or a villain, but tragically, another victim. He thought of her, alone now, in a jail filled with . . . what? Were they monsters too? Would she be electrocuted, guillotined, poisoned, hanged, shot? I guess the guards won't rape or beat her since she'll have to be shown to the cameras a lot, he tried to console himself. He prayed that the malicious old man really was Gott. If she had destroyed herself over a fake—the ultimate non-news story—the tone he would have to adopt in the piece . . . His stomach churned at the thought. He looked at Chico, talking feverishly, a dead man not knowing the killing blow had been struck, a megalomaniacal chicken missing his swelled head, and wished he could choke him. Stuff all the bullshit back down into his throat and out the right end. The rest is silence, he said to himself in bitter silence.

When they landed he realized the isolation on the plane with Chico was a blessing compared to the invasion of his brothers at the airport. The Minicams, the microphones, the notebooks rustling like autumn leaves, the pasty eager faces made bodiless by their equipment, swelled in their way, flowing with their attempt to escape the airport, a moving aggressive pack of animals unconscious of everything but the pursuit of their prey. The lights they cast followed their every step—David noticed other passengers watching the spectacle with confused expressions on their faces. Who are they? he could almost read their lips. You'll know soon, David thought to himself. He was going to make every network, every paper, every wire service, both national newsmagazines. He could see the camera photos, read the captions, hear the laughter at *Weekly*, and write their stories with just the right touch of sardonic disparagement. Two of the big boys had fucked up, rushed off half-cocked into a dubious arrangement, and were now at least responsible for the ruination of a young woman, and possibly for the death of an innocent con man.

David stared at them. He felt no panic at the press of their bodies and the thrusts of their questions. I know who you are, he thought to himself, cold passing throughout his system, numbing fear or embarrassment. Chico, however, was bursting with energetic terror: "Sorry, no comment. We'll have a news conference as soon as possible. Nothing to add." He tried desperately to behave grandly, confidently, but surely the scene must have brought it home:

Their careers were over. They'd crapped in their pants, and Mrs. Thorn wasn't going to admit she had toilet-trained them badly. They wouldn't be fired. But all the rungs of the ladder above them were being sawed off now—and eventually, when enough time had passed, they would be "promoted" to some special project away from the weekly magazine, to the book division, to work on new magazines, something on another floor, away from the barrel so their rot wouldn't spread.

"Come on, fellas, give us a break," some print reporter shouted. "We're newsies—give us a crumb. Was it Gott?"

"Everything on that point, all the information we have, has already been given to you," Chico said, sweating and speaking nervously, so that this truth sounded like a desperate lie. Every time he responded at all, as though his answers were the cries of a desperate animal, the pack drew closer, baring their teeth, tasting the meal they would soon have.

"Mr. Bergman? You're Jewish, aren't you?" Janet Halston from CBS shouted above the rest as they reached the doors to the street. It was the first question directed only to him. "How did you feel," she continued, knowing the answer to her previous question, "sitting across from one of the most heinous Nazis?"

As though a high-pitched whistle had been blown that only the dogs of the press could hear, the pack paused, their lights, their eyes, their pens focused on David.

All he could think of was the anchorman's expression, neutral, superior, after this clip of his answer would be shown.

"Did you tell Tamar Gurion of the meeting ahead of time?" someone called out.

"Oh, please!" Chico said, and tried to push them through.

But Janet Halston, holding her mike casually, her cool blond hair unruffled in this crush, clung to David, asking her question in a tone of gentle insinuation, as though they were lovers confessing sins. "Did you feel sympathy for the killer's action?"

David turned away from her—he didn't want her to get a usable clip —and addressed the print reporter. "I had never met or known of Tamar Gurion until she appeared in the coffee shop. I did not tell her."

"No more!" Chico shouted into the shouts. David smiled to himself at the panicked tones coming from Janet Halston. She couldn't use his answer. She had thought she'd get something. Chico pulled him through the doors. A limo, waiting to take them to *Newstime* to meet with Mrs. Thorn and Rounder, was there for them to dive into. David turned back and caught Janet's frantic eye—she was shouting her provocative questions at him. He winked at her while he closed the dark limousine window electronically. Fuck you, honey, he whispered. Fuck you.

Tony heard the insistent surf and felt the bobbing movement of the water. He was sleek and young, a boy lying happily on the shore, stroked with love. There were bodies beside him whom he could trust. The agony was over, the poison out of his system. I'm not hung-over, was the first clear thought.

My prick is in someone's hand, was his second.

Tony opened his eyes to see a gray light. The soft surface was bedding, not sand. The crash of the water came from outside, the bobbing was Bill Garth fucking his wife right next to Tony.

The actor moved slowly on top of his woman, sleepily, in a steady rhythm, his eyes closed, his forehead butting gently against a pillow. Helen's arms were around him, kneading his broad muscled back. One of Garth's hands was holding Tony's erection, his fingers lightly closing on the tip, flower petals closing and blossoming.

Tony closed his eyes. The lids felt rough, a harsh curtain closing. The back of his skull opened like a trapdoor and he felt he was falling into unconsciousness. Helen groaned softly. Garth's hand felt feminine, gentle, soothing. Their motion on the bed quickened. The hand clutched him. He opened his eyes, the world coming into place wobbly, a table in danger of collapse. But I could stop this, he argued to himself. What's the proper etiquette? I need you to make my picture, but get your hand off my penis.

"Ah," Garth said as he climaxed, like a runner taking a first sip of liquid after exercise. He moved off Helen and noticed Tony. "Hello," he said casually. Helen, her face soft from sleep, her body glistening with her husband's sweat, turned in his direction.

She smiled. "How are you feeling?"

"He's still hard," Garth reported, and squeezed tightly before letting go, a handshake of farewell. "That was fun," he said.

"Don't get used to it," Helen teased. They behaved like a cute television couple about the situation, as though they were involved in this week's harmless prank.

Garth got up. Helen turned on her side, revealing her spectacular figure, and put a hand on Tony's chest, lovingly, patting him. Tony was hypnotized by her body, entranced by his intimate proximity. "We're willing to have your mother killed if you want," she said.

"Damn right," Garth said, putting a robe on. "I'm gonna make Tony some more herb tea." He shuffled out, humming.

"You're lucky to be alive. That woman who brought you home could barely stand." She glanced down at his penis. Then she smiled. "Does your mother often get you drunk and then tell you you have no talent?"

"I told you about it?" Tony's voice croaked. He felt childlike, but his voice was an old man's. He looked at her with awe, flabbergasted by the perfection of her tall, full, but fatless olive-skinned body.

"You talked constantly. Even while you were passing out, you went out mumbling. It was kinda sad and wonderful at the same time." She took his hand and kissed it. "Poor baby."

Garth's voice boomed from the doorway. "You want anything?"

She turned her head to answer. Her long hair streamed like a waterfall over her shoulders. "Coffee." Tony felt her take hold of his penis, offering it to the air, pleading its case, showing an object for consideration. "Can't I do something about this?" she asked her husband.

Tony looked to Garth for an answer with mild curiosity, as though he himself were merely a spectator watching an interesting drama unfold. The sexual ache of his genitals seemed divorced from his consciousness, but he was also enslaved to the desire for her, unable to resist its needs, no matter how bizarre or disgusting the circumstance. The question seemed pertinent: shouldn't somebody do something about loving him?

"I don't know," Garth said, a hand running through the hair over his right temple. "That really kind of freaks me out. I'm pretty possessive about you." He frowned. "Do what?"

My God, Tony thought, it's a negotiation. His brain recoiled further from them and his circumstance while her hand—warm and casual, tentatively considering the value of his passion, a tempted shopper afraid the cost might be too high—made protest impossible. He not only wanted her, he wanted Garth's permission. He had slept in their bed, breaking the barrier of house servant, but that had been pity—or perversion. This might be more, a kind of acceptance into the family, an embrace of both his being and his talent. Surely Garth's agreement would be forthcoming only if Tony belonged, not only in their hearts but also in their world.

Helen turned to Tony, her long hair brushing his shoulder. He shivered. Her hand rested on the base of his penis, the fingers curling around his testicles. "What would you like?" she asked.

The question made him want to laugh, but looking into her eyes didn't. No matter how decadent, foolish, and phony the situation totaled in Tony's intellectual inventory, her soulful eyes elevated the query into a spiritual one. "I want to be loved," he said, meaning it utterly.

"We love you," she answered matter-of-factly.

"Not a blow-job," Garth commented. He moved toward the bed. "I couldn't handle that."

"I want to kiss him," she said, still searching Tony's eyes sorrowfully.

"That's okay," Garth conceded.

She came at him, her lips parting slightly. They looked pale and puffy from sleep. She closed on his mouth, her free hand caressing his cheek, stroking it. Tony put a hand on her breast and withdrew as though burned, thinking: I don't have permission. She moaned (to show approval, he thought) and pressed herself against him to resume contact. He closed his eyes and almost swooned from the heat, the relief of being touched, and the magic of her kiss: her lips accepting him, her tongue liquid and quivering.

When she withdrew after a few moments, he felt crushed, abandoned. He heard a high-pitched whistle, and until he opened his eyes, he didn't recognize it as a teakettle boiling. Helen had turned her head to speak to Garth: "Why don't you make the tea and wait? It won't take long."

Garth stood up against the bed, looming over them. "Oh, no," he said firmly. "Whatever happens, I want to see." He looked at Helen as though answering a criticism: "Not as a voyeur."

"I understand," she said so earnestly that it somehow sounded plausible.

"What do you feel comfortable doing?" Garth asked her.

Helen looked into Tony's eyes, a compensating angel. She kissed him lightly on the lips and said, "Inside me."

Garth moved so he had a clear view of Tony. "I don't know," he said. "Do you think you could masturbate?" he asked Tony almost apologetically.

Helen twisted irritably. "Billy! He doesn't need me for that." Tony noticed a small beauty mark on her long neck. Her body was so warm on the side where they touched that the rest of him felt chilled. The happiness he felt at having this beauty lie beside him made the bizarre discussion seem dreamlike—unimportant and silly nonsense. He didn't feel frustrated, he liked this passive pleasure. She softened to add to her husband: "That isn't lovemaking."

Garth nodded. "You could do it for him," he argued happily, as though a lucky notion had just flown in. "You know, he could be touching you . . ." Garth paused, holding a palm out to Tony, selling the idea. "Anything but her . . ." He lowered his head. "Not her vagina." Embarrassment seemed to overwhelm him. "I wish you'd say what *you* want, Tony," he snapped.

"You didn't ask what he wanted during the night," Helen said angrily. "You didn't bother asking whether he wanted to be touched."

"Hey!" Garth protested in an injured voice, a kid whose secrets had been betrayed by his best friend.

Tony felt his throat contract. He had assumed Garth's morning handshake had been his only imposition; the dark confused memories of the night might have curtained a hundred violations. "What did you do?" Tony cried out. He tried to sit up, but his skull seemed loaded with pronged weights that stabbed and dragged him down.

"Oh . . ." Helen embraced him awkwardly.

"You see!" Garth whined. "You've made it sound . . ."

She kissed Tony's cheek, whispering, "He only played with it—he wanted to see how long you could . . ." She bowed her head. "I'm sorry."

Something was in the voice, cracking through the perfect appearance of kindness, something calculated and mean. This was a performance, Tony sensed, a plan she had. It wasn't Garth manipulating this event, using his vulnerability and her sweetness. She was after something.

Helen raised her head. There were tears forming in her eyes. "You were so much in need. So badly wounded. We liked making you feel good—"

"Oh, don't bullshit him. I wanted to know what another man's prick felt like," Garth said. He turned and walked away. "Do what you want," he added, leaving.

Tony stared at her. He was confused. His head hurt now and his penis felt sore, unsatisfied, almost angry. He couldn't think it through, see past her outward gentleness. Most of Helen's body was on him now, and that pleasure took over. The sudden feeling that he was in power, controlling this Prince and Princess of Hollywood, sobered him. He could taste the sour bitterness of last night's wine and ugly insults. "Fuck me," he said.

She nodded, abashed.

Tony moved his pelvis against the side of her belly. "Put me in," he said.

There were no newspeople in front of *Newstime*. On the Marx Brothers' floor, things seemed quiet at first, but as they approached Animal Crackers, the noise began. Five writers were seated in the waiting area. They all gawked at Chico and David as if they didn't know them. At the sight of them, Chico's secretary pointed to Rounder's office. "They're waiting in there." She nervously continued to David, "Patty Lane has called many times. She's not at your home number."

David turned to Chico, who had paused in mid-step. "I haven't been able to get a hold of her—"

"Okay, use my office. But just a few minutes."

David took the number from the secretary and walked into Chico's office, picking up the phone. The number looked familiar, but he couldn't place it. Betty Winters answered the phone. "David? Are you all right?"

"I'm fine."

"I'll put Patty right on."

There was hardly a pause. "David?"

"Hi," he said, his voice drained of life. "I'm okay. I just wanted you to know I—"

"Have you been to the loft?"

"No, we came straight—"

"Oh . . ." she said in an interrupting tone, but nothing further came out.

"What is it? Something wrong?"

"I left," she said, and then sighed. "I found the things—I couldn't stay. Probably wouldn't have . . ." She ran out of energy to speak. "I'm sorry," she whispered. "It's bad . . ." She laughed, almost hysterically. "I guess it's bad timing, but there's no point in lying about it."

"Things?" He had been standing, anticipating a quick conversation, eager to obey and appear before the tribunal next door. Now he sat down in Chico's chair. When his automatic reaction to bow before the power structure flicked a warning light on, he coolly reminded himself he was through anyway. There was a kind of relief in that: lonely and flat though his landscape had become, at least there were no more cliffs to fall off. "I don't know what the hell you're talking about."

"Hang on for a second," she said nervously. He heard Patty speak in a muffled voice to Betty. "Hi," her voice came back loudly. "I asked Betty to leave."

"Are you staying there?"

"Yes. Look, I would have left anyway. Probably it was my fault too. I just didn't want you to come home after"—again her energy depleted into a sigh—"and find them."

"Patty, I'm tired. I don't know what the hell you're talking about."

"The magazines," she intoned dramatically. He heard her catch her breath as though she had frightened herself.

He shut his eyes hard, hoping to visualize what she meant. All he could see was the black covers on the airline magazines. The *Newstime* logo. And then he realized. "Oh . . ." escaped him into the phone.

"And the other things. I got nasty and left them out for you to find." She began to cry. "I'm sorry, I don't know why I'm crying—"

"You can't leave me because of that," he begged. He felt short of breath, and bent over, covering the mouthpiece with his free hand, feeling as though he could hold her through the electronic line. "If that's all it is—I can explain—I got obsessed with it. I can stop. Please, not over that. That's not me, Patty," he said, and found himself weeping. "It's really not who I am," he blubbered.

The Power Phone whooshed into the room. Chico barking: "David! Come in here!"

He looked up furiously at The Phone and saw that he had left the office door open. In the reception area one of the writers, Kyle Stebbins, a young star writer in the Nation section, was seated in line with the open door. He was looking down at some copy, but David knew he had been watching. Watching him plead and weep on the phone.

The Power Phone filled the room with sound: "David! Are you there?"

Patty's voice, pitying, timid, spoke into his ear: "You have to go? Why don't you call me when your meeting is over?"

The Power Phone honked: "David!"

"I'm coming!" David shouted, so angrily that Kyle Stebbins couldn't help but look up. "What the fuck are you looking at?" David shouted at him. He brushed his wet cheeks with his hands. Kyle stared for a moment and then hopped to his feet, startled, and dashed out of sight. "Why did you do it, Patty?" He spoke into the phone, dabbing at his eyes, knocking his glasses askew with his sleeves. "It was stupid and nasty."

"I know. I'm sorry, but it shocked me—"

"I'm sick and tired of what shocks people!" David yelled. "The whole fucking world is sick, Patty. Pretending it isn't doesn't make it the sweet sensitive world that you want. I'm glad you found it. Yeah, I had a better time paying for my ass to be whipped than I ever did with you!"

He slammed the phone down. His chest was heaving with despair and rage. He pushed his hands underneath his glasses and rubbed. "Fuck it," he said aloud, knowing that nothing could conceal his red eyes. He walked into the reception area—Kyle Stebbins was practically hiding behind a plant—and walked into Rounder's office.

All the Marx Brothers were there, the president, its two top lawyers, and Mrs. Thorn. Chico paused and said, "Ah! I got worried. I was telling them about Janet Halston's outrageous question at the airport."

The president, Mark Logan, spoke quietly: "Between the Jews who are outraged we are willing to pay Gott, and the people who believe we are responsible, in one way or another, for his assassination, we've got nowhere to hide."

"Hide from what?" Chico said. He actually believes we're all right, David thought, astounded,. "Surely we don't have to defend agreeing to pay for a story to CBS, or to New York *Times*, or anybody else. They've all done it."

"Not a Nazi criminal," Mrs Thorn mumbled. The bitch, David said to himself. She approved this goddamn thing.

"What about Speer?" Chico pleaded.

"He was an architect, not a torturer," the more senior of the lawyers observed with a dry smile. "Incidentally," he said to David, "I assume you didn't know her or tell her."

"No," David said. His voice was hoarse. Mrs. Thorn seemed to notice him for the first time. She squinted skeptically in his direction, almost as though she were wondering how someone like that could possibly be in her employ.

"The only approach to this is that we have a terrific story," Chico pronounced with great confidence. "An exclusive eyewitness account of Gott's death."

"We'll sell out," Rounder said, nodding.

"But at what price?" Mrs. Thorn asked dramatically. "How long will it be before we're thought of as responsible journalists again?"

"But we weren't irresponsible . . ." Chico mumbled.

"That's not the perception in Washington," Mrs. Thorn said. The mention of Washington was always used to close any disagreement.

There was a silence. At least four of the men in the room knew their careers at *Newstime* were over: that the mark of this event would be there on their foreheads for any of the initiated to see—a lifetime of snickering behind the back. David looked down at the gray industrial carpeting, worn by the nightly vacuuming. He heard Patty's pitying voice. It was then that he decided. His landsape had now flattened even more—squashed horribly. But there would be no more precarious wanderings. No more decisions. No more shame.

Garth returned and watched anyway. He stood in the door, his arms folded, his face expressionless, and stared with dull eyes while Helen, sitting astride Tony's genitals, bobbed like a rocking horse on his prick. Tony ran his hands roughly up and down her breasts, her belly, gathering the top rim of her pubic hair and tugging slightly, pulling on a nipple, watching it distend before he released it. He ignored Garth and stared angrily at her face. She averted her eyes or closed them most of the time. Neither of them felt much passion, although Tony enjoyed it immensely. Toward the end, the swelling heat of his lower body, drenched and pulled by her motion, overwhelmed his rage. He climaxed painfully, groaning as though he were a man passing a kidney stone, not consummating passion.

He closed his eyes to avoid dealing with them. She got up. He lay there, his arms resting on his chest, a dead man displayed in a coffin. His eyes burned, his head felt huge, exhausted, unbalanced. He woke briefly when he felt blankets covering him, and caught a glance of her, dressed, tucking him in.

And then there was sleep. Sleep accompanied by loud, colorful dramas; cavernous rooms, echoing theaters, brilliant parties, looming faces pleading, shouting, mocking, praising—his life came together in a grand one-acter, a cast of thousands, all mixed up, childhood friends arguing with adult enemies, characters from Chekhov and Shakespeare bantering, Ralph Kramdon fighting to the death with Laertes, Maureen accepting a Tony, his father telling him in an airport coffee shop that he was going to remarry.

The brilliant light of California roused him from time to time, flowing through the skylights, the slanted windows buffeted by the sonic thunder of the surf. He closed his eyes each time, clutching the dreams like a woman he loved, returning to the wonderful stew everything he had experienced became, nourishing his scattered consciousness. He said things he had always wanted to, he remembered his triumphs, his youthful, exquisite talent blossoming, knowing how it should be done, seeing it happen, and hearing the happy welcome of the audience, laughing with him, crying with him, a mass orgy of shared fears and hopes.

Garth, all tentativeness gone, woke him finally with the news that it was one o'clock in the afternoon, and offering a cup of coffee. He sat on the bed and watched Tony sip it, neither of them speaking.

"We can finish today," Garth said at last.

"Oh, we'll never be finished," Tony said. Hangovers must be good for me, he thought to himself. He felt totally in command.

Garth looked surprised. "Why not?"

"Come on, Bill. You people never finish. Even when you make the movie, you're not finished. Only art forms can be finished—a can of tomatoes is forever being repackaged."

Garth looked hard. Those chiseled cheeks froze, a statuary bust placed on a mountain, fiercely American. "If you believe that, you shouldn't be writing movies."

Tony nodded agreeably. "You're probably right."

"You know I get pretty sick of you New Yorkers. With your snobbery and your bullshit. You're willing to take the money, you do sloppy work, and then you complain *we're* only interested in money."

Tony smiled. "You're right. You're absolutely right."

Garth frowned at him. He wanted to fight.

Tony spoke casually. "Who are you going to get to rewrite it?"

"What?"

"Who are you going to bring in to rewrite my draft? I suggest you go for a good dramatic writer. The script's structure is okay now and I've got you a couple of cute funny scenes, but you need somebody . . . oh, just a trifle pompous, not in a bad way, to really do the heavy stuff." Tony sipped his coffee, studying the baffled look on Garth's face. It was wonderful, silly and wacky, just like his dreams. "You know what I mean," he argued. "Scenes with very few words, shot darkly, a lot of glistening tears. Meryl'll play it then. You guys'll walk off with dual Academy Awards."

"What the *fuck* do you think you're playing? A game? You think because I let you fuck her, I'll take this crap?" Garth's real anger wasn't very different from his screen fury. His face seemed to widen with internal explosive force, his lips disappeared while he clipped his words.

Tony smiled. He had an idea for the next moment in the scene. He thought it would really play nicely. He sat up more, put the coffee down, and picked up the bedside telephone. He dialed the general number for International. "Hello," he said to the operator. "Mr. Winters please."

"Oh, for Chrissakes." Garth got up nervously, his face scared, and made as though to leave, but predictably (Mike Nichols wouldn't have permitted such an obvious bit of blocking) he stopped at the door when Tony told his father's secretary, "Hi, this is Tony Winters. . . . Hi, how are you? . . . No, you're right, I have been remiss. In fact, I wanna correct that. Could you tell my father I'm going to come by—Oh, I'm in Malibu, it might take me an hour or so to get it together." Garth shook his head over and over with disgust. "Well, if he's not back from lunch by then, I'll just wait, okay? . . . Great, thanks."

Garth didn't turn to face him. He put a hand on the tall window and hunched over as though bowing to the endless expanse of the Pacific. "What the fuck do you think you're doing, Tony?"

"Nothing," Tony said, pulling the covers aside. He put his feet on the ground gently, testing the floorboards as though they might give way. "I haven't had a good talk with my dad"—he stood up and smiled—"dear old Pops, in years."

Garth pushed himself off the window, wheeling gracefully, a dancer pirouetting. The nervous look was gone. "We've still got the last scene to write."

Tony laughed—it sounded shaky. "We," he mumbled.

"Yeah," Garth answered pugnaciously. "We."

"After I talk to my dad," Tony responded.

"You're a big boy, Tony," Garth warned, readying for his exit line. "Check your arithmetic. Don't add this up wrong." He fixed Tony with a glance for a beat, and then moved out of the room confidently.

Left alone, Tony was uncertain, feeling woozy and confused. He had had nothing particular in mind when he phoned his father's office. He had done it as a prank, to throw Garth. But now it seemed like a good excuse to confront his father, to ask him the questions that he had spent a lifetime . . . avoiding? No. Asking himself. It was time to find someone with answers, not simply more questions.

In the end, Mrs. Thorn pretended they all still had their heads firmly attached to their necks. David was told to write his account immediately. He casually asked to be allowed to return home to change. Permission was granted, but they wanted him back within an hour or so, and expected a version by morning.

It was midnight when he walked out of the *Newstime* building for the last time. The radio cab was waiting. He took his carry-on luggage into the back seat and leaned on it while they drove down Fifth Avenue. He half-expected the city to look different, since he and his life had been so completely changed by the last two days. He wanted something in the architecture of New York to reflect the altered inner landscape of his mind. But, he realized, what made the town so majestic was its indifference. They passed a laughing couple on a corner, the sounds of their joy swallowed by the building's hollows. A rag-covered woman moved, head bowed, under the public library's lions—an ant crawling up an impossible stairway, liable to be stepped on by the giants who surely must inhabit such a building. Everywhere the stacks of lighted boxes suggested countless lives, at rest or restless, unaware of their insignificance.

Once he had looked at the city as a sight to conquer. He rode home from the magazine feeling the power and influence that surrounded him, certain his fate would be to move these people, to tell them what to think, what to do. Behind the mask of objectivity had lurked the even darker face of power. What a silly youthful dream. It could never have happened, it hadn't been a dream that was coming true—he was simply another doll living in these endless rows of dollhouses. Toys for giants he neither knew nor understood.

He wondered how long it would be before Patty would tell about the things she had found. At first she'd swear to keep it to herself—probably to spare herself the embarrassment. But when she got another lover, that fear would dissipate, and it would join the repertoire, another story of another crazy lover from her past. She'd use it, if not in her next novel, then in the one after.

And she didn't even know how often he had indulged his fantasy, how many times he had bared himself to the Mistress and been stripped of his false dignities, admitted his depraved longings. He loved it. Giving up all the pretenses—the relief of openly being a slave, licking to please, whimpering honestly at the whip, begging to have his silly sex stroked, granted pleasure only when thoroughly exposed as abject and humiliated. He had paid for every session—the arrangement was merely business for the Mistress—but it was leaving her, not Patty, not the magazine, that he regretted.

He arrived at the loft. The leather collar, the magazines, and the Polaroid were there on the coffee table, just as she had told him. He'd have to dispose of them, and the telephone number in his book, before finishing. He didn't want anything for Patty to cite as evidence. Throwing them in the garbage wouldn't suffice: he burned the photo and the magazines and went downstairs to the cold garbage room, putting the leather collar at the bottom of one of the bags.

Back upstairs, his phone was ringing. He glanced at the clock. He had been gone for forty minutes, not really long enough for Chico to become anxious. It was probably Patty, desperate to restore her self-respect, not wanting to face a lifetime of knowing that when he most needed her, she simply wasn't there. A long agonizing phone call would give that back to her. He didn't mind the idea of granting the favor—but the pain of life was something he no longer wanted to feel. He pulled the plug from the wall jack so the ringing wouldn't disturb him.

David hunted in the back of the loft for the tall aluminum ladders his brother had used to plasterboard the ceilings and paint the sprinkler pipes their pretty pastel colors. There were other odds and ends, including heavy ropes. David hurried his preparations. Probably no one from the magazine would react to his tardiness quickly enough to arrive soon, almost surely Patty wouldn't come down to the loft, but he wanted no mistakes, no "happy" accidents.

Climbing the ladder was scary: he felt dizzy at the height, but it was no trouble slinging the rope over the sprinkler pipe. He had a harder time making the right sort of knot. He moved one of the Breuer chairs from the dining table to stand on, and pulled down hard, swinging a bit on the rope to make sure the pipes would hold.

Then he sat and lit a cigarette, trying to imagine how it would look for the unlucky discoverer. In the vast space, his swinging body might not seem particularly ominous. He was dressed in a business suit, and death by a pastel-colored sprinkler pipe fully dressed might even look comic. Should he write a note? A final act as a master wordsmith? Tell his brother and parents why he had really done it? Dear Mom and Dad, I just couldn't face Ted Koppel. Everyone would assume the death of Gott was the cause.

Well, he thought to himself, pressing out his cigarette, maybe it was. He just couldn't decide anymore what the neat final summary should be. He got on the chair, put the rope around his neck, tightened it, and kicked the chair away—away from all the stupidity and waste.

Tony drove into the circular driveway of International Pictures' main administration building, curtly informing the nervous security guard that he was Richard Winters' son. He climbed the stairs to the second floor, past the painting of the company's founder, and on into the chief executive officer's suite. "Go right in," his father's secretary told him.

Tony was used to his father's offices being big and luxurious, but this was worthy of remark. It was larger than most studio apartments, and even had a more complete bathroom and kitchen. He wandered about noting the accouterments while Richard finished a call, opening the refrigerator stocked with everything from champagne to Pepsi, from caviar to Kraft's onion-and-garlic dip.

"I got a frantic call from Maureen this morning," Richard said as he hung up, looking Tony over. Tony hadn't bothered to shave, though he had taken a bracing shower in Garth's multihead unit, water spraying from every conceivable direction. "You don't look so bad."

"I slept it off," Tony answered.

"Apparently words were exchanged," Richard commented.

"Can't call them words. More like verbal switchblades."

Richard smiled. "I'm glad you haven't lost your wit." He raised an eyebrow. "Watch this." He pressed a button on his desk, and the heavy wooden door to his office let out a whoosh, and then slowly, haunted, closed itself.

Tony clapped. "That's fabulous!"

Richard snapped his fingers. "Don't tell me being head of a company ain't worth the effort."

"Oh, I won't. You've got power and I've learned that's what counts in this business."

"Oh, dear." Richard got up from his country French table that he used as a desk and moved toward one of the eight-foot-long couches. "Two months in Malibu and you're a cynic."

"I want to leave," Tony said.

"What's keeping you?"

"I put that badly." He looked his father in the eyes. "I'm leaving."

"Don't be elliptical, Tony. I hate that. Tell me what's going on."

"The script's not finished. There's another scene to write before you bozos get your hands on it and demand countless rewrites."

"One scene?" Tony nodded. "Don't you think writing one last scene isn't too much of an imposition?" Richard asked, a patient parent, confident of his child's ultimate good sense. "Have you had a fight with Garth? Or is this because of your mother?" he went on, sure of his omniscience.

Tony looked away. His glance fell on his father's multiline phone. Four of the six buttons were lit. "How many secretaries do you have?" he asked.

Richard followed his glance. "An assistant and a secretary." He nodded at the phone. "It never stops. I could spend all my time returning phone calls."

"Must be nice," Tony said.

Richard grunted. "It's not. It's debilitating."

"Oh, come on. To be so pursued. Must be wonderful."

"You're wrong. I'm always saying no to people's fondest dreams. It's like being a doctor in a terminal ward. The best news I can give anyone is that their death will be painless."

"You also make their dreams come true."

"Not to hear them talk. *They* make their dreams come true—I only get credit for their nightmares." Richard shifted his position. He seemed impatient. "If you envy it, try for a studio job. You're overqualified. In fifteen years you'll have my job."

Tony nodded. "That's an idea. I hadn't thought of it."

"Why are you walking out on the project?" Richard snapped, his irritation unleashed.

"Because I don't give a fuck about it," Tony answered. "I don't give a fuck about any of this, I realize. Something sick pulled me out here. I don't know what it was. I think maybe it was to impress you and Mom."

"Well, I'm not impressed. I'm impressed by people finishing what they start. I had heard the script was going well. Very well. If Garth is satisfied, and he told me he *was* last week, it's a movie this company wants to make. You'd be a fool, worse than a fool, to walk out now."

Tony bit his lip. Richard was making him nervous. He had come here convinced he wasn't giving anything up, that the project was merely a toy for Garth, just as his penis had been last night, something to keep the great actor occupied until the studio came up with a real movie for him. That wasn't Tony's reason for wanting out, but it had made the contemplation easier.

"Don't run away like your mother," Richard said wearily, rubbing his temple. He sighed. "And don't bother punishing me. Neither of us is worth messing up your life."

"Mom didn't run away," Tony complained.

"That's exactly what she did. She's converted it in her mind to political heroism, and I suppose you had no reason, being so young, to know differently. She not only wasn't called by the Un-American Activities Committee—why should she be? she wasn't a party member—she wasn't even blacklisted."

"That's bullshit," Tony said angrily.

"It's a matter of *fact*," Richard said. "Check with the people who really did lose their jobs. She was a baby in the forties and early fifties— we didn't move here until fifty-one. She knew a lot of communists, but she wasn't one. She had a nervous breakdown, Tony." He stared at his son for a moment. "After being fired off Felson's picture, she collapsed. She claimed it was because of the blacklist, because she had supported the Hollywood Ten. Supported!" He laughed. "She met them at the train station and had Dalton Trumbo over for dinner—*once*."

"She never claimed she was involved before the hearings. Simply that she helped—"

"Come on, Tony! She pretends to be the Joan of Arc of the Mc-Carthy period." He leaned forward. "She couldn't handle failure. Rejection. Unlike most actresses, she had no struggle in her career until she came to Hollywood. She was the bright young star of Broadway. She expected this town to lie at her feet. And it did for a while. But she's a stage actress. The magnification of the camera made her look like a ham. And she wouldn't adjust—she believed she was infallible, that the directors were fools. She got a reputation for being a prima donna and she wasn't a star. She forgot that 'prima' precedes 'donna.' So she was fired. And then no one was knocking down her door." He closed his eyes and swallowed hard. "And she hated me because I had followed her out here as a nothing and I became a network vice-president within a year and a half." He opened his eyes and moved his head from side to side as though it were stiff. "I was just supposed to be the handsome, smiling husband —not the big success. Between her envy and her arrogance and her failure, she flipped out."

This point of view was a collection of familiar facts arranged into an unrecognizable bouquet. Despite its newness, Tony wasn't shocked. He knew his father had a reason to justify himself, but still he didn't doubt him. He spoke painfully, abandoning years of restraint, which made his words plausible. Besides, he was a man who prided himself on accuracy. Tony knew that if he challenged his father's story, proof, absolute proof, would be submitted. "But she did make it in the business," was all that he could offer as refutation.

"Do you think her work on TV is first-rate?"

Tony lowered his head. He felt his mouth tremble.

Knowing the answer to the questions, Richard went on. "She's not a genius, Tony. And I'm not a monster."

"So what?" Tony looked up. "What the fuck has this got to do with me?"

Richard stood up and then paused as if he had forgotten where he meant to walk. "Garth rehired you after he and I had a long talk at a party. He couldn't understand why you had refused to do the rewrite last time. He liked you. Admired your work. He thought he'd been supportive. Couldn't understand why you walked away." Richard had been speaking to his empty desk chair. He moved toward it now. "I've just told you why you walked away last time." He sat down and covered his forehead with the heels of his palm, pressing. "I've got a splitting headache." He released the pressure and finally looked at Tony, his voice hoarse: "You throw another temper tantrum now and you'll never work in this town again. Maybe that doesn't matter to you. Your mother they eventually forgave. But she'd had a breakdown and then worked in the theater for fifteen years. What's your excuse?"

"My God," Tony said, feeling outraged. "You talk about me like I'm a spoiled piece of shit! I'm one of the best young playwrights in the country—"

"No you're not," Richard said quietly. "Stop kidding yourself. New York is loaded with tiresome middle-aged people who had a few promising early years. If you're not careful, you'll be one of them soon."

"You really don't give a shit about me," Tony blurted. "You talk cold . . . coldly about me. Like I'm an employee—"

"Yeah, sure, if I loved you I'd support your deluded image of yourself. Academy Award-winning screenwriters don't walk off projects! Tom

Stoppard wouldn't walk off! Nobody!" Richard shouted, his face reddening. "Even if you had achieved what you think in your head you have,
even then!" He quieted, grabbing his head in one hand and furiously
massaging each temple. "I feel it's my fault—leaving you with her." He
pointed out the window. "There is a real world out there, Tony, where
curtains ring down on tragic lives. People don't stand up at the end and
wipe off ketchup. *If* you humble yourself, *if* you work hard for *years*—
then perhaps, at the end of your life, you will be treated like a prince."
As though he caught a glance of himself in a mirror—enraged, his arm
thrust out—Richard resumed a tranquil pose. "Being a great artist,
Tony, means you answer all the crap the world dumps on you with your
work—not with more crap."

Tony felt frozen in place. His hurt had been chilled, the fire of his
outrage doused. His father's words sobered not merely his brain, but the
world as well. "If you admired my plays, you wouldn't say that. The truth
is, you think I have to pay dues because my work isn't great."

Richard shook his head, not to contradict Tony, but sadly to himself
—giving up on a hopeless case. "Even if I thought they were works of
genius—*especially* if I thought they were—I'd want you to finish. If
you're as great as you think you are, then this script, and all the rewrites
in the world, should be child's play for you. I know you're smarter than
Bill Garth and Jim Foxx, I know you're smarter than me. So what?"

"I don't think I'm smarter—" Tony stammered.

"Yes you do! You think you're smarter, handsomer, wittier, more
talented. But that's the point. You only think it. You haven't proven it
to anyone."

"All right!" Tony pleaded. He put his hands up in surrender. He felt
his mouth weaken, his eyes fill. "Stop. I'll go back. I'll finish the script.
I'll shut up. I'll sleep in the fucking servants' quarters. Just shut the fuck
up."

Richard slumped into his chair, his hands holding his head, as
though he were keeping two broken pieces in place until the glue
hardened. "I'm sorry," he mumbled.

"I've gotta get back to my boss," Tony said. And he walked back into
the sun, the Hollywood sun—glaring pallidly over the studio lots, as
though weary of its ceaseless duty.

The police, the press, David's family, and his friends all assumed
that David must have heard the news on television—the startling flash
that Chico had tried unsuccessfully to break to him by phone on the
night he killed himself.

The old man wasn't Gott. He was a former German soldier, unimportant and unwanted, who had hung about Neo-Nazi circles in Europe and South America. He might even have known Gott, certainly he had obtained genuine documents that he used to fool *Newstime*. From interrogations of a young man who had helped in the con, it came out that the plan was hatched not only to get money but also to create favorable publicity for the new Nazi movement by denying the charges outstanding against Mengele and Gott. These details hadn't been broadcast on the night David hanged himself, but the shattering fact for a proud professional like David, the ghastly irony that everybody assumed had overwhelmed him—that the victim had been a foolish deluded old man, that his killer would pay for a pointless crime, a crime which might have been prevented if *Newstime* had doubted the story more (Tamar Gurion had learned of the meeting because of careless gossip by the stringer)— had come over the airwaves at roughly the time David slung his rope over the pipes and ended his life.

Patty's efforts to reach David, combined with *Newstime*'s expectation that David would return to the office, led to an early discovery of the body. Patty had regretted their phone conversation the moment it was over, but had assumed he was avoiding her repeated attempts to reach him at the magazine, and went there. After two hours passed without an answer at the loft, a nervous Chico escorted her downtown.

Chico fell apart at the sight of the body. He frantically tried to cut him down, talking inarticulately, unable to keep the ladder steady, pulling desperately at the shoes, until he finally collapsed, alternately screaming and weeping on the couch.

Patty's first thought was to look for the collar and magazines. She was going to destroy them if they were present. She didn't know why, but even if David had left them behind, she assumed he would want her to. She couldn't find them. Then she phoned the police. She felt nothing. Not even surprise. She *was* shocked. But somehow it made sense. In the cab, Chico had talked about the situation with the Gott story in incoherent snatches. Obviously he and David were vulnerable, and in her talk with David on the phone she had heard how truly scared and alone he must have been for a long time.

I'm sorry, she said to his body. She held Chico's head in her lap while he sobbed, hiding from the sight, and spoke in the still emptiness of her mind: I'm sorry, David. She looked at the huge abstract yellow painting, no tears, unafraid, and apologized. She waited for her own tears to flow. But sitting in the loft with the great Chico, this great man whom David had worked so hard to please, weeping like a child in her lap, she understood. The joke life had played on David was both too horrible and too funny to live through. I'm sorry I didn't try harder, David, she said silently.

Betty nursed her and the magazine protected her through the cleanup that followed over the next few weeks. Although David's suicide was a marvelous side-bar to the whole episode, as though finally acknowledging there was a brotherhood of the press, almost everybody kept a distant, even dignified distance from that aspect of the story. The gossip was furious, an item or two did appear in the real rags, but an unknown journalist's idealistic suicide was dull compared to the field day they could have with the old man and his killer.

Her parents came to town for a few days. Betty convinced her to see a psychiatrist at least for a while. To the doctor she told the fact of David's sexual secret, a secret made even more frustrating for her by the fact that she didn't know its extent or importance in his life. The more she talked about him, the more the realization that she had lived with him and known precious little about him horrified her. Not because of what it implied, the desperate lonely sorrow he must have lived with, but because of what it meant about her. The therapy consoled her, forgave her, explained to her, but the fear that she was incapable of loving anyone without the distorting prism of her self-absorption keeping her a stranger to the secrets of his soul stayed with her.

Her novel came out. Of course it didn't sell. But it got great reviews. Paula Kramer didn't write about it in her devastating piece on Fred, but she did review it for the *Times Book Review*, hailing Patty as providing a remarkable combination of humor and tragedy, a writer who "is too intelligent to rely on the dogmas of feminism, but rather manages to remind us of the real effects sexism has on our lives, to *feel*, to understand with our hearts and not our minds."

Gelb tried to phone right after the tragic news, but Betty, on Patty's instructions, told him not to call again, and he obeyed. She made it. Without him. And without David.

Although in her eyes the fog of mystery and sorrow from David's death obscured her docking in the literary port, all who knew her soon thought of Patty Lane as a brilliant talent whose ultimate success was only a matter of time. The tragic story of her lover only added to the fascination with which she was now regarded. She carried alone, in her weary heart, what she knew of the sad story. Now that the world believed she had no secrets, she possessed the first true secret of her life—a keepsake and a punishment, she believed, for completing the lonely journey of creation.

CHAPTER

18

On the fifty-second week that Fred Tatter's *The Locker Room* appeared on the New York *Times* best-seller list (it had sunk from the number-one position recently, but was still in the top five), his agent held a party to celebrate the one-year anniversary. Bart didn't stint on the cost—after all, Fred was a client whose earnings exceeded a million dollars a year.

Most of the publishing industry was invited, along with dozens of writers, as well as movie and television people—*The Locker Room* was scheduled to be a mini-series the next fall, and Fred's new novel, although still unfinished, had been optioned for a feature film. Even enemies such as Paula Kramer, who had burned Fred on the interview, were asked. (The way Paula had suckered Fred, Bart explained to people, into a confessional that *The Locker Room* consisted of an account of cheating on Marion was that she pretended intimacy and then betrayed confidences, probably irritated that Fred didn't make a pass at her.) More significant than these invitations to the people who had attempted to slow the juggernaut of *The Locker Room* was the fact that they all accepted—gladly. It became *the* publishing party of the season. Not to be invited was shameful.

The caterers used all five floors of Bart's town house elegantly—two of the large rooms were finished for the party, providing a windfall of tax write-offs for Bart. Fred and Marion, at Bart's request, arrived early and were installed in an upper bedroom which had been made the control center for the disc jockey selecting the music for the dancing on the third floor. Several of the Hollywood people who were involved on the mini-series and the planned film of Fred's second book had not yet met him and Bart wanted them to chat intimately before the crush of the party.

Marion sat near the electronic boards, sipping champagne, and watched the disc jockey prepare. She had long since become bored with the slavish attention paid to Fred. She no longer simmered with quiet rage at the curious first looks she got from people when being introduced.

The television people, she thought, seemed to look particularly snide on meeting her—no doubt thinking of the amusing fact that plump, round-faced, mousy-haired Marion was being played by Farah Fawcett in the mini-series. Go ahead, laugh, she answered them silently. I'll console myself in my million-dollar co-op. Most women just get heartache from their husbands fucking around, she once told her shrink. At least I get furs.

Fred had them laughing in moments, the nervous eager-to-please hooting that seemed to be a reflex since he had become a favorite of the talk shows. The media had fallen in love with his unpretentious joking about publishing and his engaging guffaws at his self-deprecating stories. A recent carping piece on him in *Town* magazine called Fred the first stand-up-comic novelist. Marion was sick of the standards of his reper-toire by now—his embarrassing moments before he made it: spilling coffee on himself before an important meeting; stepping on Pete Rose's foot minutes before a World Series game; meeting Isaac Bashevis Singer at a writers' conference, becoming confused, and complimenting him on writing *Portnoy's Complaint* (Marion suspected he had made that one up for Johnny Carson); and then the sudden switch to an earnest but humble discussion of his new book's themes.

"It's about a strong woman," Fred said to the rapt Hollywood crowd. "Not just because she's an athlete—and great in bed," he added with a guffaw that triggered a round of laughs from the movie and television people. "With both sexes!" he added when their chuckles waned, trigger-ing a new explosion. Then he slapped himself playfully. "I've gotta be serious. No, not just 'cause of that, not just 'cause she challenges the sports establishment, but 'cause she's a kid from the wrong side of the tracks, playing tennis, the rich people's game."

"It's got everything," the producer who had optioned the novel said.

"It's a female *Rocky*," another said.

"But more serious," the producer said. "Much more serious."

"Oh, yeah," Fred said with a broad wink. "I'm thinking of writing half the book in German."

Ha, ha, Marion said to herself while the rest split their sides, outdo-ing each other in showing enjoyment.

Downstairs, they could hear that the party had begun in earnest, and started to move. The movie producer of the new book, Jim Foxx, took Fred by the elbow as they approached the stairs and pulled him aside, practically knocking Marion to the floor. "I'm sorry," he said, and then continued to Fred in a whisper: "I'm thinking of Tony Winters to do the adaptation."

"Oh, yeah?" Fred said with woozy surprise. He's already tipsy, Marion noted.

"He wrote a terrific movie for me."

"Yeah, with Bill Garth, right?" Fred asked.

"Oh, that's right," Foxx said, pretending he had just remembered. "Tony said you two are good friends."

"Oh, yeah?" Fred said with a gleam in his eye. "Well, you know, in the last year, a lot of people have suddenly become my good friends."

Foxx laughed hard—but nervously. "Of course, of course. Isn't the world terrible? But he's a good writer."

"Yeah, he's good," Fred said with a tone of critical omniscience. "But in his plays he's never really put it all together. Someday he'll have a big smash." Fred started down the stairs. He looked back at Marion and smiled. "Though Betty's probably getting tired of waiting, right?" He guffawed and moved toward the noise of the crowd.

At the sight of him, they applauded good-naturedly. A few shouted mocking toasts, but many stared at him with glistening, fascinated eyes, as though trying to decode the mysterious formula that had made him a star.

In the rear of the front room, smiling but not applauding, stood Patty Lane. To the publishing people she was a familiar sight and provoked much gossip. She wore a black silk men's shirt, just covering the tops of her naked thighs. The buttons were open halfway down her chest, so that anyone standing at an angle to her could thoroughly view the sheer black bra she was wearing. Her escort was Raul Sabas, the Broadway musical-comedy star whose obvious effeminacy and open admission of homosexuality had led to a ceaseless flow of gossip that he was in fact experimenting with women. Raul was dressed in an identical silk shirt (though he wore black leather pants with it), also open halfway down his chest, and he and Patty seemed very chummy, Raul's arm often gathering her for a delighted squeeze at one of her witticisms. Their presence together intensified the talk about them, but the five or six people in the room who were "really in the know" about the mysterious Patty Lane (her status as a cult author was growing daily due to the surprisingly strong sales of the quality-paperback edition of her first novel) whispered to others the current rumor that Sabas was a beard—in fact, they suspected she was flirting with lesbianism.

Standing with this unusual couple was Tony Winters, tan from another long trip to Los Angeles, wearing jeans, polo shirt, and a blue satin windbreaker with the title of his forthcoming movie on the back. Leaning on him wearily was his wife, Betty, looking, by contrast with her husband

and friends, absurdly conventional and out of sync, dressed in a demure enormous maternity dress that visually inflated her fifth month of pregnancy to eight-month proportions. Betty, the ones "in the know" explained, had quit her job, intending to devote herself to raising the child, and that was the reason Patty Lane's new contract wasn't with Garlands. Betty cited her husband's frequent absences in LA as the reason she felt her baby would need a nonworking mother, but those "in the know" mumbled that the couple's move to the West Coast was only a matter of time.

This foursome huddled together while Fred made his way through the crowd, greeting people boisterously, pumping hands like an electioneering politician. Something Tony said caused his group to burst out laughing, a quartet abruptly playing a different sheet of music from the room's orchestra.

"What's so funny?" Fred called out, following the curious glances of people around him toward the two couples. "Hey, Patty! You look great." The crowd parted for him to walk up. "Tony, Betty, how are you? Raul Sabas!" Fred said, putting his hand out enthusiastically. "I love your work."

"Thanks. Don't you love our matching outfits?" Sabas asked, putting an arm around Patty and posing like a chorus girl.

"We're twins," Patty said with the unsmiling but sly expression that had replaced, during the last year, her formerly eager, wondering style.

"Where's Marion?" Betty asked.

"Marion!" Fred shouted like a vulgar situation-comedy character calling for his wife to bring him a beer. People laughed and parted to reveal a somewhat flushed and bedraggled Marion, stuck at the other end of the room, having been cut off by the congratulatory press of the party. Fred didn't wait for her arrival to continue. He waved his glass at Tony. "I was just talking about you."

Tony nodded. "Yes?"

"My movie producer, Jim Foxx, is here—"

"Yeah, I saw him." Tony smiled. "He produced *Concussion*."

"Is that your movie?" Fred asked.

"Right," Tony said, and turned his back to show the title sewn on the back of his jacket. "In a theater near you this summer."

"Hey!" Fred said, and nudged Marion, who had just then arrived at his side. A little of her champagne was jostled out of the glass. "I should get one like that for *The Locker Room*, don't you think?"

"Fred, you spilled my wine."

Fred glanced down at the floor. His eyes widened with delighted surprise. "This is right near the spot where I spilled coffee before meeting with Bart!"

Tony nodded solemnly. "So it's a tradition."

Raul Sabas laughed. "You told that story on Carson. It was a scream."

"Oh, Fred's a hoot," Patty said, her pale white face glowing out of the dark black of her outfit, her eyes glistening, but her expression flat.

"Anyway," Fred continued to Tony, taking a hearty slug to drain his glass, "he said you're interested in adapting my next novel."

"I am?" Tony looked aloof and surprised.

"Uh-oh!" Fred covered his mouth. "Maybe it's a secret." He smiled at Betty. "Anyway, you won't have to worry about baby's new clothes."

"Fred!" Bart called from the other end of the room, gesturing for him to join him.

"Oops! Gotta greet people," Fred said, and left them, taking Marion's hand, dragging her with him.

"I'll talk to you later," Marion said to Betty before the crowd swallowed her.

Tony looked at Patty and rolled his eyes. She smiled slyly. "Don't we all just love our Freddy?"

"I think he's cute!" Raul Sabas exclaimed. "Just like a corn muffin! I'd love to butter him all over."

"Oh, cut it out, Raul," Tony said. "You're with us. You can be yourself. Button your shirt, have a beer, and talk baseball."

Raul roared and put out his long arm, touching Tony on the shoulder with the tip of his index finger, as though knighting him.

Betty groaned. "I have to pee again."

"My God," Tony said.

"Shut up," Patty said. "It's your fault."

Betty moved toward the crowd, saying, "If I don't come back soon, I'll be asleep in a bedroom."

Patty turned her back to the crowd, edged near to Tony, and said in a low voice: "Stop being so crabby with her."

Tony stared down Patty's shirt at her breasts, making no attempt to disguise his look. "Conventional ethics from you? I'm supposed to sit home with a ballooning wife making soufflés while you go to literary soirees and fuck everything in sight?"

"Excuse *me*," Raul Sabas said, only he wasn't speaking with mock flamboyance, but genuine irritation. "For your information, she isn't sleeping with anyone."

Patty smiled at Raul. "Thanks for clearing that up, Raul."

"I was only kidding, Raul," Tony answered. "I know all about her vow of celibacy. I'm married to her best friend, remember?"

"It's not a vow, Tony," Patty answered, frowning.

"You should be writing for the theater," Raul said to Tony, still angry. "Hollywood's turning you into a humorless vulgarian."

"Tony is writ—" Patty began to Raul

"Quiet!" Tony said sharply, and then spoke in a rush. "Don't knock being a humorless vulgarian. Look what it's done for Fred." He looked down Patty's shirt again.

Patty began to button it. "Be nice to her, Tony, or I'll cut your balls off."

Like you did with David, Tony thought to himself. He turned away, searching for the bar. He was going to get drunk. "I'm going to get a drink," he said, and moved away bumping into an elegantly dressed man.

"Excuse me," the man said. He was Brian Stoppard, Paula Kramer's husband.

Paula moved around them both to greet Patty with breathless enthusiasm: "You're not going to believe what Fred said to me at the door! He forgave me for my piece. He said he knows what it's like for free-lance magazine writers—to be noticed, they have to do hatchet jobs."

"Freddy the dope," Patty mumbled with a sly smile. *He's right*, she thought to herself. "It's good to see you, Paula."

"I'm Brian Stoppard," Paula's lawyer husband said, putting his hand out to Raul Sabas.

"Hello!" Raul said in a vaguely mocking way. "Raul Sabas."

"Oh, I know," Brian said in a neutral tone. "I'm a great fan of yours."

"Well, I don't have to worry," Paula continued. "Brian's going to get my revenge for me. Freddy made the mistake of asking Brian if he wanted to play in his high-stakes poker game."

"Are you a good poker player?" Patty asked Brian.

"Good!" Paula answered for him. She scanned the room. "Soon this will all be ours!"

At the rear of the room, Tony got himself a Scotch at the bar and sipped it, watching Fred greet admirers. Jim Foxx waved to him and walked over. "Where's Betty?" he asked.

"Peeing."

"Ah, I remember what it's like. When's she due?"

"February."

Foxx nodded. "Did you talk to Fred about doing the adaptation?"

"He brought it up." Tony crunched an ice cube, the cold radiating through a tooth and sending a frozen bolt of pain to his brain.

"Pity we have to wait for him to write the damn thing." Foxx smiled nastily.

"Poor Fred," Tony said sardonically. "No one here has any respect for his talent."

"Talent?" Foxx said as though he had never heard the word. He laughed. "Don't pity him. He's done great for himself."

"Don't worry," Tony answered.

"Say!" Foxx said, and grabbed his arm. "I just heard from some guy —theater producer . . ." He pointed toward a small man huddled in a corner with an overweight woman.

"Ted Bishop," Tony supplied the name.

"He said he's doing a new play of yours in the fall."

"Yep," Tony answered, and crushed another cube, enjoying the hurtful cold.

"How come you didn't tell me about it? He says it'd make a great movie."

Tony grunted.

"When did you write it?"

"While I was rewriting the script for the eighteenth time." Tony put his empty glass down. "I'd better find my wife." He started to move away.

"Can I read it?" Foxx called after him.

"I don't know," Tony called back. "How are the remedial courses coming?"

Foxx's obscene answer was drowned out by a hubbub coming from the windowed end of the room. There, shouting for quiet, stood Tom Lear. He was on a chair, holding a glass aloft to make a toast, while next to him Sam Wasserman, Bob Holder, and Karl Stein were shushing the crowd.

"We come to praise Fred," Tom called out. "Not to break his eardrums." After some laughter, he had their attention. "We all know why we're here," Tom Lear said in a solemn, hushed tone. The room became piously silent. "To tell Fred to please get his damn book off the bestseller list and make room for one of us!"

Hoots of laughter. Scattered applause. And then, shocking the crowd into a wild outburst of hilarity, Fred let out a wet, loud Bronx cheer. "Never!" he shouted.

"No, seriously," Tom Lear said. "No one deserves this success more than Fred." Tom lowered his head—to keep from snickering, Patty Lane thought to herself—and the crowd returned to the enforced reverence of a school auditorium. "Success, especially when it happens to someone who's young, usually spoils them. They start to believe their reviews—"

"Not me!" Fred called out, and everybody laughed, relieved that the author had been the one to point indirectly that his reviews had been either very mixed or outright pans.

Lear pressed on, holding a hand up for quiet. "They forget their friends, lose interest in the struggle to write well, and only care about the interest on their money. It's ruined more than one brilliant young American writer. Fred has too much good sense and good feeling for that. More than anything, that's what I love about him." Tom lifted his glass: "To another year on the list, Fred."

"To another year," most of the crowd mumbled, and there was scattered, desultory applause. Fred felt the urge to cry. Bart and Marion flanked him while he listened. Indeed, the town house contained the sum of all his relationships: all of his New York friends, even the old gang from Long Island; his parents were standing shyly in a corner with their best friends; his brother and sister were over by the hors d'oeuvres stuffing their faces. He loved them all. Even Tom and Sam and the other writing boys who had treated him like a piece of shit—the struggle to win their admiration had only made it a more valued prize.

At his worst moments he suspected none of them would care about him if he hadn't made it so big, but tonight he felt, in the warmth and noise of this room, that it wasn't so. They had all helped, after all. Even if sometimes they had been reluctant, or envious once things began to go well, despite all the insults, they *had* taken him to their hearts. Marion kicked him out, but she took him back. Holder asked for a lot of rewrites, but he never lost faith in Fred's ability to do them. Bart was cold and bossy, but he sure came through on his promises.

At times Fred had felt as though his heart would break, like a child wandering in the cold, unable to find his way home. But the villains had all turned out to be benevolent under their dark mustaches, and the brightly wrapped packages beneath the glowing Christmas tree in that distant window were for him after all. He leaned drunkenly on his wife and felt his eyes moisten. I love these people, he said to himself.

Holder's blustering, mostly self-congratulatory speech followed, embarrassing the group. People shifted restlessly from one foot to another, a few deserted to the bar, until Bart, correctly judging the limits of the party's endurance of honoring *The Locker Room*, interrupted to say the buffet on the second floor was ready. There was ecstatic applause and a stampede upstairs on the old staircase that rumbled in the frail house's chest like a death rattle.

What horseshit, Tony thought to himself, draining another glass of Scotch while he watched the eager faces go by. Keep it to yourself, he said as a reminder, going over the long list of vows he had made on the fateful drive back from his father's office to Garth's Malibu house a year ago. This party was a sore test of his fidelity to the new Tony. No carping at the success of others. No discussion of his own projects, no predictions of either success or failure. He had slipped twice already, allowing sarcasms about Fred to escape. Sarcasm was worse than an outright complaint. He had taken a swipe at Foxx, probably undoing a year of studious politeness. Sarcasm—the consolation prize of failed talent. His mother, now the ultimate symbol of a loser to him, used it often. And then he had been sexual with Patty, breaking another of his monk's orders. Learn to be a good bit player, Tony, he ordered himself. Don't step into the center spot; stand aside in the shadow and do your work. Do your work and one day the brilliant light will find you.

"Jim!" he called, spotting his producer edging toward the stairs

Foxx looked at him, his mouth tight. "Yes?"

"I'd love you to read my play, but . . . come here." He gestured. Foxx, still wearing the cool look of a hurt parent awaiting an apology, stepped out of the flow. "I'm very insecure about it—especially being read cold in script form. There'll be a reading in about six weeks—for me to discover what else needs to be done. I'd love you to come and help suggest revisions."

Foxx's face relaxed. "Sure. I'll be in town for the sneak in Long Island."

"That's right!" Tony snapped his fingers. "Terrific. Will you really come? I'd appreciate—"

"Definitely! Why did you act so weird about it?"

"I'm scared . . . you know. It's been a while since—"

"I understand." Foxx put a hand on his shoulder. "Don't explain."

"Hi!" Betty said, appearing. "You want to have some food? Or can't you stand any more?"

Tony looked shocked. "What do you mean? This is terrific. Are you feeling all right? Can you stay?" he asked with nervous concern.

"Yeah, I'm starving!" she said. They joined the slow mass moving up the stairs to the buffet.

Patty had spotted Tony and Betty a few moments before and now pushed her way toward them. She had looked forward to spending the party with them—Tony had been so wonderful during the past year, so full of calm good sense; he seemed to be losing it in the face of Fred's triumph. It *was* hard to bear.

While they toasted Fred, Patty had looked idly at the men in the room. She didn't envy the women their male possessions. Most of the men talked away to other men, interrupting their women's dialogue, joking whenever the subject of their wives' or dates' work came up, only to resume babbling nervously about *their* work, *their* hopes for promotion, and to indulge in graveyard humor about the failures of rivals. She had no desire to capture them with her cunt, soothe their restless yearning for a flattering all-encompassing embrace. She knew she was better than them. And she no longer planned to conceal it.

"Hey!" she called out to Tony and Betty. "Wait for me!"

"Patty!" a cheerful Tony called down, waving his hand to urge her up. "Sorry I bitched at you," he said, sounding like his good self.

"Don't worry," she called back with a brilliant smile. "It'll happen to us too."

"Well, anyway," Tony said with a sad look, "let's eat his food."

Patty squeezed in next to them and they continued their ascent on the rickety staircase, feet stamping, a herd in synchronous movement. Together, among the anonymous others, they continued their climb up —up to their only nourishment: the feast of success.